Humor Me

ALSO BY CAT SHOOK
If We're Being Honest

Humor Me

Cat Shook

CELADON
BOOKS

NEW YORK

HUMOR ME. Copyright © 2024 by Shook Not Stirred LLC. All rights reserved. Printed in the United States of America. For information, address Celadon Books, a division of Macmillan Publishers, 120 Broadway, New York, NY 10271.

www.celadonbooks.com

Designed by Michelle McMillian

Library of Congress Cataloging-in-Publication Data

Names: Shook, Cat, 1993– author.
Title: Humor me / Cat Shook.
Description: First edition. | New York : Celadon Books, 2024.
Identifiers: LCCN 2023052952 | ISBN 9781250904713 (hardcover) |
    ISBN 9781250904720 (ebook)
Subjects: LCSH: Stand-up comedy—Fiction. | Grief—Fiction. |
    Friendship—Fiction. | LCGFT: Novels.
Classification: LCC PS3619.H6525 H86 2024 | DDC 813/.6—dc23/eng/20231121
LC record available at https://lccn.loc.gov/2023052952

Our books may be purchased in bulk for promotional, educational, or business use. Please contact your local bookseller or the Macmillan Corporate and Premium Sales Department at 1-800-221-7945, extension 5442, or by email at MacmillanSpecialMarkets@macmillan.com.

First Edition: 2024

10 9 8 7 6 5 4 3 2 1

For my mom, Alise, and Carrie, who taught me everything
I know about friendship

Humor Me

CHAPTER 1

I would be deterred by the length of this line, stretching all the way down East Nineteenth Street, if it weren't a matter of life and death. Which, considering the severity of my hangover and the healing properties of the bacon, egg, and cheese sandwich that awaits me at the end of this string of other grumpy New Yorkers, it is.

"Presley!" I turn at the sound of my name and am relieved to see Isabelle in line, already having made some progress. "You look like hell."

I groan. Not because of the insult, which is undeniably true, but because her chipper disposition, which I usually appreciate, does the impossible and worsens this already lethal hangover. Then again, that same morning energy is what has already gotten us halfway through the block-long line at Daily Provisions, so the last thing Isabelle deserves from me is attitude.

"What did you get into last night, doll?" Isabelle asks as I slouch over to stand next to her. Only Izzy can get away with calling me shitty little pet names like that, as if it's 1950 and I'm her secretary. She picks a piece of lint off my black denim jacket. It's the first time I've broken it out this season—fall took its sweet time getting here. Add it to the list of 2017's insults.

"How did you beat me here?" I ask.

"Oh," she says, rolling her eyes. "I *had* to get out of there."

"Hinge Hannah didn't live up to the hype?"

"She was sweet," Isabelle says. "But I could feel her trying to sink the damn hooks in already. She tried to take me to the farmers market this morning."

I wince. I'm not sure which horrifies me more: the kind of commitment an invitation to the farmers market suggests or the idea of fresh vegetables at this moment in time.

"Yeah," Isabelle says, clucking her tongue in sympathy for the poor girl, who we both know will get her local-produce-loving little heart broken. Even though Izzy is constantly going on dates, none of her prospects ever really stick. She loves the meeting people part of dating, the commitment part less so, unfortunately for the single queer women of New York. Looking at her, it's clear how anyone could instantly fall in love with her. Even though she, presumably, had some cocktails last night and came here straight from an apartment that isn't hers, her blond hair still holds just the right amount of wave, her mascara remains unsmudged, her black tank-top-blousy-dress thing is wrinkle-free. She looks more put together than I would even if I'd spent two hours getting ready. Not that I've ever spent more than fifteen minutes getting ready for anything in my life.

She narrows her eyes at me as I massage my temples, willing the tension pounding in my head to release. "You didn't answer my question."

"What question?" I ask, fully knowing what question.

"What did you do last night?"

"Oh, just went to a show."

"You seem awfully hungover for just going to a show."

"Yeah, well, you would have been pounding drinks, too, if you were there," I say with a sigh. "It was just Weinstein, Weinstein, Weinstein. Which is great if people are going to, like, say something original or insightful about it. But I don't know . . . it somehow already feels like it's too late to say anything new about it?"

"I get what you mean," Izzy says. "It's been just enough time for a subject to be exhausted on Twitter, but not enough for actual societal or cultural thought."

"You talk smart," I say.

"I'm quoting a tweet, sadly. Who did you go to the show with?" she asks.

I clear my throat and study my short, jagged fingernails. "Adam. We had some drinks after, so I guess that explains the hangover, too." Isabelle sighs deeply and looks up to the sky, as if an explanation for my behavior might be written on a Gramercy rooftop.

"Should I even ask?"

"Ask what?" I ask, like I don't know what.

"I believe you know," she says, eyebrows wiggling up and down suggestively.

"Jesus, Izzy," I say, feeling a bizarre twitch in my shoulder. "Of course not, you know that. Adam and I are just coworkers." Her crazy blue eyes widen like she's going to yell at me, which I can't handle in my current state. "Friends!" I correct myself. "Very close friends!"

She shuts her eyes and takes a yoga breath, pressing her hands together at heart center and everything. "Presley?" she says sweetly. "Can we just not with the 'close friends' bullshit? You two are just blatantly in love— *Ow!*" I slug her on the shoulder, which is meant to be gentle. She makes a pouty face and hunches her statuesque five-foot-ten frame. I pat the spot.

"My bad."

"Violence is never the answer," she says mock seriously. I crack my neck, which makes Isabelle shudder, and both of us laugh. The line inches forward.

"Should we split a cruller or each get our own?" I ask.

"Good question. All I know is that if they don't have maple, I will literally—"

"Presley Fry?" I hear someone say. I turn and look into the face of a woman so glamorous she couldn't possibly know me. She's wearing a white jacket over this blue dress that looks like it costs more than my rent. She pushes her fancy-looking sunglasses to the top of her head, which helps me recognize her.

"Oh, Mrs. Clark, hi," I say, clearing my throat and trying to channel Isabelle's cheery energy.

"Hi, hello!" she says, grinning like we're old besties and she just can't believe her good fortune to see my hungover face on this hinting-at-autumn day.

"What, uh, what brings you downtown?" I ask.

She holds up a heavy-looking Daily Provisions bag. "It's Lawrence's birthday today. Twenty-six." She shakes her head and looks down at the ground, smiling. "I can hardly believe it."

"Right on," I say. Isabelle shifts next to me. "This is my roommate, Isabelle."

"Hi," Isabelle says, giving Mrs. Clark an up-down. "I *love* your outfit."

"Thank you! Susan Clark," she says, shifting the bag to her hip and reaching for a handshake. She turns her attention back to me and her smile falls slowly (even with the considerable amount of Botox she's clearly had), like a shadow is passing over it. I've learned to recognize that look over the last year and a half. The frown, the concerned eyes. There's pleading in it, too; people's need for me to smile, laugh, or make a joke is undeniable. They want me to prove I'm all right, so that I can save them from both their own concern for me and the awkwardness of the moment.

"How are you holding up, Presley?" Susan asks, shaking her head, her glossy brown bob brushing against her shoulders. "I'm happy to be running into you, but gosh, I can't believe I haven't invited you over for dinner or taken you out or anything since . . ."

"Oh, all good, Mrs. Clark," I say, since I guess *I'm* the one who's supposed to comfort *her* here. "I'm doing okay. I just visited my grandparents, actually, and they seem to be holding up pretty well." This isn't exactly true, but it does the trick. Susan looks up, visibly relieved. But not for long; that damn shadow returns quickly.

"You know, I really am sorry to have missed the funeral."

I shake my head, wishing it were my funeral she had missed. Death seems preferable to this conversation. "It wasn't a big thing. Small. You know . . ." I rack my throbbing brain for the right word. "Close." Well, probably not the right word, but it's what comes out. "Anyway. How's Mr. Clark?"

She does this weird head twitch, as if a bee were swarming around, and suddenly I feel like *I'm* the one who said the wrong thing. She clears her throat, takes a breath, and rights herself. "Great, thanks for asking. He'll be glad to hear I ran into you, and that you're doing well."

A wave of nausea passes over me. Every moment of this unfed hangover is worse than the last. "Well, I hope Lawrence has a good birthday."

She brightens up again at the mention of her son, which irritates me for some reason. "Thank you! You know, he lives down in the West Village now. You two should hook up, what with you being the same age and everything." Isabelle snorts at Mrs. Clark's word choice, then tries to cover it with a fake cough.

"Totally," I say, even though I'm sure the one thing I have in common with Lawrence Clark, native Manhattanite and probable finance bro, is a mutual lack of desire to hang out.

"Well, I'd better be going," Susan says, to my extreme relief. Which is short-lived, because like some kind of Elmo ninja, Susan comes in quickly for a hug. Her bag full of doughnuts squishes awkwardly against my jacket, and she's, like, runway thin and very short, so her ribs knife my hip bone. She's also surprisingly strong, so breathing is no longer an option. I feel Isabelle wince next to me; she knows I'm not big on hugs. Susan trembles and I start to panic that this lady might actually fucking cry.

She pulls back almost as quickly as she dove in, returning her shades to cover her eyes and saving me from having to confirm my suspicion. But I'm thinking she was, in fact, crying, considering how quickly she turns on her sneakers, the kind that come pre-scuffed and I'm pretty sure cost six hundred bucks a pop.

"Strange woman," Isabelle says, looking after her with something like confusion, something like awe. "Who is she?" she asks wistfully.

"She's from Eulalia. She and Patty grew up together."

"Ah." Isabelle nods, practiced enough to not offer a reassuring hand on my shoulder or some sympathetic look that will inevitably convey not sympathy but an invitation for me to spare her from the awkwardness of having to talk about my dead mother. "You okay?" She bends to retie her shoelace, saving me from eye contact. Because she's the fucking best.

"Yep," I say.

"Wanna talk about it?"

"Nope." My evergreen answer to that question.

"Mmkay," Izzy says, standing back up. "Is it just me, or was she weird when you asked about her husband?"

"Very weird," I say. "She's married to Thomas Clark. He runs the American Network. Absolutely loaded. He pushed my résumé for *Late Night Show*, which is one hundred percent how I got that interview. And the internship, probably."

"And now look at you, soon-to-be associate producer," Isabelle says. I nudge her with my shoulder and roll my eyes. I'm still an assistant, the promotion to associate producer just a dim light at the end of a long, underpaid tunnel. Izzy continues, "What's the deal with her son? Is he hot? I hope so, since you'll be 'hooking up' with him soon." She slaps her knee in an exaggerated fashion.

"No idea. Mr. and Mrs. Clark had me over for dinner when I first moved to the city, so I guess, like, four years ago. But he wasn't there. The last time I saw him was when we were both in, like, middle school or something. They came down to Eulalia for Christmas. He was very . . . chatty. Freaked me out."

"Ah, southern emo teen freaked out by gregarious, fancy New Yorker. Sounds cute."

"It wasn't," I say.

I picture calling Patty to tell her I ran into Mrs. Clark, then remember that's not an option. My heart does the jump-start thing it does when I realize I've forgotten she's gone. I read an article about phantom limbs a few years ago, the sensation amputees have where they can feel an itch on an arm that isn't there, soreness in a long-gone shin. That urge to reach for something that's no longer part of you. Feeling something impossible.

....

My name is Presley because *Viva Las Vegas* was on in my mom's hospital room when she gave birth. While I do appreciate that I don't have some girlie bullshit name, it's a bit much, I think. Which makes sense, because "a bit much" is what we should have put on my mom's headstone. But, as it turns out, when your mom suddenly has a stroke (well, as sudden as a stroke can be considering the damage that daily heaping cups of Burnett's vodka will do to a liver), you don't exactly have the time or mental capacity to workshop the perfect epitaph.

One evening a year and a half ago I had been walking down First Avenue at night after scouting an up-and-coming comedian. Scouting was a new responsibility I had just been given at work and one that I was psyched to get to do. No pay raise came with this, just reimbursements for tickets and two-drink minimums. Bringing comedians in to do a set on the show is a necessary step in being considered for a promotion. I was feeling distinctly like I had my shit together. Or, almost. Like I was on the right track.

That's when Grammy called. I knew right when I saw her name on my phone that something bad had happened. I'm always the one to call her, because she says she doesn't want to bother me or have my phone go off at an inconvenient time. She doesn't quite get the whole "vibrate" thing.

My mother was in a coma. I needed to get on a plane to Georgia if I wanted to say goodbye to Patty before they pulled the plug. As Grammy told me all this, in her measured, calm southern lilt, I stopped walking abruptly enough to really piss off the gaggle of drunk girls stumbling behind me. Either it was new or I hadn't noticed it before, but spray-painted on the metal door leading to the speakeasy Isabelle was always suggesting we try was a life-size painting of Elvis, dressed in his iconic all-white Vegas show outfit. Head bent, crooning silently into a mic, pointing to the filthy patch of wall next to it.

In some small corner of my mind, the part that wasn't numbed with shock, I recognized the irony. But nothing about it was funny.

CHAPTER 2

Mondays have an unfairly bad reputation. I like Mondays at *Gary Madden's Late Night Show*, where I'm an assistant in the talent booking department. I like signing off on the expensive boxes of treats we fill the goody bags with for famous guests who absolutely don't need them. I love looking at the full lineup for the week and anticipating which interviews will go well, which ones will be boring or stilted or uncomfortable. And seeing which comedian will fill the Friday slot.

The Friday show, which is filmed every Thursday afternoon right after the Thursday show, always ends with a stand-up comedian doing a tight five-minute set instead of a musical act. It's a tradition for any late night show, but we're the only one still doing it, and according to my boss, Emma, "owning" that Friday-night slot is the best thing I can do to make a case for a promotion. I spend most of my weeknights and weekends bopping around the Village, the Lower East Side, and the various and spread-out clubs in Brooklyn looking for the next stand-up comic who'll get their shot on TV. This was already my preferred method of spending time; now I just have a new motivation. If someone I pitch ends up on the show, and they do well, I'll finally be considered for the promotion to associate producer (a job I already do, but without the added responsibilities of Emma's administrative bullshit and the corresponding meager pay). The assistant to associate producer pipeline usually takes two years, meaning I'm six months out from being considered a geriatric assistant.

I've been sitting at Emma's desk for half an hour, syncing her calendars and going through her mail, when she blazes into her office at ten a.m., glamorous (per usual) with her cropped Afro and navy-blue blazer, intimidating despite the fact that she stands at a puny five foot two. She tends to rush everywhere she goes, which is partially why I was so afraid of her as an intern and for the first few months after she hired me to be her assistant. And while she is undeniably crucial to the show's success, I now diagnose her constant quick pace as a strategic choice. Acting like she always has somewhere to be casts an aura of importance around her.

"Good weekend?" she asks after catching her breath, plopping down on her pink velvet couch and taking off the sneakers she commutes in to replace them with one of the several pairs of shiny, unscuffed heels she keeps in her office.

"Yes," I say, arranging Emma's calendar and email windows the way she likes on her desktop. "I saw Agatha Reddy again at Union Hall, that really talented comedian I mentioned last week. Her set is getting so good, I think we should reach out if she keeps at this pace."

"Your dedication is noted, but I haven't had coffee yet. I meant that question in a friendly way, not in a work way."

I shrug. "I'm just excited about her, is all. Weekend was good, otherwise. Yours?"

"Cara somehow lost Ellie, so I'm sure you can imagine how the weekend went."

I wince. Cara is Emma's two-year-old, whom I occasionally babysit for extra cash and also because she's the cutest kid on the damn planet. Ellie is her stuffed elephant, a first birthday gift given by yours truly. Emma recently sent me a photo of Cara, eyes closed with a death grip on her short braids, mouth open in a scream, with a message: This is what happens when Ellie has to have a bath in the washing machine. Thanks for ruining my life. ☺ So I can only imagine how horrifying an entire weekend with a lost Ellie would be. "I'll get your coffee."

"Good woman."

Just before rounding the corner to the kitchen, I catch myself doing that subconscious thing I do: a quick (and hopefully subtle) check in the hall mirror that hangs next to the framed photo of Gary interviewing Barack Obama. My dirty-blond hair is pulled back in its usual ponytail, but I'm wearing a gray T-shirt with black jeans instead of my standard black T-shirt, so I'm really stepping out today. Makeup-free, shoulders hunched, all five foot six of me plain and unnoticeable.

As I enter the kitchen, I try not to peek into the production assistant's office, which is hardly an office and more just a cramped little mildewy room right next to the fridge. I'm pretty sure it was originally meant to be a pantry. I sneak a look anyway, like I always fucking do. Adam is sitting casually at his desk, leaning so far back in his chair that the ancient thing looks broken. He's flipping through a copy of *The New Yorker*, laughing at something Mike, another PA, is saying. The only word I catch is "Franzen." Adam's dark brown, nearly black hair has recently gotten long enough that he could probably put it in a man bun, something I would love to mock him for. He's worked at the show for only six months, so I don't know if this is a new or returning look. I try not to smile as I realize he's wearing a gray T-shirt, like me. Stupid.

I start making Emma's latte with the machine that looks more like a spaceship than a coffee maker. I jump when a voice behind me says, "Tall! Decaf! Cappuccino!" I turn to find Adam leaning on the counter, grinning. My heart starts doing the uneven-hammer-uncomfortable-drum thing it tends to do when I see Adam for the first time after some separation (if one day counts). It also happens when I'm alone with Adam sometimes, when I think about Adam when I *am* alone, when he compliments me, or when he wears this white shirt he has that stretches across his (admittedly pretty narrow) shoulders in this very specific way.

"Tall decaf cappuccino," I echo, just like the man behind Meg Ryan in line at Starbucks does in *You've Got Mail*. We discovered our shared love of that movie (and all nineties rom-coms) when I caught Adam lingering outside our theater's biggest greenroom when Tom Hanks was a guest. It was Adam's second week at the show. Instant bonding ensued.

"Big Emma undercaffeinated?" he asks.

"Always," I say, turning my focus back to the machine.

"Does she care that people call her 'Big Emma'?" asks Adam, who I'm guessing (I'm not guessing; I know, because I know him surprisingly well considering we met only six months ago) would not like a nickname like that. The kid can be pretty sensitive, particularly about height stuff (he's only one inch taller than me), which makes negging him all the more fun.

"She doesn't mind." Gary Madden gave Emma the ironic nickname himself, which makes it special.

Adam leans against the counter. "Did you talk to her about Agatha?"

"Mentioned her. But I think she needs a few more weeks to perfect her set."

"That's why they pay you the big bucks, Fry," Adam says, nudging my shoulder, sending an irritating little shock wave down my arm.

"They pay me nothing," I say, which is, unfortunately, basically not even an exaggeration.

"They pay everyone nothing. How was your Sunday?"

"Fine."

"Whoa, slow down, cowgirl, no need to overshare. This is a place of *work*, you know," he says.

"Just didn't get up to much." Susan Clark's weirdly tight hug flashes quickly in my mind, but I shove it out. "How was yours?"

Adam raises his messy eyebrows suggestively. "I ended up going on a date with that girl my buddy Ethan wanted to set me up with."

I swallow and force a smile and an eyebrow raise. "Your 'buddy,' nice. First of all, I *know* Ethan. Secondly, we aren't living in an eighties sitcom."

"Whatever," Adam says. "Do you want to hear about it?"

I absolutely do not, but at the same time I feel an almost physical starvation for details so I can analyze them. Which Adam and I will do together, although for admittedly different reasons. He has a tendency to overanalyze every date out of a professed hope that he can find something that will work; I tend to analyze for evidence of the opposite. Not that I don't want him to be happy, but we'd probably hang out less if he started dating someone.

"Hm, friend of Ethan's, you say? Let's see how much I can guess first," I say.

He folds his arms and rocks back on his heels. "Oy, let's hear it."

"I'm gonna guess this girl lives in Bushwick," I start. "No purse, but a *New Yorker* tote, or some other kind of publishing tote. She doesn't work in publishing, though. She works at, hm, some kind of marketing thing? But she doesn't lead with that. I'm guessing she's a performative reader, like the kind of girl you would see walking down the street reading a book, which makes absolutely no sense. I can only assume she doesn't wear a bra and has a very nip-forward Instagram. Badly-on-purpose-cut bangs, maybe?" I look to the ceiling, give myself a moment to see if any other details come to mind. I shrug, satisfied. Adam is bent over, shaking with silent laughter. His hand covers his mouth, which he only does when he finds something truly hilarious.

He calms down. "Nip-forward Instagram. You're a wonder, Fry."

"So? How right am I?"

"She doesn't work in marketing."

"Oh?"

"She works at a razor subscription start-up."

"Which I'm guessing she loves to *not* use?" I ask.

He laughs again. "Damn, you really have me pinned down, huh?"

She sure would like to. I can hear Isabelle's voice in my head, which I shake.

"So," I ask, "you in love?"

"You know, no, but I think there's potential there," Adam says with a shrug. "Ashley was cool." My stomach tightens. "Then again . . . if I fall

in love with someone and can't talk to you about all my dating escapades anymore, what fun is there to be had, really?"

I smile tightly, validation settling over me, tainted with a pinprick
of hurt I don't care to explore. "We'll have to see, I guess," I say, nodding to one of the two coffees in my hands. "Gotta get this to the boss.
Can't have her drinking cold coffee, now."

He grins, the pale skin around his blue eyes crinkling, and unfortunately, it's beautiful. "Later," he says, strolling back into the PA's office.
I concentrate on not spilling either coffee as I round the corner and
carry them back to the talent department. I try to focus on the task hard
enough that any thought of a braless girl named Ashley with shabby
chic bangs, laughing away her Sunday night with Adam, is pushed away.

....

While I wait for the goody bag deliveries and the all-staff Monday-
morning meeting summons, I catch up on my guilty pleasure: *The Snap*'s
advice column. There's nothing wrong with reading *The Snap*. Everyone in the office does, especially during the last week, when it seemed
to always be the first outlet flashing name after name of men in show
business called out for shitty behavior. But I think any advice column is
inherently trite, and reading it suggests I'm the kind of girl who loves to
talk about nail polish and obsess over *The Bachelor*. To be clear, I couldn't
give a shit about either of those things.

But the woman who writes the column is smart and something of
a personal hero, because she's from the same shit town in Georgia as
me: Eulalia, which might sound charming but I can assure you is not.
In this week's column, the person writing in is seeking advice about the
impending wedding she doesn't really want to have. Apparently, this
bride's father has a terminal illness, so there's pressure to go ahead and
get married so her dad can witness it. But now she feels rushed, and
she's choking. I can't exactly relate. I don't know who my father is, I
think all the patriarchal dad stuff surrounding traditional weddings is

bullshit, and I don't really understand why anyone would get married anyway. I ditch the column.

When I refresh *The Snap*'s home page, a new headline flashes and my blood goes cold:

ANOTHER ONE BITES THE DUST: THOMAS CLARK, PRESIDENT

OF AMERICAN NETWORK, BECOMES LATEST MAN IN MEDIA

ACCUSED OF SEXUAL HARASSMENT

Thomas Clark. Susan Clark's husband. I nearly jump out of my skin when I hear Emma's voice behind me. "Oh shit," she says, reading over my shoulder. "Thomas Clark? Gary's gonna have a field day, and Wes is gonna have a heart attack."

I shake my head and try to come back into myself. "Well, would that really be the worst thing?"

"Touché," Emma says, straightening her pencil skirt. Wes Smithson is the CEO of United Broadcast Company, which airs our show and owns the cable network at which Thomas Clark has apparently been harassing women. Wes is older than Father Time, and, to be frank, I'm sure it won't be long before it's his name that's flashing in block letters on *The Snap*. He strikes me as the kind of guy who would grab a handful of ass at a holiday party after a few martinis, claiming that in his day, none of the office gals minded. Emma nods to my screen. "Dumbass or Devil?"

It's the question we ask whenever a soon-to-be-formerly powerful man is publicly outed as a creep. What we mean is: Was this guy Weinstein rapist-level evil? Or was he the kind of guy who said something he shouldn't have about an intern's dress and called his female colleagues "sweetheart"? Neither is good, but the difference feels worth noting.

"I haven't read it yet," I say. I swallow, which brings my already dry mouth to a Sahara level. My stomach feels wildly tight.

"Who now?"

I turn and look into the freckled face of Peanut, my coworker whose real name I no longer remember. He's the other talent assistant, a tiny human being from Los Angeles whose sweet and jumpy energy took time to get used to. One time, I said hello to him before he saw me and he screamed so loud an intern hid under a desk, assuming there was an active shooter. Peanut is the exact spiritual counterpart to his boss, Mark, who thinks he's the Second Coming of Christ because he worked for Gary's agent when Gary was an unknown improv student surviving solely on ramen and dreams of comedy stardom.

I rotate my screen so Peanut can see the headline. He lets out a low whistle, turning somehow even paler. "Wes might finally croak over this one," he whispers, and Emma snorts.

The bell chimes, meaning it's staff meeting time. Mark catches up with us before we head downstairs to the conference room, and as usual when I'm in his presence, I hold my breath—I'm convinced the amount of cologne clinging to his eerily perfectly tailored suit could kill a small animal. Or maybe it's all the hair gel caked onto his swooped-over brunette helmet head. Either way, I wouldn't suggest lighting a match near the man unless you wanted to see an explosion.

"How was your weekend?" he asks Emma.

"Oh, fine. Cara had some tantrums, but what can you do," she says. I always feel a small bloom of pride at how Emma's usually energetic voice deadens when she speaks to Mark, like the fact that she doesn't bother to be polite to him is a rebellion.

"Oh yeah, you're telling me. Melissa had some girls' trip, so I babysat all weekend."

"I don't know if taking care of your own child can be considered 'babysitting,'" Emma says back. Peanut and I give each other a little side grin.

Per usual, it feels like the big, overly lit conference room is going to burst with the whole staff crowded in here. Yet the seat at the head of the conference table remains empty as everyone quietly asks each other about their weekends and waits for the head honcho to arrive. Adam gives me a nod from across the room, leaning against the wall with the other production assistants, all in the same jeans and T-shirt uniform

I'm in. He tilts his head and gives a performative eye roll—he's stand-ing near Justin, the writers' assistant, who is speaking embarrassingly animatedly to a group of writers, undoubtedly managing to work the fact that he went to Harvard at least three times into whatever asinine anecdote he's telling them. I try to smile back nonchalantly, but my heart is racing and I feel anxious, like I have to give a presentation I'm not prepared for. I'm annoyed with myself for having such a physical reaction to the news about Thomas Clark. I haven't seen him in years and barely knew him when I did.

Soon enough, Gary Madden saunters in and takes his seat, look-ing significantly more haggard than he will this afternoon, when his makeup artist will reverse time on his face in the name of show busi-ness. A reverent silence falls over the room.

"G'morning, team," he says as he does every Monday, in this casual voice, like the obvious fact that he's being worshipped has no effect on him. "Hope everyone had a good weekend." The staff nods. "Know who didn't have a good weekend?"

Some of the staff chuckle and look around knowingly, while some look confused at first, then quickly mask their confusion with the same knowing looks as everyone else. I sneak a peek at Dan, the showrunner, who has to go between the suits at the network and Gary. Days like these are his nightmare. A pang of sympathy reverberates in me, but I quickly shoo it away. If Dan has a problem with his show calling out creeps, then fuck him.

My mind jumps to the encounter with Susan yesterday outside the bakery. Now her bizarre response when I asked about Mr. Clark makes sense; she must have known this story was going to break. How shitty this must be for her. But like I do with all these stories in which the perpetrator is married, I find myself wondering whether Susan had any idea about Thomas's behavior. Maybe this thought is a result of some internalized misogyny, some sick, subconscious need to blame the wife. Most of all, though, thinking about Susan makes me feel like my chest has a bowling ball in it. Whether or not she knew, this must be painful.

My shoulders stiffen as the inevitable memories start creeping in. Memories of how after a few too many (and there was never anything less for my mother), when Susan came up in conversation back in Eulalia, Patty would call her childhood friend "uppity," would go on about how Susan abandoned all of them for a "hoity-toity New York life" with a Yankee who thought too much of himself. On *really* bad nights, Patty would say to anyone who would listen (her less-than-enthusiastic audience consisting of just me and my grandparents) that she thought Mr. Clark was probably gay. At this point, Pops, my sweet, gossip-allergic grandpa, would usually clear his throat loudly and try to change the subject. I always thought Thomas seemed nice, especially when I was a kid and I'd see him every few Christmases. Then again, as a fatherless, not-yet-jaded child, I found all dads pretty intriguing.

After an email chain started by Pops led to my dream New York internship here at *Late Night*, Susan and Thomas invited me for dinner at their apartment at East Eightieth and Madison. I could see during that dinner how someone like my mother would think that Thomas might be gay—just because he was outgoing, smiled a lot and laughed generously at others' jokes, and clearly dressed with intention. It was small-town thinking. Over Sfoglia takeout rigatoni, I skewered Patty in my mind. How embarrassing for her that she had no idea how the world works.

I snap back to the present, where Gary sits at the head of the table, cracking himself and the entire room up (genuinely or not, who could say) with jokes about the soapy, over-the-top TV Thomas's network makes in an attempt to keep up with the prestige television trends of the day and the wordplay about sexual harassment he could work in there. The network had a show called *Skirts* about the secretaries who worked in advertising in the 1960s, so there was no shortage of material to draw from.

I paste a smile on my face and chuckle along with everyone else, like the good employee that I am.

CHAPTER 3

I'm pushing my Trader Joe's frozen dinner (sweet potato gnocchi, TJ's most criminally underrated item) around a pan when my phone dings with a text. I don't usually keep my phone volume on, because I'm not a boomer. But Adam normally calls or texts after work, and he hasn't yet today. I reach for my phone much more quickly than I would have had Isabelle been home to witness it. But of course, like she is most weeknights, Izzy is out at some happy hour or dinner or show, her presence lingering in the egg-covered pan and plate and the stained coffee mug she's left in the sink, which I'll hand-wash along with my dishes after dinner, because our shoebox East Village apartment doesn't have the luxury of a dishwasher.

My shoulders sink and I roll my eyes in disappointment when I see it's not Adam but a text from an unknown number—probably a spam account or political faction—and in disappointment with myself for being disappointed at all. I open the text to delete the message, and my finger is halfway through dragging it across the screen when I realize that it's not automated after all.

> Hi Presley. This is Susan Clark. It was great running into you,
> and I'd love to make a plan to take you out for dinner or a drink
> or anything, really xx Susan

I pause. Who, in their right mind, the day that their husband's name is dragged across the internet, follows up on an invitation to meet up that was obviously never going to happen?

On the other hand, part of me gets it. When something horrendous is happening, the easiest thing to do is look away. To finish folding your laundry, or send that email, or go to an exercise class (although not one where they make you meditate). Something like empathy claws through my chest.

Then I think about the effort that would be involved in actually hanging out with Susan. The woman is already experiencing her own traumatic shit, which would be quite the addition to the mess of her attempting to console me in mine. I don't want to talk about Thomas's cancellation, and hopefully Susan wouldn't want to either. And I *certainly* don't want to discuss Patty or Patty's death, so what does that leave? Small talk. I'm not good at that under normal circumstances.

My phone buzzes in my hand, and a photo of me and Adam outside Village East movie theater pops up. He insisted on taking it before we saw *Dunkirk*, complaining that we had no photos together, and took the liberty of assigning it to his contact in my phone. I sigh, relieved, even though my heart rate also spikes. "Yes?" I say, as if I'm annoyed. We both know I'm not.

"What are you doing right now, Fry?"

"Making dinner."

"What are you having?"

"Why is that information you need to know?" I ask, turning off the stove (no small feat considering how rusty the knobs are).

"Rawr," he says. "Why so testy?"

I exhale. "Sorry. I'm having TJ's gnocchi."

"Sweet potato?"

"Yeah, you know, because of the—"

"Because of the sauce, Fry, I know," he says.

Look, I know it's weird that Adam and I work together all day, then keep our conversations going into the evenings. But it's damn near impossible to finish a conversation when there's an hour's worth of television to throw together. It's also nearly impossible for us to finish a conversation in any circumstance, really. With us, there's always something more to say, an inevitable spark one of us can always catch off the other's latest comment. It feels like an endless conversation, the one between me and him.

"You never finished telling me about your date," I say, even though doing so makes me feel like a wrecking ball has dropped into my stomach.

"Eh, is that worth talking about? Dude, what I want to hear about is your relationship with Thomas Clark." After the staff meeting, I had mentioned to Adam over Slack that I knew Thomas, right before Adam got tasked with hunting down an inflatable dragon for the cold open and I got sent to Chipotle to pick up three very specific burritos for Aubrey Plaza, all of which I had the pleasure of gifting to the interns when I found them untouched at the end of the day. I feel a small ribbon of relief unfurl in me and I choose not to analyze it, not to think about what it means that I would rather talk about my family friend who has recently been outed as a predator than discuss the potential success of one of Adam's dates.

"Please don't call it a relationship, considering what that now implies," I say. "I don't know him super well or anything. His wife—well, wife for now, I guess—grew up with my mom and they were really close when they were kids. They kind of kept in touch, enough that Thomas put in a good word for me when I was applying to the internship a few years back, and he and Susan had me over for dinner at their apartment, like, once."

"Did he seem like a creep?"

I consider this as I scoop some gnocchi into a chipped bowl Izzy and I got at Century 21. Maybe I can be a bit more objective now that the initial shock has worn off. "No. He never did anything, like, overtly weird. He was always really nice. But he had this big personality, he's old money, I don't know. I would be shocked if he were a full-on rapist, but isn't the allegation just that he made some comments he shouldn't have and stuff?" I hadn't done much research after seeing that first headline. Partially because of all the running around the office and theater (and to Chipotle) the day required and partially because reading about it had made me queasy.

"There was an affair with a colleague," Adam says. "He released a statement admitting that. She hasn't said anything. She wasn't blatantly age *in*appropriate, but she wasn't his equal at work, either. Maybe a VP or something."

I exhale. Poor Susan. "Fuck."

"What's the wife's vibe?" Adam asks.

There's no room for a regular kitchen table in our apartment, so I take the six steps that separate the stove from the couch and put my bowl on the glass Craigslist coffee table in front of me. I know my gnocchi's going to get cold. I don't want to eat while I'm on the phone, though, and I'm rapidly losing my appetite, anyway. "She's, you know, Upper East Side. I mean, she wasn't always. I ran into her yesterday, actually."

"What were you doing on the Upper East Side?"

"No, I saw her at Daily Provisions."

"Jealous."

"Don't be. She hugged me for an uncomfortable amount of time," I say.

"I think, according to you, any amount of time in a hug is an uncomfortable amount of time," Adam says. I choke out a little laugh involuntarily. Does Adam think about hugging me? Touching me?

"Whatever," I say.

"I guess she needed a hug, yeesh," Adam says. "What with all this."

"I think she thought the hug was more for me than for her. It was very . . . condolence-y. I haven't seen her since, uh, my mom."

I don't talk much about Patty's death, but recently I've found myself toeing the line a little bit with Adam. Just a comment here or there

acknowledging it. No idea why. Because Adam started working at the show six months ago, he's only known me post–Patty's death. I'm glad for that. In those first few months after, I was basically a zombie, and it's occurred to me more than a few times that Adam and I might not have become friends so quickly had he come to the show earlier.

"I'm sorry, Fry," he says.

"Oh, it's fine," I say quickly.

"Okay, well, I'll leave you to your gnocchi. I'm about to walk into a bar anyway."

"Another hot date?" I close my eyes.

"Nope, just meeting Billy, unfortunately for the single ladies of New York." He puts on an overly suave voice as he says this, like he's introducing a jazz trio or something. It's stupid, and we both crack up.

"Jesus, you are such a—"

"I know, I know, I'm the worst," he says. "I'll see you tomorrow, Fry."

"Bye." I hang up. I always make a point to hang up first on our calls. As if that changes anything.

....

I met Isabelle in a freshman-year political science class at UGA. The number of students in the lecture was twice that of my entire high school graduating class. "Hi," she said as she sat down next to me. "I'm Isabelle." She reached over for a handshake, which I thought was a pretty schmucky thing for an eighteen-year-old to do. Her oversize sorority T-shirt certainly didn't help.

"I'm Presley," I replied, gingerly shaking her hand before turning back to the new laptop my grandparents had given me for graduation. After class, Izzy asked if we could exchange numbers in case one of us ever had to miss lecture or had questions. Her overt friendliness put me off, but I typed my number into her phone; I didn't have much choice with the way she shoved it in my face. She texted me immediately. I didn't reply.

But the joke was on me, because I fucked up saving my notes on my fancy new computer and we had an upcoming quiz. I panicked and knew my only choice was to text the pushy sorority star and ask for her notes, which she sent over immediately. This put me in her debt, so I started chatting with her more before and after class. Soon, we figured out our dorm rooms were only one floor apart, she dropped her sorority (some of her "sisters" were a bit squeamish about Isabelle's sexual preference for sorority members over fraternity), and we started having lunch together in the dining halls most days. The rest is fucking history.

Her effortless ability to turn her friendliness into networking, knowing how to do shit like take good notes and save them properly, plus the fact that she's whip-smart are all reasons why Isabelle has a highfalutin job at a fancy PR firm where she is the youngest person there to have her own office with a view of Bryant Park. She's already responding to emails now, at eight forty-five in the morning, sitting next to me as the D train takes us soaring beneath Manhattan.

Without looking up, she asks, "So, what did you do last night?"

"Nothing. You know this," I say. Isabelle has my location tracked on her phone, which she tells me she checks regularly. I roll my eyes whenever she mentions this, but the truth is it makes me feel safe. She nods, semi-listening as she types on her iPhone like there's a gun to her head. "What did you do?" I ask her.

"Took a potential client out to dinner, then got a drink with Hannah. Your lights were out by the time I got back."

"Hinge Hannah lives to see another day!"

Isabelle shrugs. "Yeah, we'll see." Izzy goes on a shitload of dates but has yet to commit to anyone. At the risk of perpetuating a lesbian stereotype, pretty much every girl ends up trying to, like, marry her, but their love tends to go unrequited. I think she likes playing the field too much, which is fine by me. I get to hear about all her entertaining escapades and don't have to deal with the horrifying prospect of having to share her or our apartment with someone else.

"I did try to stay awake for you. Yesterday was actually pretty wild and I wanted to tell you about it," I say. Isabelle looks up from her phone, giving me her full attention. I tell her about Thomas Clark.

"Whoa," she says when I finish the part about Susan texting me. "Sounds to me like that is some . . . next-level avoidance."

"I guess," I say, ducking my head to avoid decapitation by some dude's gigantic backpack. I feel Isabelle staring at me.

"Again, *avoidance*. Is that something you would be familiar with, Presley?" Isabelle loves feelings (after much happy hour sangria recently, she told me one of her most vivid and most returned-to fantasies is sitting in couples therapy with her future wife) and riding my ass for me not loving mine. We both know she's referring to Adam, but we also both know that deep beneath it, she's talking about Patty. I glare at her, and she pokes me in the ribs jokingly. She knows better than to push any further.

"So, what do I do, though?" I ask.

"You didn't reply?" Isabelle asks, eyes widening. She sighs. "I guess I shouldn't be surprised. But, P! You gotta reply. Think of how sad she must be."

"All right, all right, but, like, what do I say?"

"When you're free?"

I groan loudly. "But I don't wanna!"

Isabelle gives me a stern look and puts her hand on my knee, bouncing along with the shaking of the aluminum can we're in. "Presley Fry," she says, "if you want to make up some excuse and blow this woman off, that's your prerogative. But your connection to her helped you get your job, a job that you love. She seems like a nice lady, who is currently in pain, and *she* reached out to *you*. Plus, she wants you to hook up with her son, which we know you won't do, so you may as well toss her this one small bone. Have a little drink with her, get it over with. That's my advice."

"I hate your advice," I lie.

She stands as the train pulls into the Bryant Park station. She looks down at me, pats me on the head, and smiles. "That's very sweet coming from you, Presley, considering that you pretend to hate everything you love. Mwah!" She blows me a kiss as the doors open and she saunters off the train.

CHAPTER 4

Susan Clark's Upper East Side apartment is pristine. This shouldn't come as a surprise, but for some reason, it's strange to come to terms with the fact that a woman whose life is basically unspooling is watching it unspool from such a clean, fancy place. Then again, I'm sure it's not like she's the one actually cleaning it. I'm sitting on a couch so stiff I must be the first person to ever sit on it, but it also somehow looks like it's thousands of years old. Susan is sitting across from me in an armchair that looks similarly uncomfortable.

Thankfully, she gave me a much quicker hug this time upon opening her apartment door after Roger, the smiling, portly, middle-aged doorman, admitted me up here.

"Anyone ever tell you you look like Scarlett Johansson?" he asked me as we ascended.

"No," I replied, cheeks pinching in a scowl. From the way he smiled and shrugged, though, I don't think he meant it as any kind of come-on.

Susan has on a silk blouse and slacks, which gives me pause. Her shoulder-length brown hair looks professionally blown dry. She looks like she should be going to an interview, click-clacking through a marble lobby, not chilling in her own home. She's wearing makeup on her one-shot-shy-of-too-Botoxed face. She's definitely pretty, though, which always killed Patty (no pun intended).

"So, what can I get you to drink?" she asks, motioning to a heavily stocked bar cart, this golden antique thing that looks like it would more likely grace the cover of an Edith Wharton novel than exist in someone's home. "We also have wine in the kitchen, red and some white in the fridge."

This question. The first thing my mind jumps to is what I can afford, then I remember I don't need to offer to Venmo this woman for offering me something of her own to drink. I never drink vodka—that was Patty's poison, and the smell makes me curl inward and shiver. I like wine, but my favorite drink is beer. Or whiskey. But I don't know if it's kosher to ask for a whiskey on the rocks at a lovely ladies' happy hour.

"Glass of wine sounds good," I say, even though it doesn't.

"Red or white?" Susan asks, standing.

"Uh, what are you having?" I ask as Susan starts to walk away, disappearing into the cavernous apartment.

"White! It's a sauvignon blanc," she offers, pronouncing it all French and shit.

"Sounds good," I say again, even though it still doesn't.

I check my phone and see a text from Adam, which I scramble to open. He says: Let me know how it goes tonight! with the double-eye emoji.

I tuck my phone back in my jacket pocket as Susan reemerges with two goblets of wine. She hands me one and clinks my glass, gives me a big grin, like we're both doing really well and just tickled to be here. I chide myself for not using my Tinder date trick: setting an alarm on my phone for twenty minutes from now, an alarm that can pass as an "emergency" call and an excuse to leave.

"So," she says, returned to her perch on the armchair. "Tell me everything!" I blink. I do not know what she could possibly mean by this. Her neck twitches a little, though her smile doesn't falter. It's unsettling, but

I think she's realizing I don't know what to do with that open-ended prompt. She tries again. "How's . . . work?"

I'm not sure this is better. Am I supposed to drag Gary, say something about him going too far in the way he publicly went after Thomas? Should it even be acknowledged, or can I get away with acting like my boss didn't make a joke on national television that Susan's husband went after Emmys and younger female colleagues in the same way ("unsuccessfully")?

"You know," I say, even though she doesn't, which is why she fucking asked. "It's good. I'm just an assistant, so not much to brag about there, but I really like my boss, Emma." I take a sip of the wine. Damn, that shit tastes crisp. Expensive.

"That's great! Lawrence is an assistant, too," Susan says. "And what does your boss do, exactly?"

"She books talent, like the guests for Gary to interview on the show. The celebrities."

"Oh, that's probably interesting," Susan says. "Although, maybe disappointing, too. I've never really been a big celebrity person."

"Yeah, me neither," I say. "But every Friday we have a different up-and-coming comedian on to do a five-minute set, and I've been given a lot more responsibility with booking them. It's cool because it means I go to a lot of comedy shows, which I enjoy." "Enjoy" is one of those words I use only around adults. I know I'm technically an adult, but I'm also still on my grandparents' phone plan and sometimes have ice cream for dinner.

"Oh, now, that's fun," Susan says. Her accent shows a little sometimes, but it sounds classy and sweet. Like she's from Charleston or somewhere people in uptown Manhattan would describe as "quaint." "When I first moved to the city," she continued, "I shared this small apartment not too far from here, actually, with a few other girls from Vanderbilt, and one of them *loved* going to see stand-up comedy downtown. It was back when downtown was seedier, so I'll admit, she sometimes had to fight to get us to go with her, but I was always glad every time I did. We had so much fun."

I nod and feel myself smiling a little, picturing Susan in a bar where people smoked indoors. "That's cool. Ever see any legends?" I ask.

"What do you mean?"

"Never mind," I say. We sip our wine in silence for a minute, and I'd very much like to break it. I go with: "So, did Lawrence have a good birthday?"

She smiles again, but it's not the forced one she's had on. Her whole face lights up, and her posture perks up, too. "He did, thanks for asking. I gave him your phone number, I hope that's all right. I really do think it would be fun for you two to get to know each other."

I nod, knowing full well this UVA frat boy is not about to text the family friend whose number was forced on him by his mother. God, Susan really must think I'm some charity case. I do wonder how he's holding up, though, with everything with his dad. Speaking of, is it weird that I haven't said anything about Mr. Clark yet? Holy shit, what if he comes home and I have to talk to him?

"Are you single?" she asks, then rushes forward with, "I don't mean that in relation to Lawrence. I'm not trying to be . . . to put pressure on . . ." She clears her throat, and I would like very much for the floor to swallow me whole. "I just wondered, is all."

"I am single, yes." I don't have much more to say about this. I've never dated anyone, never had a boyfriend. I hook up with the occasional Tinder dude every now and again just to keep the wheels greased, but nothing more. "You know, guys in the city my age aren't always . . ."

She chuckles a little. "Oh, I remember," she says. I'm scared she's going to say "Boys will be boys" or some shit, and then I'll have to laugh like I think that's funny. Like that's not exactly the kind of thinking that set the stage for situations like Thomas's. But instead she says, "Your roommate seemed like a cute, fun girl. I should've told you to invite her tonight, I'm sorry."

"Oh, that's okay," I say. "She wouldn't have been able to come anyway. She's one of the busiest people on earth."

"Oh," Susan says, eyes bugging a bit at my hyperbole. "Well, that's fun! Is she single, also?"

"Yes," I say. Susan nods. "And how's Michael?" I ask, thankfully remembering the existence of her older son.

"He's great, thank you! He works in Los Angeles as a graphic designer," she says, smiling that same smile from earlier, when she talked about Lawrence. It sets off a little twinge in me, when I see mothers light up and twinkle at the mere mention of their children. Probably because I immediately assume it's fake, though of course it isn't. That kind of shiny maternal pride is just not something I have much first-hand experience with. "He just started dating someone new, and it must be serious, because Michael let me meet him on FaceTime." She giggles a little bit with actual pleasure, and I'm pleased to hear that Susan is so accepting of having a gay son. "And how are George and Doris?" she asks me.

I tell her they're good, that my grandmother recovered well from her hip surgery. And thank God she did, because my grandfather can't do anything without her. As in, making himself a damn sandwich would have his brain in knots. It's a good thing he's so lovable.

"Oh, my parents were the same way," she says. I don't remember Susan's father, who died before I was born. I sort of remember Susan's mother, a sweet lady in my grandma's bridge club who lived a few neighborhoods over from us. I must have been nine or something when she died. Now that I think about it, I'm pretty sure Lawrence and I played *Pokémon* on our Game Boys next to each other after her funeral.

"Yeah, men are—" I stop myself when I remember I'm not sitting in my apartment shooting the shit with Isabelle, that it isn't cool to casually say things like "Men are trash" to respectable women, especially since bad male behavior is not a can of worms I'm trying to open right now.

"Helpless, they can be helpless," Susan finishes for me, taking a lengthy sip of her wine.

I chuckle in an attempt to be polite and wonder when I can leave. Maybe finishing my glass of wine can spur my exit. I gulp down a big mouthful.

"You know, Presley," Susan says, her face finally rid of that fake smile, though its absence isn't exactly a relief. The small talk was grating, but I'd rather that than talk about something real. "I just have to tell you I'm so sorry you lost your mother. It's a terrible loss, the deepest loss. I know that personally, and I can't imagine how painful it must be at your age. And will continue to be. So, I want you to know, my heart is really with you."

Her heart is with me? Any feelings of sympathy or concern that I had for Susan in the aftermath of the revelations about Thomas dissolve like Alka-Seltzer. My throat feels like it's closing. My body's gone numb, which usually happens when Patty comes up. But I try to snap out of it. The quicker I respond, the quicker this whole thing can be over. "Thanks, Mrs. Clark. I appreciate it." I try to offer a little smile, to put her concern to rest. But I can feel it not reaching my eyes; it's just a mechanical movement on the bottom half of my face.

"Patty was really special. To this day, I've never met anyone like her." I can't help but snort; this is a very diplomatic thing for Susan to say. But I appreciate that she isn't sugarcoating, exactly. A bunch of our neighbors in Eulalia tried to tell me how much they loved my mom, bullshit about how "sweet" she was. The only times she was ever sweet involved the perfect amount to drink and just the right thing on TV. And it never lasted, she always quickly crossed over to her usual disastrous, overserved self. She was nice when she was around a cat or dog, actually. She was always, like, Steve Irwin–good with animals.

Susan smiles to herself, and I feel a tug in my chest that is entirely unfamiliar to me when it comes to the mention of Patty. It's the same little yank I feel when Adam mentions that he went on a date or when Emma calls me into her office with "big news." It's wanting to know more, with the realization that knowing more could also suck.

"She taught me so much, your mother did," Susan tells me.

I stiffen, try to shove my curiosity down and away. "Like what, how to cover liquor breath?"

The joke sits heavy in the room, growing sour with each passing moment. I'm not sure why I said it. The only thing rarer than my talking about Patty is my talking about Patty's drinking. It's not difficult to get away with, because hardly anyone up here knew her, except Izzy, who met her only a handful of times and knows better than to pry. But I guess Susan would know. Everyone from Eulalia knows.

I take another sip in response, like the true child of an alcoholic. Susan exhales. "No," she says. "Although we did get into some trouble. . . ." She shakes her head and chuckles. I feel that tug again. Maybe it would be funny to hear about Patty's antics back when they were acceptable, back when it was the weekend and she was young and wild and childless. Susan continues, "She was just one of those girls, I feel like I come across them even now, especially in a city like New York. One of those girls who somehow knows things. Things I wouldn't have known on my own." I almost laugh, assuming she's talking about sex stuff, then remind myself to grow up and get my head out of the gutter.

I get what she means, though. Isabelle is like that. She somehow always knows which clothes will pair well together and how to do hair and makeup. And it's more than just traditional girlie shit. She strikes the perfect tone in emails, always knows at what point in the night to stop drinking, and plans the right balance of chill and bustle when she has guests visiting New York.

Patty was nowhere near the level of competent I associate with those kind of women. Patty, who couldn't hold a job, who blacked out every night without fail (I don't count her bouts of sobriety, so brief and pathetic were they), who couldn't even raise me on her own. Someone like Susan looking up to my shell of a mother is impossible to imagine.

"I had such a hard time when I first started at Vanderbilt. I don't know what I would have done had she not been there," she says.

I open my mouth to correct her. My mother didn't go to college, much less Vanderbilt. But then I remember. Vanderbilt is, of course, in Nashville, which was where Patty ran off to after high school. What happens when you mix together God-given narcissism, overly supportive parents, and a decent choir voice? A woman who's convinced she's a star. So off to Music City, USA, Patty went, sure she would Be Someone, only to blow her high school savings on studio time to record a demo she dropped off at record labels, to absolutely zero results. This is usually where her drunken telling of the story would peter off, but I know she tended bar for a while, until I suspect the outgoing booze money exceeded the incoming booze money and she had no choice but to return to Eulalia, her 1980s big-haired head hung in shame. It's very difficult to picture Susan mixed up in any of that.

"Street smarts," Susan says. She's staring at the Persian rug, but it doesn't look like she's seeing anything. "A level of street smarts I've never seemed to have. There was this one night, that . . . Well, this one day that turned into this night . . ." She trails off. Her voice starts to thicken, like tears are gathering in her throat. She takes a breath and shakes her shoulders a little, looks up at the ceiling, and swallows. "She saved my life once, your mother did."

My eyes narrow. That damn tug of curiosity is back stronger than ever, yanking on my chest. What the fuck is she talking about?

"Anyway!" Susan says, sitting up straight and pasting that freaky smile back on, like she's just woken up from being hypnotized, with no recollection of the past few moments. "She was special, is all I'm trying to say."

I'm too stunned to respond. I pinch my arm to force myself back here, to this sparkling apartment, to this empty conversational space I'm supposed to fill. "Yeah, well, she marched to the beat of her own drum, that's for sure," I manage. A platitude I developed in the days following Patty's death. I figured it was the truest thing I could have said about her while remaining pleasant. Susan nods.

Ready to be out of here, I guzzle down the last sip of wine. I stand, awkwardly looking around, wondering what I'm supposed to do with the empty glass. "Well, I'd better be going. Thanks for having me."

Susan stands, too, and takes the glass. "Thanks for coming, Presley. It was really nice to see you, and it was really nice to . . ." She swallows and cocks her head to the side, looking for words, ever so briefly dropping that bulletproof composure. "It's nice to spend time with an old friend."

"Old friend" is more than a stretch, and I shudder to think that maybe she's talking about Patty, implying that I'm some kind of extension of her. I don't say anything in response, just nod and do that tight-lipped smile I do when I'm biting back a sarcastic comment. She leads me to the door and pulls me in for a hug. It's not as tight as the Daily Provisions hug, but it does last longer than the one she greeted me with tonight. When she finally lets go, I practically sprint down the hallway and into the mirrored elevator, holding my breath until I spill out onto Madison Avenue. I make myself slow down as I walk toward the 6 train, make myself breathe deep. I picture gathering up Susan's words like they're bricks, taking "this one day that turned into this night" and "saved my life once, your mother did" into my arms, and chucking them out to sea. But the wind brings them right back, flying at me.

CHAPTER 5

Thursday night at Black Cat LES. Objectively, this open mic is shitty: shitty drinks, shitty folding chairs, in a shitty basement. But I'm here almost every week. It would probably be more productive to go to shows with actual lineups, where comedians perform sets they've carefully honed and are already closer to being ready to appear on *Late Night*. But I love the idea of finding someone with undeniable talent at an open mic, of being the person who can say they discovered someone who will go on to become big. Maybe I could be the one to help fast-track their career.

And there's the energy of an open mic. You can feel the nerves. You'd think they would be coming from the comedians, but they're mostly all pretty high off their own supply. The nerves come from the audience, the people who have been dragged here to support their roommate or college friend or significant other (yikes), with the precarious possibility (likelihood) of jokes being met with silence. Considering the quality of most of the performances, the audience dynamics are usually the most entertaining part: the loud, fake laughs given in support, the drunk wannabes heckling the comics.

The audience member I love watching squirm the most is Adam, whose own self-consciousness really wiggles its way to the forefront on open mic nights. Adam likes comedy, as most people who work at a late night comedy show do, but his real love is film. He's nice to come to as many shows as he does with me, and in return I go to the Angelika with him and see all the subtitled indie movies he breathes like air. Adam wants to make movies—or, excuse me, *films*. His passion occasionally ventures into the pretentious, which is fun to mock. I can't help but respect it, though, his obsession. There's some quote from one of those self-help white ladies Isabelle is always trying to get me to read about interested people making interesting people. That applies here.

Emma recently gave me two tickets to an early screening of this new movie *Call Me by Your Name*. I didn't know anything about it, but Adam loves the director, so I brought him. We didn't say a word to each other the whole time the movie played, and silence between us is rare. After, we intentionally took the local train, on a line that doesn't particularly make sense for either of our apartments, just so we would have more time together to geek out over how excellent the writing was, how much the dad's speech at the end moved us. The next day, I found an envelope on my desk, the word "Scrapbook" written on it in Sharpie, with hand-drawn stars and hearts all over it. The ticket stub from the night before was in it, along with a sticky note that said, "For all the mems to come."

"You owe me for this," he mutters into my ear as a pasty guy walks in wearing a T-shirt with Seth MacFarlane's face on it.

"You're the one who's been begging me to hang out all week. This was my available time slot," I say.

He rolls his eyes but throws his hands up by his shoulders. "Whatever," he says. I hadn't actually been that busy this week, but I don't want to seem available every time Adam wants to hang out. "Where's your girl?" he asks.

Agatha Reddy isn't here yet, and I know, because my eyes are peeled for her. The first time I saw Agatha perform was about a year and a half ago, my first comedy show back after returning from that awful trip to Eulalia for Patty's funeral. It was an open mic, not unlike this one, and she was far and away the best comedian there—had clearly put effort into her set, was referencing a little notepad on the stool she stood next to instead of just riffing on arbitrary subjects like the other (all-male) comics that night did. I followed her on Instagram and Twitter, started trying to see her as much as possible at shows around town, and eventually introduced myself to her. When Emma told me I had the green light to start really scouting for the show, I knew immediately Agatha would be the first comedian I would pitch. She is perfect: talented, professional, unknown (for now), in search of a bigger platform. I could both give her that platform and get credit at *Late Night* for being the one to find her, and use that credit to get promoted.

Speaking of, there's a tap on my shoulder, and I turn around and look right into Agatha's face, her blue eye shadow shimmering under the light of the disco ball hanging above us. She's crouched below me. This is the one thing I don't like about her: how close she gets when she talks. "Hey, Presley!" she says.

"Hey," I say. Adam shifts next to me. "This is Adam, he works at the show with me."

"Hi." Agatha nods in his direction briefly before turning back to me. "What's the latest?"

I know what she means. "We're getting there, dude. I'm so excited to see you perform tonight. I'm gonna film, just in case. And if this is the one, I'll show my boss, and then hopefully we're one step closer to getting you on the Friday spot."

She nods enthusiastically, her ink-colored bob swinging by her ears. "Okay, good to know," she says. "I'm gonna feel it out tonight, but I've been cutting the pork chop bit from the set."

"Oh, really? Okay. I like that bit, but it's obviously up to you. Follow your instincts. I know you'll do the right thing when you're up there."

"Thanks, dude," she says. "Priya also told me not to cut it. Hm." Priya is Agatha's older sister and the recipient of all Agatha's original joke ideas in the form of voice notes. Agatha and I have recently started texting about ideas, too. She may be unknown now, but the collaboration feels like an honor. She stands and hikes up her high-waisted jeans, bringing them closer to the hem of her camo crop top. "See ya." She nods in Adam's direction. "Good to meet you."

It pleases me that she barely acknowledged him, like the only person she's here to impress is me. I try to hide a smirk as I feel Adam looking at me, the satisfaction that he saw me doing my thing, in my element, unfolding and expanding in my chest like a microwave popcorn bag. As a production assistant, and one who's newer to the show, his responsibilities mostly include fetching things for people. And while there's a certain pleasure in feeling more important than him, I also don't want to make him feel bad, which, judging from the way he's shifting in his seat, he just might.

I nod to the guy with the Seth T-shirt. "Next beer says that guy humps the mic stand."

Adam laughs, which, no matter what kind of day I'm having, is a consistent mood lifter. He tends to throw his head back and look up at the ceiling, and his shoulders really shake. But my favorite part is this look he gets on his face right as he's tossing his head, this look of almost surprise, almost appreciation, for whatever it is he's laughing at. Then, he usually covers his face with his hands, hiding. Though I have absolutely no stand-up ambitions of my own, the serotonin rush I get from his laughing at my jokes is a specific, tingling gratification. "You're on," he says. "Though I have a feeling I'm about to be one beer poorer."

The emcee is this guy Woody McCloud, whom I see around town a lot. He opens with some jokes I've already heard (mostly about his name), but I force laughter anyway (just like I did the first time I heard them). I may as well be supportive. "So, I have a girlfriend," he says, holding dramatically for applause, which gets a good chuckle. "She is blind, yes, thank you for asking. And she and I were talking about birth control recently, like what her options are. *Her options*, obviously. I'm a man, why would I help with that." Some guy whoops, which Woody, bless him, makes a disapproving face at. "Cool, I see we have a misogynist with us tonight, great. So anyway, she was like, 'Do I get the IUD, do I go on the pill, is it cool if we just stick with condoms,' and then she got kinda frustrated, you know. She was like, 'Ugh, it's so annoying that I have to sit here and think about all this shit, and you don't really have to.' And I was like, 'Babe, I *think* about birth control.' Recently I was on a flight, a Southwest flight. You know how with Southwest, there are no assigned seats, very equal for all, very Bernie." A small laugh. "So, I was getting on the plane, and I saw this woman, this mom, she had two kids with her. And because she's a mom, she loves her kids, and that was made clear when she said to them, she said, You know what, kids, I love you two so much, I'm going to let the two of you choose seats. So, one kid picks the window, another kid picks the aisle, and her sad ass is relegated to the middle. And I looked at that, at how when you have kids you love them so much that you become willing to suffer extreme amounts of discomfort, to sit in the fucking *middle* if it makes them happy, and I said . . . that's birth control!" He gets a decent laugh here. It's a warm crowd, considering the tepid response that monologue probably *should* have gotten. "I have that thought, and I can't get a condom on fast enough."

Woody introduces the first comedian, who is none other than Seth MacFarlane T-shirt guy. He gets up and immediately starts making fun of himself and how quickly he comes when he has sex. If I'm not mistaken, he's just directly quoting Louis C.K. It's under two minutes before he humps the mic stand, and Adam and I look at each other and burst out laughing. Probably helpful for the comedian's ego, misdirected as our laughter may have been. Adam gets up, hunching a bit so as not to make a scene squeezing himself out of our row. Not that he needs to. He's hardly the Incredible Hulk.

By the time Adam returns from the bar, Woody is up introducing the next comedian. Adam hands me a Coors Light tallboy, and I take the can and knock it against his. We smile at each other. He has these blue eyes that shine even in the darkness of this Lower East Side basement. It's distracting enough that I forget the little jangle of nerves I had before, when I realized that Woody was doing crowd work.

The jangles return violently when I feel the crowd's eyes on me. "Ooh, they were staring too deeply into each other's eyes to hear me,

I guess. I'll ask again. How long have you two been together for?" It feels like all the blood is draining out of my body and probably pooling around my feet.

"Uh . . ." I blink. My mind is blank, heart racing.

Before I can even think about it, Adam says, "Two years next month!" He has this goofy, dumb, lovestruck smile on. He turns it to me, and all thousand watts of it are blinding.

"Oh, wow, congratulations," Woody says. I realize I've been going on about how much I love stand-up, but let the record state that I detest crowd work. I'm not here to talk. And I get picked on more than one would assume, considering how often I'm told my resting face is a scowl. And this time, there's the added anxiety of whatever shit Adam's trying to pull by playing into it. "Two years, wow, that's a good while, huh," Woody says. He nods curtly at me and says, "Babe, I'm gonna do you a favor." Turning back to Adam, he says, "When the hell are you gonna propose, man?"

The crowd *loves* this. There are actual hoots of laughter, guffaws that feel deafening. I swear I can feel my intestines twisting around themselves. I may burst into flames, spontaneously combust, bringing the whole building down with me. No way this place is up to code.

Adam, on the other hand, snakes his fingers through mine. I didn't realize I was shaking until his hand steadies me. He pulls my hand up, performatively presses his mouth into the back of it. His lips are dry but warm. My entire being has somehow compressed into my hand, and the rest of my body is weightless. My heart stops beating.

"Any day now!" he says, grinning. When our eyes meet, I'm brought back to myself, no longer weightless, just another person in this crowd that's having a wonderful time at my expense.

"Oh, wow!" Woody says. "Awesome. I feel like I'm usually instigating a huge fight with that, but congrats on the health of your relationship, I guess. Anyway, please put your hands together . . ." And the next stand-up, an incredibly nervous-looking ginger who can't be older than twenty, shuffles to the stage.

I'm laughing and shaking my head and forcibly jerking my hand out of Adam's, and his shoulders are heaving so violently his folding chair is rattling. He laughs like this, face in his hands, all silent and hunched over, only when he thinks something is truly *hysterical*. I'm laughing, too, all the energy that had been wound so tightly in me from our moment in the spotlight uncoiling and releasing.

But then a lick of anger splashes across my abdomen. Is it really *that* funny, the idea that he would be with me? Is it that outrageous? I stop laughing. He wipes the corners of his eyes, having laughed so hard he *cried*. He takes a deep breath, calming down, and looks over at me. He opens his mouth to say something, but I shake my head and pointedly look up at the ginger onstage, who is now fully quivering. Agatha will be up next. I go ahead and pull out my phone in preparation to film her, remembering what it is I'm here to do.

CHAPTER 6

My body is on fire. Not literally, but it may as well be, as I try to think about anything other than how painful it is to remain in the plank position that a white woman with culturally inappropriate braids and the most gorgeous abs I've ever seen is screaming for us to hold. I sneak a look at Isabelle, who is taking deep, measured breaths as she balances, still as a statue, on her elbows and toes. Meanwhile, I'm shaking as if I actually am a plank, being strut on by a pirate. I can barely see anything else, considering it's nearly pitch-black in this ridiculous workout studio, except for any white clothes. Day-Glo or whatever.

"Four! Three! Two! One!" the instructor screams. I collapse onto my rented mat, which is already slick with sweat, but I currently lack the wherewithal to care. I'm too drained to even dredge up any sass for Izzy, who dragged me to this workout on her dime and under the guise that it would be a kickboxing class. Hitting stuff is good for me, we've realized.

This class was more of a shadowboxing situation (aka idiotically pummeling the air) for the first half, then it became a hot yoga kind of thing. I was looking forward to punching shit, not getting quiet with myself. Luckily, the poses we had to hold were so hard as to completely consume my mind, pushing me into a kind of oblivion. It would've been pure bliss if I weren't so out of shape.

I turn over so I'm lying on my back, like the instructor tells us to do. Now we're told to close our eyes, and I lie here, so tired, and I see, just as if she were sitting right in front of me, Patty's face. Her frizzy dirty-blond bangs, blue eyeliner ringing her big brown eyes, the wrinkles she earned way before she was old enough. A golf ball–sized lump announces itself in my throat, and I feel the tears waiting to rush out. I refuse. I snap my eyes open and, quietly as I can, get up, roll my mat, and avoid eye contact with the instructor, who's shooting daggers at me. We were told specifically in the beginning to "do our best to stay in the room" until we were dismissed. Well, Braids, my best does not include lying prostrate and weeping.

I'm sitting on the benches in the locker room, catching up on Comedy Central's stand-up Instagram, when the rest of the class files in. "Are you okay, P?" Isabelle asks as she rushes over.

"Yeah, yeah, just time for me to make my exit," I say. Izzy narrows her eyes but nods and turns to open her locker.

A ding on my phone. I look down, hoping for Adam, and instead see a text from Susan Clark. "Ah, Christ," I mutter.

"Hm?" Isabelle asks, raising her eyebrows.

"Susan Clark texted me. . . ." I open the text and sigh. "She's inviting me to see *The Band's Visit* with her."

Isabelle slams her locker shut and turns to me, eyes bugging out of her head, blond topknot lurching forward.

"Oh my God," she says. "I'm so jealous. I'm dying to see that. The tickets are hard to get!"

"Aren't you, like, well-connected and fancy these days?" I ask. Not ungratefully, considering she paid for the overpriced workout class. Which also eased the frustration I felt last night when I spent half an hour scrubbing Pyrex bowls and a sticky cake pan, left in the sink from Izzy's effort to bake a birthday cake for our super. How she even knew it was Luis's birthday is beyond me.

"Not enough to get me to that show. It's *the* show of the season. Tickets are, like, astronomical." I grimace. "Not that face. You're going."

"I don't really want to hang out with her, though . . . ," I say. "She's, like, a random lady."

"She's fabulous."

"She seems to want to, like, talk about Patty," I say. I study my beat-up five-year-old Converses.

Isabelle sighs. "Is that such a bad thing, P?"

I look at her, then look away. The lump is back. The thing is, Gary himself just saw the show and loved it. Tony Shalhoub came to *Late Night* to promote it, and the reviews have been amazing. And it's not like I can afford to go on my assistant's salary, obviously.

"I mean, it's the theater. It's not like you'll be talking a lot," Isabelle points out. Per usual, she's right. I throw on my ratty UGA sweatshirt and grumble in agreement. I text Susan back and tell her I'd love to come. She replies immediately with a string of musical instrument emojis. God help me.

....

When Susan asked if I wanted to get a drink and "snack" before the show, I didn't feel like I could say no. I'm pretty sure these tickets are hundreds of dollars, and it feels like refusing a preshow hang is the equivalent of dining and dashing or something. Anxiety has been building in my chest all day at the idea of more small talk. Getting a text this afternoon that Lawrence would be joining us certainly didn't help.

We agreed to meet at the InterContinental near Times Square, which sounds dreadful. Isabelle made me borrow one of her dresses— apparently my customary monochrome jeans and T-shirt wouldn't do for the "theatah." It's simple and black, so I can deal with it, except for the fact that it's from one of those brands that's just one name and definitely costs more than I make in a week. When I ran into Adam in the office kitchen today, his eyebrows shot up into his hairline and he started to say, "Hubba-hub—" until I punched him square in the shoulder, harder than I intended to.

"Jeez, Fry. Can't a guy just tell his friend she looks beautiful?" When he said this, my soul left my body. I am many things: resourceful, loyal. But beautiful I'm pretty sure I'm not, and pretty sure I don't want to be anyway. What does it even mean to be beautiful? That you've perfectly smushed yourself into the narrowly imagined, standard idea of beauty decided by men?

Unfortunately, though, judging from the warm and fuzzy pleasure blooming in my chest area, maybe I don't mind it. Being called beautiful. Being called beautiful by Adam.

I choked on my coffee, and Adam thumped me on the back until I glared at him, then chugged down some water. I didn't know what to say, but Adam saved me with "You got a hot date tonight or something?"

"Please," I said, annoyed to feel a drop of satisfaction click in my chest again. Would it bother him if I was on a date?

I try not to think about this interaction now as I walk into the swanky lobby of the InterContinental. Susan waves to me, perched on a little pouf under an intricate chandelier. The idea of sitting on a pouf is humiliating, but I have no choice but to take the one next to her. "Hi, Presley!" she greets me. "Thank you so much for joining me!"

"Thanks for inviting me, Mrs. Clark," I say. "I'm pretty amped to see this show."

"Please call me Susan," she says. I nod, knowing that won't be happening.

"I'm so glad Lawrence can join us for drinks," she says. "I've had these tickets for a while. Lawrence was supposed to come to the show with me after . . ." She casts her eyes down into her lap, and I gulp. I had wondered if it would be possible for us to pretend that Thomas Clark didn't exist, and I guess I have my answer. "Well, Thomas is staying at our house out east. He will be for some time, what with . . ." She clears her throat, reaches for a water glass, and, seeing that it's empty, sets it back down. She smooths the collar on her navy-blue silk dress. "Um . . ."

"What with everything, yeah, that makes sense," I say, rescuing her. Watching Susan struggle with the words was like watching a middle school band performance: so uncomfortable it could be classified as torture. American Network released a statement that Thomas will be on temporary leave, news that was quickly overshadowed by revelations of some high-profile restaurateur's rampant abuse. Susan forcibly blinks and straightens up in her seat, like she's a marionette whose string just got pulled tight.

"I really like the cosmos here!" she tells me. "Cosmopolitans are probably out of fashion these days. But Thomas had this aunt who drank them, and I always thought she was so chic."

"Nice." I nod along. Of course Susan Clark will be drinking something pink from a martini glass in midtown Manhattan. Suddenly, she waves to someone behind me, smiling like she's just won a million bucks. Well, if she considered that to be a lot of money, which she probably does not. I turn around and a very tall, goofy, khaki-clad dude with Susan's chestnut-colored hair is making his way toward us, flashing her a grin.

"Lawrence!" she says, standing on her tiptoes to plant a kiss on his cheek. He preens, glowing with mama's-boy energy, and I judge him for it. He leans down toward me, and I realize he thinks we're going to hug. This would have worked far better had I stood, but how the hell was I supposed to know we would be embracing? The last time I saw him all we did was silently play *Pokémon* next to each other.

I start to stand, but he's already on his way down, so we do this sort of squat, stiff, side-hug thing, and it's uncomfortable for both of us. Though you wouldn't know it as Lawrence Clark plops onto the pouf next to me and flashes a smile a bit too bright for someone whose family name is being publicly dragged through the filthy streets of New York City.

"Hey, Presley!" he says. "Been way too long. How are you?"

"Fine," I say, looking away from his big brown eyes. Between those peepers and his shaggy hair, not to mention the smile and the way he sort of galloped over to us, I'm reminded of a golden retriever. "You?"

"Great, great," he says, reaching for a cocktail menu while a waiter fills our water glasses. Susan orders a cosmopolitan, Lawrence and I old-fashioneds. As soon as the waiter leaves, he says, "Damn, Mom, you know you're gonna have to let me get a sip of yours." He turns to me. "Cosmos are my weakness."

"Why didn't you get one?" I ask him.

He looks at me. "Because you got an old-fashioned. But I guess that's a dumb reason, huh?"

Susan is positively beaming at the two of us, like we're sitting here solving world hunger instead of discussing cocktails. "How was your day, hon?" she asks her son.

"It was good, it was good," he says, nodding and reaching for his water glass. He spins it around a little. Fidgeting. Then he grins and actually blushes as he says, "I talked to Mason about that promotion today. Sounds like they'll be making it official in the next month or two."

Susan claps her hands together and smiles so big I can practically feel her dermatologist clenching. "That's great, honey, congratulations!" Turning to me, she says, "Lawrence works at CAM, Creative Artists Management. It's one of the biggest agencies, and they do sports and literary representation, and actors!"

"Mom," Lawrence says, "I'm sure Presley knows what CAM is if she works with talent at Gary Madden's."

I nod. "I do, yeah." I hate dealing with most agents and managers. They're annoying and entitled, the way they send their clients' riders and then show up and act like they're as important as the people they represent, as if their clients are successful because of *them*.

"Oh, of course," Susan says. She throws her hands up by her shoulders. "Look at me, out with these industry professionals!" She actually giggles.

There's a moment of quiet, which I break with "So, you'll be promoted to agent, or . . . ?"

"Oh, no," Lawrence says, resuming his fidgeting with the glass. "I'm an assistant now, and then in a month or two I'll be promoted to coordinator. I mean, I basically do that job now, but it'll be nice for it to be official and to be off the desk of the agent I currently work for. It will free me up to get more involved with actually representing athletes instead of just, like, rolling calls."

I nod in solidarity. Assistants share a code, like we're in a secret society or something—even the ones who wear khakis and have loads of family money. "Yeah, I feel that," I say. "I'm an assistant, too."

He offers a hand for a fist bump, an action I don't think I've participated in since 2006. I bump him back, and he smiles. "Mom, what'd you get into today?" he asks.

An interesting question; I do wonder what this woman fills her days with. "The annual Women in the Arts luncheon was today. It was nice to see some old friends," she says. I know at some point Susan was connected to the gallery world, but I'm not quite sure how. I can't help but doubt that seeing "old friends" was nice, what with the stares and whispers she must have been treading on. Good for her for not retreating, though, for showing face.

Our drinks arrive and we clink glasses, which I hate. Not because I don't like the act generally, but because it feels stilted and staged right now. "It's cool to see you, Presley," Lawrence says after he takes a sip and tries to hide his wince. "Thanks for keeping my mom company tonight. I'm bummed to miss the show, but I have a friend's birthday dinner downtown I felt like I shouldn't miss."

I turn to Susan. "Are you telling me I wasn't your first invite? You invited your *son* before you invited your old friend's kid?" I pause. This was a bold move; it's not like Susan and I know each other well enough to be yanking each other's chains. But sarcasm is my primary conversational currency—with my friends and at work (it's not like *Late Night* is some beacon of professionalism).

The color drains out of Susan's face and her eyes widen, but she relaxes when she sees that Lawrence is laughing. "Oh, well," she says. "I should have invited you first, considering this one is always too busy for his mother." She reaches across the little coffee table and lightly slaps his knee.

"Yeah, whatever, Mom," he says, though he's smiling, too. But unlike Susan's smile, his has nothing pinched or forced about it. There's a brightness to his eyes, like a searchlight is beaming out from his face. No wonder he's getting promoted. It would be a tough smile to say no to.

Lawrence asks me about my job at the show, and I power through the small talk until Susan checks her Tory Burch–banded Apple Watch and announces we *must* go to be on time for curtain. We walk out together, and Lawrence gives his mom a hug, which looks comical considering how he towers over her, and a peck on the cheek. It makes the woman practically glow.

He hugs me again, too, and it's a bit more natural this time around. I accidentally inhale when we embrace, and I would describe his scent as Clean Boy. Tide and pine deodorant. I don't remember the last time I hugged a guy, or a tall guy. I'm surprised that I don't hate it, being enveloped like that. Held for a split second. "Great to see you, Presley," he says. "Don't be a stranger."

"Yeah, same to you, Lawrence," I say, not meaning it.

He leaves us, walking backward and smiling at me. "Everyone calls me Clark," he says. Then he actually *winks*, which I can't help but grimace at. He catches it and throws his head back and laughs, skipping away from us, hustling to the Times Square subway station, disappearing into the crowd.

Despite the show's overwhelming praise, my favorite thing about it turns out to be the short runtime. I forgot a crucial detail when I agreed to accompany Susan, which is that I hate musicals. What could ruin an emotional, impactful moment more than breaking into song? Exactly one thing: the woman who sponsored your ticket to the show weeping for the entire second half. Susan tried to be subtle about it, which I appreciated, but she kept having to fish in her Chanel bag for more tissues, and it's hard to effectively keep a sniffle quiet in a spellbound theater. We're walking out together now, and she's blinking her eyes and checking her reflection in her iPhone camera, dabbing at her smudged makeup. I check my phone, too: a text from Izzy telling me she's home from a work dinner and can't wait to hear about the show. Nothing from Adam.

"Well," she says, slipping her phone into her bag, a bag that could probably feed me for a year should she sell it. "I thought that was just astounding. What about you?"

"Totally," I say. "Shalhoub forever." Susan chuckles but also looks confused.

We walk to the corner of West Forty-Eighth and Broadway, side-stepping and concentrating to avoid running into all the people around us. We have to press ourselves against a brick theater wall to avoid a family of tourists in *Frozen* merch taking up the whole width of the sidewalk with their hand-holding. Susan turns to me. "How are you getting home, Presley? Can I call you a car?"

"Oh, no," I say, even though the luxury of taking an Uber over navigating the Times Square subway station sounds nothing short of heavenly. I don't want to accept any more favors from this woman, not that I think a twenty-five-dollar Uber would take any skin off her back. "The train will be faster. Thanks, though." It's not necessarily true, but I know it's the only way to get her to lay off.

Susan nods. "I gotta say, I understand the convenience of Uber and Lyft and everything, but I always do my best to ride yellow. Taxis make New York, New York."

"Totally," I say. "Plus their whole medallion thing is so fuck—is so, uh, messed up."

Susan gives a naughty smile at my profanity. Look at us, being bad! The subway station comes into view, and I turn to her, praying she won't hug me, knowing the prayer will be futile. "Thank you so much for taking me tonight, Mrs. Clark," I say. I hope it sounds genuine, because I really am grateful.

"Please call me Susan," she says, which makes that image of her son spinning around and laughing cross my mind. "Um, Presley, before you go, I wanted to ask you something."

Oy. When I'm this close to a subway station, all I want to do is rush underground. There is no pain greater to a New Yorker than barely missing the train and having to stand on the platform in shame, thinking about all the tiny things you could have done differently on your walk that would have shaved off those extra few seconds and allowed you to make it. It's also already pretty late; the trains are probably on a stilted schedule. But what am I supposed to say? Also, what is *she* about to say? I turn to her and can't help but be a bit taken aback by how short she is. My Doc Martens give me a little extra height, but she barely comes up to my chin, and I'm hardly some Amazon woman. "What's up?" I say.

She looks nervous and shifts her weight (all ninety pounds of it) on her sensible flats. "Well, I was thinking. I'm sure you're very busy, what with your exciting job and being young in the city and all that. But I was just wondering, well, it was so nice running into you, and having you over, and getting to have a girls' night tonight, even if Lawrence did come for some of it." She smiles at this, but without showing her teeth. "I suppose I was just wondering if you would like to be friends?"

I can feel a blush rising up my neck and into my cheeks, which is not something I'm prone to do. Maybe I feel like I owe her because of the pricey theater tickets. Maybe I feel a little bad for her because of everything with her husband, not to mention how desperate a person must feel if they're straight-up asking someone thirty years younger to be their friend. Maybe it's because, even though the shared part of the Venn diagram is infinitesimally small, there is overlap between her and Patty. I hear it sometimes in the lilt in Susan's southern accent, feel it when she looks at me with real curiosity, like she's searching for something (or someone, rather) in me. And there's that tug, anchoring me to stay, even when my impulse is to bolt.

I hear myself say, "Sure, Susan. Of course I'd like to be friends."

CHAPTER 7

The next day, I choose to walk home from work. Certainly not the most practical decision, but I wore sneakers today, and it feels like fall is actually here. I can practically smell the buzzing pheromones of all the pumpkin spice latte girls, not to mention the smell of actual pumpkin spice lattes even though it's eight p.m., as I wind my way through the West Village, heading east. People balk when I tell them I sometimes like to walk the three miles home, like I don't know that the subway's faster. Like it's about anything other than getting to be in this city, to feel its energy pulsing as I'm swallowed up in it. New York City robs me of every measly penny I make, so when it's nice enough outside to experience it, I will, dammit!

I'm probably twenty minutes from home when I feel my phone buzz in my pocket, Lorde's *Melodrama* interrupted in my headphones. I smile and answer by clicking the button on the wire. I don't need to check the screen; I know who's calling me. "Hi," I say.

"Is less than an hour after work a new record for me to be calling you, Fry?" Adam asks.

"Might be," I say. "But I'll cut you some slack since we didn't get to chat much today." Today's show involved a more elaborate pretaped cold open than usual, which meant Adam was running around helping make things happen, so there had been no kitchen chat, no me-wandering-into-the-production-office chat, no him-sitting-on-my-desk-while-I-send-emails chat. I'll admit, I had missed the camaraderie.

"I know. I didn't even get a chance to tell you about my new shirts." I roll my eyes, even though he's not there to see it, and it's not like I actually hate the intimacy here. He launches into a story about how his grandma sent him money to buy new shirts, specifically, even though it's nowhere near his birthday, because she's starting to lose it a little. I do end up having to take my phone out of my pocket after all, to look at the photos of seemingly identical button-downs in different colors, while he asks my opinion about each of them.

"The red and green ones are fine," I say. "Don't think this yellow is quite doing it for me."

"Ah, of course, Presley Fry, Queen of Darkness."

"I am not a queen of darkness. You should have seen me this after-noon. I held the door open for John Cena and he *bowed* to me."

"Queen of something, then."

"My point is that Emma told me afterward that I was glowing."

"I'm pretty sure I'm taller than John Cena," Adam says.

"Congratulations. Would you like a certificate or a trophy for that?"

"Both. Anyway, I'm surprised you can even tolerate the green or red shirt. I wouldn't be surprised if you were actually color-blind."

"Ouch!" I say, annoyed that I am a bit stung.

He might sense this. "Fry, you literally only wear black. Besides, don't act like you care about my approval. It is I who needs your affir-mation for everything—that's our dynamic. Therefore, the yellow shirt will be going back to the store."

"My mom always wanted me to wear yellow everything. I thought it looked shitty on me, but she and my grandma told me I looked like sunshine." I bite my lip, hard, and the shock of pain helps bring me back to earth. Why did I just say that? Adam is quiet on the line, and I want to dissolve onto Eighth Street, fizzle into a million pieces, and disappear. I didn't know I was going to say that, didn't know I even remembered.

The Belk dressing room in the fifth grade, Grammy and Patty waiting on the bench outside, dragging me through the process of finding a dress to wear to elementary school "graduation." It must have been one of my mom's bouts of sobriety, which is somehow more painful to think about than the more usual times. The overhead fluorescent lighting of the store, the color in her cheeks. Seeing myself in a dress and trying not to preen, finding myself actually enjoying a rare time when my knees weren't dirty and I wasn't sweaty from running around outside with the neighborhood boys, wanting to be tough and wild like Caddie Wood-lawn or Jo March, girls I read about in books who were in charge of themselves.

Grammy likes to talk about how when I was a toddler, I was really into girlie shit. Princesses, makeup, dresses. Pink. Pops was a very willing Prince Charming when we played pretend at their house. Then I learned to read, and I was much more interested in being like Caddie or Jo, who were consistent each time I visited them, dependable. Even though it was fiction, it felt more solid than my reality. Especially before third grade, when Patty and I left our apartment and moved in with Grammy and Pops.

I shake my head. "Anyway—"

"I bet you did."

"What?"

"I bet you did look like sunshine. But, uh, for what it's worth . . ." Adam clears his throat, while my heart leaps into mine. "I think you're sunshine now. Even in all black and your scary boots."

I scoff a little, and it makes my throat burn. Despite the chill in the air, I'm sweating. My fingers suddenly feel very light, like they're filled with radioactive electricity instead of blood. My pace quickens, and I swerve around an old couple holding hands. I feel an almost physical need to say something that will break the tension of this moment. "If you think Doc Martens are scary, you really need to grow up."

He chokes out a little laugh, but I can still feel something like anxiety crackling between us. "Another thing, Fry. It's clear to me it's not

something you're super interested in talking about, but I want you to know that if you ever do want to talk about your mom, I'm here. I want to be someone you really trust, you know?"

I don't realize I've stopped walking until someone actively bumps into me on the crosswalk on Sixth Avenue and tells me to "fuckin' watch it." My feet sputter into action, carrying me to the sidewalk, and I let out something between a laugh and a choke, the odd little sound ringing in my ears. Before I can stop myself, I picture it: sitting on my couch with Adam and everything spilling out of me like I'm sliced open. The vodka, the humiliation, the screaming (mine and Patty's), the way I could see past my grandfather's eyes and all the way down into his broken heart when she would get wasted, the hospital, the funeral, the way my chest hasn't been able to fully expand in eighteen months. Everything that was Patty, or, rather, everything that was me and Patty, would just pool between us.

And maybe Adam could take it, could soak up some of it. And I wouldn't feel like I was on the verge of busting open. And maybe he would wrap his arms around me, and I would cry on his chest. A little at first, trying to hold on to some semblance of dignity. And then he would tell me it was fine, to let it all go, and then I would really let it rip, and he wouldn't mind at all. And later I would be embarrassed, I would be livid for allowing myself to show so much emotion, but before I could even apologize or walk it back or laugh at it, he would reach out to me and reassure me it was okay.

I swallow, push that mental snapshot down. I don't want to do any of that. Or maybe it's that I don't want to have done any of that. There's a difference.

"Thanks, man," I say, half proud of myself for saying something so casual, having the wherewithal to loosen a bit of the tension, and half mortified that I couldn't just pretend to be something like refined for even a second.

"Of course . . . bud," he says, and I can feel the warmth of his grin through the phone. We talk some nonsense and then say bye, and I rush to hang up. I move through the crowded sidewalk, headed east still, close to home, surrounded by people who don't know me and don't give a shit about me. The freedom of that anonymity buoys me. I wish I had three more miles to walk.

CHAPTER 8

It's the best when Emma doesn't want to go home at the end of the day. Sometimes she calls me into her office as the day winds down, naughtily revealing that she has a bottle of wine or whiskey from a manager or publicist, and we'll sit in her office and drink and talk shit. If she were a man, it would be red flag galore; but she's not, and so it isn't. In fact, because she's a woman who doesn't feel ready to go home and face her toddler and husband (whom I happen to know handles most of the domestic stuff in their household anyway), it's actually an act of feminism.

At least, that's what we tell ourselves as Emma tips another "at-home pour" (a quarter of the bottle) of Drew Barrymore's pinot noir into my *Late Night* mug. We tell ourselves we deserve it: we've had to deal with our least favorite manager not once but twice this week, which is the third week in a row we've had to see him. He calls both of us "honey" and is always asking me to go fetch him things: cups of ice, extra napkins, Tide to Go. As though *he's* the one starring in an Oscar-bait biopic or the one who has a new special on Netflix. Emma does an uncanny impression of him and the way he says,

"Thankyousomuchhoney," like it's one word. This bit is the only thing that makes him tolerable.

"After Mark and I first met him, Mark tried to start calling me 'honey,'" Emma says. "Which I'll admit was a step up from 'diversity hire.'" She bares her wine-stained teeth in a growl.

"Jesus," I say. When I first started working for Emma, I thought that her banter and bickering with Mark was friendly, collegial even, in the way that in the entertainment business calling someone an asshole can be collegial. It wasn't until Emma realized Mark was trying to get me to handle all the greenroom cleaning so that his assistant at the time (some douchebag named Jeff who, to my dismay, now writes for *SNL*) could skip it that she finally revealed her hatred to me. Mark and Emma met at Gary's old show, where they were both assistants. Mark's previous job had been working for Gary's agent, and he got promoted to producer a full year before Emma did.

"Anyway," Emma says as we finally stop laughing. "How's everything going for you? How's your search for the next great comedian?"

I steady myself. "Good," I say. "I really think Agatha is getting close for us to formally pitch her." Agatha and I had both decided her recent set at Black Cat was close but not the piece we wanted to put all our money on. She had texted me earlier today, just the words Gnarled fingers . . . ? and I knew immediately which joke that was meant to be slotted into and sent back the crying-laughing emoji.

Emma nods. "Fantastic," she says. "Look, I just want to say I know how hard you're working. You've obviously got your responsibilities here super fine-tuned, and I know you know how much I, and the whole department, frankly, know we can rely on you. And that's huge. I know how hard this hustle part is, but you're doing the right thing: focusing on the Friday segment, trying to make it the best it can be."

I nod back, setting my mug down. "Thanks. I just, like . . . I care about it, you know? I want to get great comics on the air here. For their sake, and for the show's. Keep it honest to what it's supposed to be: a comedy show."

"Yeah, instead of just lining up vapid celebrities to talk about the next Marvel rip-off or whatever, like what I do, right?" Emma asks, taking a gulp from her mug.

"No, no, that's not what I meant at all!" I say. And I mean it: I think every segment is important, in both the tradition they hold up, the potential of a celebrity interview to promote art worth seeing, and the clicks the top interviewees get us (which are now, sadly, the lifeblood of shows like ours).

Emma waves her hand. "Yeah, yeah. I don't mean to sound jaded." Her face softens a bit. "Anyway, I just wanted to say I see you working your ass off, and I know it can feel like you're treading water, working so hard and still making no money and having to pick up greenrooms and all that shit. But I think you're gonna really make this work for yourself if you want it to, and it's cool to watch. I'm proud of you."

Something blooms in my chest, her affirmation more elevating than I would have expected. Part of it is that there's no one in my family, or even Izzy, who really understands what I do, what the dynamics of this place are. The other thing is just Emma herself. I don't mean to sound like a creep, but when a person is placed in charge of you, standing exactly where it is you want to be someday, and they manage to be nice to you on top of that, it's difficult not to worship them a little bit.

Emma finally packs her things up to face her family, and we separate outside the stage door; she heads north to the Q train as I head east to the B/D train. My phone buzzes. Izzy's sent me her location, and as she's typing a message, I see she's at a bar we've been meaning to try in our neighborhood. It claims to be a dive. COME!!!! Izzy says. I'm tipsy enough that I actually shrug and say "Why not?" out loud, even though I'm walking alone to the Seventh Avenue subway station.

Only in Manhattan would a "dive" bar serve seventeen-dollar cocktails. When I arrive, Izzy is standing at the bar, preemptively ordering me a beer, and I spot Sammy, Izzy's former-coworker-now-friend, sitting in a booth in the back. Sammy lives in the neighborhood, so she's something of a regular for me and Izzy. She's got on a shimmery halter top, and her naturally curly brown hair is straightened. We'll make quite the juxtaposition, what with my greasy ponytail and wrinkly T-shirt. She waves me over.

"Presley Fry, the scariest, secretly nicest, funniest girl in town!" She gives me finger guns, which alerts me to the fact that she's clearly already been drinking. Which works for me. Izzy sets down my beer, what I'd guess is a vodka soda for her, and a margarita for Sammy. She presses her pointer finger to the middle of my forehead.

"Hello, friend," she says.

"Hey."

"Presley, I want your opinion," Sammy says, sliding her phone over. It's open to a man's Bumble profile. I scroll. It couldn't be more basic: group photo of him at some sort of sporting event, him and some other guy in banana suits in a tiny living room, clearly a city Halloween. I can't even tell which guy is her prospective suitor until I see a photo of him and his grandmother that looks like it was taken seven years and twenty pounds ago. And of course, there's one of him on a little boat, holding some fish out to the camera like an offering.

"We know it's basic," Izzy confirms. "The question is, should she go or not?"

I shrug. "Totally up to you, Sammy."

"That's so helpful, thank you so much," Sammy says. Izzy smirks.

"What!" I say. "I just mean, like, this guy seems fine, right? Like you could have a nice chat, maybe hook up with him if you wanted to. But I think it's like, do you really want to give an evening up for that? If you do, go for it. If you don't, don't."

"You're such a romantic. It's embarrassing me," Sammy says. She sighs. "Though I'm sure you're right. According to this"—she points to her phone—"I'm currently a person who actually is interested in texting with a stranger about the best Halloween costumes we've ever worn."

"'Tis the season," Izzy says.

I throw my hands up by my shoulders. "This is why I like Tinder. Way less bullshit. You just kind of cut to the chase."

"BC," Izzy says, shaking her head.

Izzy likes to joke that I have a "business casual" approach to sex. As Chimamanda Ngozi Adichie (and Beyoncé) confirmed several years ago, women are sexual beings. Feelings don't have to be involved for that to be true. I was eighteen the first time I had sex. Senior year was ending and I didn't want to arrive at college a virgin (I didn't yet know that virginity is a social construct). Logan Whitt, my grade's resident douche lord, was throwing a graduation party while his parents were at his great-aunt's funeral, and I went into the night with the singular goal of getting laid, armed with a Trojan I found in one of Patty's old purses and a water bottle filled with the whiskey my second cousin had surreptitiously given me at Christmas. I was met with a decent opportunity early on when one of Logan's meathead friends, Grant Williams, hit on me, which was a bit insane as we had never spoken and I was fairly sure his cup of tea was Cindy Truett, head cheerleader.

He drunkenly put his arm around me, said something about how he had always found me cute beneath all my "goth." Being called cute turned me off enough to know immediately that Grant Williams would not be my partner in accomplishing the night's goal. Across the party I spotted Aaron Jenkins, a quiet kid in my grade who was freakishly good at math. When we were ten, we had to do a writing exercise about someone in our family, and I remembered he wrote about this bird he had named Frosty who would sit on his shoulder when he took a shower. Though undeniably bizarre, that had always struck me as kind of sweet. We made eye contact as he took a sip from a red Solo cup. I wriggled from under Grant's arm, crossed the room, took his hand, led him upstairs, and spent the next two and a half minutes crossing "have sex" off the to-do list.

"But it's *fun* to meet new people," Izzy says, twirling her straw.

"Not for everyone," I say. Izzy grins. I've never been able to understand the appeal of spending hard-earned evenings and weekends on people I don't know, just for the sake of meeting them. I suppose it's the best thing to do when looking for a relationship, which is another thing I struggle to understand, that invitation to complicate things. And as for Izzy, who claims to go on all these dates in order to land a relationship, I don't see how that would work. Her schedule is sardines as it is.

Sammy moves her phone away from me and over to Isabelle. "Can you help me just set up the date? You're the queen of this shit."

Isabelle nods, pushes her drink to the side, and picks up Sammy's phone, squinting at it. She taps it a few times and pushes it back over to Sammy, who reads it and rolls her eyes. "It's not even that creative," she moans, slapping her hand down on the sticky dark wooden table. "But you just make it seem easy."

I crane my neck to see that Izzy has written: Anyway. What day are you free week after next to meet up for a drink?

"She gets it done," I say.

"Are you seeing anyone these days?" Sammy asks her.

"No," Izzy says, sighing. She ended things with Hinge Hannah over text two weeks ago. Hannah responded by immediately Venmo charging Izzy sixty bucks. The request read: That salmon I cooked you was *local,* you know. "Got a date tomorrow, though," Izzy says. "Meeting up for a late afternoon drink in Brooklyn with this girl Georgia." Sammy holds an empty palm out to Izzy, who pulls Georgia's profile up on her phone and slides it between me and Sammy.

"Cute," I say, and mean it. Curly red hair, tasteful tattoos, a puppy.

Izzy shrugs. "We'll see." We both know this will go like it almost always does: she'll have a fine time on the date, the girl will follow up, Izzy may see her again but will end up gently telling her she wants to be friends. And she'll probably actually mean it and might even make it happen. Izzy's kept in touch with several failed dates, attends their dinner parties and goes to concerts with them.

After some more drinking, bitching about dating apps and tiny apartments, and hearing a crazy story about two of Sammy's coworkers who everyone in the office knows are having an affair, Izzy and I start walking west on Fifth Street toward our place. Sammy is going out dancing on the Lower East Side and tried to get us to come with her. It's Friday night, after all. But Izzy and I just want to go home, eat an edible, and watch a movie. We're passing a vintage shop and she presses her nose and flat palms to the glass like a child at a Christmas display.

"I fucking love this store. Hidden treasures galore," she says. She turns to me with a pouty face. "You never go shopping with me."

"I never go shopping, period."

She hooks her elbow through mine and leans her head on my shoulder as we walk. It's not particularly comfortable, and I can't imagine it is for her either, considering how far she has to lean over, but I've had enough beers that I don't mind. "All this talk about dates and dating," Izzy says. "It's fun. But I'm starting to feel like 'What's the point?'"

"Don't tell me you're coming over to the dark side."

She gently shoves me. "I just mean, at this point in my life, I work, I hang out with you, I see friends, I do what I want to do when I want to do it. What more is there? Why complicate shit?"

I gently shove her back. *More.* I picture Emma and what it must be like to go from a crazy day at work to toddler chaos instead of a blissfully quiet apartment. And Susan, who probably thought she had everything she wanted but is only just learning how fractured it was. Patty weeping in front of a "Movies We Love" marathon on E! And then there's this: me and my best friend, tipsy, in a city and at an age where the different versions of ourselves and the different versions of our lives feel infinite. Linking our paths to someone (other than each other, that is) seems only limiting. Like we're denying ourselves freedom, that pristine taste of endless potential.

CHAPTER 9

I don't know what it is about me that gives Susan the impression that I'm a lady who lunches, but here I sit, in the restaurant inside Bergdorf's. It's my first time here, if you can believe it. The carpet and wallpaper are neutral, but there's a glitz to everything else: wooden tables so polished you can see your reflection in them, rainbow prisms the light makes bouncing off the framed art I don't recognize. It doesn't even smell like food; it just smells like rich people. I'm early. With its utter lack of predictability, the MTA makes it nearly impossible to get anywhere exactly on time, so I always give myself a cushion.

Susan arrives and her birdlike body floats toward me. She's wearing a fuzzy little cardigan and a khaki dress that would seem appropriate at a safari photo shoot. The way she moves through this room would have seemed almost obscenely graceful anywhere else, but anything short of that kind of poise would be out of place here. Like when *I* clomped in, for instance.

She arrives at our table, and I realize, based on our last few interactions, I'm probably supposed to stand and hug her. But it's too late, and I can tell she's contemplating how unladylike it would be to bend down and over me. Not that she would have to go far considering how minuscule she is. But she saves me from this, blowing an air kiss as she sits down and leans forward, patting my hand that's resting on the table. It's very chic.

"Presley, thanks for meeting me! What a treat to have a girls' lunch," she gushes. I know that I agreed to be her friend and everything, but I don't know if I would call this a treat, considering I'm a bit too hungover to be socializing with anyone, much less an actual woman-about-town. I know twenty-five isn't old, but considering that switching from wine to beer has me feeling this bad, I can say I certainly don't feel young.

She shrugs off her cardigan and places it daintily on the back of her chair. "How 'bout that autumn chill in the air! I just got out all my sweaters this morning. In those moments, I do become jealous of my friends in other cities, with houses and big closets that don't require a switchover every season," she says, rolling her eyes in a good-natured way.

I nod and try not to scoff at the idea that our living situations are comparable. I haven't seen her closet, but mine is about two feet wide. Izzy doesn't even have one, though her bedroom is big enough for a clothing rack that she classed up, topping it with a shelf of plants. Even though the lack of closet definitely downgrades the value of her room, Izzy still pays significantly more rent than I do, chalking it up to the size. We both know it's because we want to live together, she wants to live in the East Village, and I would not be able to afford it under any other circumstance. It's why I don't mind cleaning up after her so much: I'm working off my debt. "I have to keep my jackets and stuff around nearly all year. The office is usually pretty cold, and the theater is basically an arctic tundra."

"Oh, no," Susan says, golden-brown eyes widening.

"Yeah, I mean, the theater temperature makes sense, because with all the lights and bodies it would get pretty hot. But the office being so freezing is really annoying. It's because most office temperatures are based on keeping a hundred-seventy-pound man in a suit comfortable, which obviously sucks for women. Yet another way the patriarchy is running train on us." I blame my hangover for my grumpiness and the fact that I'm clearly having trouble keeping it to myself.

Susan furrows her brow thoughtfully and nods. "You know, I didn't know that, but that makes a lot of sense." She doesn't press further.

We catch up. She tells me about a book she read this week that she thinks, for God knows what reason, I would like. It's about some Mafia family who ran Red Hook in the twenties. I'm nodding along, skimming the menu that does not contain the greasy food my hangover demands, when I realize she's just asked me something.

"I'm so sorry, what was that?" I ask, hoping it may seem like I actually hadn't heard her instead of that I just zoned out. She's pretty soft-spoken, so it's not hard to believe.

"I asked if you read? I know you're really busy," she says.

I do read, but I don't love to admit that. As soon as you do, the person asking wants to know everything you've read, ostensibly looking for overlap but probably just to judge. Susan doesn't seem interested in judging me, but I have a hard time imagining we're reading the same stuff. "I read some," I say.

"Have you read anything good lately?" she asks me.

"Uh . . . ," I say. The last thing I read was a four-hundred-page memoir this white dude in his twenties wrote, published by some tiny press Adam worships. He's the one who recommended it to me, and I had a hell of a time busting his balls for being into something so masturbatory, so self-indulgent, so gratuitous. This kid's great tragedy was that his parents divorced when he was a child, as if that didn't put him into a category with exactly half our generation. I doubt Susan has heard of it, plus I don't really think the topic of divorce is one I'm too keen to gab about with her right now. "Not anything good, no. I'm kind of in the mood to reread *To Kill a Mockingbird*. I just heard they're adapting it for Broadway."

Susan nods vigorously. "I heard that, too," she says. "One of my favorites. Have you read *Go Set a Watchman*?"

"Hell, no," I say, my hangover continuing to dissolve my filter. My eyes bug out a little at my profanity, and Susan actually *blushes*, which I find oddly satisfying. "Sorry," I say anyway.

She waves her hand in front of her. "Oh, please, we're both adults here. But may I ask why not?"

"Yeah, so this guy I work with is dating a girl who works in publishing, and apparently Harper Lee had written *Watchman* and shoved it in a drawer or whatever, like, forty years ago or something, and never wanted anyone to read it. And then when she got older, like, senile, her publisher and her estate lawyer convinced her to sell it and have it published, and I just think that's shady. So it's not really something I want to support. Plus, I hear it ruins Atticus Finch, whom I not only love but actually named a cat after."

Susan grins at the mention of Atticus the cat. May he rest in peace after Roy Henderson, my grandparents' son-of-a-bitch neighbor, accidentally ran over him with his car. When Roy knocked on my grandparents' door and told me what he had done, not looking nearly as ashamed as he should have, he said we both had something to mourn that day. See, the University of Georgia Bulldogs had just lost to Auburn.

I'm not a big crier, but the loss of a beloved pet stands outside any habits or rules. The thought that I would never again wake up to the comforting weight and warmth of Atticus's body on my chest, to open my eyes right into that black-and-white floof ball's unblinking (and admittedly a bit creepy) peepers, the fact that I would never again hear him scratching at my door as I watched *Late Night* in my room, hiding from Patty as she drunkenly screeched on the phone downstairs, the absence I knew I'd always feel on my legs from the figure eights he would make around my ankles as I brushed my teeth were all too much for fourteen-year-old Presley to bear.

Patty was working at the Winn-Dixie at the time, which she found shameful. You'd think the fact that she did it hungover every day would be the shameful part, but it wasn't. Her delusions of grandeur made her resent stocking frozen Tombstone pizzas under the buzzing fluorescent lights, ringing up her former classmates as they did the weekly shopping for their healthy, complete families. The day Atticus died, I heard her toss her red vest on her bed when she got home that evening, and I tried to quiet my crying sounds, to no avail. She peeked her head in my door, pink lipstick slightly smudged, blond-from-the-bottle bangs askew. I remember that when she saw me, so atypically emotional, she looked afraid.

"What's wrong, honey?" she asked. I told her, and she rested her eyes in the heels of her palms. She loved Atticus, too. But instead of crying, she shot her head back up a moment later. "We'll get the bastard back."

That night, under the cover of darkness (and Patty under the cover of Burnett's), we crept out of my grandparents' house, each of us with a carton of Winn-Dixie eggs that Patty had gone back to work just to retrieve. We looked at each other, her brown eyes sparking with mischief, a look she wore well, a look she wore often. My face did not mirror hers: my rule-following tendencies meant I was a lot closer to shitting my pants than I was to emitting a glint in my eye.

She threw the first egg. The sound it made, the crack, was quiet but satisfying. The streetlamp gave off enough light that I could see the yolk dripping down the brick. It was too late in the fall for the eggs to start immediately rotting, but I knew it would smell by morning. She nodded once. "Still got it," she whispered, more to herself than to me.

I threw next. It was much louder, hitting a window instead of brick, and we doubled over, attempting to keep our laughter silent. I looked at the house, adrenaline coursing through my veins, waiting for a light to come on. It didn't, so we emptied our cartons, *smack smack smack*. We high-fived and stood there, admiring our work. I remember it with high-def clarity: the protection of my Eulalia High sweatshirt against the chill, Patty panting next to me like she had just run a race instead of tossed some eggs, the satisfying thud I felt in my stomach that we had scraped together some justice. We took the fifteen-step walk back to our house in silence, until Patty said quietly, "For Atticus."

I'm guessing Mr. Henderson knew immediately who had done it. I'm guessing there was a confrontation, maybe there were consequences of some kind. I'm guessing because any kind of fallout was kept from me.

"Yes, it does not reflect well on Atticus," Susan says, jolting me back to the moment. "I hadn't heard that about the publishing drama, but it's a shame. I'm so glad to have young people like you in my life who can keep me up-to-date on what's hip!"

I laugh a little. I hope it comes off politely, but I'm straight-up scoffing at the idea that me giving her the skinny on Harper Lee's latest novel makes either of us hip. Our waiter comes. I would have to google what Susan ordered to know what it is. I order a burger. Probably not the most ladylike choice, but I need to make the most out of a free meal.

"What are you up to this afternoon?" Susan asks when our food arrives, as she's cutting into what I'm guessing is a piece of fish.

I shrug. "Don't know. Probably gonna meet up with my roommate, Isabelle. I have a show later."

"A show?"

"Yeah, a comedy show. For work."

"Oh, that's right! That'll be fun. Gosh, I haven't been to a comedy show in so long. I bet they don't even let people my age in the door!" she says as she takes a sip of her sparkling water.

"Well, that's definitely not true," I say. And without thinking, "Maybe you can come with me sometime."

The idea of sitting next to Susan Clark while some asinine NYU student humps a microphone stand or Agatha Reddy talks about getting her asshole waxed makes me want to disappear. But I can't help but be heartened by the way Susan's eyes light up at the invitation. You'd think I asked her to the prom, not to risk asbestos exposure for corny jokes. "I would just love that," she says solemnly, eyes wide.

"Sweet," I say. "What are you up to this afternoon?"

"I have some shopping I need to do. I'd love to take you, if that doesn't sound too miserable. We can pick something out for you, maybe a new sweater or something, since you're so cold at work? My treat!"

It does sound miserable. Like torture, actually. And there's that word again: treat. But how can I say no, when she just acted like my invitation to go to a comedy show was like asking her to be my maid of honor? But I also don't want her charity. Sure, I make minimum wage and wouldn't mind some new threads, but the way she's looking at me with her starving, boy-mom eyes, she'll probably try to put me in a tutu or something. Between this ladies' lunch and an afternoon of shopping, I'm starting to feel like Carrie fucking Bradshaw. And let me be clear: I am a Miranda. Proudly.

"You don't need to buy me anything," I say. "But yeah, I can chill." As much as I don't need—well, want—her charity, when the check comes after I've wolfed down my burger and Susan has taken three bites and artfully rearranged the food on her plate, I don't bother acting like I'm going to pay.

We make our way down to the third floor, which has what the buyers at Bergdorf's seem to think are "fun clothes." A distressed-denim jacket catches my eye. I check the price tag and nearly lose my lunch when I see it's $425. I shove it back on the rack like it's poisonous.

"What kind of office outerwear are you looking for, specifically, Presley?" Susan asks as she starts sorting through a rack of coats that look so fresh off a lamb I wouldn't be surprised if there was a farm in the back.

"Uh, whatever works," I say. The cardigan I keep by my desk was purchased by Grammy at the Lord & Taylor outlet in Eulalia, Georgia, nearly four years ago. I've worn holes in the elbows. Anything here would be an upgrade.

She takes in an excited breath of air and pivots to sort through some dresses that seem appropriate for a fancy party or a dignitary's funeral. "Do you have any events coming up?" She asks this as she holds up a blush-colored, chiffon-looking thing that I would sooner shave both my eyebrows off than wear. She's inspecting it at arm's length, tilting her head to the side, setting her jaw, and sort of narrowing her eyes. I still don't fully understand what her job was before, but this is a look that would feel very at home in an art gallery, I'd guess.

"No events," I say, trying not to laugh. What kinds of "events" does she imagine broke twenty-five-year-old assistants attend? She spins the god-awful princess thing around to me.

"You wouldn't be caught dead in something like this, anyway, would you?" she asks, and she's really smiling, almost like she does when Lawrence, or "Clark," as he said people call him, comes up in conversation.

I laugh a little, then cover my mouth. I don't want to seem like I'm laughing at her, but she starts laughing, too, and suddenly we're in on the same joke and everything between us shifts. My shoulders relax a little, and something in my center loosens. "Probably not," I say.

"I should've known," she says, replacing it on the rack. "Your mom was never one for girlie clothes either." I wait to stiffen up, for that roaring thing that rises in my belly whenever Patty comes up, but it doesn't. I snort.

"Yeah, no shi—no kidding," I say. While Patty was nowhere near my grunge level, she was hardly super feminine, almost always in shorts and a plain shirt or tank top, no matter the season. To be fair, it's not like it ever gets actually cold in Eulalia, but there are times when it's too cold for shorts. I'm convinced Patty would have had to visit Antarctica to put actual pants or long sleeves on. See, my mom had this perfect, toned athlete's body. She ran track in middle and high school before booze started running her, and even though she went for runs only occasionally then (during bouts of sobriety or attempts at a hangover cure), she never lost her figure. Or her speed: the woman was fast. One of the few things I would have been glad to inherit from her, but, considering my noodle arms, dimpled thighs, and inability to run a mile in under eleven minutes, most certainly did not.

"Oh my goodness, I'll never forget when I practically dragged her to the outlets to go shopping for prom, and she pitched such a fit when I put her in this big purple taffeta thing, with these sleeves—" Susan's really laughing now. "It was the seventies," she says, wiping her eyes and shrugging.

Something in me sinks, achy to think about the part of my mom's timeline that didn't overlap with mine. Her before me. Now that she's gone, now that I can look at her life as a complete and dormant thing, instead of a stick of dynamite with the potential to blow up my day, I find myself more curious about who she had been before.

I have a memory from when I was little of begging to watch my mom put her makeup on before she went out. A yellowed toilet, chipped green paint on the walls. Squeezing myself to fit on the tiny bathroom sink in the little apartment we shared before we moved in with Grammy and Pops, unable to take my eyes off her as she grinned hard in the mirror with lifeless eyes, powdering blush on her cheeks and applying a pink lipstick to her thin lips. Susan's right that my mom wasn't some girlie girl, but she always, *always* wore lipstick, and blush most of the time, too. I avoid the makeup aisle of Duane Reade now—my stomach drops every time I see a Maybelline product.

"Ah, yes, our mission," Susan says, marching over to some tables with folded sweaters and cardigans. The sign says they're all cashmere.

"Oh, Susan, I don't need anything this fancy," I tell her as she starts holding up different options, thankfully all in black or gray.

"Of course you do," she says, folding and replacing a gray one as soon as she sees it has little flowers sewn into the sleeves, which I appreciate. "You know what they say. Dress for the job you want."

I wonder if she's right. I don't think that my casual clothes reflect poorly on me at work. I'm dependable and efficient, and in such a fast-paced workplace, that's the only thing people seem to care about. But maybe there is a secret world of judgment buzzing beneath my feet at the show that I'm just unaware of. I know I'll have to get better clothes if I get promoted and start actually greeting and interacting with the guests, but that has yet to happen. Based on what they pay me, I don't see how they can expect a glamorous transformation to happen before then.

"How about this?" she asks, holding up a dark gray cardigan. It looks fuzzy and inviting, so I reach out and touch it. It feels like butter that's been infused with one thousand hugs.

"Whoa," I say.

"Cashmere is a must," she says, unbuttoning it and holding it open for me to slip my arms into, like she's my handservant or something. I oblige and walk over to a nearby mirror. Yep. It's a cardigan. But I don't think I've ever worn something so cozy and luxurious. Susan catches me smiling a little in the mirror and smiles approvingly, like this is a makeover show and I'm wearing a gown instead of frayed black jeans.

"I'm buying it for you," she declares.

"Susan, you really don't have to—"

"Hush, it would be my pleasure," she says, reaching her hand out. The thing is, as I take it off and hand it to her, she does look happy, sunshine bursting from the inside of her. I like how it feels, to do something nice for her, to take part in something that clearly brings her joy. Then I have to laugh at myself, thinking I'm a hero for allowing this woman to purchase luxury clothing items for me.

"Were you not looking for anything?" I ask her after she pays, the cardigan nestled in wrapping paper in the Bergdorf's bag dangling off my arm and making me feel like a fraud.

She sighs and cocks her head to the side. "I have an event coming up. It's just a little cocktail fundraiser, but it'll be my first time . . . I'll be going, you know, alone. But it's funny," she says, giving me a little grin. "I don't particularly want anything new. There's this dress I had, oh gosh, probably twenty years ago. I got rid of it spring-cleaning a few years back, not thinking I would miss it, and it's just really been on my mind lately. I keep thinking it would be perfect for this, for some reason, even though I'm probably misremembering it. I doubt it would even fit me anymore." I smirk to myself; there's no way this compact flea of a woman would have trouble fitting into anything.

I feel a flicker of compassion, though, hearing about this obsession with some dress. I understand missing something when it's gone, even though you thought you wouldn't. When it felt, at the time, like it was more trouble than it was worth.

"Have you ever thought about shopping vintage?" I ask her, picturing Isabelle pressing her face to that East Village shop's window last night.

Next thing I know, Susan and I are stepping out of a yellow cab and onto Fifth Street and First Avenue. I warned Susan that I don't really know what I'm doing. I don't even know the name of this shop; all I know is that my roommate likes it. She gasps as we enter, immediately confronted by a print of a Dolly Parton portrait. "I love her," she says, exhaling, looking at the plastic-covered cardboard like it's the *Mona Lisa*.

"She's a certified badass," I say, nodding. "I met her last year when she was on the show, and I can confirm that she's also one of the nicest guests we've ever had on."

"That's wonderful," Susan says, and then she claps her hands together and looks around the store. It's like hundreds of sewing machines combusted in here, the racks bursting and sagging with fabric. "Where to begin," she mutters to herself as she marches over to a rack holding dresses. She starts sifting methodically on one end, and I notice her nose is pinched from the store's musty smell.

I mirror her movements on a parallel rack, even though I have no earthly idea what I'm supposed to be looking for. My phone buzzes in my pocket—a text from Adam. It says, Our man—busted!! and I open the accompanying photo. Next to Tom Hanks's floating head reads the fake headline ANOTHER WOMAN COMES FORWARD AND ACCUSES TOM HANKS OF BEING NICE. I smile to myself, despite the fact that I've already seen this joke on Twitter.

Suddenly, Susan gasps again, her mouth in a perfect little O. She slowly pulls a long-sleeved little white number off the rack. It looks like a nightgown.

"Presley," she breathes, like she's just found buried treasure.

"Susan . . . ," I say back, not bothering to hide my lack of enthusiasm.

She spins the dress around so it's facing me, and I see it has some kind of, I don't know, bodice thing? It looks very Brontë sisters to me. "Do you know what this is?" she asks, as though the fact that I don't isn't obvious from my blank stare.

"I sure don't," I say, pocketing my phone and covering the short distance between us. I hold up one of the silky sleeves, which has tiny buttons on it.

"I cannot tell you how much I wanted this dress back in the day," she says.

I look at the price tag and my eyebrows shoot up my forehead. "It's five hundred dollars," I say, horrified that something *used* and, frankly, hideous could be that expensive.

"I *know*," she says, nodding, mistaking my horror for awe. "And for *Chanel*."

"You should get it," I say.

"Oh, Presley!" she says, actually putting a hand on her chest, jaw dropped, eyes bulging. She looks horrified, like I had suggested she strip naked and run through the streets. "This is way too young for me."

I snort. "Young, like, a baby going to their christening, maybe." She lightly smacks me on the arm and gives me a disapproving look, but something like laughter flickers in her eyes.

She replaces the dress on the rack like she's parting with a dear friend she won't see for a long time. "Aw, come on, Susan," I say. "Just get the dress."

"No, no," she says, already moving on, sifting through the racks with renewed interest. She doesn't end up buying anything, but I'm pleased with myself for taking her somewhere she liked. Showing her around the East Village was almost like having an out-of-towner visit, all wide-eyed and giggling when we passed the sex shop window next door to the vintage shop. I wait with her until she hails a cab going uptown on First Avenue, and she gives me one of her suffocating hugs. I walk west toward my apartment, appreciating the near disappearance of my hangover, but it isn't long before I feel something else nagging at me.

It's guilt, an all-too-familiar feeling. Patty would be horrified to know that I just spent an afternoon putzing around Manhattan with Susan, that I let Susan buy me something expensive, something Patty would never have been able to afford or even understand. I think about the call I would receive from Patty if she knew, how thick her voice would be with disapproval and Burnett's and Ocean Spray. "Did you have fun with your new best friend?" she might ask me mockingly, before I would hang up on her and try to shake it off. Then she'd text me the next day, something innocuous, but I would know it was because the vague recollection would be eating at her and she'd be checking in to make sure we were good. I would reply like everything was fine, because it wouldn't be worth the fight.

CHAPTER 10

Realtors in the city have a particular euphemism for when an apartment's common living space is actually just a hallway or a rat-infested two-by-four: "The city is your living room." Even though every Realtor in this town is about as trustworthy as a Death Eater, this makes sense to me. We don't live in New York City to sit on our small secondhand couches and watch TV. We live in New York City to go out in New York City.

But occasionally, Izzy and I find ourselves preferring the coziness (tininess) of our actual living room (area next to the wall that houses a fridge, stove, oven, and way too few cabinets). She stretches out on our Facebook Marketplace couch and I curl up in the yellow armchair we inherited from her parents. Apparently, one of Izzy's former-dates-now-friends is throwing a rooftop party in Williamsburg, but it's too chilly for that. We could meet up with Sammy in the West Village, but the thought of crossing town is hard. We could park our asses at the Gray Mare, our neighborhood pub, but that would require changing into real pants. And for the moment, still somewhat in hangover recovery mode and definitely in shopping recovery mode from my day with Susan, real pants are a bridge too far.

A colander full of popcorn rests on the table. We both continually reach for it while *Miss Congeniality* plays on the TV, which we talk over.

"What's Adam up to tonight?" Izzy asks.

"Fuck if I know," I say truthfully. I haven't heard from him since the Hanks meme, so I can only assume he's with Razor Girl. It's why there's a closed door between me and my phone, which I left resting on my bed. I'm sick of checking it.

"Well, okay then," Izzy says. Her eyes flick up from her phone to the screen just as Sandra Bullock reveals her post-makeover look. "Sandy truly can get it, can't she."

"For sure."

"I kinda prefer her when she's rougher around the edges, though."

"Definitely."

"I think I'm gonna delete Hinge."

My eyes swivel from the screen to Izzy and a piece of popcorn falls out of my mouth in the process, which makes her burst out laughing. I laugh, too, before popping the soggy kernel between my teeth. "What's that, now?"

She shrugs, lets out a sigh. "It's like we were talking about on the walk home: I've just been on these apps for so long. And take my date today—it was totally fine, but I know it's going nowhere."

"*But it's so fun to meet new people,*" I say in an extravagant impersonation of her, which earns me a pillow to the face.

"It *is*," Izzy says. "I've had lots of fun, and met lots of great women I'm lucky to be friends with now. And can hook up with, occasionally. But between them, and the rest of my social life, and work, it's just like . . . I'm good, you know? Like I was saying last night. The only reason to keep doing this is if I'm really looking for a relationship, which I think I'm good without right now."

"Damn, I mean, yeah, that sounds reasonable," I say. "Who the fuck needs a significant other."

"Easy for you to say, you already have one."

"Izzy! For fuck's sake! Adam is just my—"

"Not Adam, P. Me." The incorrect assumption spreads heat through my face and chest. She continues, "And I'm a great girlfriend. I plan fun outings for us, introduce you to new restaurants, et cetera."

"Fine. True. But don't act like I'm not your wife. I clean up all your shit and make sure our bills are paid on time and check that you sleep on your side when you're drunk."

She looks over at me, corners of her mouth turned down, mirth extinguished from her eyes. "You do?" she asks quietly.

I readjust in my seat, focus on tucking my arms under our UGA blanket. "I mean, it's not a big deal. Just, like, leftover paranoia from D.A.R.E., I guess." This is true, but we both know where else the paranoia stems from.

My eyes are back on Sandy, but I hear Izzy take in a big breath and slowly release it. A dull anxiety is rising in my belly that she'll push, but she just says, "Thanks, P. I love you."

"I love you, too."

CHAPTER 11

I'm adding notes to the living document I keep of promising stand-ups (I was impressed by this dude I saw at an open mic last night who made a lot of sharp jokes about how abnormally long his neck is, so into the log he goes) when Emma pulls me into her office. Emma calling out, "Presley, will you come in here?" will never not shoot a shiver of anxiety through my limbs, even though I've been doing this job long enough to know that if I had fucked something up, I would have caught it on my own.

I plop down on her couch. "What's up?"

She has one pencil behind her ear and one in her hand, which means we're going to be concentrating. "For the Halloween show cold open, Gary wants to do a parody of 'Monster Mash,' and all the 'monsters' will be men accused of shitty behavior. I'm looking at the guests for next week to see if we already have a guest coming in who could do this with him, who could maybe come in early to tape. But in case not, do you mind making a list of New York–based friends of the show who you think would be a good fit and who might be able to swing by and do the bit?"

"Sure," I say, grinning, both because I like the idea and because whenever we bring in a guest to help with the cold open, it means I get to work with Adam. "Male or female okay?"

Emma groans, then sighs. She throws her hands up. "I'd say yes, but these men are dropping like goddamn flies. Would be pretty unfortunate to tape it with someone hours away from being accused of predatory behavior." She looks at the lineup and sighs. "I swear to God if Dev Patel turns out to be a creep it's over for me."

"Female preferred, got it," I say.

I sit down at my desk and already have a Slack notification from Adam.

> Adam: Howdy partner
> Presley: Yes?
> Adam: So excited to work with you, too! Let me know the talent shortlist, just so we can start making what plans we can?
> Presley: Will do. Am I crazy for thinking Laura Linney would participate?
> Adam: That'd be sickkkk
> Adam: Justin (he went to Harvard. Did you know that????) just sent the writers' rough draft of the lyrics
> Adam: Sorry to report your guy is getting called out in it
> Adam: TC

I scrunch my face up at my screen in confusion, before realization dawns: Thomas Clark. And then that dread rising in my belly, thinking of Susan. My new friend and benefactor, apparently. I'm also surprised—the gossip mill reported that Wes gave Gary and the writers a wrist slap, and Dan a straight-up tongue-lashing, over last month's Thomas-centric monologue. Much as I dread it for Susan, I can't help but be proud to work for Gary, holding bad guys accountable despite the trouble he'll be in.

Presley: He's hardly "my guy"

Adam: Who is your guy, these days? Anyone?

Presley: ??

Adam: My stupid way of asking if you've got any dudes on the hori-
zon. Any crushes these days?

I swallow, my fingers suddenly feeling strangely cold. Of course I don't, but would Adam care if I did?

Presley: Stupid indeed

Presley: And funny you should ask

Presley: I do, and it's your mom

The comment had seemed funny in an ironic way in my head, but it couldn't look dumber on my screen. I'd very much like to disappear, or turn back time, or both.

Adam: HA, GOOD ONE! Have you submitted a packet yet? You're
comedy's next big thing, aren't you

Presley: Yep

Presley: What about you, how are things going with Ansley

Adam: Ashley

Presley: Right

Adam: Good actually

Adam: Kinda ended up spending the whole weekend with her.
Probs a relief for you to not have to deal with me blowing you
up 24/7

I knew it.

Presley: Ah yes, my compliments to Ashley then

Presley: JK, missed you

Fuck!

Adam: Damn, I should start giving you space more often . . .
Presley: Whatever. Don't you have work to do?
Adam: I s'pose. Later, dude

Dude.

....

It's Sammy's roommate's birthday, and also "Halloweekend," so Isabelle has decided we are going to have a "big night." Sammy's roommate is a girl named Jeanine, which may sound weirdly grandmotherly,
but just know she is one of the most beautiful girls I've ever seen in
real life. She's rented out the basement of a bar only a few blocks from
us, and costumes are required. Izzy has decided that we are going to
be Kat and Bianca Stratford from *10 Things I Hate About You.* She
suggested I go as the fashionable, bubbly Bianca and she go as the
edgy, jaded Kat, as a subversion of our personalities, but I unequivocally refused to wear the fluffy pink dress she ordered on Amazon for
the Bianca costume. So Izzy wears the pile of blush tissue paper and
spends forty-five minutes pinning her hair with dozens of tiny butter-
fly clips, while I'm going essentially as myself but with crimped hair
(made possible by Izzy sitting me down on her bed and styling it while
I loudly complained but secretly enjoyed the pampering). I heat up
Trader Joe's frozen appetizers and we play Beyoncé and guzzle some
tequila cocktail Izzy found the recipe for online.

My phone buzzes with a text, and I'm relieved to see Adam's name
lighting up my screen. He's sent me a photo of himself in front of a
TV, showing that the UGA football team beat the Florida Gators
today. While I don't particularly care about football, I appreciate the
gesture to my home state. "Who are you smexting?" Izzy asks from the
doorway to her bedroom.

I wipe the smile off my face immediately. "No one."

She saunters toward me and peers over my shoulder. "Oh my God,"
she says. "What a lame excuse to text."

"It's not an excuse, Adam likes football, whatever," I say, suddenly sweaty in my jacket. I'm actually pretty sure Adam has never mentioned college football, or any sports, to me. I guess he's not with Ashley if he's texting me, since apparently he can't do both at the same time. "Are we going to this party or what?"

Izzy narrows her eyes. "You know, Sammy and Jeanine said the more the merrier. I think there's a tab number they have to hit in order to rent the space, or else Jeanine has to make up the difference. So it wouldn't be weird for you to invite anyone you may want to see there." She blinks her eyes in faux innocence and smiles.

"I'm not inviting Adam to this party."

"Ugh." Izzy slumps her shoulders forward and rolls her eyes. "Why, are you too embarrassed for him to see you be basic in the basic East Village with all your basic friends on basic Halloween? Where is he? Warehouse party in Bushwick? A horror film screening at the Angelika or something?"

"I actually think he said he was going to be in Ridgewood today."

"I literally don't even know what that is."

I pat Izzy's shoulder. "There, there," I say. "No one's judging you for being basic."

She scoffs. "I'm fabulous," she says.

"Can't argue with you there."

"Shall we?"

And we're off. Walking down the buzzing, chilly East Village streets where girls with cat tails and mouse ears and devil horns and hardly any clothes huddle together and their overgrown frat-boy counterparts call out to each other. A toothless man in a hat that says "I LOVE PUSSY" offers to sell us cocaine. Rowdy costumed groups burst out of bodegas, six-packs peeking out of black plastic bags. A Pomeranian in a tutu struts the sidewalk seemingly alone, its owner trails so far behind. The waitstaff at San Marzano wipe down tables while one group of people still sits at a table, singing loudly. There's a line at Veselka, consisting of both the drunk and the sober waiting for pierogi. A little bit of life spills out of every doorway we pass: a pulsing beat, a barking dog, a triumphant, drunk "I love you, bitch!" and a tearful, drunk "You said you wouldn't do this shit anymore."

When we tell the bouncer we're here for Jeanine's birthday, we're able to skip the line of vampires and sexy nuns and a dude in a Trump mask that's halfway down the block. I don't mean to sound like a snob, but please shoot me dead if I ever wait in line to get into Drexler's, a painfully average bar. We descend into the basement, where neon dots of light from the disco ball instantly render us spotted. I don't recognize the song blaring from the DJ's speakers, partially because it's too loud to make sense of. I follow Isabelle to the bar, where she opens a tab with two tequila shots for each of us, as if we hadn't just downed enough tequila to kill a small animal back at our apartment, and a beer for me, some liquor and soda with lime for her.

Embarrassingly, bile immediately rises in my throat as I cough down the tequila, anchored back into my stomach only by the rush of lime I usher into my mouth like it's lifesaving medicine. Old work friends of Izzy and Sammy's rush up to her, engulfing her in hugs and exclaiming over her costume. I pull out my phone, which opens automatically to my texts with Adam. Go dawgs was all he had written along with the selfie.

Yeah, was on the edge of my seat for that one, I write back.

The three dots appear immediately, Adam typing a response. Then they disappear, a text probably soaring through the air to land on my phone. But nothing comes up. Clearly, he started to reply, then decided against it. I wonder briefly if I should take Izzy's directive and invite him here, to this crowded bar where it's too loud to have a conversation, where he would see finance bros and basic girls waiting in the line to enter. The shots are working their way through me, too, meaning I'd also be inviting him to the place where I'm drunk. Now, *that's* spooky. I refuse to put myself in a situation in which I'm tempted to even toe the line we spend our days dancing around and say something regrettable. Plus, there's the fact that I've consumed enough tequila for my southern accent to come out, which Adam gave me shit for when he heard it over postwork drinks once. As a guarantee that not even my fingers will be able to do any damage, I switch my phone off, making any contact, or even any obsessive phone checking, a non-option.

A knock on my shoulder, and it's Sammy. She pulls me into the middle of the room, and I make sure to pull Izzy with me. Khalid, who was a musical guest on the show recently and makes me feel old, blares loudly through the speakers. Izzy, still holding my hand, spins me around.

We somehow wind up at a packed, deafening bar in the West Village, so that Sammy can meet up with Banana Boy. He's worth pursuing tonight, what with the combination of Sammy's need to get laid and the fact that the date was "fine, whatever." He clearly recycled last year's costume, making him easy to spot, the tip of the banana suit hovering above the crowd. I half wonder if we'll run into Lawrence Clark here. Seems like the kind of place he would frequent on a Friday night. Isabelle and I find a corner, where we laugh as a wasted guy in a football jersey hits on a girl dressed as a cheerleader (the pickup lines write themselves) who's clearly not interested. It would maybe be creepy if he had any kind of hold on himself, but soon enough his head is on the bar and he's asleep in his stool and the bouncer has him by the elbow, removing him. Men are so embarrassing. After he's gone, the cheerleader and her friends bump hips in celebration. Isabelle and I are charmed enough by this to try the move ourselves, which makes us laugh harder.

We meet Sammy's banana, who, as Sammy promised, seems *fine, whatever*, and then Izzy and I are falling into a cab headed east. Not home, but to Proto's, the pizza joint a few blocks from our apartment, so we can get a slice (realistically, several slices) to bring home. We call the man who works the counter at this hour "Proto Papa," and, per usual, he lets each of us pick out a free can of soda from the fridge. We'll wake up tomorrow morning and briefly wonder why there are magically two cans of Coke in Isabelle's purse before we remember. And we'll toast to Proto Papa, for his preemptive help in curing our hangovers.

"Let's do the thing!" Isabelle says when we're in the cab.

"Fine," I groan, as though I don't love the thing, as though I weren't just about to suggest the thing. We roll down our windows and swivel so our backs are pressed up against either door, put our feet in each other's lap, legs bent at odd angles to make ourselves fit. We lean back, heads out the windows, and admire the city at this angle as our cab crawls east. We love this: the breeze on our faces, the dark, starless night sky, the upside-down sharp angles of the rooftops we glide past. A different geometric tour of something we see every day.

"I love New York!" Isabelle yells. I smile. Our cabdriver doesn't react. "Do it, Presley!" Izzy says, her head still tilted back.

"I love New York!" I scream. Because I do.

CHAPTER 12

The following Tuesday, I'm sitting at my desk contemplating whether I feel like a star or a fraud in my Bergdorf's sweater when Adam messages me. Ray's? is all he says. Ray's is a bodega down the block from the theater, and it has two stools by the window, and sometimes, when Adam and I aren't too busy, we sit, people watch, and sip the coffee (which is really more like sludge that smells faintly of old coffee beans).

We actually have some near competent interns this semester who have already set up the greenrooms to my approval (fresh flowers, boxes of gourmet doughnuts, properly assembled gift baskets, fully stocked mini-fridges), and Emma is in a meeting, so I tell Adam I'll meet him there in five. I don't love walking out with him when we go to Ray's. People at work know we're friends, but I don't want to get a reputation as an office flirt, even though that would be completely unfair, since he's the one always begging me to hang out and his reputation isn't susceptible to the same risk. Adam accused me of paranoia, but I just had to say the magic words ("male privilege") and he shut the fuck up.

I get held up chatting in the hallway with Steve, one of the camera guys. He's always showing me pictures of his one-eyed husky, who's apparently been having diarrhea, as if that were information I needed to know. I pass the writers' assistant, Justin, in the hall and successfully avoid an interaction—no time for a Harvard anecdote.

By the time I get to Ray's, Adam, eyes bloodshot, hair a mess, is already slouched on a stool. He holds a bodega coffee cup out to me. Sitting next to him, I say, "You look like shit."

He offers a half grin. "Thanks, Fry."

"What's wrong?" I say. I choke on a sip of my foul coffee and hope that'll make him crack a real smile. It doesn't.

"Just tired."

"Oh, so you're gonna make me pry."

"No, no, I just . . . I don't know."

"Girl problems?" My stomach tightens uncomfortably. Probably similar to what Steve's husky is currently experiencing.

"Something like that," he says.

"Oh, woof, are things going south with Ashley?" I ask, trying to look concerned.

He sighs. "No. But I'm wondering if they should."

"I thought you wanted to have a girlfriend. To be in love," I say, rolling my eyes.

"Those are two different things," he says. "I just . . . Can I be honest here, Fry?"

My heart stops beating. I feel my cheeks blush in anticipation. Of what, exactly, I don't know. I nod, pulling my coffee cup up to my face to hide it.

"So, with Ashley, and I know you're gonna give me shit for saying this out loud, but I can tell she likes me, or whatever. I can feel her"—and he puts his hands up in little claws—"trying to sink the hooks in, you know?"

"Sure," I say, choosing not to tease him for his cockiness here, because I may not be a good enough liar to act like I don't know how someone could want to be with him.

"And it's not that I definitely *don't* like her, but I just can't make up my mind. And it's driving me crazy," he says, raking a hand through his hair, further mussing it up. I swallow.

"I'm kind of shit at advice in this arena," I say. Adam knows I've never had a boyfriend, even though he jokes that he refuses to believe that. The closest I've come was letting Herbert Grove, my friend in high school who had come out only to me, imply that we were dating to the rest of our class. "But Isabelle's not, and I think what she would tell you is that if you're gonna date someone, you should probably be sure. Then again, you're one of the more indecisive people I know, so . . ."

"Exactly!" he says. "What if I'm never sure about anything? What if I've ruined my own life with rom-coms?"

"You haven't ruined your life with rom-coms. You're not that dumb," I say. He cracks a little smile.

"Okay, like last night," he says. "I was talking about the new Simon Curtis film—"

"More context, man."

"Right, sorry. That movie about A. A. Milne, who wrote *Winnie-the-Pooh*, and his son, the real Christopher Robin. And it wasn't that great of a movie or anything, but it really got me thinking about art, and using your own life for art, and involving other people. Like, how much responsibility does the artist have to the people in their personal lives when it comes to what they want to make? I wanted to, like, engage on this topic, you know? So I bring it up, and you know what she says? She says, 'Yeah, life's crazy.' Life's crazy. Like, how can I be with someone I can't even have a real conversation about a film with?" he asks, eyes growing manic.

I snort. There's an urge to agree with him—"life's crazy" is a pretty brutal response to what was clearly meant to be a conversation starter. Not to mention what lurks behind that: the need to even propose a conversation starter. For me and Adam, there is no pause, no blank space begging to be filled. The conversation never stops. I open my mouth to validate him, but the worry over how it will look if I disparage her to him won't let me vocalize any of this. "Well, if she's not asking you to make any decisions now, why stress yourself out over it?

Just keep giving her a chance, if that's what you want to do." Shoving toothpaste back into the tube would have been easier than shoving those words out.

"I guess. I just don't want to hurt her when she's making herself pretty clear." Why does he have to be thoughtful? Sensitive? Sometimes, I wish he were just an asshole. That would make things easier. "Also, last night, we were . . ." His eyes dart to mine, then down to study the yellowed countertop. "Never mind."

"Oh Christ, Adam."

"What?"

"We're gonna play that game? We both know you're gonna tell me. So just tell me."

"Okay, I mean, it's weird. I swore to myself I wouldn't tell you."

"Cute."

He smirks, but his eyes linger on mine for a second. It's intense, but I don't look away. Physically, I don't think I can. "Fine. So last night, we were . . . you know." He raises his eyebrows multiple times in a row suggestively, and my insides rearrange themselves.

"Ew."

"You said I could tell you anything!"

"That's not what I said, but we're in too deep now," I say, trying to keep my composure. I'm too curious at this point anyway.

"So. She can't really, um . . ." He waves his hand in a little circular motion, à la Billy Crystal. "Come from, you know, penetration."

I mime gagging. "I certainly didn't think I was going to hear you say the word 'penetration' today."

"Be serious! I'm trying to tell you the story."

"Okay, sorry, sorry," I say, torn between wanting to know more and wishing I could teleport out of Ray's. "But lots of women don't. Jesus, does that annoy you or something?" Anger flares in my chest.

"No, I know, I know—"

"Think of how much worse that is for *her*!" I say, hearing my voice rise. "*You* want to sit here and complain that *she* can't *come*?"

Adam starts laughing hysterically, face in his hands, and I don't think it's because he thinks I'm being funny. I can feel discomfort radiating off him in waves. "No, no! That's not what I'm trying to say."

"Well, what the fuck are you trying to say?"

"Now, now, no need for that kind of language," he says, uncovering his face and patting my shoulder. I swat his hand away and growl. He continues: "So, last night, after we had sex, I'm of course feeling guilty, because I knew she hadn't . . . you know. And I'm all, you know, *spent*, and I can feel her laying next to me, all . . . alert. And I feel like she's waiting. And I know I need to go down on her or finger her or whatever, but I was just so *tired*, and I just . . . Fry, quit looking at me like that!"

I can feel that my face is twisted in disgust, but I throw my hands up in surrender. "Fine, I'll try to keep it neutral. I just—"

"I *know*, I know it's bad. That's what I'm trying to tell you," he says. "Do you think that's a sign? Like if she was someone I was super into, don't you think I would be, like, jazzed to take care of her in that way?"

Ah, Adam. Adam, whose parents are still together and who has a family group text, active enough that they know who I, his best work friend, am. He has probably never doubted for a single second that his parents love him, and each other, completely, fully, unconditionally. And then he injects all these rom-coms into his veins (which he so obviously not guiltily calls his "guilty pleasures," by the way), and, combined with his own idealism, a perfect alchemy is created in which no woman will ever be good enough for him, in which hesitating to finger someone signals doom, because he's searching for perfection. I do not like this about him, but unfortunately, knowing that does not make the tight coil of jealousy that's lodged itself in my throat unspool.

I'm also mortified to feel jealous. What am I jealous of? The idea of having sex with a guy who doesn't care if I have an orgasm?

I shrug slowly and shake my head. I feel like I've been skinned alive, all raw and hurt and embarrassed. Desperate for cover, I say, "I don't necessarily think that just because you didn't want to put in extra work, much as she might deserve it"—I lift a finger for this point—"that that has to be a deciding factor here. People get tired sometimes. I guess, just, see if it becomes, like, a pattern or something."

He's looking at me now, like really looking, and he finally looks awake, his eyes somehow less puffy. Like talking to me has turned him back into himself. I catch him staring at me like this sometimes, tender yet probing. Like there's something in him that's beeping out Morse code to something in me, and he's checking to see if I got the message.

It also feels like he's trying to extract something from me. Like, my soul, or something. Not because he wants to take it, but just because he wants to see it. Though I'm not sure there's a difference.

"That's not what I thought you'd say," he says.

He doesn't usually surprise me. "What'd you think I'd say?" I ask.

He smiles a little and actually blushes, which I haven't seen him do before, ever. He stops giving me the tender look and grimaces. He shifts on the stool, shoulders scrunched up by his ears, and I can tell he's more uncomfortable than I have ever seen him. "I *really* didn't want to tell you this next part. I swore to myself that I wouldn't."

"Yeah, I'm kind of getting that vibe," I say. He doesn't say anything. "Well, now I have to know. Out with it."

"I thought about . . . you," he says. Every nerve ending ejects itself out of my body.

"What do you mean?" I ask.

"When . . . Oh God." He starts laughing hysterically again. Not his Adam laugh, which starts with that look of surprise, the one I like so much. His face is immediately in his hands and his shoulders are shaking. "I'm sorry, this is so humiliating to admit, and this is gonna sound so weird. But I just mean that, I thought of you, when I was there, and she was lying there, wanting more. It wasn't in a weird, sexual way! I just thought of how disappointed you would be in me. I just thought I'd get more of a lecture from you."

My body is completely frozen and feels flat somehow, like someone has pulled all my blood, bones, and organs out and I'm just squashed skin. "Um," I manage to croak out. My throat feels like someone lit it on fire.

He's waving his hands around like he's trying to cast a spell. He looks insane, frankly. "I didn't mean it, like, don't take it . . . Ah! I'm sorry! I shouldn't have said anything! I made it weird."

I shake my head, and my instinct to make everything okay pushes itself to the forefront of this whole mess. "It's fine," I say, taking the top off my coffee cup and securing it back on just for something to do with my hands. I fix my attention on a circular rust-colored stain on the linoleum floor. "It's fine. I get it. We're friends who talk about this kind of stuff. It's fine. It's fine." But I'm shaking my head, and I can tell with the way I'm repeating myself that this is actually anything but fine.

"Oh God," he says, mussing up his hair again. "I'm such a freak, I'm sorry."

I take a deep breath. "It's fine." A small chuckle squeezes itself out of me. "But good to know you think of me as some kind of, I don't know, disciplinary figure or something just shaking my finger at you, trying to shame you."

"That's not how I think of you," he says, exhaling. "You just . . . You make me want to be good, is all."

What does that even mean? We're both just nodding at each other like this is normal, but I think we both may want to die. We leave, and I make up some excuse about needing to stop by the fancy doughnut store to make sure we have enough for our guests later, so that we aren't stuck walking in the same direction. He disappears into the theater side entrance, and I immediately press myself against the brick building, trying to summon calm. I want to shove this whole thing down and away, to bury it and act like it never happened. But I also feel an urge to call Isabelle, to tell her everything and ask her what it means, so we can hold it in our hands together, pull it apart, and figure everything out. I even start typing a text to her, but I shake my head and pocket my phone. She won't let me forget it; she'll make me think about this and deal with it. As if it's something real. And I don't know if I can handle that.

CHAPTER 13

Before the host even steps up to the mic, I already regret bringing Susan to the Comedy Cellar. Because of how iconic this venue is, and the (relative) notoriety of these comics, the odds that I will find an act for the show here are pretty low. Most of them have already done the *Late Night* Friday segment at some point. But I wasn't about to bring Susan to one of my usual dank basements, where God only knows what would happen. I'm sure at either place comedians will cover topics that will make Susan uncomfortable, which will make me uncomfortable by proxy, but at least here the jokes will be met with tourists' vacation laughter instead of a shifty silence.

Clark is here, too, which is a bit of a relief; now it's not solely my job to make Susan feel comfortable. "I don't mean to crash," he had said as he ambled up to us waiting in line before the show (in khakis, of course), "but I couldn't believe my mom wanted to come to this. I had to see it for myself."

She smacked him on the arm, not unlike she did to me the other day when I was making fun of the Chanel dress. "I used to come to clubs like this all the time in my youth."

Clark gave her a big grin and pulled her in for a little hug, which was silly looking considering their height difference. It clearly made Susan happy, though. She gave him the squeeze I'm getting familiar with, and Clark faked suffocation, wheezing and bugging his eyes out. His brown eyes are big, and so is his mouth, and his expressions wear him more than the other way around. It's not unattractive, though, as indicated by the glances he was getting from the girls'-night-out group ahead of us in line.

Inside, we sit at a small table near the back, likely out of the crowd work zone, thankfully. "Oh, a two-drink minimum, just like the old days!" Susan exclaims as she holds a fake candle close to the menu. I chuckle, and Clark pats Susan's forearm.

The host, per usual, is some doughy white guy I've barely heard of. I can respect a lifer, someone who loves comedy so much they're fine with barely scraping by financially, with minimal hope of a half hour on Netflix or a green light on their pilot, as long as they get to spend their days sleeping and their nights in these dank basements making fun of themselves to a room full of people who will laugh along with them. I do want him to hurry up, though, so we can get to the first comedian on the lineup. When he finally calls her to the stage after some cringewor- thy crowd work, Susan leans over to me. "Do you know her?"

The first comedian is Martha Green and she's a regular at the Cel- lar, and she actually does have a half hour on Netflix. She opened for Chelsea Handler on her last tour. "Not personally," I tell Susan as I clap.

"So, I'm single," Martha says, to a few drunken whoops from the same girls who were checking Clark out on the way in. "And I'm straight, which is horrifying, because it means I'm out here dating men." Susan laughs and looks at Clark and me, like *Can you believe this girl?* I nod and smile. "And you know, for all the progress feminism has made and for all the woke boys out there, something that keeps happening to me is this: I'll be on a date, being myself, you know, making jokes, being charming and hilarious. And the guy will stop and kind of look at me like this." She cocks her head to the side like she's appraising a piece of art. "And he'll say, 'You know, you're *funny*.'" She gets some titters here. "And I'm like . . . 'Yeah. I'm a comedian. Kind of comes with the territory, don't know why that should hit you as some surprise.' Like, if I'm on a date with an accountant, which, yeah, I've stooped that low before, and the check comes, and then he calculates the tip, I'm not like, 'Wow, George, oh, George, I can't believe it, you're so good at math.'"

The crowd bursts into laughter, very warm. I sneak a look at Susan, who is laughing, with a big smile plastered on her face. Clark is hootin' and hollerin', which surprises me. I wouldn't have thought that he would be the key demographic for Martha Green. The show continues, and thankfully, no one humps the microphone, though I could tell that Susan was unamused by Liz Borstein, who loves to tell jokes about her daughter's lack of intelligence.

There are no drop-ins, which is unsurprising for the eight forty-five p.m. (early) show. It's a little past ten by the time we emerge into the chilly night, the chaos of MacDougal slapping us immediately. "Well, chickadees," Susan says, smiling, "that was fun. Thanks for bringing an old lady into your world for the evening."

I smile back. "Next time, I'll take you to an open mic. That'll really be something." She claps her hands together and emits a little squeal. It's all very girlish.

"That I also can't miss," Clark says. Susan shoots her hand in the air as a taxi, numbers lit, creeps down the street, and she sprints toward it.

"Love you . . . well, both!" she calls over her shoulder in a harried way as she leaps into the back of the taxi, eager to escape the Greenwich Village filth. I'm glad for her speediness, which saved me from having to reply to that last comment. Clark smirks a little after her, not unkindly.

"Oh, Susan," he says. "You gotta love her."

I nod. "Yeah." I'm already thinking about what I'm going to listen to on my walk home. I won't be calling Adam, I guess—I had expected to emerge from the Cellar to a missed call from him, but I haven't. I try to swat away the creeping disappointment but am worried that something misshapen has settled between us after our Ray's conversation. Clark also looks up from his phone.

"I didn't realize we'd be out so early," he says. "Do you want to get a drink or something?"

"Oh, um . . . ," I say, automatically casting about my brain for an excuse not to. Why is this family so insistent on becoming my friends? I had planned on going home, hitting my weed pen, crawling into bed, watching *Veep* on my laptop, and passing out by eleven thirty. But then I think about walking home, not knowing what I want to listen to, not having Adam to call. He probably hasn't called because he's with that girl. *Ashley.* Ashley, whom he can't bring himself to finger. The girl he laid next to in bed while he thought about me. "Yeah, why not."

Clark lives in the West Village (of course), and considering that I'm in the East, we decide to go somewhere close by, in the relative middle. "Amity Hall?" he suggests. I can't help it—I make a face, and he laughs. "Too bro-ey, I should have known," he says, and I can see in the city lights that he actually blushes, and a bit of guilt pinches in my chest.

"It's probably super crowded," I say, to make him feel better. But he was right. I absolutely do not want to guzzle Bud Light surrounded by white dudes in vests screaming at TVs.

"I know a place," he says, jerking his head and walking in that direction. I text Izzy that I'm going to be out later than I thought. We walk a few blocks north to a bar called Analogue, and it's quiet and probably fancier than something I would have picked. But then again, Clark is a fancy guy, I guess.

"Are you gonna get a cosmo?" I ask as we take seats at the bar and pull menus close to us. It's almost too dark to see them; the walls are painted navy blue, the wooden bar is a dark mahogany, and only a few lamps give off soft light. It's relaxing to feel a bit hidden.

"Thinkin' about it," he says. "Are you gonna get an old-fashioned and emasculate me?"

"A real man would just get a cosmo and own it."

"I didn't think it was cool to say things like 'real man' anymore."

"Oh God," I say, rolling my eyes. "Am I about to get a you-can't-joke-about-anything-anymore lecture? Are you about to spit some

Tucker Carlson at me?" Clark tips his head back and laughs. He has a deep laugh, like it comes from his gut, like he can't help it.

"No," he says. "I'm just messin'. And"—he leans conspiratorially toward me—"this place is known for their whiskey anyway." He points to the top of their menu, where it says "Cocktails and Whiskey" to prove it.

I shrug. "When in Rome." We both order old-fashioneds, which I can't really afford, but I'm already two drinks in from the Comedy Cellar, which is right around the time that the chasm between what I can and can't afford starts to seem narrower. My phone buzzes with a text from Izzy: Love that, party girl! See ya tomorrow! I send back a thumbs-up.

"So, Presley Fry, comedy expert," he says. "Who's your favorite comedian?"

I don't know why the question surprises me so much. I suppose most people have a favorite song or movie or whatever, so most comedy lovers probably have a favorite comedian. It's just that it's such an overarching question about something complicated, something living. If comedy is vast like the ocean, then I'm a marine biologist, intensely studying one reef at a time. I could pontificate on the difference between the Brooklyn and Manhattan comedy scenes for at least twenty minutes straight, if prompted, and that's not even getting into individual comedians. "You mean, like, ever?"

Clark nods. "Is that a dumb question?"

"No, no," I say honestly. "I'm just not sure how to answer it. I guess I just spend so much time thinking about who the next big comedian could be and thinking about what's going on in comedy, like, right now, that I don't really think about it in any kind of extreme way."

"That makes sense, I guess," he says. "I just would have thought you had a favorite or something, like, when you were a kid."

"Well, yeah. Gary," I say. Embarrassment immediately prickles my skin. "I guess that sounds kind of lame. Like: I loved Gary Madden growing up in my small, hick town, so much so that I moved to the big city and work for him now, or whatever."

"That's not lame. That's cool," Clark says earnestly. I resent his approval of this sentiment: like he's this big-city boy and I'm satisfying him by fitting into a stereotype. Adam would have made fun of me for admitting my childhood obsession, like he made fun of me for my southern accent, and I would have appreciated it. Because he understands the difference between where I come from and who I'm trying to be. "And did you just call my mother a hick?"

I laugh. "Your mother is the opposite of a hick."

"It's funny, her accent. Like, it's cute and sweet most of the time," Clark says. "And then you can see when she turns it up to charm a waiter or be let into Bergdorf's even though it's about to close or whatever. And sometimes, when she's had a few, you know, it does actually swerve a little into hick territory. My dad does this really funny impression, but it drives her crazy." He thoughtfully takes a sip of his drink and I'm not sure what to say. I'm sorry your dad cheated on your mom and was a low-key misogynist?

"Well, I can relate to that. And you should've heard my mom after a few. That would really have given y'all something to talk about." Wow. I guess I feel awkward enough that I'm willing to use Patty and her alcoholism as a conversation pivot.

Clark smiles. Not his big grin, but a sad little smile. It's polite but doesn't seem practiced. Good for him. "I'm sorry about your mom," he says.

"Oh, thanks," I say, picking up my glass, then setting it back down again, for something to do with my hands.

I can practically see them sitting there between us, all the words we aren't saying about our parents. I'd very much like to say something, to break this tension, when Clark's phone, resting on the bar between us, lights up with a Hinge notification. He quickly darkens the screen, and I can't help but laugh.

"Shut up," he says, and I think he may actually be blushing again, though it's a little too dark in here to tell.

"Who's the lucky lady? Or man? Or person? Aren't you gonna check?"

"No," he says, shaking his head and avoiding eye contact.

"All righty," I say, shrugging and staring straight ahead, just like he is. I catch our reflection in the mirror behind the bar, sitting quietly side by side, whiskey glasses in front of us. We look like proper pals.

"I don't really use it," he says, looking into his glass.

"What are you, like, embarrassed?" I ask, genuinely wondering. He doesn't strike me as the type who would be embarrassed to be on a dating app. Might even be the kind of guy who brags about paying for the upgrades, the ones where they send only people with six-pack abs and/or who went to Ivy League schools and/or who have famous parents.

"No," he says, still studying his glass, like a funny retort might scurry out from beneath the big, melting ice cube. He slides a glance over to me, looks at me like he's testing the waters, like he's weighing how I'll react to whatever he might say. He shifts in his seat and I smell that scent again, that one from when we hugged before Susan and I saw *The Band's Visit*. The Clean Boy smell. Tide and pine.

"What?"

"No, it's . . .." He shrugs. "Never mind."

"Okay, you don't have to tell me." We both take a sip of our drinks, but he quickly puts his glass down and blurts out:

"I'm just kind of going through a breakup, is all."

"Oooooh," I say, nodding. There it is. "I'm sorry. Breakups are hard."

He shakes his head and lets out a puff of air. "You're tellin' me. When was your last one?"

"Oh, uh . . . ," I say, suddenly not wanting to look at him. "I just meant, you know, generally." He gives me a quizzical look, and I practically see the brain waves undulate in his mind that make him decide not to ask me anything more. I'm glad. Not that I'm embarrassed to have never had a boyfriend, but I'm not really trying to get into the business of sharing that kind of personal information with Lawrence Clark. To shake the spotlight off, I ask, "Do you want to tell me what happened?" I am interested to know, is the thing.

He sighs, sort of hunches his shoulders over the bar. "College sweetheart situation. I saw her, like, our very first fraternity party." I can't help it: I scoff, and he rolls his eyes. "Yeah, yeah, whatever," he says. "So, she walked in and I was just like . . . whoa. It was like a movie. Time just kind of stopped." He puts his hands up for effect, and I make a conscious effort not to roll my eyes. "We barely talked that night, but it didn't matter, the deal was already sealed for me. I knew I wanted to be with her, that I wouldn't want to be with anyone else. Like, maybe ever."

"Wow," I say. "Some hunch punch your frat must make."

He lightly taps my shoulder in a joke swipe, and I'm reminded of his mother batting me away when I suggested she buy the weird Victorian dress. It's a comfortable move, like we've been close for a long time. That's obviously not the case here, but it doesn't bother me for some reason. Maybe because I knew him when I was young, and our families are from the same place. I don't know him, but I also do.

"*Anyway*, she didn't feel the same way, at first. But I stuck around, we became friends. Junior year she decided to give me a shot. Senior year, she got a full ride, still at UVA, for law school, so she stayed in Charlottesville, and I got an internship that I was told would likely become a job at CAM, so we decided to do long-distance. Which everyone bitches about, you know, but I thought we could handle it. I thought the people who complained about it just didn't have what we had. Which is pretty cocky, I'll admit."

I shrug. "Well."

The light shoulder tap again. He's quiet, and I want to ask for more details, but before I can even open my mouth he continues. "We made it work for two years, and the plan was that she would come up here for an internship between her second and third years, get an offer at some top firm, and then we'd be together again. She's so smart. So much smarter than me, which isn't that hard. But she's smarter than everyone, like genius level. She got internship offers from everywhere. And she decided the one she wanted to do the most was in San Francisco. Which, like, not the plan, but I wanted to be supportive, right, so I'm like, well, this is a longer distance, and the time difference will probably toss a wrench into this whole thing, but for her?" He lets out a puff of air. "For her, you do that, you know. But she didn't want to do the distance this time."

I nod. I wouldn't have made it even half as far as he did. The inconvenience of long-distance is highly prohibitive. This is something I, and Isabelle now, too, have trouble seeing past, the unwieldiness of being in love, of having to organize your life while also being considerate of someone else's, like we don't have enough to take care of with our own shit anyway. Seems like a tall order. Not that either of us knows firsthand.

"But I was like, well, we've made it work for two years, surely we can handle one summer with a time difference. The firm she was going to had offices all over, and so does CAM, so I thought by the time her offer came around and she was deciding where to move permanently, I may be able to work out of a different office anyway."

"And not live in New York?" I ask. I don't mean to sound horrified, but as the words leave my mouth, I know I do. But it does baffle me: the idea of wanting to live anywhere else. Especially if you're someone like Clark, with the resources to rise above a lot of the daily inconveniences (atrocities) that come with living on this absurd, magnificent island.

He laughs. "Yeah, there *are* other places, you know." I give him a look. He smiles. "I know," he says. And I instantly like him by ten more degrees. It always happens when I realize someone loves New York as much as I do.

"She started by saying she didn't want to do long-distance. But turns out, it wasn't just that," he says. "She just . . . didn't want to be with me anymore." He taps his pointer finger on the bar, looking down at it as he does. Not signaling the waiter or anything chic like that, just fidgeting.

"Damn," I say. "That sucks." Because it does. I don't have the answers for Clark, I don't know the perfect thing to say to make him feel better. It is wild to me how people think they, whoever *they* are, no matter their relationship to the person they're speaking to, no matter what their personal experience has or has not been, will have the words. It's narcissistic, really. Someone sharing something is not an opportunity for a hot take. Losing Patty has taught me that the only thing to do is acknowledge other people's pain.

"Yeah, thanks," he says.

"When did all this go down?" I ask.

"Eighteen months ago," he says solemnly. I will my eyes not to bug out of my head, but a little choking sound accidentally escapes me. I mean, the kid is acting like this wound is fresh, and it practically happened in another lifetime. "Hey!" he says, hearing my scoff, turning to face me. "Heartbreak stands outside of time!" I don't feel myself doing it, but I would guess, based on my, you know, entire personality, that I give him some sort of look of disdain. He grins at me, though, seemingly acknowledging his own cheesiness. Then a shadow passes over his face. "It wasn't like it was a clean break, though."

"Ah, yes, that would be a crucial detail," I say. "Also, fuck that." I mean it. People going back on their word pisses me off. If you're going to dump someone, commit. The whiskey lends weight to my clawed feeling of indignation on his behalf.

Speaking of which, Clark asks if I want one more. I do. "On me, by the way," he says. I give him a look. "You'll get it next time," he says. I shrug; I'll allow this. It's especially easy to swallow considering that I sort of doubt there will be a next time. It's not even like we're intentionally hanging out, it's more just like we're two lonely people without plans who happen to be drinking in the same place at the same time. I shudder, pinched by the realization that that's how Patty met most of her "friends."

"Yeah, it took a while for the breakup to really stick," he says.

"That is fucked up," I say, taking a sip of my fresh drink. "If you're gonna break up with someone, you have to just break up with them. It's cruel to fuck with people like that."

He nods. "Yeah, but I also get it. I mean, we had been together for a long time, I get why she second-guessed. And it's not like I was really . . . enforcing boundaries."

"Oh, so it's your fault she jerked you around because she knew you were in love with her? Sorry, but no," I say. He smiles, but there's a question in his eyes. "What?" I ask. I kind of spit the word out, by accident.

He throws his hands up in innocence, and I can tell that he's a little drunk, too, based on the looseness of the movement. "Nothing, you're just, like, fired up here. Which I appreciate, make no mistake."

I think I may feel a blush rising up my neck. It's not like we know each other well enough to get worked up on the other's behalf. But I shrug and say, "Whatever. Weak people like that just grind my fucking gears, is all."

"Was some guy, uh, *weak* to you?" he asks.

"No."

"My bad—or girl," he says.

"Nope. I'm not much of a . . . dater," I say. Of course, at this exact moment, my phone lights up with a call. Adam, and that stupid photo.

"Well, well, what do have we here," Clark says, craning his neck to get a closer look at the photo. I quiet the call and let it go to voice mail, flip my phone over on the bar, even though a roaring part of me wants to step outside and answer it.

"Just a friend from work," I say, not looking at Clark and taking a sip of my drink, taking my time returning the glass to its coaster.

"Okay," he says. "Sure."

We finish our drinks, switching to less personal topics, like how shitty the apps can make you feel and how tragic (annoying) it is that people keep throwing themselves on the subway tracks during rush hour. He tells me he's going "leaf-peeping" upstate next week and I nearly do a spit take, which makes him throw his head back and really laugh, and his face is open and unbridled. It's nice to look at.

He pays the bill and we go our separate ways after a quick little side hug that is thankfully much looser than his mother's. I start walking east, pop my headphones in, swerve to avoid some drunk touristy people on the sidewalk. I listen to Adam's voice mail just as I walk across Fifth Avenue and see Washington Square Park's arch, all lit up in the night. It makes me smile. What a fucking cliché I am.

Adam's voice in my ears: "Hey, I just wanted to make sure we're good after today. I'm sorry for being weird . . . yeah. Bye." I also have three texts from him, his desperation to make sure I'm not mad or judging him clear. I feel a twinge of regret that I missed his call, that he's been feeling anxious. It's met with another feeling I don't want to deal with: relief that he clearly went home alone tonight. Just like me.

CHAPTER 14

Hump day, and I'm sorry to report that I mean that in more ways than one. I've been in a sexual dry spell. The truth is there are only four ways of being, sexually, that I ever am: in the act; starting a dry spell; in the middle of a dry spell; or nearing the end of a dry spell. Then the cycle repeats. The way I see it: I'm a human being with sexual needs. I am not interested in a relationship, and I am not interested in hooking up with someone consistently, because according to movies and also the volatility of men, there's a sky-high risk of the latter leading to the former.

As a woman of the twenty-first century, my preferred method of finding sexual opportunities is Tinder. I can essentially sort through a menu of guys and chat with ones I find reasonably attractive, mostly to confirm that they're literate. I try to swipe right only on guys whose paths I don't think I'd cross normally: aka guys in their thirties. I also find an increase in the likelihood that guys in their thirties know their way around a clitoris. And don't mind exercising that knowledge, unlike, ahem, some people.

I'll match with someone, exchange a few texts about getting a drink, hopefully that night or in the next few days. I'd love to skip the drink part and just cut to the chase, frankly, but I'd also love to avoid being brutally killed, something a guy seems far less likely to do in a bar than the privacy of his own home.

It's been three months since I drank cheap beers with Greg, an app developer who lives in Greenpoint. Greg was perfect for my purposes: boring, droning on and on in the dive bar he picked in his neighborhood about his job, while I nodded and asked polite questions and shared nothing about myself except to make one joke-not-joke about how my best friend had my location on her phone and also there was mace in my purse, so he better not try anything weird. We went back to his place, did the deed, he fingered me afterward until I came, and then I left. I unmatched him while switching from the G train to the F train (wordplay unintended), but I sent a message thanking him for a fun night first. I'm not totally heartless.

Business casual sex, Izzy calls it. It's a rebellion against the horseshit I heard in Bible study growing up: that as a woman, I would find it impossible to separate my feelings from sexual interactions. That it was critical I save sex for marriage, because who would want to marry me (the assumption, of course, was that being marriage material was the ultimate goal) if I was damaged goods? Our youth pastor actually used a violin as an example: he claimed it was a Stradivarius, then threw it into the audience casually. This was meant to symbolize that our virginities contained unbelievable value (as much value as a Stradivarius!), and would we really just casually toss that around?

I now realize that virginity is a social construct built to restrict women's personal freedom, and it pisses me off to know that such an effortful attempt was ever made to convince me otherwise. Especially when I think about the fact that that particular Stradivarius sermon was for girls only.

Now I find the idea of love being inherently tied to sex hilarious. As dark as this may sound, I don't really see what love and sex have to do with each other. Maybe I'd get it if I were Izzy, who came back from Christmas break last year telling me (while cringing) that she had overheard her parents having sex in the hotel room next to hers when they went to the Bahamas for New Year's.

Patty dated, but her relationships never lasted long. Hugh, the butcher at the Winn-Dixie, was the leading man, in that he appeared sporadically but over the course of many years. He'd pick her up at the house, take her to dinner or the movies. She'd usually return wasted (she'd also *go* wasted), grumbling about how men don't commit anymore. Hugh was around as long as I could remember, and for a while there I was a bit worried he was my biological father. But Patty, oversharer that she was, informed me when I was twelve that he was sterile, bringing me as close as I think I'll ever get to confirmation of the my-dad-was-a-man-passing-through-town story. Anyway, Patty was susceptible to intense crushes. Like there was some guy named Bryan in one of her AA groups, and she'd come home and tell me about him. I didn't give a shit about who he was, but I appreciated that he was incentivizing her to go to meetings. Otherwise, I'd overhear her complaining about men on the phone to Rita, a drinking buddy of hers whom I saw in person only about five times.

A lot of my mother's love life existed in movies, like the clichéd lonely woman she was. She'd stay up late watching *An Affair to Remember* and its spiritual grandchild, *Sleepless in Seattle*, and I'd sometimes stay up with her, when her drunken commentary didn't get under my skin too much. I didn't have a bedtime; a perk of having an alcoholic mother is that there aren't really rules.

Anyway. I made progress on accomplishing my mission of getting laid today when I hid out in one of the greenrooms after I cleaned it more quickly than expected (Timothée Chalamet brought quite the crowd but didn't leave a mess) and began swiping. Poorly lit close-ups of biceps, smoldering selfies where you can practically hear the guy's inner dialogue screaming *Do I look sensitive?* and shirtless mirror pics. I tend to swipe right on the thirtysomethings who I think look nice, if a bit basic. Bonus points if he has a dog, the only downside there being that he is likely aware of the bonus points. I half hoped I could get a match undisturbed and half hoped that Adam would wander in and see that I was making plans with someone. Or trying to, anyway.

I matched with a dude named Matt, who apparently has an ancient beagle, a tattoo sleeve, and nine more years on Earth logged than I do. And now here I am, sitting across from him at a pub in downtown Brooklyn, and I've already managed to make my standard joke about his not being able to easily get away with murdering me. He did chuckle appreciatively, which is about the only individual attention I've gotten so far. I'm asking questions: what does he do, where is he from, how many siblings, whatever. And he's just going on and on, thrilled at the chance to talk about himself. About how he's biding his time at his day job in advertising, but his real passion is music, and once he puts together a band with *just* the right dynamic, he knows he'll be able to do it full-time.

"It's all about finding the right group of guys," he says.

"Or women," I say.

"Right." He nods.

He pays. I offer to Venmo him. He accepts.

His apartment is just down the block from this bar, so it would be easy to have one more drink at his place, he tells me. I make a show of sending Izzy the address. It's so practiced, all of it. And I appreciate that. We're items on each other's checklists, and it feels equal and democratic. He doesn't pretend like he's going to fix me a drink once we cross the threshold into his spacious, sparsely IKEA-decorated apartment. We don't even go to the bedroom, just the couch. And by "couch," I unfortunately mean futon. We pause making out so I can unlace my combat boots, and we undress ourselves. He lays me down, one knee leaning against the back of the futon, the other splayed out into space, which pulls at my hips uncomfortably. He goes down on me, and, as his age had led me to hope, he does in fact know his way around a clit.

He keeps a condom in his wallet. He sits on the couch, rolls it on wordlessly, and thus I receive my cue to begin. At one point, when I'm straddling him, I think of Adam, not in any kind of articulate way, but his face just appears in my head, and he settles all over my brain like freshly fallen snow. As soon as I register that I'm thinking of him, I hate myself so much I lose my breath. Matt asks if I'm okay, I say that I am. I imagine pulling blinds down in my head, and we continue. He pecks me on the forehead when it's over. I take a deep breath, get dressed, give him a weird quick salute I immediately regret, and leave. I unmatch with him on the F train.

CHAPTER 15

I think I'm the only person at *Late Night* who isn't grateful the Thanksgiving holiday grants us an entire week off. Last year, I went home to Eulalia to be with my grandparents. It was our first year post-Patty. This year, flights were even more astronomically expensive, so my grandparents are just going to eat with their neighbors. And I won't be alone here: Isabelle's family is coming. I thought I would be excited for a whole week off, to catch up on Netflix specials and read and maybe go catch the Central Park fall vibe, but now that it's here, I'm in an unparalleled funk.

Except for last night. Because holidays like Thanksgiving tend to thin the New York City crowds, Izzy had an easier time scoring us a reservation at Lilia, this Italian restaurant in Williamsburg that immediately elicits a groan of jealousy anytime anyone mentions going there. Like most things, it's out of my price range, but Izzy had a gift card from a client and insisted we use it. We gorged ourselves on wine and prawns and cacio e pepe and ragù, and Izzy demanded I hold her stomach when we took the L train back home afterward, because she was so full.

A major topic of conversation was Sammy, who is not only still see-ing Banana Boy from Hinge and Halloween but has, according to Isabelle, fallen head over heels in love. Izzy had a drink with Sammy last week before she went home to Dallas for Thanksgiving, and apparently "Sean" was all they, well, Sammy, talked about. Sammy told Izzy some elaborate story about how she had cooked him dinner and he found one of her hairs on his asparagus and according to Sammy it was just *so funny*. She also spent thirty minutes explaining how Sean is trying to extract himself from the banking world, as if Izzy gives a shit. Sammy herself didn't even know what the man's job was a month ago. She didn't even like him that much after the first few dates! "If there isn't a spark immediately, I'm out," Izzy said. I agreed, though the whole idea of a "spark" isn't something I buy into. We pressed our glasses of wine together and vowed never to bore each other with stupid stories about the significant others we don't even have. And won't anytime soon, what with Izzy's swearing off dating and my allergy to romance.

Now I toss two Tums into my mouth in an attempt to regulate my stomach after all that richness. I took up our showrunner Dan's offer to come in Monday and Tuesday of this week for extra pay and do the random shit no one has time to do when we're busy putting on an hour of television every day. Really sexy stuff, like organizing the storage closet, archiving footage and guests' preinterviews from the last few months. It's eerie being here alone. Earlier I went into the PA's office to leave Adam a creepy, funny note for when he gets back from Philly, but I couldn't think of anything to write. I felt like a stalker being in there anyway.

As I'm scanning preinterview transcript notes, my mind wanders to Thanksgivings past. Two years ago, I lived off mostly ramen noodles for months to save up for my plane ticket home. It was a memorable occasion in retrospect, what with it being Patty's last Thanksgiving. And also because she called me a bitch at the table. It was the first time I had seen my family since I moved to New York after graduating the previous June. My grandparents rarely touched booze but liked to have champagne (cheap prosecco) with Thanksgiving dinner, to be festive. Patty made a show of refusing the prosecco, as if she were sober, as if we were unaware that she'd been guzzling Burnett's all day.

At the table, the talk had centered on yours truly. Grammy and Pops wanted to hear all about my life in New York, reacting to everything I shared as though we didn't talk on the phone every single week. I should have known this would cause an outburst from Patty, who was tiptoeing the line of avoiding her parents and commanding their full attention.

I could tell she was two miles past wasted when she scooped the mushy sweet potato casserole out of the glass bowl with her bare hands and flicked it onto her plate with a splat. I tried to wipe the disgust off my face when her lazy eyes looked up into mine, but I must not have been fast enough. "What, too fancy for me now, bitch?" she slurred. Patty may be gone, but I can still feel my chest pierce open at that one. Like she had thrown a knife instead of a drunken sentiment.

I steal up to the studio roof to clear my head. It's chilly, but the sky is blue and cloudless. I rest my elbows on the stone wall, look out over the city. Horrifyingly earnest as it is, I feel a sense of wonder, totally in awe that humans made all this. In Eulalia, my grandparents dragged my ass to church every Sunday, where I was forced to hear about the splendor of God's creation. And while I'm certainly not a Christian, sometimes when my grandparents would drive me through the mountains of North Carolina to visit my second cousins or when I would see the purple sky when the sun set over Eulalia, I'd get the hype. Some higher power must have dreamed all that up.

But God didn't make Manhattan. People did. And they aren't finished, never will be; it's built upon every day. And while sunsets and mountains are beautiful, that fact is what takes my breath away. That this city is a living monument to what people can accomplish, what they can overcome.

After researching from our couch, Isabelle and I found a restaurant in the East Village with good reviews that does traditional Thanksgiving food, though of course with a bit of froufrou spicing-up bullshit Isabelle finds exciting. Looking at photos of brown-buttered sweet potatoes some food blogger seems to think must have been cooked by the breath of angels, I couldn't help but ache for my grandma's sweet potato casserole and the way my grandfather laughs about turduckens every year.

Izzy and I arrive at the restaurant at the same time as the rest of her family. There's George, who's a junior in high school; Daniel, who's a junior in college; and Isabelle's parents, whose names are, God bless them, Harry and Harriett. They got in from Maryland late last night. The whole blond family looks very much alike, and I would find it creepy if they weren't so likable. "Look at us!" Harry says, stretching his short arms out proudly. "Showing up at the same time as the real New Yorkers!" At his full height, Harry can't be taller than five foot nine. Harriett's got three inches on him, at least. Harriett is a bigwig at Lockheed Martin, all schedules and smiles and blazers and handshakes and being secretly (and sometimes not so secretly) the smartest person in every room. Harry is a teacher and worships the ground Harriett, and by extension Isabelle, walks on.

They're essentially the dream family. Exotic, occasional vacations. Don't drink on weekdays. They sent their kids to camp, gave them allowances growing up that were helpful but not overly generous. Lots of family inside jokes, but they also like meeting new people and opening their doors to strays, like me.

I hug Harry, then Harriett, who gives me one tiny, short squeeze that thankfully doesn't crush my bones the way I've come to expect from my time with Susan. Possibly the only thing more consistent than the force of Susan's hugs is the way she signs her texts, still, xx Susan. Like the one she sent me this morning: Happy Thanksgiving, Presley! I'm so thankful I get to call you a friend. Xx Susan.

"Christ, look at y'all," I say, briefly hugging George and Daniel, who were essentially children when I first met them on my freshman-year spring break and are now something like men.

"Hey, Presley," Daniel says with a bit of a smirk. He followed in Izzy's footsteps, from Maryland to UGA, and joined a fraternity, though unlike Izzy he has stuck with it. And given the swagger with which he greets me, I can tell he's *really* stuck with it.

"Hey," George says with a little wave, even though we're standing two feet apart. He's all splayed limbs, skin, and bone. He reminds me of a baby deer, if that baby deer had acne and pants that were four inches too short.

We sit and order and Harry pours wine for everyone except George, who rolls his eyes, as if pinot noir is something a seventeen-year-old boy would want anyway. Harry, who loves Gary Madden, peppers me with questions about the show and about Gary himself. Questions he also asked me on their last visit to New York and the one before that as well. Is he nice? Does he know my name? How much of the monologue does he come up with himself? Yes, barely, and I don't know—they don't let anyone other than the writers and the writers' assistants within a twenty-foot radius of the sacred writers' room.

Harriett raises her glass. "To family, both blood and chosen." She gives me a little wink. "To New York City, to our health, to all that we have to be thankful for." We clink glasses and take a sip. Except for George, who stares at the table sullenly. "And of course," Harriett goes on, "we acknowledge the people we love who aren't here with us today, like my father." Isabelle's grandfather died eight months ago after years of fighting cancer. Harry puts his arm around her, and she looks at him, teary. Isabelle reaches across the table and covers her mother's hand with her own.

Then Harriett looks at me. "And Patty, whom I only met a handful of times, but who clearly brought a lot of joie de vivre to the world."

I silently raise my glass again, and my throat becomes scratchy, my skin hot. Next to me, Isabelle squeezes my shoulder, then quickly pulls away. The warm force of it, the blood that pools there for a split second, the way my shoulder instantly loosens, brings me back, and I take a sip of water and will my body to cool down. I remind myself to call my grandparents after we eat.

Conversation moves on to where George will apply to college next year, and George asks if, please, since it's a holiday, could they not talk about this. Daniel mentions some study-abroad program he wants to go on this summer, and I remember it from my days at Georgia as being the one known less for studying, more for partying. He tells us his girlfriend is also going, which prompts Harry to ask me and Isabelle if we're seeing anyone at the moment.

"I'm not," Izzy says proudly. "It's the year of me."

"It's been the year of you since 1994," Daniel says. Izzy sticks her tongue out at him.

"What about you, Presley?" Harry presses. "Seeing anyone special?"

I got a text from Adam this morning. It said, Happy Thanksgiving, Fry, with a string of emojis: turkey, prayer hands, potato, and heart eyes. Three dots had appeared below, and I'd accidentally gone lightheaded, holding my breath. The next text: Seriously, I'm thankful for you, dude. Don't know where I'd be without you.

Multiple reactions had churned in my stomach. There's the sentiment, which is nice, but there's also the "dude." I wrote back, Back atcha, bud.

"Nope," I say to Harry, pointedly avoiding the look Izzy is surely giving me. "Just me and Izzy, taking the city by storm." Harriett gives a nod of approval, which fills me with an unexpected pride.

I'm forced to admit the brown-buttered sweet potatoes actually *do* taste like they've been cooked by the breath of angels, and by the time the waiter clears our plates, we're all holding our stomachs and can't focus on anything other than how full we are. Harriett suggests a walk along the East River to help digest, which I decline to join. They should have at least one pocket of this day that doesn't involve an outsider. I pick my way along the sidewalk, dodging a family of tourists in mittens, a young boy screaming that he liked the inflatable SpongeBob the best of the parade. I make eye contact with a grungy dude leaning in a doorway, smoking a cigarette. We throw each other quick head nods, acknowledging that we live here, they don't. I pull out my phone, pop my headphones in, and make a call.

"I was just fixin' to call you," Grammy says as soon as she picks up.

The southern lilt and the softness of her voice are so at odds with the filthy flock of pigeons blocking my route on the sidewalk, pecking at discarded bread crumbs and completely unbothered by me, I can't help but grin. "Happy Thanksgiving."

"Is this Miss New York City?" Pops asks. I can picture them so clearly: she on the corded phone nailed to the kitchen wall, sitting on the stool just beneath it, he in his recliner, the cordless in his liver-spotted hand. Football on the TV, Grammy bustling around the kitchen. The way that I know she won't accept that my grandpa is done eating until he's practically comatose at the table later.

"Hi, Pops." My grandpa asks me what I'm doing. I tell them about eating with Isabelle's family, which they're glad for. They met Izzy's family every move-in and move-out day in Athens, and my grandparents liked them, despite the fact that they're Yankees. My grandparents tell me they're going to be heading over to the neighbors' soon. They were told not to bring anything, but Grammy made three different casseroles. It'll be different this year, that's for sure, they tell me. I swallow hard when they say this, my throat knotty.

My grandpa must sense it, because he says, "We wish you were here, but we're glad you had a happy Thanksgiving, and you know we're doing fine down here. S'long as I've got my girl with me, we're all set." The "girl" he's referring to is my grandmother. I nod, even though they can't see me. I pull my keys out of my pocket, approach my doorstep.

"I'm so thankful for y'all," I say quietly, knowing any added volume will force the knot in my throat to rise and spill over onto my cheeks.

"Oh, honey, we are thankful for you, and we love you so much," Grammy says. I press my pointer fingers against my eyelids, the shakiness in her voice getting to me.

"Love you, Presley Pie," Pops says.

I tell them I love them, too. Then I climb the five flights of stairs to my apartment, collapse on our fraying couch, and stare at the ceiling until the quiet becomes too overwhelming. I open my phone and scroll to my audiobooks, and soon enough Nora Ephron's voice reading *I Feel Bad About My Neck* is bouncing off the peeling-paint walls. And like a tide, or a hairline, the loneliness slowly starts to recede.

CHAPTER 16

It shouldn't surprise me that Peanut's boss, Mark, thinks Chris Munson is some kind of heavenly gift to the up-and-coming comedy community. Munson is a young, straight white guy, and the first time I saw him do stand-up at Carolines, I didn't get half his jokes—his set was very Jets-heavy. His audience is probably Lawrence Clark and Co., which is to say fratty and boyish. Chris keeps it pretty clean, but I get the impression his locker-room talk would likely make my skin crawl. Such judgment may be unfair, since I have been his audience member for a combined total of merely twenty minutes, but know what else is unfair? That he is mediocre at best yet gets to perform stand-up on television's number one late night show (even if I do really like that one joke he has about white quinoa looking like used condoms).

Of course, one of the managers Mark is always having drinks with and referring to by last name was the one who pitched Chris Munson to us. Based on Mark's loud anecdotes, I'm pretty sure he and this manager play pickup basketball together every weekend. Mark is one of those people who can't seem to work out without mentioning it at least seven times.

Because I'm working on owning the Friday segment, and in an attempt to make Thursdays less hectic for the actual producers, I'm handling Chris today. I walk into his greenroom to find him sipping a Bud Light—which, at four thirty in the afternoon before the nerve-racking opportunity to be on national television, I can't say I judge him for. For his big debut he has chosen to wear jeans and a plain gray hoodie. Perhaps the most frustrating thing about Chris Munson is that despite the fact that his features don't quite *work* (weirdly large mouth, beady eyes), he is somehow, admittedly, attractive.

"Hi, I'm Presley, here to walk you through everything. Welcome to the show," I say, going in for the handshake. In order to make this work, he has to switch his Bud Light from his right hand to his left, and he wipes his newly free hand on his jeans before clasping mine.

"Yeah, thanks, Todd should be here soon," he says, clearly annoyed by his manager's tardiness.

"Can I take you to the stage? I'll show you your mark. One of our interns will bring your manager in when he arrives."

Down the hallway we go, dodging a clothing rack bursting with colonial garb for a cold open shoot. It's so full I don't even realize that Adam is the one pushing it until he's almost past us, and when he sees me with Chris, he shoots his eyebrows up and smirks. Adam knows how I feel about Chris being here. He Slacked me earlier, All the more reason for you to be the one handling the slot, Fry. Getting the comedians up there who really deserve it. And he's right.

"Gary will throw to commercial, and that's when you'll come out here and find your mark, so when Gary intros you when we come back, you'll already be standing here," I say as we enter from stage left. We walk to where there's a masking tape X on the ground. "And here's your mark. I'll hand you a mic backstage, so you'll already have that, but, here, if you want to do a sound check now . . ." I jog over to the mic closet, switch one on, and hand it to him. He bends his knees quickly a few times, standing on his mark, like he's getting ready to do a free throw. He stills, holding the mic, and looks out into the theater. It's mostly empty, except for a few interns milling about, making sure the Thursday-show audience hasn't left a mess before the Friday-show audience is loaded in.

He has this dreamy look on his face, and I see his Adam's apple bob as he swallows. He clears his throat, says, "Hi, Chris Munson, check one two, one two," and I could swear his voice sounds a little choked up. His eyes rove over the ceiling, which is ornate and gold trimmed and painted fresco style and beautiful. Which I forget, because I see it every day. But this is rarefied air, sacred, the theater in which Elvis performed for the first time on late night television, in which a young Chris Rock did his first late night five-minute set. An opera was apparently performed here in the early 1900s. Anyone who watches the show in its entirety would have seen images of the theater, as they show them as intros and outros to the segments, but these days so few people see that unless they're actually here, because the show is mostly watched segment by segment on social media. That shouldn't depress me, considering that's undoubtedly how I would consume the show if I didn't work here, but it does.

I look back at Chris and catch him aggressively wipe his nose. He catches me catching him and laughs a little, instantly endearing himself to me. "Sorry," he says. "Embarrassing. This just . . ." He shrugs and swallows again, and even though I can't tell for sure because, again, I can't overemphasize how beady his eyes are, I would put money (if I had any) on them being filled with tears. "This is just so cool, you know? It's like . . . it's dream-come-true shit."

I nod and look back out over the theater. Just like that, I find myself hoping his dumb Jets jokes kill.

CHAPTER 17

I have been bamboozled into shopping again. Several weeks ago, I would have told you that shopping was my nightmare. If I had to get specific, I would have said parading around Bergdorf's with a friend of Patty's was torture. But this? Christmas shopping for Adam's girlfriend-not-girlfriend? This is the seventh circle of hell.

Adam seems to agree. He groans loudly as he mopes around this junk store in Chelsea, which he insisted on visiting because he had heard they had some original movie poster he wanted to buy himself before figuring out whatever he's getting *Ashley*. The store does have the poster. It's ripped, and also twelve hundred bucks. Everything in here is out of our price range; also, everything in here is crap. Tiny desks, Betty Boop lamps, and bent postcards as far as the eye can see.

"I told you we wouldn't find anything in here," I say. "Is there anywhere else that would have something she'd like?" I watch my helpful words pull themselves out of my mouth. Apparently, Adam wasn't planning on getting her a gift, but she's dropped some unsubtle hints that she was getting him one. He's decided to get her something small, something silly. Something that acknowledges her, but not something that says, *I love you, let's date*. Or so he tells me.

"Ugh," he says. "I don't want to be doing this at all."

"That makes two of us," I snort. "You know how I feel about shopping," I add quickly.

Adam bends down to closely examine a typewriter, which makes me snort again. "What?" he asks, tugging self-consciously at the worn hem of his pilling green sweater.

I shake my head.

"What?" he asks again. "Come on, I'm not gonna buy it! I could never be *that* pretentious. I'm not Greg Kinnear in *You've Got Mail.*" It's criminal, the way he can make a perfect Nora Ephron reference.

I cock my head to the side and pretend to ponder this. "You know, there really are some similarities, actually—"

I swerve as he closes the gap between us and lunges to whack my arm. He misses. He sighs and swivels a ceramic desk chair that would have looked at home on the *Mad Men* set. Eyes on the chair, he says, "I could totally see you with a guy like that."

My jaw drops in mock (well, kind of real) offense. "That guy's a tool!"

"Sure, sure, and I don't think you'd be into that," Adam says. "But I just mean the vibe. Glasses, supersmart. Wants to make a difference in the world, call out injustice or whatever."

"Thanks?" I say.

"Though I know he's no Balto." He can't even get halfway through the sentence without starting to laugh. I will forever regret telling him that the cartoon wolf was my first crush. I've lost track of how much Adam knows about me, what with the way he bombarded me with questions when we were first becoming friends. Who was my first fictional crush? Did I ever run for class office? (Hell, no.) What was my family like? (Ha.) What did I think of the news? (That it was shit.) Who was my favorite feminist icon? ("Pander much?" I had said.) It was a bit strange at first, but I discovered that I didn't mind receiving such laser-focused attention from him.

I wave my middle finger in his direction, and his laugh slows. "What?" I ask. He's looking at me strangely, sort of wistfully, eyes unblinking. That tender look.

"Nothing." He slowly shakes his head and looks down again at his finger still spinning the chair.

"Adam," I start to say, not even sure what the rest of my sentence will look like, just wanting to say his name, just wanting his gaze on me again. He does look back up, but eye contact is more than I'm capable of handling. "What about the Strand?" I ask. He blinks. "For the gift? For the girl?"

He arches an eyebrow and says, "Is this your way of trying to judge her? By her taste in books?"

"No," I say as we walk out of the store and head east on West Sixteenth, cold wind instantly seeping through my black denim jacket. We're nearly knocked over by some brunette hurrying out of a building with sex hair, in last night's makeup. "Ugh, I did it again," she's saying into the phone pressed to her ear. I continue, "They have fun little gifts even if she's not into reading. Since you're opposed to getting her something *serious*."

He cuts his eyes at me and nudges my shoulder with his as we walk in lockstep. "Why did you say it like that?"

I want to make sure I phrase this delicately. I don't want to seem like I have skin in the game. "I guess I just don't understand why you're getting her a gift at all."

"I told you, because she's getting me one," he says.

"But don't you think . . . ," I start. I can feel him refusing to finish my sentence for me as we cross Seventh Avenue. There's an uncomfortable silence.

"Don't I think what?"

"Come on."

"Just say it."

"Fine." I turn and face him as we wait for the light to change. "Don't you think if you get her a gift you're sending her a message that you like her and want to date her? Regardless of what it is? Which, if you do, then great. I just raise this because that is not the impression I've gotten from you."

"I don't know how I feel," he says.

"Okay."

"But then it's like . . . if I don't know, does that mean I really do know? Like not knowing is knowing? Like if I'm sure, I would know, and anything else is a no? You know?" he asks. Then we make eye contact and burst into laughter.

"I don't know, man," I say once we finish laughing. "That's what I'd think, but maybe it's like you said the other day. Maybe we're just sick in the head from too many rom-coms. In real life, this stuff always seems kind of complicated, right? Like, who is ever actually sure?"

Adam shakes his head. "I hear you, Fry, but I just . . . I don't know. Like, when I was a freshman in college there was this girl on my hall, and I took one look at her and was just like, no way is she as cool as she looks. Someone that good-looking must have a horrible personality. But then I got to know her, and nope, she was great. I had the biggest crush on her, and I just think about how I felt then, how sure I was I wanted to be with her." He pauses. "And that's just not how I feel now."

I gag as we sidestep a dead pigeon. "What happened with her?"

"We dated for a while, then she broke up with me for someone on the tennis team. I'm sure you can imagine my fragile, broken eighteen-year-old heart."

"Sad."

"Yeah."

"There must have been something in the water when we were eighteen. Someone was telling me just the other day about how he met someone their freshman year, and he took one look at her and fell in love."

"Who?"

"You don't know him."

"Okay, but who?"

"Just a family friend."

"What family friend?"

"Oh my God," I say. "Susan Clark's kid."

"Susan Clark? Like Thomas Clark's wife?"

I use looking both ways before jaywalking across Sixth Avenue as an excuse to pause. I feel Adam's judgment sitting on his shoulder, waiting to leap over onto mine. "Yeah," I say.

He shakes his head. "Weird."

"What's weird?" Venom and defensiveness in my voice.

Adam throws his hands up, slowing his gait after our brisk walk across the street. "I don't know, I'm just wondering why you're suddenly spending all this time with a middle-aged Republican."

"She's not a Republican," I say. Completely unfounded, as I have no idea where Susan's politics fall. She's much too proper to discuss something like that. Last year, American Network printed out these brochures for interns, and we assistants were charged with passing them out. The brochures depicted the whole C-suite and all the top execs at the networks and streamers, the higher-ups. We were all chilled by seeing that many white men with unrealistically pearly smiles grinning up at us from the glossy paper. Thomas had been on it, and with the way the production assistants were all looking up the men's political donations online when we were bored, I had kept my mouth shut about the fact that I knew him. Not that they found anything on him anyway.

"Sure she's not," Adam says, and my shoulders tense. I hate this about him, that he can be so holier-than-thou, so judgmental. I'll admit, it's a relief to hate something about him. "And now you're hanging out with her son? What is he, like, a mini Thomas?"

"No," I spit out. Though I keep the details of Clark to myself; if Adam was going to judge my hanging out with a possibly conservative mom, he might actually smite me for hanging out with a West Village frat bro. But you know what, let him. Fuck this. "We had a drink after I took him and Susan to the Cellar. I wouldn't exactly say we're 'hanging out.'"

"Whoa, whoa, whoa," Adam says, slowing to a stop, shaking his head, and turning to face me. I cross my arms and avoid eye contact but also stop walking. "Fry. This is serious." I look up now and see that he's looking at me, mischief dancing in his blue eyes. "Did you go on a date and not tell me?"

"God, no," I scoff, and instantly regret my knee-jerk honesty. Was that a hint of jealousy I heard in his voice?

Adam's eyebrows travel up his forehead. "Does Presley Fry finally have a crush?"

I smack him on the arm, which I realize only makes it look like I just might, in fact, have a crush. I recognize this is all very elementary school, but I wonder, with a twisted pleasure, how it makes him feel. The idea (however incorrect) of my wanting to be with someone. Someone who isn't him. "No," I say. "We're just family friends, is all."

"What did you guys do? Slam champagne at Trump Tower?"

"Jesus, Adam," I say, and I hate how shrill my voice sounds in my ears but don't care enough to stop. "Shut up. I barely know Clark, but I actually *like* Susan, okay? She's going through a hard time, and it's actually *nice* to hang out with someone who gets excited about things, who isn't so cynical about everything all the time the way I am and everyone I know is. Plus she's the closest thing I have—" Oh God, where is this going? My throat catches. I start again. "I don't have any other connection here to . . ." I find I am incapable of finishing the sentence.

I glance up at Adam and see that he looks chastened, eyes wide, because we're both realizing I just might do the unthinkable and cry in front of him. His phone dings with a text. He checks it, and his eyebrows shoot up his forehead. He exhales, deflating. "Ashley just texted asking when we're exchanging gifts this week," he says, not looking up at me. "I guess we're done with the hinting phase."

I blink, confused. Surely that didn't just happen? Surely he didn't just change the subject exactly when I'm on the precipice of being vulnerable with him, as he's been practically begging me to do for months now? And surely, *surely*, the subject change didn't involve the girl. This girl, whom he doesn't even fucking like. There's a part of me that can recognize the absurdity of this and is aflame with anger. There's another part of me, though, that's riddled with humiliation. The two parts, the anger and the shame, swirl together, ricocheting off each other.

Through gritted teeth I say, "Well, clearly, it's not like you can judge me for who I spend my time with. Look at what we're doing *right now*. Picking out a Christmas gift for someone you don't even seem to like."

Adam's face is fully red, and I know him well enough to know that *he* knows he's really stepped in it. This whole moment could not feel more fucking wrong.

"I didn't— Ugh." Adam takes a breath and rakes his hand through his hair. A familiar guilt sprouts through my limbs. I always *hated* when my mom was mad at me, which was unfortunate, because alcoholics are famously prone to anger and irrational behavior. Growing up, I knew better than to provoke an outburst from her, but when I hit puberty, my rage would overpower my good sense. Like the time I was trying to study for a calculus test and she was drunkenly screaming into the cordless phone at Hugh, the Winn-Dixie butcher. I snuck downstairs and unplugged the phone cradle but wasn't fast enough in my escape upstairs, and she caught me. A screaming match of epic proportions ensued, broken up by Pops begging us to "cool off." I was the one who apologized less than an hour later, because I couldn't stand to have her mad at me, even though my rage could have fueled a rocket launch.

And now, even though fury is radiating out of my fingertips, there's still something in me that refuses to accept Adam and me being at odds. I can feel an apology, or an explanation, or an excuse, rising in my throat, anything to make the tension that's simmering between us dissipate into the gray air.

Adam puts his hands on my shoulders, and a ball of tears knots together in my throat, which only heightens my fury. I refuse to look at him, focusing on a piece of alarmingly green gum stuck on the ground near his shoe. At least some karma might manifest in that I'm too choked up to warn him not to step in it.

"Fry," he says. I raise my eyebrows in acknowledgment but keep my eyes trained to the ground. "I'm sorry. I shouldn't be such a judgmental dickhead about you hanging out with Susan. Even if she is socially liberal, fiscally conservative, which we both know isn't a real thing."

I shake my shoulders roughly so that his hands fall off, but a small laugh rises and releases the tension in my throat, saving me from the humiliation of crying. We start walking. He's not even apologizing for the right thing. Somewhere in the center of my gut I know what he should say. He should say, "Tell me what you were going to say about your mom." Actually, what should have happened is that he shouldn't have interrupted my almost bringing her up with his fake Ashley problem in the first place. But that place in the center of my gut is too deep inside, and I don't have the energy to gain access to it, to pull it out and consider it. So here we are: nestled in the safety of not actually talking about my grief. And I know, with absolute certainty, that we'll act like none of this ever happened.

We've made it to the Strand. "Well," I say. "Shall we go in and pick something out for your girlfriend-not-girlfriend?"

He gives me a sad smile with just one corner of his mouth. I know we'll also pretend like I never said that he doesn't seem to like Ashley, and my shoulders drop in the warm glow of the unspoken mutual agreement. Or maybe it's relief that we're both going to keep tiptoeing around the things we aren't saying to each other, choosing cowardice over anything else.

We enter the chaotic, colorful store and he picks out a cookbook from some Food Network personality. I learn that Ashley is vegan, as if I needed another reason to resent her. We part ways by the door, him heading to Union Square to catch a train to Bushwick, me heading east. I don't even put my headphones in. There's nothing I want to listen to.

Our conversation replays in my head. How accusatory he was, how defensive I got, the underlying annoyance (pain) of even helping him shop for another girl in the first place. Like I want to pick out a gift for some *vegan* I don't know, who probably loves that their names start with the same letter. And most piercing, the hard pivot when I brought up Patty. Or almost did, I guess. My chest feels heavy, like my heart is actually a wheelbarrow full of misshapen rocks. I pull out my phone as I turn onto Second Avenue.

"Sup," Isabelle says on the second ring.

"Hey," I manage to croak out, even though that ball of whatever it is has lodged itself in my throat again.

"Oh, P, honey, are you okay?" she asks, and I hear the ambient sounds of her standing up and separating herself from whoever it is she's with. I feel pathetic for interrupting her.

"Yeah, I'm fine," I say, trying to surreptitiously clear my throat. I can't help but hear myself through Isabelle's ears, how hollow the lie is.

"Where are you?"

"Uh, about to be home. I was calling to see if you, uh, needed me to get toilet paper."

I hear her tapping on her phone, undoubtedly looking up my location.

"You're too far out from the dollar store to be picking up toilet paper. What's wrong?"

"Nothing, I—"

"You're walking home?"

"No," I lie.

"I'll see you there."

"Izzy, don't—"

But she's hung up. By the time I make it to our apartment, she's already waiting on our stoop, fresh out of an Uber, shivering a bit in the cold. Izzy's always a late adapter to the right outerwear for the colder season. She's a summer hanger-on.

She immediately envelops me in a hug, and I don't even flinch, which is how I know I must really need it. We walk up the stairs to our little home without saying anything. Inside, I sit on our small gray Facebook Marketplace couch, and she fills her Anthropologie kettle and turns on the stove.

She sits down on the couch and waits. She looks right into my face and says, "Oh, fuck the tea," switches off the stove, and starts making me an old-fashioned with the bitters she got me for my birthday this year. She hands it to me and says, "So. What happened?"

I tell her about how Adam was being something of a judgmental douche about me spending time with the Clarks, and I don't acknowledge her raised eyebrows when I get to the part about him asking if

I had been on a date with Clark. I tell her about how defensive I got, about how hanging out with Susan feels like a connection to Patty I didn't know I would appreciate but do.

She squeezes my shoulder. "And what did Adam say to that?" she asks.

I shake my head. "Not really anything. He got a text from the girl, so the subject changed."

She gives me a long look, lets out air. "Presley, that really—"

"It sucks, yeah," I say. "It sucks a lot." She continues looking at me with raised eyebrows, his dismissal (betrayal) hovering in the air between us. She opens her mouth to say something. But she closes it and thankfully doesn't press. I tell her about the vegan cookbook.

"I mean, it was just a lot." I try to wrap it up. "And he doesn't even like this girl. Like, why are we spending the day buying her a Christmas gift? I told him I thought it was fucked up, him getting her something. Would send the wrong message."

I take a sip of my drink and feel Izzy's eyes narrowing on me. "Well, for starters, I agree," she says. "And also, can you please, *please* just consider why else this is maybe frustrating? Like . . . maybe because the girl is not you?"

I swallow and sink back into the couch, noticing how the drink has relaxed my shoulders and slowed the emotional drawbridge that usually comes up at this point, the point where Izzy is trying to get me to admit that I have feelings for Adam.

Because of course I do. And after today, it feels like, finally, the pain of having to pretend I don't, of having to smile and nod and be a pal while he jabbers on about the girl he's sleeping with, has finally eclipsed my fear of admitting it. Well, to Isabelle anyway. And myself, I guess. I put my face in my hands and a groan spills out from between my palms. "Fuck."

Isabelle puts a tentative hand on my shoulder, then rubs my back in slow circles. Despite my usual allergy to touch, it feels warm and comforting, a reminder she's here. I guess that's the point of contact—to make a person remember they're not sitting alone.

"Finally." Isabelle exhales. Which makes me try to shove her shoulder, blindly and unsuccessfully, because I don't take my face out of my other hand. We both laugh a little bit.

"Yeah, I mean . . ." I take a deep breath with the sudden realization that, for whatever reason, I want to say it out loud. "I guess I'm basically in love with the motherfucker."

Isabelle gives me a slow clap. "Very good, P. Very good!" This earns her another shoulder shove, successful this time. "So now," she continues, clapping her hands together sharply, "we strategize."

"What?" I ask, then knock back the rest of my drink, shaking the ice, before unceremoniously holding the glass out to her for a refill.

She blinks, takes the glass. "It's time to figure out what you're gonna do."

"What I'm gonna do about what?"

She looks at me like I'm an idiot. "Um, what you're gonna do about the fact that you're in love with Adam."

"There's nothing to do."

Isabelle's jaw drops, but she quickly shuts it. She stands, starts silently and thoughtfully fixing me another drink. When she's done, she sits back down on the couch, recomposed. She takes a long sip of her own old-fashioned. "Presley," she says in a gentle yet condescending tone.

"No."

She holds up a hand. "Presley," she repeats. "You need to tell him."

"Oh, fuck off," I say, taking another sip of my drink, which seems stronger this time. I set it down. Whiskey isn't going to help.

"I will not. You just admitted, finally, that you love him. It seems very clear to me that he loves you, too, but also don't you want to know how he feels? Don't you want answers? I mean, babe, the alternative is to just know that you love him, and to keep doing this, to keep feeling"—she moves her hand in a circular motion around me—"like this."

"And completely ruin our friendship? Our friendship is important to me. I can deal with this. I can just bury it and move on."

Isabelle winces, closing her perfectly cat-eye-lined eyes, like a gory scene in a movie just started. "That's not how it works. And besides, it really seems like the guy has reciprocal feelings. Dude—no offense, but you're not *not* intimidating. He may have no idea you feel this way, and he's probably hinting to you on purpose that he doesn't really like this girl to see if you'll react!" I thank my lucky stars I haven't told Isabelle about the thinking-about-me-in-bed thing. "If you tell him, I bet he'll be like, 'Wow, thank God, same here,' and then you can, like, ride off into the sunset together."

"Ew," I say. I shake my head. "Besides, haven't we just agreed we're in our single-girl, fuck-everyone-else era?"

"Nah, babe," Izzy said. "I'm in that era, newly. You've been in that era for, like, twenty-five years. And maybe it's time to get out of it. For you to be with Adam."

"He's told me multiple times he wouldn't date someone he works with," I counter.

Izzy rolls her eyes. "People always say shit like that until they meet someone. The right person."

I search for the words, wanting to explain something to her that I know in my bones to be true. "I just . . . I feel like I know him, like I *really* know him, right? And I think that if he had these . . . *feelings*"—I mime gagging as I say the word—"he would have told me by now. He's shit at keeping things from me."

Isabelle shakes her head, frowning. "Disagree, babe. You won't know until you hear it straight from him. And I do not think you're going to hear what you seem to think you're going to hear."

"Izzy, I just can't," I say, and more force comes out behind the words than I intended. She puts her hands up and shrugs, then looks at me, scooches over the few inches on the couch that have separated us, and puts her arms around me. I lay my head on her shoulder, and it eases me to just let it rest there.

After a moment I pull away. "Dude," I say. "I'm so sorry you left whatever you were doing to come to my dumb ass."

"Oh, shut up," she says, gently shoving my shoulder. "I was just with Sammy, hearing about adventures with Banana Boy. No way I wasn't going to come here. I could hear it in your voice."

I nod, because even though it's outlandish, the idea that Isabelle would drop everything to come see me, even though she knew she would be seeing me later tonight, even though I hadn't explicitly said I needed her (in fact, I'm pretty sure I had said no more words than maybe "hey")—it's what we do. It's who we are to each other. It's the one thing I know for sure, and despite the maelstrom of emotions swimming around in me, I know that it's enough.

CHAPTER 18

B ack when I was a working gal in the city," Susan tells me as she leans over the Michael's menu, manicure glistening, "our boss would take us out to a fancy holiday lunch every year, and I always thought it was such a fun tradition. So I thought it would be fun to take you! Especially since you don't get a lunch break at the show." I'm impressed she's managed to say this without turning pale.

Susan has tried, multiple times, to take me to lunch during the workday, and I've had to repeatedly explain to her that we don't really take lunch at the show. It's more like a race to wolf down one of the burritos I keep stashed in the freezer or panic-fill a plate with a catered lunch between running around and getting doughnuts for the greenrooms or transcribing preinterviews or fielding calls from agents and publicists to Emma or whatever else the day calls for. When I explained this to Susan, you'd have thought I told her they beat me with a stick every day.

So here we sit, on a Saturday, at Michael's, a restaurant I'd never heard of but should have, judging from the enthusiasm with which Susan texted me the reservation. I googled it and read this fantastic oral history of the place in *The Hollywood Reporter*. The best part about the article was Lesley Stahl's lunch group, who instead of a "ladies lunch" call themselves "Smart Bitches Consuming Protein." I didn't recognize any of the other names in that group, but one of them, a literary agent called Esther Newberg, had some very memorable quotes and apparently represents Chris Rock and Steve Martin, so clearly I should have known her. Which is all to say, the article got me excited until Weinstein was quoted and I had to stop reading immediately.

Anyway, I guess this is *the* spot to lunch if you're a fancy person who works in media. Half of which is true for me. It's sweet of Susan to try to shout out my job this way, even if being in midtown on a Saturday is giving me the heebie-jeebies and this restaurant is about as stuffy as my nose in pollen season. The Cobb salad is a cool thirty-four dollars.

"When are you headed to Eulalia for Christmas?" Susan asks. "Or, I'm sorry. The holidays."

I sip my iced tea, which I ordered just because Susan did, to hide my smile at her earnest attempt to be politically correct. "I'm not, actually. My grandparents have been wanting to go on this Caribbean cruise forever, so I'm just gonna stick to the city."

Susan is aghast. "You didn't want to go with them?"

I shake my head. Much as I miss my grandparents, I can't imagine anything more depressing than being on a cruise designed specifically for retirees, crawling through the Caribbean, especially when it would have cost an arm and a leg to get there. My grandparents offered to treat me to the cruise, but flights around the holidays are unreasonably expensive even for people who make actual salaries. They also offered not to go, but I wasn't going to hear of that. They've been talking about this cruise for a decade.

And that's not even touching the Patty of it all. Last Christmas, our first without her, was not easy. Even though she would have made a show of making eggnog for everyone that only she would drink, or gotten me something pink just to piss me off, or cried about being single, it was a pretty bleak day without her. My grandmother, who rarely cries, had tears streaming steadily down her face all day, and that's not an exaggeration.

Izzy's parents invited me to spend Christmas in Maryland, and they offered to pay for my tickets and everything, which is kind but feels too much like charity for my liking. So here I am, left with the choice of being a loner in the city or a freeloading invader. Merry Christmas!

"Well," Susan says, sitting up straight, "if you'll be in the city, I am going to have to insist that you come over. Michael is coming to town, and the boys and I are keeping it low-key at the apartment. I'd love it if you spent the night, or if you just want to come over on Christmas Eve, or Christmas Day, whatever suits."

"Thanks, Susan, that's really nice," I say. "But—"

"If you're in the city, you're coming over." She pats my hand sweetly but says this with a finality that's honestly a little scary. It's clear that I don't have a choice, and the thing is, I'm not mad about it. I also have to respect Susan's method: donning her sweet southern-lady charm to forcefully get her way.

We move on to other topics, like when Michael (her son, not the owner of this restaurant) is getting into town, how hard "Lawrence" seems to have been working lately. "He and I had a drink after the Cellar," I tell her, and she smiles so brightly I'm surprised she doesn't burst into flames. I instantly regret saying it, can practically see her transforming me from "new friend" to "daughter-in-law" in her mind. I haven't even seen the guy since we had drinks after the show, though he did invite me to a birthday party on a West Village rooftop last week. I wasn't particularly into the idea of socializing with a bunch of people I don't know, especially people who probably, like, wear pearls and don't pay their own credit card bills.

"He told me about his ex-girlfriend," I say, hoping the fact that he had confided in me about this clearly indicates he isn't interested in me romantically.

Susan sighs and looks to the ceiling as though for help. "She seemed like a nice girl at first," she says, and I feel a sick spike of excitement at the possibility of hearing Susan talk shit. "But, between you and me, her being in touch with him as much as she was after she broke his heart really turned me against her."

"Makes total sense," I say. "That kind of in-between stuff . . . like, just make up your mind."

"Exactly," Susan says, nodding. Our food arrives, and when the waiter leaves, Susan goes for the kill. "I don't mean to pry, but since we're on the topic, may I ask what's going on in your love life?" I nearly drop my burger bun, which I had been spreading ketchup on. I don't want to talk to Susan about my love life, but I'm not actually sure of my own rules anymore, now that I've admitted the whole Adam dilemma to both myself and Isabelle. Susan starts shaking her head violently. "I'm sorry!" she says. "I didn't mean to make you uncomfortable."

Instant guilt. We're supposed to be friends, right? "No, it's cool," I say. "I'm sort of . . . the truth is, I . . . uh, I'm pretty into this guy, Adam, but it's complicated."

"Why?" she asks, leaning forward, like I'm the most interesting person in the world.

"We're just really good friends, and I wouldn't want to mess that up. But I also can't tell how he feels. Sometimes . . ." I pause and think about his phone calls, how he called me "beautiful" in the kitchen. "Sometimes, it feels like he likes me as more than a friend, too, but sometimes not."

Susan cocks her head to the side. "Hm," she says, and she directs her attention to the pieces of lettuce she's pushing around on her plate.

"What?" I ask, surprised at my desire (need, actually) to know what she's thinking.

"Well . . ." She rests her fork on the side of her plate and looks at me. "Of course, I don't know everything about the situation, but I'm struck by what you just said, about how in-between situations are always unfair to someone."

"It's complicated," I say again quietly, feeling myself shrink.

"I'm sure it is," she says. Then she sighs. "I know I'm just some old lady with outdated opinions, but I would just like to stress to you that you are the kind of girl who should be swept off her feet immediately by the man you're interested in. Not left to wonder where you stand."

I blink. Something in what she said strikes me at my center, and I'm instantly uncomfortable. I think about last night, when Izzy and I were watching *Die Hard* and I texted Adam a photo of our TV, strung in Christmas lights, the title page on the screen. He instantly "liked" the message but sent no other reply. Adam loves that movie, but apparently, he didn't love that I was watching it enough to send an actual response. Apparently, he doesn't love it at all. He "likes" it. I quarantined my phone in my bedroom for the rest of the night, too embarrassed to even look at it.

I open my mouth to explain that we got to know each other through work, and it isn't really my style to play into the traditional gender roles of male as pursuer, when a balding, sweaty man in a suit (friendly reminder that it's Saturday) approaches the table. I recognize him from the upper-level brochure we give the interns each semester. He smiles and touches Susan on the shoulder, and she looks up at him. I'm fully staring at her, so I'm able to catch her lightning-quick succession of expressions: surprise, wide-eyed panic, something like indignance with a pursing of the lips and a swallow, before settling into her forced smile. "Chris, hi," she says, standing up quickly and air-kissing in the vicinity of his cheek before sitting back down.

"Hi, Susan," he says. "I thought it was you from across the restaurant, and I had to come say hello before I left. How are you holding up?"

"I'm fine, thanks. Enjoying a nice holiday lunch with my friend Presley Fry." She nods toward me. I try to smile at the man, but it probably looks like a grimace. I'm not good at pretending like I don't hate someone's vibe. "And how are you? How's Viv?"

"Good, all good," he says.

There's an uncomfortable moment of silence, which Susan breaks with "Don't tell me you're working on a Saturday," pinching his sleeve, indicating his outfit.

He rolls his eyes exaggeratedly and smiles. "Always a rush to wrap everything up before the end of the year. You know. Or remember. Or . . . know." He gesticulates with his hands like he's trying to explain something complex. Good God, this is a nightmare, but Susan keeps her composure.

"Of course," she says with a smile. "Well, don't let 'em work you too hard." Such a smooth dismissal.

"Great to see you," he says, that hand on her shoulder again, and I see him give her a little squeeze. Maybe he meant it to be comforting or something, but I find it strange. As if squeezing her shoulder is going to undo how awkward this was. "And meet you," he says, tipping his head toward me. I try to move the corners of my mouth up, but I can feel how dead my eyes are.

He walks away and Susan takes the napkin that had been resting in her lap, brings it up, and presses the corners of her mouth primly, even though she hasn't taken a bite in ages. I'm not sure what to say.

"That's Chris Lemming," she says.

I nod. "Yeah, I know." I'm not sure if it would be interesting or helpful to mention that I have the higher-ups of American Network memorized. In all our hangs, Susan and I have mostly managed to avoid talk of Thomas. If his name casually comes up in an anecdote, Susan skates right over it. Other than that one time she mentioned he was "out east," which Isabelle informed me is rich-people code for the Hamptons. I literally thought she had meant, like, China or something.

"I'm afraid I don't quite know what to say or how to act around Thomas's colleagues since October," she says. Ah, so that's what we're calling it. October. "There's a woman Thomas hired, who specializes in helping with this sort of thing when it's . . . public. But I didn't have any interest in media training."

"Ah, so she's like Olivia Pope," I say, nodding.

"Who?"

"Never mind," I say. I suppose network dramas like *Scandal* aren't exactly Susan's taste. "Well, for what it's worth, you handled that like a champ. Totally unruffled."

She exhales a short little syllable of a laugh. "There's just, there's not really anything to say. At least if we were getting a divorce, I would have something definitive to tell people. But I don't think there is a polite, casual version of 'Yes, hi, hello, my husband is in the Hamptons for now, while I try to figure out if I want to stay married to him after he humiliated my family. And me. Not to mention the other women he humiliated, and not to mention the woman he had an affair with. I hope business is well.'"

Color rises in her cheeks, and her eyes look a little wild. I've never seen her anything other than perfectly composed. It's like seeing your teacher in the grocery store—inexplicably jarring. "Can't you just say you're separated?" I ask dumbly, out of my depth.

She shakes her head. "While that is factually accurate, I hate the sound of it. 'Separated' is just a pit stop on the way to divorce. And I don't know if that's what will be happening."

I nod, though I have no idea what to think. From where I'm standing, her husband was inappropriately flirty with women at work. He cheated. Probably more than once. His name, her family's name, has been stomped on, degraded, pissed all over on national television and across the internet. Also: he is her husband of however many years, the father of her kids. I'm twenty-five years old. I have no idea how any of this stuff works.

"Oh, Presley, I'm sorry," she says. "I don't mean to put this on you."

I shrug. "We're friends, right? Friends talk about these things. I'm just sorry I don't have advice. My husband is yet to have his first scandal. Or exist."

She laughs at this, which makes me relax a bit in my seat. I didn't realize how tense I had been. I hope she doesn't take my comment as a chance to turn the conversation back to Adam. But she just shakes her head, says, "I do wish I could get Patty's take."

"Oh, that I can give you," I say. "She'd tell you to leave him." Susan nods, and she looks so upset that I momentarily wish I could unsay it. It's the truth, though. When I was seven, I had a crush on my best friend, Herbert. It went unrequited; neither of us realized at the time that he was as gay as the day is long. I tried to hold hands with him after a neighborhood game of tag, and he sprinted away like I had electrocuted him. I still remember the slippery feel of his sweaty palm sliding against mine. When I walked through the front door in tears, Patty asked what happened. I told her, and she got down on eye level with me and said, "That's bullshit. But you may as well learn now, men are going to give you bullshit all your life. But girls like you and me? We don't settle for that." I swallow, the memory punctuated with other memories of Hugh the Winn-Dixie butcher honking his horn in my grandparents' driveway, too chickenshit to pick her up at the door. Reaching for levity, I say to Susan, "Then again, I only ever took Patty's advice as instructions for exactly what *not* to do, so who knows."

She takes a breath and says, "I know your mother wasn't always the . . . easiest. But I hope you know that I really loved her. Owe her everything, in fact."

This thing again. It's crossed my mind a few times since that first night I had drinks at Susan's: this supposed incident in which Patty saved Susan's life. I don't really see how that's possible, and I'm not sure that I want the details. "Well," I say, over talking about my trauma and ready to return to Susan's, "I know you'll do the right thing."

We finish our meals quietly for a few minutes (I disappear my burger, while Susan pushes her food around and nibbles at some leaves), then she asks me about work, and then we get to talking about the new Guillermo del Toro movie, which, surprisingly, she wants to see. Her ability to steer a conversation is masterful, but I still feel it wedged between us: my inability to give her good advice, her inability to get through to me on the Patty front. The chasm of our generational difference.

CHAPTER 19

New York City gets the best and worst of me every day. It gets every last dollar I make, it gets my MTA-provoked middle finger when the subway doors close in my face, it gets my stupid little shimmy when I'm leaving work and Gary's jazzy walkout song is stuck in my head. The embarrassing smile I can't help but crack when I walk around in the fall and listen to the Cranberries' "Dreams," the time I stomped on a man's foot on the subway because I found his manspreading so appalling.

But tonight, walking around on Christmas Eve, its emptiness is making me feel like, for just this one tiny moment, it's *mine*, instead of me being its. There's even a light fall of snow, though it's not sticking and just makes the pavement and the trash wet, but I allow myself to think there's still something magical about it. Until a rat the size of a pit bull sprints in front of me and the spell instantly breaks.

Maybe if I had stayed with Susan tonight, and was walking around on the Upper East Side, I'd be able to peer into brownstone windows and see families huddled around trees, lighting the menorah, sitting down to a meal, dancing around in footie pajamas. But downtown, which I'm told by every city person over the age of fifty was *so different* twenty, thirty years ago, is deserted. Maybe back then all the artists everyone talks about would be milling around, too broke and inspired and out of touch with their immediate blood families to go home. Maybe there would be parties, drugs; maybe it would feel like any other night.

But here, now, all the yuppies are home with their families, wherever they're from. Taking a sip of the hot toddy I'm clutching because, hey, it's Christmas Eve (and cold), I realize I don't really know what my home is anymore. I know what it *was*: my grandparents' place in Eulalia. Even before Patty and I officially lived there, before the rent on our tiny two-bedroom apartment became too much responsibility, it was the yellow house, the needlepoint pillow with John 3:16 on it, the worn, pilling leather on Pops's La-Z-Boy. The lumpy mattress that had been my uncle's, the deafening roar of the cicadas in the summer. The smell of toast that Patty would nibble on, hungover. Patty singing Céline Dion in the living room, sloshing Burnett's onto the shag carpet as she spun in circles, tilting her head back: "And that's the way it is . . ." Patty, Patty, Patty.

But New York is home now, too. Mine and Isabelle's socks on our hissing radiator that takes up half the wall in our living room. Drunk girls' giggles floating up into our apartment. Feeling like a guppy in a sea of people surging upward out of the subway and spilling onto the streets, where interns rush into skyscrapers, adjusting ill-fitting pencil skirts and blazers. The way everyone rips their clothes off and lies spread-eagle on the grass along the West Side Highway, in Central Park, anywhere, really, on that first day of spring when the city is soaked in sunshine. The shouting, the screech of the subway brakes, the calls of "Chanel, Chanel" from the women in Chinatown, the occasional cry of a seagull that makes you remember you're on an island. All that noise.

It's quiet now, and other than a distant ambulance, it's peaceful. I wish I could call my mom, even though I know it likely wouldn't end well, were calling a real possibility. There's something gentle and warm about this longing to talk to her. Nestled in the safety of wishing for her, without the possibility of it coming true.

....

I should have known I wouldn't be able to get away with a low-key Christmas brunch at Susan's, even though that's exactly what I was promised. The tree is massive, Christmas music jangles out from the surround sound speakers, and there are nibbles everywhere, like this is a cocktail party and not a Christmas morning for four (one of whom is an outsider). Not to mention enough presents that the word "capitalism" blares in my mind like a siren.

It's not like I showed up empty-handed. I baked a cinnamon monkey bread that may be straight from the Trader Joe's box but is pretty damn good. "Smells delicious," Susan's doorman, Roger, had said as we made our way to Susan's floor. "By the way, I think I realized it's Jennifer Lawrence you look like." It was a ridiculous thing for him to say, but it's Christmas, so I let it slide. Anyway, I scraped together little gifts for all three of the Clarks, even though I'm just shooting in the dark for Michael, whom I haven't seen in probably ten years: mugs that have the Clarks shoe logo on them, with little make-your-own-cosmo kits Isabelle pointed out to me in our local liquor store. I don't know who will be more excited about that one, Clark or Susan.

I knew it wasn't much, but when I see the monstrosity that is the pile of gifts Susan's gotten me, I'm straight-up humiliated. My embarrassment isn't eased by the fact that Susan is wearing a Mrs. Claus costume pajama set thing. Michael, who warmly hugged me upon my arrival and immediately offered me a Bloody Mary, is wearing silk pajamas; the pale blue of them goes well with that trademark Clark chestnut hair. Clark himself is in plaid flannel pants and a UVA T-shirt. I feel like an idiot in the tights and ill-fitting black sweater dress I've had since 2012, but how was I supposed to know this was a goddamn pajama party?

"Okay, Presley!" Susan says, clapping her hands together like a cruise director. "We are *so* glad you could join us. We waited for you to open gifts, and I know the boys are just chomping at the bit to open theirs." She smiles big but also rolls her eyes a little, as if the boys need to calm down.

Clark, not unkindly, smirks behind her, and Michael gives his mother side-eye. He leans close to my ear and performatively whispers, "She thinks we're still five and nine years old."

We all sit down in the living room, and I'm back on that old-and-new-looking couch I first sat on when Susan and I had drinks here in October. I jump a little when Susan practically shoves a gift down my throat. "Start with this one, Presley! It's just a little gag gift."

It's certainly not wrapped like a gag gift—it looks professionally done. I want to be the first person to open a gift about as much as I want to stick needles in my eyes, but Susan's just not a woman you say no to. I start, carefully as I can, unwrapping the gift. A Bloomingdale's box, which contains fuzzy pajama pants with little moons on them and a matching long-sleeved light blue shirt that says "If he loves me, he'll let me sleep."

I must look about as baffled as I feel, because Susan explains, "You know, like Snow White? Or Sleeping Beauty? The prince kisses her to wake her up? I know how much you hate girlie kind of princess stuff, so I thought this was just cute. You know, let me sleep and all." My face softens as she explains. If she were anyone else, I would probably make a snarky comment about how fucked up it is that Prince Whoever the Hell would kiss anyone who was asleep, essentially normalizing and commercializing sexual assault—for *children* to watch. But now doesn't feel like a good time for a lively conversation about consent in the media. "It's just meant to be silly," Susan says, "but I thought you could change into them, so that you can be comfy like us!"

Michael takes a long sip of his Bloody Mary, and Clark and I make eye contact. I can see him trying not to laugh, before his eyes flick over to his mother, whom he looks at with a kind of sympathy. It's nice, having this little inside joke moment without there being any real malicious intent behind it. "Thanks, Susan," I say. "They're great."

An hour later, odd family that we are in our mismatched pajamas, we've finally gotten through all the gifts. The boys mostly got clothes, though they were very different in style. Michael is all jazzed about some fancy running watch and is sitting in the kitchen on his laptop, programming it. Susan squeals and Clark lets out a big guffaw when they open their cosmo kits, and Susan immediately goes to the kitchen, cleans her new Clarks mug, and pours her remaining coffee into it.

"Nice work," Clark says, holding up his mug overflowing with the mini triple sec and vodka bottles and grinning big at me. The resemblance to a golden retriever really is astounding—I want to pat his head and toss a ball for him.

"Thanks," I say. "It was this or Rolexes."

"Sure. I mean, with our assistant salaries? Endless options," he says. He leans forward. "Mike sponsored most of our parental gifts, thankfully." I wonder if they got gifts for their dad, if they've spoken with him today or are planning on it. My Patty phantom limb is aching, and I wonder how strange it must feel, to technically be able to speak to your parent on Christmas and actively choose not to. But I don't even know if that's the case.

There's a big catered brunch: buttery croissants, a quiche so light it could float, fatty bacon. I'm starting to realize Susan doesn't cook, which is surprising given her whole housewife vibe. But I suppose that's not so weird in New York. I sit next to Michael, and we quickly figure out we have a very similar podcast diet; *Las Culturistas* is our favorite. He watches *Saturday Night Live* every week, as do I, and we geek out over our favorite writers and sketches, how we hope Kenan never leaves. We acknowledge how unfortunate it is that times like these, when the country feels like a dumpster fire, are when the show seems to be at its best.

"Although, with everything with Al Franken, it seems like maybe some of those guys should stick to making fun of the politicians, instead of becoming them," Clark says.

"Why, so he could only have harassed women who work in comedy? Do they deserve it more than women who work in politics?" It launches out of my mouth like a rocket. Susan's grip on her fork tightens, and a tense silence permeates the room like a fog. It doesn't last long.

"That's not what I meant at all," Clark says, his face red with embarrassment. "I just—no, yeah, I just wasn't thinking. Obviously it isn't . . . I'm sorry, yeah, dumb comment from me, surprise, surprise. . . ." He forces out ripples of laughter.

A corresponding apology rises in my throat but gets stuck. I didn't mean to ruin the jolly vibe, especially when I'm the outsider being included here. And I don't believe that Clark meant to say that pretending to grope someone, or actually groping them, is ever okay in any workplace. And I get it: the discrepancy in behavior between what's acceptable at a comedy show and what's acceptable in the Senate. But it's also not like I'm going to apologize for pointing out that women's bodies aren't just low-hanging fruit for the humor of their male counterparts, regardless of where they are. "All good," I say. "Anyway, I really wish I could *go* to *SNL* one of these days."

"Same," Michael says. "Though the odds decrease significantly when you live in LA. American Network tried to do a late night sketch show out there for a while, actually."

"*America's Sketch Show*!" I say, laughing. "I remember."

"God, that show was a disaster," Michael says. "We got to go, because of Dad."

Susan drops her fork, and it clatters loudly. She stretches her fingers over her plate and holds them steady, like she's willing the china to calm down, like that's what caused this mess—not the discussion of bad media men and the mention of her conspiuously absent sort-of-husband-sort-of-ex-husband.

"Whoa, whoa," Clark says.

"Sorry," Susan says, looking up at all of us and blushing a little, plastering that semi-terrifying smile on her face. "Clumsy me. . . ."

"You okay, Mom?" Michael asks, reaching over and placing a hand on Susan's pencil-sized forearm.

"Yes," she says, nodding. "Yep! Just gonna head to the restroom." She gets up and marches off to somewhere in the back of the apartment.

"Woof," Clark says under his breath as soon as she's out of earshot, looking at his brother with wide eyes.

Michael shakes his head. "Not great."

"Sorry, Presley," Clark says.

"Oh, no," I say. "*I'm* sorry. Should I go?"

"No," Michael says. "I think it really helps that you're here. It feels more like a fun new occasion and less like . . . an old one with someone missing."

Clark nods in my direction. "You're good. Plus, guaranteed, she comes back smiley. She just needed a sec." Sure enough, Susan swirls back into the room, just as smiley as Clark predicted.

"What did I miss?" she asks, sitting.

An hour later, after Clark and Michael do the dishes, which they will not let me or Susan help with, which I (somewhat frustratingly) find charming, Susan is insisting I try on the pile of mercifully neutral-colored, expensive-feeling clothes she absolutely did not need to buy me but absolutely did. "I want to know if I can make any returns for you!" she insists. "Use my room. First door on the left." I can't overstate how much I do not want to have a fashion show with the Clark family, but I'm also not sure how I can say no.

Her bedroom is clean, and not as grand as I expected. I guess New York is too small for everyone. I slip into a black shift dress that is thank-fully frill-and-ruffle-free. The brand name is just a common-sounding man's first name, and the fabric feels like butter. When I walk back into the living room, they're all sprawled out on the furniture, Michael and Clark looking at their phones, Susan's eyes locked on the TV as *It's a Wonderful Life* plays. When she turns to look at me, I see that her eyes are filled with tears, and I get a bizarre urge to reach out and pull her into one of her own signature bone-crushing hugs. Except she's so small I worry she may actually break.

She swallows and claps her hands together, startling the boys into looking up at me. This is horrifying. I feel my face grimace but try to stop it, and I can only imagine how the expression looks. "Well, I don't know about you, but I think that fits wonderfully. It's perfect on you!" Susan says.

The truth is, I am in need of a not-shitty dress like this for days when

I take on more of Emma's responsibilities of actually dealing with the guests. Dressing for the job I want, as Susan pointed out to me in Bergdorf's. And I do like this dress: it's plain enough that it won't get in my way or, worse, attract unwanted attention, but I also know it doesn't look cheap.

Clark lets out a whistle, which according to the feeling in my cheeks makes me blush but also makes me want to slap him. I narrow my eyes. "Shut up," I say before I can stop myself. He throws his head back and laughs, that laugh that comes from his gut, hearty and genuine.

Michael looks up from his phone for just the amount of time it takes him to scan me from top to bottom, back to the top again. He nods curtly. "Keep," he says, returning quickly to scrolling. His approval, as a handsome gay man, does happen to be the only one I care about in this scenario.

"Thanks, Susan," I say.

"Of course," she says back. We smile at each other, and maybe it's nice to feel this way. To have been given a nice gift, and to feel gratitude for it, while also knowing buying it didn't put Susan out in any way. Like maybe I did Susan a solid by allowing her to spoil me. And for a second, I'm not thinking about my dead mom and it doesn't seem like she's thinking about her deadbeat husband. For a second, it's just Christmas.

When all the wrapping paper has been stuffed in the recycling bin and all my new threads have been folded into reusable Zabar's tote bags, I say my goodbyes. "Lawrence will walk you to the subway," Susan says as she hugs me, stifling my ability to insist this won't be necessary with the way she's restricting my access to air. By the time I regain it and open my mouth, she cuts me off. "It's dark out."

It's also five p.m. "He really doesn't need to do that," I tell her. "You really don't need to do that," I repeat to Clark, who's already shrugging on his puffy coat.

"Air will be good," he says, zipping up, and next thing I know, I'm standing in the elevator as he and Roger discuss college basketball. "Maybe a young Greta Garbo?" Roger calls after me as the doors close. I shake my head, and thankfully, Clark doesn't ask.

"Thanks for coming over today," he says as we hunch our shoulders against the freezing December air. "I think it helped her, for real."

"No, thanks for letting me crash," I say. The truth is that this Christmas Day, awkward avoidance of Thomas and feelings of intrusion included, was preferable to the gaping and screaming absence of Patty back in Eulalia and likely preferable to a seniors' cruise as well.

"It was weird without him," Clark says. I'm glad we're both facing forward, that if the panic of not knowing how to respond to that is written all over my face, he won't see it. I rifle through my mind's file cabinets, searching for the right thing to say, then remember my whole ethos around talking about Patty: there is no right thing for me to say.

"I know," I say, because I do, of course, know what it's like when a parent is supposed to be there and isn't.

"Yeah, I guess you do," he says, and I like that there's no sense of grief Olympics here, just a shared ache.

"Are you talking to him?" I ask as we turn to walk south on Lexington. The question is a bit invasive for my taste, but I want to know, and for whatever reason, I don't find myself walking into any proverbial closed doors when I'm talking with Clark. He just seems so open.

"Yeah," Clark says. "Michael and I are going to FaceTime him tonight. I'm obviously, like, mad at him. But totally cutting him out right now just doesn't seem . . . I don't know, it's just not what I'm going to do. Especially when Mom won't talk to him at all." I nod. I figured Susan had iced him out, what with him being away still, and especially on Christmas. "Anyway, Christmas, families, man."

"Christmas, families, man," I repeat as we approach the Seventy-Seventh Street stop. He turns to me, takes me by the shoulders, and pulls me in for a hug, our coats pressing into each other. This family and hugging. My hands remain in my pockets, and it's pleasantly warm.

"Merry Christmas, Presley," he says as he pulls away.

"Merry Christmas," I say back quickly, before descending underground. I've barely checked my phone all day, and once I sit down in a mostly empty car, I pull it out of my pocket, a slight boil rising in the simmer of constant hope that I'll have a text or a missed call from Adam. A missed FaceTime from Izzy, nothing from him. The disappointment squeezes in my chest like a fist. I toss my phone in one of the Zabar's bags, shaking along with the train as it takes me home.

CHAPTER 20

It is a truth universally acknowledged that New Year's Eve fucking sucks. Especially in the city: the trains barely run, cabs are next to impossible to get (not that I can afford one anyway), it's cold and usually wet. And that's just the evening itself: I haven't even touched New Year's resolutions. I will be partaking in no dry January, will maintain my fairly bad eating habits, will continue working out only when forced by Izzy, and will be nicer to exactly no one. I will neither journal nor cleanse. I will just continue trying to get by.

Speaking of Isabelle: she's about the only person who can make New Year's fun. Last year, we rang in 2017 at this bar near our apartment called Whiskey Town, which features a photo booth and music from our teen years. It was fifty bucks to get in that night, but the tickets made it less crowded than usual and there was a champagne toast. Worth it. We danced, we drank, we screamed "Mr. Brightside." And then we rang in another year, hoping it would be slightly less shitty than the one before it. Possible only because 2016 had been such an unparalleled parade of insults.

This year, Izzy stayed in Maryland. Her high school friends, a group with whom she's remained close (a key difference between me and her), are all going to someone's lake house or something. She sent me a selfie from a boat earlier, wrapped in approximately one million blankets, even around her head, shades on.

I will spend my last evening of 2017 in Bushwick, a Brooklyn neighborhood I pretend to like because a bunch of my friends from work live there. Peanut is having a party. He lives in an actual town house with, like, seven other people or something, and tonight they're opening their doors to anyone they know or kind of know who's "down to rage." Adam's going, so at least I won't be flying solo. As I put mascara on—it's a holiday, after all—my heart freezes in my chest. It hadn't occurred to me until now that Adam's girlfriend-not-girlfriend might be making an appearance at this thing.

Before she went home for the holidays, Isabelle tracked *Ashley* down on social media, but I refused to look. I don't see how it would be helpful in any way to know what she looks like, what kinds of captions she writes. To know what I'm up against, I guess, though that makes it sound like I haven't already waved my white flag in surrender. Which I have.

I get off the M train at Wyckoff and walk through the charmless streets of Bushwick, huddled against the cold. I'm wearing tights, which aren't exactly doing the trick, and one of the short black dresses Susan got me for Christmas, but this one's vaguely shimmery. Susan's eyes lit up like her own Christmas tree when I tried it on for her, and she cooed over me like I was a pageant queen. That woman really should have had a daughter.

Adam texted me that he is inside, in the kitchen, apparently. I pull my coat sleeve over my hand that's clutching the six-pack of beer I brought, more for appearances than anything else. In my coat pocket, I have a water bottle filled with the Maker's Izzy got me for my last birthday.

There's no need for me to pull up my phone to double-check the address: I can hear the party raging inside the house as soon as I turn onto the block. I walk in, and the temperature immediately rises by one thousand degrees. I look around for someone I know but am unperturbed when that doesn't happen. It's not like anyone is looking at me.

If you were to make one collective hole the size of every piercing in this party combined, it would swallow the Earth. Hardly anyone's gender is clear, and I'm guessing there's not a single underwire bra in this whole house. There's more tattooed skin than not. I am not cool enough to be here. Inexplicably, I picture Susan here, and the thought makes me laugh. She would be so out of place, but the thing I dig about Susan is that I don't think she would judge. I think she would be fascinated, peppering me with questions.

I weave my way to what I'm hoping is the kitchen, through people holding cups and smoking joints and someone snorting a key bump the size of an anthill. Sure enough, Adam is leaning against the counter, talking to Peanut and a girl I don't recognize.

The girl is gorgeous. Her pale skin looks like it could have been grafted off a newborn baby, and she's got these full, rosy cheeks, too. Her hair (featuring badly-on-purpose-cut bangs, of course) is pulled up in this messy bun, but it does nothing to disguise the fact that she probably couldn't go to the mall as a child without getting scouted. Her nipples poke through a nearly sheer, body-hugging turtleneck, and she touches Adam's arm and laughs as he finishes saying something.

It feels like I just got punched straight in the chest by someone who knows what they're doing. I can't feel my fingers, weirdly. Embarrassment washes over me suddenly—why am I wearing an almost sparkly dress? What do I think I am, starring in a sitcom about being a twentysomething in New York? A sour swell of anger also roils in my stomach. Who does this girl think *she* is? I fear I might cry.

In short, I want to die. I need to go to the bathroom immediately to collect myself. Maybe I can leave and act like I was never here. I hadn't asked Adam if he was bringing Ashley or not, because I didn't want to seem like I cared. I know I do care, but this level of hurt is still shocking. It feels like betrayal, and it's staggering, utterly dehydrating. I'm ninety degrees into my turnaround when Peanut spots me. The friendly bastard.

"Presley Fry!" he says, beckoning me over and leaning in for a hug, somehow smelling like peppermint. He looks at me with his bright green eyes, his freckles seeming to glow.

"Hey," I say, swallowing and forcing my soul to return to my body, my heart rate to slow, my lungs to take in and expel air. "Great house."

"Thanks!" He tips his head in the direction of the hot girl. "This is my cousin Jessica. Jessica, this is Presley, she's an assistant at the show, too."

It's like I've been dipped in spa water. Cousin. The girl is Peanut's cousin. *Jessica.* I suddenly appreciate her beauty without an ounce of jealousy, admire her gumption for wearing such a revealing shirt. I smile, and I can feel how big it is on my face. This girl is going to think I'm *very* friendly.

"Hey, good to meet you!" I say.

"Yeah, likewise," she says, her voice raspy. "I always meet such great people at Brian's parties." Her eyes slide over to Adam a bit flirtatiously, in my opinion, as she says this. But I'm thankfully momentarily distracted by the reminder that Peanut's real name is Brian.

"Hey, Fry," Adam says, tipping his head in my direction and not hugging me. He thinks I hate hugs, which I largely do. Though I do feel like hugging him for coming to this party alone. I also just feel like hugging him most of the time.

"Hey," I say.

"Jessica, is Naima coming?" Peanut asks. Before she can answer, he turns to me. "Naima is a stand-up, you should check her out, Presley. She played Union Hall last week."

I turn to Jessica. "You know Naima Ross? She's great," I tell her.

Jessica nods. "Yeah, we went to college together. She's killing it, I'm so happy for her."

"Fry is basically our comedy scout," Adam tells Jessica. I hate the way he tilts his head toward her as he speaks to her, being outside the force of his magnetic field. She's shorter than me, which is allegedly supposed to give me some advantage, but the truth is guys love short girls. I'm sorry to make sweeping generalizations (not really), but the patriarchy has infected people's minds, and the truth is straight guys like to be bigger, with as much of a gap as possible, than the girls they want to flirt with, date, fuck, etc. So, much as I hate myself for looking at the situation this way, Nipple Jessica's tininess is another strike against her in my eyes.

"That's sick," she says to me with the enthusiasm of someone who absolutely does not think it's sick. "You should totally have her on."

"I'd love to pitch her, at some point. She's one I've been watching. Could be good to give her some time to really perfect a tight five, but yeah."

Jessica rolls her eyes and smiles and looks at Adam like he's the person she should respond to instead of me, the person who just spoke. "Tight five. You industry people."

I feel color rising in my cheeks. She said it lightly, but I don't know her well enough for her to be making fun of me. I don't know her at all. "We're insufferable," Adam says. "Fry, let's get you a drink. Good to meet you, Jessica." He taps my shoulder and we turn away as I give a small nod goodbye.

We move through the crowd to the other end of the packed kitchen (this place really is huge), where the sink is filled with ice and the floor is littered with overflowing coolers. "What'll it be, Fry?" Adam asks.

"Officially, this," I say, holding up the Bud Light six-pack. I start placing the bottles into the nearest Styrofoam cooler, shoving them down into the packed ice. "Unofficially?" I pull out my crinkled plastic bottle, shake the amber liquid within it, and Adam smiles, wiggling his eyebrows.

"Maker's?"

"Maker's."

He finds two Solo cups, which makes me feel like we're in college, which I honestly don't hate. Given that it's New Year's, given the emotional roller coaster that I just went on thinking Nipples was Adam's girl, given the proximity of Adam right now, getting college-level drunk just may be in the cards for me tonight. An image of Patty, chin on her chest, snoring loudly in her chair, flickers in my mind, but I quickly shove it away. Adam pulls chunks of ice out of the coolers, plops them in our cups, and I do the honors of tipping my Poland-Spring-that's-not-Poland-Spring contents into them.

He raises his cup. "To 2018," he says. I touch my cup to his, and we keep eye contact, and I forget to breathe. We sip, and the essence of the liquor fills my mouth and bites my throat, and I'm calm again. I nearly do a spit take, though, when I look across the room and see Justin, just as he's saying to some bored-looking girl, "Well, at Harvard, where I went to school . . ." I whack Adam on the shoulder and nod in his direction. Adam turns around, then whips his head toward me again, bending over and filling his cup with his laughter.

And it's this: it's us trying and failing to cover the fact that we're cracking up, sharing this joke, that laugh that I know so well at this point, even though this time last year I hadn't even met him. It's the way the skin around his eyes crinkles, the way he covers the lower half of his face with one hand when he's laughing this hard at something we're in on together, which no one understands but us.

We mingle. We meet some new people, successfully avoid Justin, mostly talk to each other about our winter breaks. After I've drained half of my cup, I hear myself ask, "Didn't bring the girl?"

He shakes his head. "She's still back home in California."

"Sounds sunny," I say, and we both giggle a little. We're drunk. "Did she like her cookbook?" I ask, like a friend would. Like I care.

"She did, she did," he says, nodding. "Thanks again for helping me sort that out."

"No problem." I take a big sip of my whiskey.

"We actually, um, are, like, you know," he says, rhythmically tapping his cup with his hand.

"Is that supposed to mean a sex thing? I don't want to know," I say.

He tips his head back and laughs. "No, no," he says. Then he looks at me again, and he hesitates. Like he's embarrassed. "We were FaceTiming on Christmas and we decided to give the whole thing a try. Like the real thing. Like a relationship. Like . . . she's my girlfriend."

My body goes numb. Something inside me—my soul, I guess—

exits. I feel it pass through my skin, and suddenly I'm nothing but air, a cloud hovering above this conversation, threatening rain.

I take a large gulp of my whiskey, and I'm back. I busy myself with strategizing how I can look the most normal. Am I leaning too much on one hip? Holding my cup at a weird height? Another sip. I realize I'm supposed to say words. "Wow" is the one I choose.

He nods slowly and purses his lips, and I know he's bracing himself for whatever I'm going to say. Because we both know the things he's said about her, we both know how unsure he was.

"And I feel really good about it," he says thinly, taking a noticeably big gulp out of his Solo cup. He starts nodding to himself, again and again, like a dashboard bobblehead. "It's the right thing. I know I had talked to you about not knowing exactly how I felt, and I realized that trying is probably the only way to find out. You know me, I can obsess over something forever. Better to just . . ." He does a low-level fist bump to no one, like he's telling someone he's A-OK. "Go for it. You know?"

Adam has a girlfriend.

"Adam has a girlfriend," I say out loud. It comes out heavy. I try again: "Adam has a giiiirlfriend." I pinch his shoulder and will the corners of my mouth to move up, for my eyebrows to raise. Like I'm teasing him, like this is just another one of our shared jokes.

"Off the market, as they say," he says. "Devastating for women everywhere." I roll my eyes but feel my features settle back into something probably downcast. He pokes my forehead with his pointer finger. "What's happening in there?" he asks.

I look up at him and try to lift my features into something resembling the happiness you're supposed to feel for your friend when they tell you they've started a relationship. "I just hope she isn't, like, the jealous type. I don't want for anything . . . I just hope she won't be weird about us hanging out. And I hope that you'll, you know"—I take another sip of my drink, willing the burning in my throat to come from whiskey, not tears—"still have time to hang out."

Though I am sharing only a small portion of my actual feelings on this matter, what I'm saying is still true. Even though I don't necessarily know firsthand, considering Isabelle's perpetual singledom, it's common knowledge that when your close friend starts dating someone, things change: they have less time for you, may not be able to relate as well on single-person shit, you're not their first call anymore, etc.

I've loved being Adam's first call.

And even though we're hopefully moving into a post-men-this-women-that world, I know that enough people worship at the altar of *When Harry Met Sally* to know that most people don't believe men and women can be friends. I hope Adam's girlfriend isn't one of those people, that she won't make Adam feel weird about hanging out with me. I hope she isn't suspicious.

Though, of course, she would be right to be. But only of me, not us. Adam's made his choice. Not that I think I was ever even considered, which is both better and worse.

His face has softened, and his eyes are all wide, like I caught him looking at me in the junk antiques shop, like I catch him looking at me sometimes at work. Like I'm filling up his vision, like I'm all he can see. "Fry, come on, never," he says.

I cast my eyes down to my Solo cup, which is dangerously close to empty. I have consumed a lot of whiskey. More would be good, though. Not looking at him, I press my cup into his, and he returns the pressure. "Well, cheers to your new relationship," I say, trying to make my voice sound light and airy and rainbow filled. We both tip our drinks into our mouths and I shake my head a little, willing all these feelings to loosen and fall out.

"You know, it's funny," he says. He's actually blushing and looking a bit bashful, and I'm unfortunately reminded of what he told me in Ray's, about thinking of me when he was with her. He shakes his head, stumbles a bit. "Never mind."

"You're obviously going to tell me. As we've leeearned." We both laugh, and as only a good joke can (not that me elongating the word "learned" is a good joke), it breaks some of the tension. Still, despite my tipsiness (drunkenness), I feel my nerves chasing themselves around in little whizzing circles.

"Just, I was telling my family about you helping me pick out the cookbook, and stuff," he says. "And they all were like, 'Adam, what are you doing? Presley is clearly who you should be with. Why aren't you dating Presley?' and I just told 'em, you know, I told 'em the truth. I said, 'Guys, relax, I know, okay? When it comes to Presley, I'm playing the long game.'"

The alcohol slows the words as they travel from his mouth and make their way, single file, into my brain. They float around like dust particles, then settle down and establish themselves. *Playing the long game.* I'm confused and reeling, but I also instantly know what he means. I manage to choke out, "What?"

He finishes the sip of whiskey he started taking right after he said the phrase that's snaking its way through my body like poison. "You know, like, Ashley's fine for now, but the end goal is you."

I blink. I mean for it to be a quick motion, but the whiskey is slowing everything down. I sway a little on my feet, aware of both how drunk I am and how drunk I must look. A voice in my head: Patty. *Girls like you and me don't settle for that bullshit.* Anger is clawing from inside my rib cage. How can he say something so sacred so casually? This thing that I've been carrying around, this hope for him, he's felt it, too. But he can just let the sentiment spew out of him at a shitty New Year's party in Bushwick, while I couldn't even admit it to my best friend for six months.

And he's dating someone who isn't me! How can he do that? He can't feel what I feel. Does he think that I'll just be sitting around, forever single, waiting on him to be ready to be with me? "Playing the long game" just sounds like code for running around town fucking girls who are hotter and less emotionally stunted than I am.

Humiliation settles over me like a poncho. Because beneath this anger, there's a metal satisfaction clicking into place, a fire of recognition. He wants me. It hasn't all been in my head, our connection. I hate myself for feeling anything other than pissed.

He's looking at me expectantly, blushing. What the hell am I supposed to say to this? The only thing I know is that between the maelstrom of feelings buzzing around my chest and the blood alcohol content flowing through my veins, I can't be trusted to say something I won't regret tomorrow, if not instantly.

For reasons I cannot explain, I do a two-finger salute, say, "Well, happy New Year," and turn on my heel, leaving him to ring in 2018 with Peanut or Nipple Jessica or Harvard Justin for all I care. Isabelle. I need Isabelle. But she's in Maryland, and God only knows what I'd say on the phone right now. I push past all the chic partygoers and out into the harsh night air. I try to take a deep breath in, but it catches in my throat, turning my chest to ice. It's time to go home.

CHAPTER 21

If my life were a rom-com, Izzy would return to our shoebox apartment on January 2 to a home I've let become filthy in my distress over Adam, to piles of takeout containers, to a sweaty, smelly me who hasn't left the couch in days, too busy obsessing over what Adam's "long game" comment meant to bathe. But the reality is I've tried to avoid obsessing by deep cleaning our apartment. I've eviscerated the dust bunnies behind and beneath the radiator, erased the olive oil splatter stains on the wall next to our stove. I can practically see my reflection in the hardwood floors. I lint-rolled the fucking rug. There isn't a takeout container in sight, because according to my bank account, takeout is a non-option, and I myself am squeaky clean because the shower is the only place I feel warm enough, though I can't stay in there long, because that's when the thoughts creep in.

"Damn, P," Izzy says as she drops her carry-on and immediately begins to remove the Canada Goose coat she bought before she knew how inhumanely that company treats the geese. Her eyes rove over the place. "It's *so* clean in here, thank you!" Then her eyes come to rest on me. "What's wrong?"

I open my mouth to say that nothing's wrong but snap it shut again, because I know there's no point and because I suddenly feel deeply exhausted from two days of scrubbing and pacing and listening to old episodes of *Las Culturistas* at double speed. I knew things were bad when not even Matt and Bowen could bring me out of my funk. "Maybe you should unpack first," I say.

"Fuck that," she says, shoving her carry-on and gigantic roller suit-case into her room and shutting the door, so the awaiting task won't be staring at her. She sits on the couch and looks at me expectantly, her blue eyes scanning my face as though I had gotten a tattoo that would explain everything. Which I have not, so I tell her what happened.

I can practically see her thoughts whizzing around in her brain as I tell her the story. When I get to the end, she lets out a long breath, then leans over and buries her face in her hands. "Oh, P, honey, no."

"Yeah," I say, snuggling deeper in the UGA blanket I have wrapped around my shoulders, like that can protect me from the complications of this shit show.

Izzy suddenly stands up and starts pacing, furiously twisting her blond hair up in a knot and tying it off with one of the wristbands she always has on hand. She's shaking her head back and forth as she says, "I don't like this. I don't like this one bit."

"Yeah, I don't exactly love it."

"I'm just . . . I mean, honestly, my gut reaction is who does this motherfucker think he is? If someone wants to date my best friend, they don't mess around with someone else first. They try to date her *now*. They *sweep* her off her *damn feet*," she hisses. She sits back down on the couch in a huff and plants her feet firmly on the ground. "Okay," she says. "How do *you* feel about this?"

I can feel my impulse to say it's not a big deal spring up like a cartoon daisy, no matter how ridiculous that lie clearly is at this point. I squash it and say, honestly, "I don't think there's one answer there."

"Then tell me all of them," Izzy says.

And I do. I tell her about the shock that he could casually express a sentiment I couldn't admit even to myself for months. About the thud of disappointment that came next, from realizing that the thing we have doesn't carry enough weight to make him think twice before he confessed to me, that the gravity doesn't pull him down the way it has me since the first time I saw him lingering outside that greenroom. About the pinpricks of light that shone through the comment—that it wasn't all in my head, that he did feel the same way, at least a little. The sickening crunch that even if that's true, the feelings were warped and bent so differently in his head than they were in mine. Because, sure, I was playing the long game with him, too, but that meant putting everything else on hold, that meant him soaking up every ounce of my attention, that meant waiting by the door like a fucking dog. Whereas for him, the long game means taking me for granted, doing whatever he wants with whomever he wants now, because when he's tired of that and wants to have a conversation with someone who says more than "Life's crazy" when he tries to talk about something real, the assumption is that I'll be there, because no one else could possibly want to scoop me up in the meantime. And, of course, the shame of allowing a *man* to send me into this tailspin. The shame of being my mother's daughter. Though I keep that thought to myself.

I tell her about how strangely violated I feel. I thought there were boundaries, things we wouldn't admit to each other, because they were too real, important, life-altering, risky. Adam paraded right across that boundary, like admitting this thing was no big deal, because my response was either guaranteed agreement or didn't matter at all.

Izzy listens to me actively, nodding vigorously and saying "mm-hmm" and making pained faces and clapping her hands and rubbing my shoulder. "Well," she tells me, "I hope you know that you are absolutely entitled to feel all of those things." She shakes her head. "Dude, I'm gonna be honest here. I was rooting for him, but I've been a little out on him ever since you told me he shut you down when you almost brought up Patty." I swallow. She gives a slight shake of her head, assuring me we aren't going to linger there. She continues, "And I know that you didn't exactly make your feelings crystal clear, but this just makes me feel like he's been leading you on. Like, keeping you in his back pocket or whatever. And the fact that he admitted you're endgame for him and doesn't seem to think it's a big deal, or maybe even"—she genuinely shudders here—"thinks that that would be somehow good enough for you or *appealing* to you, when he's newly *with* someone else, is just . . . beyond. Have you heard from him at all since?"

"Not a peep." I don't admit that at least twenty times a day I had pulled up his contact in my phone, seen that stupid photo of us outside the stupid movie theater, finger hovering over the call or text button, before darkening my phone screen, with no idea what I would even say. And then I wonder why *he* hasn't reached out to *me*. Shouldn't he apologize? Clarify? At this point, even make a joke out of it, so that I can at least have confirmation that he wasn't too drunk to remember what he said?

But I know Adam, and he wasn't drunk enough to forget saying that to me.

"Look," Izzy says. "I know you said before that you wanted to just bury this, and try to move on without having a conversation with him. But I just . . . I really hope I don't have to convince you that he's thrown a big fat bomb into that and not speaking with him doesn't really feel like an option anymore."

I nod and pull the fuzzy blanket over my head, groaning. "What do I even say, though!"

"We'll figure it out. We don't have to decide right now," she says. Her arms encircle me, and I lean my covered head on her shoulder.

CHAPTER 22

Well, if it isn't the elusive Presley Fry, Adam had replied with what I can only guess was forced nonchalance when I texted him this morning. I felt a stab of anger at his word choice, as if he had made any kind of attempt to reach me. As if he had thrown me anything other than radio silence. Winter break ends tomorrow, and I want the air cleared before we're back at the show. After a strategy session with Isabelle, I know it's time to get this damned thing over with.

We need to talk, I had texted him earlier, intentionally choosing words I knew would spike his anxiety enough to drop whatever he was doing and meet me. Though after what happened, it should be no surprise to him that we're due for a chat.

So now we're having an afternoon beer at a stupid pub in Flatiron, partially because meeting somewhere near Union Square is easiest for both of us, mostly because I want this to happen at a place I'll likely never visit again. Our nerves are buzzing back and forth across the sticky high top at which we've parked ourselves. The Christmas decorations, up past their deadline, twinkle around us. "So," he says. "What's up?"

"Nothing, what's up with you?"

"Come on," he says, fiddling with the hem of his navy-blue sweater. I try not to notice how it emphasizes his eyes. "You have to know I've been an anxious wreck all day since you texted me."

"Yeah, sorry," I say, though there's about as much apology in my voice as there are hops in my Bud Light, which I'm drinking because while liquid courage is necessary here, I can't be sloppy. I take a breath and plant my hands on the table, steadying myself. "Though I'm guessing you know what this is about."

A flush creeps up his neck and I doubt it has much to do with temperature regulation. "Uh . . . ," he says, taking a long sip of his hard cider, which I would love to mock him for were we here under different circumstances, ones in which chumminess wasn't strictly off-limits. "Well, I noticed you left Peanut's pretty suddenly the other night."

I scrape a handful of bravery out of my gut. "Yeah. My night was pretty much ruined by your whole, um"—and I can't resist throwing up air quotes here—"'long game' comment."

He nods and turns his attention down to the table. He starts pulling at the label on his bottle of Magners, then stops. "Yeah, I saw on your face pretty immediately that that wasn't a cool thing for me to say."

I blink, fury swirling around my abdomen. Making this about my face, like we're here to discuss my reaction to the thing he said instead of the thing itself. "Yeah, not cool. At the very least."

"Totally," he says, looking into my eyes, fearful, like he's in the principal's office. "And I'm sorry, Fry. It was a weird thing to say, and I shouldn't have said it."

My eyes narrow, and his fear level seems to go from principal's office to electric chair. Does he think the conversation is going to end here? That a simple apology will return everything to how it was? That I won't hold him accountable? Well. Of course he does. It's all I've done so far.

"For starters, it's a pretty shitty thing to say to someone who's not your girlfriend." I take a deep breath, mortified to feel a lump rising in my throat, my anger suddenly replaced with a nauseated fear. "And also . . . I mean, come on, dude. You must know."

Just when I think he can't get any paler, the remaining tidbit of color leaks out of his face. He swallows, the bob of his Adam's apple pronounced over the neckline of his sweater. He says nothing, and I'm disgusted by his cowardice.

"Fine," I say, leaning in, fury taking over my fear. The fury that he's hung me out to dry like this, to handle this all on my own, like we're not in this mess because of his insistence on becoming close to me, his constant attention and flirting. "I've caught feelings for you, Adam. And I felt embarrassed about that for a while, told myself I was spinning a fantasy out of a perfectly normal friendship between two adults, two coworkers. But then you made your long game comment, and you confirmed something I think a part of me had always suspected, which is that the idea of something more happening between us is not something I've completely made up. It's actually something you've created, this relationship that's flirtier, that's . . . I don't know, *more* than a normal friendship. And it's fucked up that you did it, it's fucked up that I let it happen, it's fucked up that you so jokingly, half-heartedly acknowledged it, it's fucked up that you have a girlfriend, it's all just . . . it's all just really fucked up."

Adam's formerly fidgeting hands clutch his cider bottle, and he looks as stricken as if he had just witnessed a fatal car accident. He seems to have shrunk in his chair somehow, and it occurs to me, quite satisfyingly, that the last thing on earth I want to do is have sex with this man. Not that it had ever been about that, but still. "Fry, I didn't . . . I didn't know."

"Bullshit." The word shoots out of my mouth before it had even registered in my brain. His eyes fly open wider in surprise, and the satisfaction of somehow shocking him with the truth, instead of tiptoeing around everything that really exists (or existed) between us, overrides any potential humiliation.

Adam opens his mouth, then closes it quickly, wheels spinning, going nowhere. I can't help but laugh at myself a little, remembering how I felt outside the Strand when I mouthed off to him in a real way, not our usual joking way, and how terrified I was of the possibility that he was mad at me. How, even after he butchered my almost bringing up Patty, I had walked my vitriol back, stood on Broadway until we returned to our equilibrium. Here, in this shitty bar designed for finance bro happy hours and tourists, with Oasis playing softly in the background, whose only offering is warmth in the cold, I have zero interest in walking anything back. Or even hearing what he has to say in response. I want him to have to sit with this.

He takes a deep breath and pushes his hand through his hair, a gesture that might have made my heart skip a beat a mere few weeks ago and now makes me want to flip the sticky table our beers (excuse me, my beer, his *cider*) rest on. "I'm trying to figure out what to say here," he says, wasting his breath, as if this is news.

I sigh. "Honestly—"

"No, Fry, listen." I flinch at his interrupting me. "I'm just . . . now that I'm sitting here thinking about it, I can see how things . . . I can see how things could have been confusing. And I agree that a lot of that is totally on me, I mean, I'm always calling you and stuff. Asking you to hang out. But I'm just so . . . I'm just so torn as to what to say here. Part of me wants to apologize for leading you on when I didn't mean to. And also I thought I had plenty of evidence that you weren't into me." I open my mouth (to say what, I don't know), but he holds up a hand. He continues, "But I also would be lying if I said that everything you're saying makes no sense to me, now that you're . . . now that we're talking about this. Like, I know what you mean. I guess, what I'm trying to say is . . ." He leans forward on his elbows and takes a deep breath. Looks up at me. "Just, as to where it all came from . . . it hasn't always been easy for me to just be your friend. But I know that's not exactly . . . helpful at this point."

I nod, our eye contact scalding. Every feeling is playing out, the film sped up to a dizzying pace. Satisfaction that it wasn't all in my head—the warm thud of confirmation that this wasn't just a friendship for either of us. Humiliation, and the quick follow-up of anger at his apology for leading me on, at the allowance I've made in admitting that he's hurt me. Frustration that even now he is throwing all his feelings at me without parceling them out on his own first, like I'm going to help him sort this shit out, like we're both huddled over his phone in the kitchen at work, helping him draft a text to a girl he's trying to ask out on a date.

Something that's conspicuously missing: hope. I'm gloriously air-lifted without the weight of it, mortified that I let it hold me in place for so long.

"Right, it's not helpful because you have a girlfriend," I say. "It sucks that you said what you said, that I guess you thought you had the chance to just keep me on the hook." He opens his mouth to say something, but I hold up a hand. "But I'm glad you did, because it's time for all that to end."

His face is starting to turn green, and I worry momentarily that he may actually vomit. I know what's going on in that head of his: I know he's beating himself up for saying what he said, for inviting this chaos. But I mean it: I'm glad he said it. This shit is past its expiration date.

"Here's what's gonna happen," I say, rescuing us both from uncertainty, from having to make choices together, from having to ask each other questions and wait for responses. "We're gonna stop talking, other than when it's absolutely necessary at work. I need space. I need to know that you're not going to call me, Slack me, ask me to get coffee at Ray's." He's blinking furiously at the table, and it occurs to me that he may be trying not to cry. A heaviness anchors me. I miss my earlier anger—something breaks in my chest at his sadness. At how even though he's been an asshole, I know I'm going to miss him.

He clears his throat. "Can I send you memes?" He refuses to look at me, so I actually do not know if he's joking.

"No," I say. He nods once, solemnly.

He finally looks up at me, and I get that Morse code feeling I've gotten from him before, like he's trying to communicate something to me without words. I thought it was romantic, this idea that, I don't know, our *souls* were in cahoots or something, that we could be in on the same thing without having to say anything out loud. But I see now, with the kind of clarity that can only come retroactively, that I was just dressing up his cowardice, his greed, as something bolder, deeper, special. I feel the pre-ache of a deep sadness coming on, partially for how much I know I'll miss talking to him and partially that I've wasted so much of my fucking time on this clown.

I withdraw a premeditated ten-dollar bill from the front pocket of my jeans and place it on the table, pat my hand on it once. "Well," I say, wishing I could fast-forward this part. "Bye." I stand and he stands, and he reaches out for me—how ironic that he hugs me the one time I really don't want him to. He pulls me in close, and even beneath his sweater I can feel how bony he is, how even though I'm technically in his arms, I am not protected from the chill blowing in from outside. I step out of the hug and turn away quickly. I don't want to see his face.

I leave the bar, walk the planned two blocks east and south, burst into a Starbucks, where Izzy sits in a corner, scrolling on her phone. She looks up at me and immediately stands. I practically sprint toward her, into a hug I know will be warm.

CHAPTER 23

The Bell House is a venue in Gowanus, Brooklyn, that regularly hosts some of my favorite comedians, but goddamn does it feel like a hike to get there from the East Village. I couldn't be more excited for this show, though: two of my favorite comedians, Matt Rogers and Bowen Yang, are hosting their "I Don't Think So, Honey!" show. "I Don't Think So, Honey!" is a segment on their podcast, a sixty-second rant against something the participant is bothered by or hates. Topics can range from proposed legislation to the paucity of stew in fast-casual restaurants. For the live show, Matt and Bowen do a short set before turning the spotlight over to other comedians, allowing them the chance to spend a minute comedically railing against something they've either chosen in advance or pull from the "Troll Bowl," which is filled with universally beloved or agreed-upon topics, like Julie Andrews or the fact that Santa isn't real. Agatha is on tonight's lineup.

The crowd inside the Bell House is piping hot, and the audience goes wild for Matt and Bowen. They, and the comedians they've lined up, are fantastic. I never knew hearing someone scream about half-empty cans of LaCroix could be so funny; Greta Titelman makes Izzy laugh so hard she cries. It's loud and it's nonsense and it's all so joyfully and boldly dumb. Izzy and I whoop and holler and smash our hands together when Agatha steps up to the mic.

"I don't think so, honey, *weed*!" The room immediately fills with cheers and boos alike. "Because I'm an undeniably cool girl, I'm supposed to like you, weed. It's expected that I like you, weed, but like most things that look chill on other people, you make me feel like *shit*! Why must you play me like you do, weed? The last time my sister smoked you, she had a cathartic experience watching *A Bug's Life*, then slept like a baby for ten hours. The last time I smoked you, I had a panic attack because I couldn't stop thinking about a weird joke I made to my prom date. Prom! As in an event that occurred a decade ago! And then I became terrified that I was stuck in a time loop! Sorry to sound like a Republican, but maybe you're illegal for a reason, weed! Not really, but I am one person for whom weed should *always* be illegal!" The audience *loves* this, and hearing their unfettered joy, I'm so proud I could burst. "I don't think so, honey, weed!" she finishes triumphantly.

The D train back to Manhattan isn't nearly as crowded as our ride here was, now that it's late and we're reverse commuting. Izzy's back on her phone, and I'm mentally reliving the show, jotting some thoughts down in my Notes app, names of comedians onstage I hadn't been familiar with and liked. Ones that could be a fit for the Friday slot. I'm pleasantly tired and buzzed from the Bud Light tallboys and the hours I spent among people I know nothing about but with whom I share a sense of humor, listening to people spin ideas into something we can all laugh at. I crane my neck to see the Statue of Liberty when we go over the bridge back into Manhattan and hit Izzy's leg so she can look and see, too. When we make it to the NYU stop, we bundle ourselves as much as we can before emerging into the freezing January air. When we get home, I send Agatha a congratulatory text. I'm smiling at my phone like a fool, alight with pride, with possibility.

It isn't until I've closed out of my messages that it occurs to me what I didn't look for: a text from Adam. A small thud of grief, followed by a long, unspooling exhale. For the first time in a long time, I feel free.

When I told Adam to stop speaking to me, there were plenty of things I worried about. I worried about the humiliation of having to admit my feelings for him. I worried about social stuff with coworkers I'd miss out on by refusing to be in the same place as him. I worried about other people at work noticing us avoiding each other, wondering what happened, and assuming something far more nefarious than the truth, which was that *nothing* happened and that was the problem. And sure, it's been awkward at work: avoiding eye contact, trying to time my trips to the theater to ensure our paths don't cross. Basically, the exact opposite of what I've done ever since he started. I'll say this, though: I have seen him, and he looks like shit. Especially that first day back. Puffy eyes, hair disheveled, the works. It's not dissatisfying.

Anyway, all my worries were fair, but fuck me for not anticipating the most painful result of all: the splitting caffeine headache I get from purposefully waiting to get coffee until I can safely assume he's already gotten his. This headache is not helped by the fact that I used to escape my cubicle for coffee every day just as Mark made his grand entrance into the office and would make loud, obnoxious small talk with Peanut.

"Did you watch?" Mark calls out to Peanut's cubicle as he nestles himself down in his office, undoubtedly referring to the Golden Globes, which aired last night.

"I did," Peanut calls back, though we all know Mark doesn't give a fuck about whether he's seen it. He asked just to create an opening for himself to share his opinions.

"Some speech from Oprah, huh?" Mark asks, voice cloaked in a smirk, and my hands involuntarily clench into fists. I see the skin between Peanut's freckles turn scarlet. Poor Peanut, who is in no position to tell his boss off but will surely be unable to stomach a bad word spoken about Oprah and her impassioned speech about how time is up for abusive male behavior in every industry across the country, how women found power in the collective this past year.

Peanut, bless him, gulps and says, "I thought it was really amazing."

Mark snorts. "I mean, I don't disagree with her sentiment. But it's an acting award. Is this really the forum for a political discussion? For a history lesson? It felt like posturing to me."

"Um, well . . . do you want coffee? I'm going to get some coffee," Peanut says, standing quickly.

"Yep, the usual." Peanut, shaking his head, wide green eyes staring into mine in both solidarity and disbelief, practically sprints toward the kitchen.

I press my hands into my desk in an effort to exorcise some of the anger vibrating through my body. Isabelle bawled when Oprah was finished speaking, and I was verklempt myself. I felt inspired, and seen, and maybe even hopeful that the exposure of so many atrocities last year was a necessary step in expunging all the bullshit. Hearing Mark dismiss it feels like confirmation that change is impossible, that our voices, whether we're calling shit out or encouraging people to be better, will always be accused of being something else, something sinister or nefarious or stupid. Posturing.

Perhaps this is why I stick it out as an assistant, making minimum wage and doing Emma's expense reports and cleaning up greenrooms: in the hope that one day I'll be the one in charge, instead of dipshits like Mark. I'll be able to promote women like me and Emma and guys like Peanut who understand that we have a responsibility to take people seriously, that culture depends on listening. There won't be room for people unwilling to change. If Mark cares so little about this industry, or half the population of the world, why does he work here? Why be a part of a show that's committed to poking holes in existing power structures, especially abusive ones? Hell, fighting tyranny was the initial goal, the entire reason for the creation of comedy in ancient Greece, for fuck's sake. And why be a part of a show that promotes inclusive art? That's weaving itself into the fabric of culture while staying on the right side of history? I mean, why even—

Emma's here. She needs her coffee.

CHAPTER 24

Over the past several months, Susan Clark has surprised me. She's surprised me with her willingness to be open-minded, with the fact that she doesn't cook, with her generosity. But nothing is more surprising than the text I received a few days ago, inviting me to come to her apartment and take shrooms with her. I think she may really be losing it.

The text read: Hello, Presley! I was recently at a dinner party with Tracy Pollan, who gave me a galley of Michael's latest book, which is all about how good magic mushrooms are for you. Do you know about magic mushrooms? Would you like to come over this Saturday and eat some? My Michael is overnighting them. Xx Susan. This was immediately followed by a text that said: Please delete my last message, though the invitation still stands. Xx Susan.

I assumed, at first, that she had been hacked. Or that I had been hacked, that somehow this text was only *appearing* to come from Susan Clark. But then I googled Tracy Pollan to figure out who Michael Pollan was, and then I remembered that Susan, despite her crisp pleats and perfect lipstick and refusal to allow her face to do anything other than smile, is going through one hell of a hard time, which is when people typically become interested in trying new substances. Speaking of substances, I remember also that she was, once upon a time, close with Patty, and I suddenly think she may not have been hacked after all.

Izzy and I tripped once in college, when this dude she had become friends with (in an accounting class, of all places) offered her some homegrown shrooms. We went to this park in Athens on a beautiful, though pollen-saturated, spring day and had ourselves a time. We were on our hands and knees, rubbing our fingers through the grass, marveling at how beautiful it was, how had we never noticed how beautiful grass is? How *silly* grass is? It was spectacular.

We would occasionally talk about wanting to take them again, but it also wasn't exactly a top priority. I read the text to Izzy when we were sitting on the couch watching *The Office*. "Jealous," she said, keeping her eyes trained on Dunder Mifflin's chaos.

It's not like I have plans this Saturday. I could use an escape from how awkward the return to work has been with Adam. Plus: What am I going to say to the woman who just sponsored basically an entirely new wardrobe for me? No? So I write back, Sure lol.

....

"Did you eat a hearty breakfast?" Susan asks as she ushers me into her apartment come Saturday, quickly closing the door behind her like she's running a meth lab in here instead of preparing to eat something that occurs naturally and will probably be legal in the next decade. "I think it never hurts to line your stomach."

I think back to the piece of bread I toasted in the oven an hour ago because we don't have room in our "kitchen" for a toaster. "Yep," I say.

She claps her hands together and nudges my shoulder once I get my coat off and hang it on the coatrack. There's a little sparkle in her eyes, and I marvel at the fact that this woman put on makeup to do drugs with a friend in the comfort of her own home. She's wearing a clean button-down and khaki pants, office casual. "Can you believe we're doing this?" she asks, giggling.

"Nope."

I follow her into the kitchen, where a USPS box sits on the counter, opened. There are Ziploc bags of chopped produce all over the counter, including one with a star sticker on it, like it was the student of the day. She points at it. "Those are the mushrooms," she whispers as though the cops are in here. "I had Michael send a bunch of vegetables so it wouldn't look suspicious. Or so that we could say we didn't know if we got caught."

"Genius," I say. I find it very endearing that Michael has become Susan's drug dealer. "Does Lawrence know you're doing this?"

She sighs. "No. I've been calling him, but he keeps texting saying he'll call me back the next day. Busy boy."

"Hm," I say, wondering how he would react if he knew his prim mother would be trying psychedelic drugs today.

"I just didn't think it would be a good idea for me to wait as soon as I decided I wanted to do them," she says. "Knowing me, I'll overthink and end up not doing it, and I just . . . I just want to have the experience!"

"Right on," I say. "So, how do you want to go about consumption?"

"I was too nervous to look up the best way to go about eating them online, you know, digital footprint and all that," Susan says, and I try not to laugh out loud. "So I asked Michael. He suggested we mix it in with some yogurt." I smile, recognizing the method. It was what Abbi and Ilana did on *Broad City*. "I wrote down the boys' phone numbers and the number to the nearest hospital here," she says, tapping a Post-it stuck to the marble countertop, as though I'm here to babysit her kids. She grabs a couple of Fage Greek yogurt containers out of the fridge, carefully mixes the mushrooms in them, and hands one to me. We sit at the counter and eat quietly, and I try not to make any faces at the less-than-pleasant taste.

"I don't feel anything," she says the second she finishes half her yogurt, the half with the mushrooms. I've never seen her eat so much.

"That's normal," I say.

"You've done them before?"

"Once. In college."

"That makes me feel so much better," she says, clearly relieved. "And you liked it? It was good?"

"Yeah, Susan, it was great. And this will be, too."

"I still don't feel anything."

"You will."

We wander into the living room and sit on the couch. "Should I turn on the TV?" Susan asks.

"Probably not," I say, thinking of the uninvited images and ideas that could pop up on it.

She nods quickly. "Totally. Just so you know, I don't feel anything. Do you feel anything?"

"Not yet, Susan."

We continue sitting on the couch for several minutes, quiet except for Susan's occasional interjections that she doesn't feel anything yet. I check my phone and am relieved to see a text from Isabelle. I woke up this morning to find she didn't come home last night, and I tracked her location to a building in Williamsburg I didn't recognize. All good! Will explain later, but having fun xo is her response to my inquiry into whether she had gotten laid or been abducted. I don't want my phone to interfere with my shrooms experience, so I power it down and pocket it. Restless, I pick up one of Susan's heavy, expensive-looking coffee table books. It's called *Audubon*.

"I love birds," Susan says as I flip through ornate drawings of North American bird specimens. She scoots closer to me on the couch, leaning over my shoulder and looking on with me. Three pages later, she says, "I don't feel anything."

"Me neither, Susan."

"Maybe we should meditate," she says. "Michael said that could be good at first."

Getting quiet with myself could not be lower on the list of things I want to do, but sitting here in anticipation, with Susan's energy buzz-ing around the room like a swarm of bees, isn't great either. "Sure," I say.

At Susan's suggestion, we move to the floor, sitting, eyes closed, on pillows that were clearly made to be shown only. My tailbone digs into the floor. She plays an app from her phone, instructing us to breathe. Just as her phone tells us that our thoughts are clouds, Susan says, "I don't feel any—"

"Yep, me neither, and that's fine, Susan."

Her breaths are shallow, but I can hear her effort to deepen them as the lady on the app instructs her to do so. That's the thing about Susan: she always does her best.

There's a buzzing warmth starting to soften things in my chest, and a little in my brain, too. "Presley?" Susan asks.

"Yes?"

"I think I might feel something a little bit."

"Me too."

"Whoa," Susan says a few minutes, or maybe it's seconds, later.

"Yeah," I say, my voice strange and hilarious and somehow lovely in my ear. The room has come alive, and it's exquisite. The winter light that comes through the windows is weak but specific, lighting dust particles in the air like they're each their own pop star, and I see now that it's because they are. Pop stars. And pop stars are dust. The pillow I sit on, and all the pillows in this room, are beautiful and soft to the touch, how had I never touched them before? And it hits me: some-one *made* these pillows. Someone dreamed them up, had an idea for a pillow, and then *executed* that idea. These were stitched together, and that fact wallops me. And now they're here, in someone's home, all because someone *else* had the idea to make them. I am completely astounded and humbled by this fact, that I get to be here, among these items.

"Susan, Susan," I say, eager to tell her about the pillows.

"I feel it a lot," she says, and I look over at her, and she looks wild-eyed and silly and her hair doesn't seem so neat all of a sudden. "Whoa," she adds.

This strikes me as very funny. That this was her idea, and she was so worried about feeling it, and now she's feeling it. I laugh, because I can't not. I hear her laughing, too, and then hear the thud of her small body hitting the carpeted floor. I ask her if she's okay and she cries out, "Yes!" She's lying on her back, looking up at the ceiling, and she raises one of her tiny arms, I believe to signal her okayness.

To lie that way suddenly seems like a brilliant idea, and I follow suit. I gasp as I realize I can put one of the gorgeous, so lovingly made pillows beneath my head, and I look up and gasp again. There are light patterns dancing all over the ceiling, in between the moldings, and the light is moving so quickly and so slowly. The meditation app is no longer blaring from Susan's phone, instead classical music is playing, and I realize it's a soundtrack—it's a soundtrack to a movie the light is playing on the ceiling for me.

I see two characters and I realize it's me and Adam; I'm seeing us meet outside the greenroom on the day that Tom Hanks came to the show. It's happening on the ceiling, in retrospect, but it's also happening right now, somewhere else, because I step into the realization that time is actually a construct, and everything is always happening, all the time, and that time is now. But the versions of ourselves that are on that ceiling meeting for the first time are unaware of this. Now we're making coffee at the coffee machine, and we're laughing, and there are shapes that are glowing with bright pastel colors in our chests, and we can see them in each other's chests, and I realize that this is what he's always referring to when he looks at me like he's trying to blink something to me in Morse code. It's that light in him talking, trying to communicate with mine.

I see it with perfect clarity: we have these pieces that were recognizable only to each other, and that is why and how we connected the way that we did. But it's not enough! It's not necessary to make a relationship or to build a life or to fall fully in love. It's just a strand of light. And it's beautiful, but it can't dictate everything.

And that's actually okay, I see now. It was gorgeous, what we got to recognize in each other. But there's nothing more to it. He isn't enough runway for me to get off the ground, there isn't a middle either of us can reach. Gratitude for having met Adam rushes my chest like a dam somewhere has broken, and it's making room for all this compassion. It's okay that I felt for him the way that I did, of course it was, because there was the light, the light. And it's okay that it wasn't enough. It's not our fault. I am both shocked and completely welcoming of the wetness I feel falling out of the corners of my eyes and down to my ears. Doesn't it make all the sense in the world? Isn't that a relief? I can let it go. I'm clean now.

I hear a sound. It's Susan, saying, "I know, I know, I know." And then she's saying, "You don't know, no, *you* don't know!" And then she's shaking her head and moaning a little and suddenly I'm scared, but then she starts laughing and then I remember that everything is okay, everything has always been okay, because all of this has already happened.

Sometime later, I realize that the pillow beneath my head is actually just a lumpy thing that was probably purchased at an uppity store and extremely overpriced and made by a machine or a child in a third world country. I lift my head up, and Susan looks peacefully asleep, though her mouth hangs open, drool oozing out of it. I've never seen her look like this: messy. I realize I'm smiling at her fondly, like she's my toddler finally down for a nap.

Slowly, quietly as I can, I rise and go to the kitchen for a glass of water, because I'm thirstier than I could ever have believed was survivable. I'm sitting at the counter, my mind pleasantly fuzzy and tired, chugging a second glass of water, when Susan pads in.

"Hi," she says bashfully.

"Hi, Susan."

"I don't think I feel it anymore."

"Yeah, I think I'm pretty much all the way through, myself."

She joins me at the counter with her own glass of water. "Want to order dinner?" she asks.

As we eat lo mein and dumplings brought to the door by Roger (he tries Goldie Hawn as my doppelgänger this time), we debrief. Susan can't get over how heavy her body felt, and I try not to roll my eyes at the idea that Susan carries more weight than a flea. I tell Susan about the pillows, and she smiles. "Well, they *are* Gucci," she says.

I leave out the Adam stuff. "What about you?" I ask.

"Well," she says, staring into her noodles, "I hope this doesn't upset you, but I had a chat with Patty."

My insides turn cold. Discomfort at this particular topic, jealousy that she got to talk to my mother and I didn't, and guilt that Patty didn't even cross my tripping mind. Just some pillows and a production assistant I can't even call an ex. I swallow my mouthful of food, a Herculean effort. "What'd you two gab about?" I ask before coating my dry throat with more water.

"She—well, I know it wasn't really her," she says. "She told me I need to make a decision. About Thomas."

"Oh," I say. "That sounds . . . direct."

"Well, she always was, you know that," Susan says.

Neither one of us looks at the other. "Do you think you're going to listen to her?" I ask.

Susan nods. "It was good advice, I think." The loud strum of a guitar ringtone fills the kitchen, and Susan walks over to where her phone is plugged in by the stove. "Lawrence," she says to me, unplugging the phone and walking out of the room as she answers with "Hey, sweetie!"

I remain sitting in the kitchen. Only minutes earlier my appetite felt vast and endless, but now the food in front of me looks lifeless and dull and I can feel it sitting in my stomach, weighing me down. My limbs are heavy, and I want to go home. The ache in my chest flares up again, thinking about Susan talking to Patty, whom Susan hadn't spoken to in years, whose funeral Susan didn't even attend. But the ache does dull with the thought that my mother was here. I chuckle at the idea of Patty knowing that she would one day, in her own way, haunt Susan. Finally give Susan a piece of her mind, in light of Thomas being a prick.

"I love you, too, I'll call you tomorrow," I hear Susan saying as she comes back into the kitchen, hanging up. She looks at me, mouth frowned in guilt. "I'll tell him tomorrow what we did," she says.

I nod, scrape my plate, rest it in the dishwasher. "Thanks for today, Susan," I say, hoping the fact that I mean it is conveyed in my voice.

"Oh, sweetie, thank you for joining me. I won't forget it," she says, smiling weakly, and I can tell she is also tired. "Sure you don't want to stay a little bit longer?"

I think of her sitting in this apartment alone and feel a heaviness I can't bear. I shake my head. "Thanks, but I better be getting back."

She nods. "Can I call you a car this time?"

I almost say no, but then I pause. "Okay," I say. "Thanks." And I'm home in twenty-five minutes, nearly falling asleep in the car because it was so warm and peaceful in there.

CHAPTER 25

I'm walking home Sunday night, trying to shake off the second-hand anxiety I just experienced due to a rare bomb from Agatha at an open mic, when I spy a frantically waving beanie-clad figure. It takes me a second to realize the person is waving at me, and that the person is Izzy, who hasn't been home since Friday. We meet in the middle of our block after I fish my keys out of my pocket; Izzy claims hers are too buried in her purse for her to locate quickly enough.

She dodges my demand to know where she's been and asks me about tripping with Susan as we climb the five flights of stairs to our apartment. As soon as I unlock the door, she collapses on the couch. "Dude," she says breathlessly, "I have news."

"Okay," I say, my nerves tangling themselves audibly in my voice. Izzy throws her head back and laughs.

"It's a good thing!" she says. She takes a breath, then dramatically rips her beanie off her uncharacteristically greasy hair, throws it across the room. "I've met someone!"

"Ooh, can I guess who?" I ask. She looks at me, confused. "Do you not mean a celebrity . . . ?"

She guffaws and grins at me, big. Her eyes look like sparklers, the kind families buy on the Fourth of July. "No, silly," she says. "I've met a girl. And I'm like . . . oh my God." She buries her face in one of our couch pillows and yells something inaudible.

"What?" I ask.

She perks her head up and groans, but she's still got that grin on. "I'm besotted!" she says.

I sink into the yellow armchair, trying to wrap my mind around this confusion. "Besotted? Did you also accidentally fall into a period film?" I ask.

She laughs, like I'm just the silliest thing. I blink. "Okay, so I went to dinner with Sammy and some of our old coworkers on Friday, and then we went to this bar in Williamsburg, and we were just playing pool, hanging out, and some friends of Sammy's friends came and met up with us, and I started flirting with this girl, Julia." Izzy sits up, fishes her phone out of her bag. Shows me a photo of a brunette with tasteful tattoos lining up a cue ball, unaware of the photo being taken.

"Flirting with her or stalking her?" I ask.

"Shut up, whatever," Izzy says. "So I went home with her, and we hook up, right? And then we spent like . . . the whole weekend together. Like, that's where I've been. We went and got bagels on Saturday, and then that turned into seeing a movie, and then that turned into drinks, which turned into dinner, which turned into Saturday night, which turned into brunch today . . . you get it."

Me? "Getting" the idea of declaring myself to be "besotted" after spending two days with someone? I most certainly do not. It took me six months of constant flirting to admit I cared about Adam, for fuck's sake. And I thought Izzy was taking a break from dating?

"I know what you're going to say," Izzy says, sitting up straight, smoothing her smile down into a more serious facial expression. "No way can I be this obsessed with someone after just a weekend. I don't know how to explain it, really, but it feels like I've known Julia forever, like she's been in my life for a long time. I think I might be falling in love." She looks into my face. "I know it sounds crazy!" she says, giving me some clue that I must look about as horrified as I feel.

"No, not crazy," I say, guilt rushing in like a tide, the need to verbally affirm my best friend stronger than any stabbing feelings of doubt that a weekend with a cool brunette warrants an L bomb. "Just . . . like something from a movie, or something."

"It *feels* like that!" she says, eyes brightening, as though I meant that as an endorsement for and not an argument against. "Richard Linklater directed my fucking life this weekend."

"Whoa," I say, forcibly ignoring the pang at the reference—Adam was the person who introduced me to the *Before* trilogy. A thought intrudes: What if Adam and I had worked out? And now, this: Izzy with someone? Would there be double dates? Would there be joy, instead of this depressive panic flooding in that Izzy's found someone and I'm going to start spending every evening alone in our apartment? I stand to get myself a glass of water, shake myself out of that mindset. This shit isn't about me. "What about taking a break from dating?" I ask the sink.

"Well, you know what they say," Izzy says as I chug my water. "The right person comes along as soon as you stop looking."

"I've never heard that," I say, returning to the armchair.

"Well, you've never been someone who was looking, I guess," she says with a shrug. The comment stings, and I'm not sure why.

"So," I say, searching for the right words, coming up short. The silence sits on me like an elephant, cutting off my access to air. "Who is this girl?" I eventually ask, genuinely curious. I've watched Izzy go on countless dates over the years, with a whole spectrum of women. Flight attendants, accountants, a chef. Chill girls, type A girls; early risers and insomniacs. A triathlete, a girl who spoke eight languages. Who is this girl, this *Julia*, who has managed to capture my picky best friend's attention and heart after one weekend?

"She's our age," Izzy says. "Obviously so cute." She waves the photo in my face again, goes on about how she has some job in coding and is from Colorado. I plaster what I hope is a smile on my face, nod along. Try not to think about how I feel something slipping. My rank, maybe? I am at once aware that this is the entirely wrong way to think about this and also wondering if my position as Izzy's first phone call is about to be usurped. I know people in relationships often refer to their significant other as their best friend, but surely Izzy wouldn't do that? When Izzy's done giving me the finer points of Julia's bio, and telling me some inane story about how this one time she thought she lost her dachshund but hadn't, I stand up and excuse myself to go to bed. I give Izzy's shoulder a squeeze on my way, hopefully indicating that I'm excited for her, marking that I recognize that this is a momentous occasion. That this is a moment of joy, and not the moment when everything changes.

CHAPTER 26

Our new interns this semester are as helpful as a litter of puppies and significantly less cute. I'm thumping up the stairs to the roof, cursing their lazy, entitled names. Ben & Jerry (as in . . . *that* Ben & Jerry) have sent the staff gallons and gallons of their new Gary Madden ice cream flavor ("Bake Night Show"), so we're having a staff ice cream social. This would be just adorable, except that we need extra tables, which are allegedly stored on the roof under some tarps from our summer parties, and apparently all the interns are too busy being idiots to handle the task of retrieving them. The darkness and quiet of the stairwell are a welcome reprieve from Mark's recounting of some long-ago Oscar party in which he and Chris Pine got "so hammered we sympathy vommed in the urinals." I lean my head on the wall for a second, take a deep breath. My phone buzzes in my pocket— Izzy, telling me not to wait up for her tonight, she's going straight from work to Julia's. The stairwell echoes with my huff, which is unwarranted considering it's not like Izzy and I had plans. I roll my eyes and send back a thumbs-up. Then I worry that just an emoji will convey my lack of enthusiasm, so I throw in a Have fun! for good measure.

Pocketing my phone, I emerge into the sunlight and icy air of the roof, wondering how in the hell I'm going to carry buffet tables back down the stairs by myself, when my eyes adjust to the light and I see a man in a puffy jacket turning to look at me. He's smoking a cigarette. Gary Madden.

We both freeze. "Uh-oh," he says. I must look confused, because he laughs a little and says, "Don't rat me out," nodding toward the cigarette. "I quit ten years ago. Or so I tell people."

I nod. "Secret's safe with me. I'm just up here to get tables." I look around for the tarps but don't see any.

He jerks his head, indicating that I should come stand where he is, leaning over the wall and looking out over Times Square. It's a good view, the exact spot where I stood when I was alone here just before Thanksgiving. I walk over and will my heart rate to slow down. While Gary and I see each other in passing every day, he's too shrouded in celebrity and importance and hosting to be pals with anyone except the writers. This is the first time we've ever been alone. My elevated heart rate does not slow down: what was at first excitement is now a horrible feeling of dread, settling somewhere in my stomach. What if he does something untoward? What if he's a creep? What if I have to tell? What if I don't want to tell?

"I'd offer you a smoke, but Cora only lets me bring one up at a time. And only once every other week," he says, smiling that dazzling, superstar smile at me. This close, I notice his thick brown hair is shiny with gray flecks. Cora is his assistant, a lifer, who's been with him for something like thirty years.

"Can't get anything past Cora," I say. He's leaning over the wall, looking out at the city, not at me. His eyes are all dopey, and he has this dreamy little smile. He's staring at the city with real love, like the way Susan gazes at Clark every time he speaks. Seeing this pure admiration on his face, the very same one I carry for the city, makes me feel safe.

"Presley, right?" he asks.

I nod. "Gary, is it?"

He chuckles, and I realize I've made Gary Madden laugh. I have peaked.

"So, what brought you to the show?"

"Oh, um . . . ," I say, torn between the pull to be truthful and my aversion to coming off like a psychotic loser. I shiver with the cold and my nerves. Nerves so powerful I don't think I can lie. "I love comedy, I guess. I've always loved comedy."

"Where are you from?" he asks. I tell him, the answer slipping easily out of my mouth. He's a good interviewer, after all.

"I'm from a small town, too," he says, like I don't know exactly which small town he's from in Pennsylvania, like everyone who works for him isn't familiar with his whole biography.

"I watched this show every night growing up. It made me feel connected. To, like, culture," I say.

He nods, and I feel like he does understand. Of course he does. He wouldn't rise to the demands of this job, the pressure, if he didn't think about this, the weird loner kids watching stand-up in their bedrooms, the depressed people who can't take the news straight, need it to be mixed into a comedy cocktail to help make sense of it, to help imbue some hope into it.

"Well, given how competitive I'm told it is to get a job here, I'm glad to hear that staying up that late every night clearly didn't affect your grades," he says.

I exhale a little laugh. "Yeah. My mom was a drinker, and so I was usually up, you know, taking care of her or waiting for her to get home, or both. So I watched the show, and it just, kind of, I mean, I said the culture thing just now, but it kind of took the edge off, I guess. Made life, uh, bearable." *Shut the fuck up, Presley. Quit spilling your guts. To Gary Madden.* Goddamn him and his world-class charisma and interview skills.

I do think, though, that there's a part of myself that's always hoped I'd get a chance to tell him. So that he can know. It feels important for reasons I can't explain. Gary's dad was an alcoholic, too, famously, something I read about in Gary's first memoir, *Put Your Hands Together*. Probably part of what drew me to him, if I'm honest. I wish my words didn't sound dingy and cheap coming out of my mouth. I can practically see them clanging against each other in the cold air.

"Was?" Gary asks me, looking at me with his bright blue eyes. I must look confused, because he says, "You said your mom *was* a drinker."

"Yeah. She passed around a year and a half ago." Much as I respect Cora, I would very much like to throttle her right now for sending Gary up here with only one cigarette. I'm not much of a smoker, but it seems like it would be very helpful in this moment.

He exhales. "Ah. I was hoping for a recovery story. Though I had a similar experience and, as much as I hate to say it, know better." His dad died of cirrhosis of the liver.

"I know. I, uh, I read your book."

"Way to do your homework," he says, not unkindly. He straightens up. "A raise of one million dollars, you shall have." I laugh, but a tack of annoyance also pricks me. He fucking should give me a raise, so that I can, you know, live. "I am sorry to hear that, though," he says, and it feels genuine. "Thank you for telling me."

We look out over the skyline together. I feel a flicker of excitement, thinking about telling Isabelle that I shared a heartfelt moment with Gary. I sneak another peek at his profile, and a grin tugs at the corners of my mouth. On second thought, maybe I won't tell anyone. Maybe this is just for me.

CHAPTER 27

Though she behaves like an old person in most respects, Susan is a texter, not a caller. So when I'm leaving work one Thursday, and I feel my phone buzzing with long vibrations, I feel a flare of anger, assuming that Adam is already disrespecting my request that he leave me alone. Though, as Isabelle says, healing is not linear, because there is also a small pang of disappointment when I realize it's Susan calling and not Adam. "Hello?" I answer.

"Presley! My friend, my old friend," Susan says, and I actually pull one of my earbuds out and my phone out of my pocket. I stare at it in disbelief, stock-still on Fifty-Sixth and Broadway. It's Susan, and it can't be Patty, and I know that. But my head is spinning. Susan is clearly wasted, and the déjà vu is real.

I can hear warbly words traveling through the cold air, and I quickly press my earbud back into my ear. Susan is laughing hysterically and saying, accent thicker than I've ever heard it, "Life is funny, ain't it? Just hilarious."

"Susan—" I say.

"Presley, will you come over? Please? Is it— Oh, look! It's dinnertime! Will you please come over for dinner?"

The last thing I want to do is have dinner with a middle-aged woman who's three sheets to the wind. I have no plans, though, so my mind starts scrambling for a lie. "Oh, thanks, Susan, that's nice, but—"

"We can order anything you want. Maybe we can even have pizza. Is that crazy? I know it's not the weekend." I try to put these two disparate thoughts, which for Susan are clearly related, together, when she cuts in again. "I'll be honest, Presley, and I'm so sorry, but I've been drinking a little."

"Yep, that's . . . yep."

"I'm sure you don't want to come uptown and have pizza on a weekday with an old lady. But I just, um . . . Well. I've been drinking since lunch if you were wondering why I sound like I've been drinking since lunch. Because I had lunch today, a very strange lunch."

I reach the B/D train station and linger by the top of the stairs. I'm realizing I likely won't be getting on it, won't be going downtown tonight to watch Netflix in my bed after heating a frozen Trader Joe's meal like I had planned. Goddammit. I take the bait. "Why was it a strange lunch?"

"It was with my husband's *lover*, if you can believe that. *Roberta* is her name. Here's what I've always thought about women with that name: I'm sorry that your parents wanted you to be a boy. I mean, really, who names their daughter *Roberta* if they're expecting a girl? No one. You name your daughter Roberta because you wanted to have a boy named Robert, then the baby comes out, and she's a girl, and you panic."

Despite the fact that she just dropped a bit of a bombshell, I can't help but pause and appreciate that little monologue. It is probably the funniest thing I've ever heard Susan say. Anyway: Roberta Shoemaker. The woman who was the VP to Thomas's president. The woman he had an affair with. "Susan, why would you have lunch with her?" I can't help but ask. I thought she was pushing it all those months ago having drinks with her dead friend's kid, but this is a whole new level.

"Come over and I'll tell you all about it!" she yelps into the phone. She giggles. "It's like, you know, it's like your comedy shows. I'll stand up here, and I'll do my speech, and you'll laugh. Because let me tell you, it is *funny*."

"Sounds hilarious." I sigh into the phone and start walking uptown to get on the Q train. "I'll be there in thirty."

Given how Susan sounded on the phone, it's a bit shocking to walk into her apartment (after "a blonder Julia Roberts?" from Roger) to find it as pristine as ever. Susan herself may be a mess, but it is not reflected in her home. Unlike Patty, whose bedroom floor was always covered in clothes, who always had the smell of Burnett's trailing behind her. *Unlike Patty.* I repeat it to myself as Susan pulls me into one of her suffocating hugs, as vodka and half a lemon slosh out of her crystal martini glass and onto the sparkling hardwood floor. My whole body tenses up when the vodka splashes, as I wait for the smell of Burnett's to waft into my nose, slingshotting me back in time to wiping liquor off my grandparents' kitchen floor, leading a mumbling-to-herself Patty up the stairs, pulling a big T-shirt over her head to wear to sleep, like she was a doll.

But the smell of Burnett's does not make its way to me, as this vodka is too fancy to smell like it should be used to clean a crime scene. "Whoopsie," Susan says as she bends down to pick the half lemon up from the floor. "I couldn't twist it," she says as she stands back up slowly, wobbling. She holds it out to me, like it's a precious gem. "You know, to have a martini with a twist. I couldn't do the twist, so I just went . . . plop! And put more in there, and more people should do that, because it helps with the flavor."

"Sure," I say. "How about we get some food? Food could be good."

Susan nods vigorously and shoves her phone in my face. "Use this, get whatever you want. As long as what you want is pizza!"

I order a large pepperoni from some place called Little Luzzo's on Seamless and we make our way into the kitchen, where I pour Susan a large glass of iced water and place it in front of her. I fix one for myself, too. I've found with drunk people, it helps to make it seem like you're not treating them like a baby, even though that's exactly what must be done.

Susan takes a prim sip of water and a big gulp of what's left of the martini. Black ink is smudged beneath her eyes, lipstick bleeds over her lip line, and her hair sticks up at odd angles. "Thanks for coming over," she says. "I wanted to gab about my lunch, you know. Girl talk! Not like I can talk about it with any of my other 'friends.'" She waves her hand around, turns her air quotes into wiggling spirit fingers, like this is all fun and not incredibly painful for her.

"What happened?" I ask, noticing that Susan's phone has lit up with a notification that our food is on the way. She plops down on a stool, leans her elbows on the marble kitchen island.

"Well, I obviously knew who she was when the news broke and all that. Of course, I knew who she was before, I mean, they've worked together for a long time. And I always thought she was very beautiful. Tall, like a model. Fifteen years younger than me and Thomas. Basically exactly the kind of woman you *don't* want your husband to be in the vicinity of every single day. But! I told myself, every time I would see her at a Christmas party or whatever, that I was being a batty little wife, which was not what I wanted to be." I nod. I wouldn't want to be a batty little wife either.

"Susan, you didn't find out on the internet, did you?" I ask. I've always wondered about that part. The idea of Susan finding out about her husband's affair at the same time as the rest of the world is so humiliating it lights my brain on fire. But there was her bizarre vibe when I ran into her at Daily Provisions the weekend before the news broke, like she knew it was coming. I've never felt like it was appropriate for me to ask, but this situation is already inappropriate enough that all bets seem to be off.

"No, Thomas got wind that the story was going to break, so he told me the week before. You know what's funny?" she asks. She keeps trying to make this comedic, but the situation is purely bleak. Which is how the best comedy is born, really. "He sat me down, all serious, all 'I need to talk to you,'" she says with a husky imitation of a male voice that sounds nothing like Thomas. "And you know what I thought he was going to say? That he had cancer. I just feel like we're at cancer age, not affair age, but then again, he's a man, so any age is an affair age, I guess. But no, something bad was not happening to him, he had *done* something bad, something very bad. He told me it had been short-lived, just a few times, and there were probably some feelings there, but they had decided to squash it for the sake of both of their careers. And his marriage, he was quick to add! But he didn't say that part first!"

"Yikes," I say unhelpfully.

"Yeah, yikes," Susan says. "Yeah! Yikes! And, you know, the other stuff, the 'sweetheart' stuff in the article, the flirty stuff, I just . . . I always liked that he was friendly and fun and the life of the party. But of course I know that's different at work, that's different when it's your boss, but—maybe this is bad and you won't like this, because you're a young woman and you young women these days seem to have a clearer idea of what's okay and what's not than I ever did—but that's not the part I'm mad about, okay? I'm from a different generation."

I feel myself automatically poised to make the "different generation" argument. How that just can't be an excuse. But I keep my mouth shut. Societal expectations around workplace behavior are not what we're here to discuss.

"But the affair, the affair," she says. "Didn't like that! Didn't like the affair. And you know, the worst part is, do you know who I was the most mad at, Presley?" She looks at me expectantly. I wait. She continues, "Me! I'm most mad at me, because it crossed my mind, like I said, and I said, 'Oh no, Susan, you're being silly. Thomas wouldn't do that. And this woman, *Roberta*, she wouldn't do it, either, because you see her at the Christmas party.' I really thought that, Presley, I really thought that because this woman saw me at the Christmas party every year, that would mean that she wouldn't sleep with my husband. Because I'm not just an idea to her, you know, I'm a person. A real woman! I thought to myself, 'This wouldn't happen, so why dwell on it? Why cause a problem when there isn't a problem? Don't want to make waves.' I never want to make waves. But I should have made the wave, because then the wave"—she widens her eyes and moves her hands up and down in a wave motion—"the *wave* got *me*."

"Yikes," I say again, because I don't know how else to respond. In an attempt to keep her on track, and because I really do want to know, I prompt: "So why did you have lunch with her?"

Susan sighs and puts her head in her arms, folded on the kitchen counter. Then she snaps it back up and says, "Because I had questions. Thomas had told me one story, but he only told me because he knew the news was going to come out. By the way, this all happened two years ago. So. It would seem that I can't exactly trust him. But he's my husband, and I don't know if I want to divorce him, so I thought, well, the first step would be to see at least if he told me the truth, even though it was late." A knock on the door. I retrieve our pizza and open the box between us. Susan picks a slice up and takes a big bite, grease dripping down her chin.

"So, did he?" I ask, reaching for a slice of my own, not bothering to get a plate if she's not going to.

"Did he what?" she asks, mouth full.

"Tell the truth."

She nods and swallows. "He told me what the truth was to *him*. But that wasn't the same thing as what the truth was to *her*. But of course her truth was the truth, because she was the only one seeing things for what they were!" She slams a tiny fist down on the counter, like a toddler pitching a fit. Her face has gotten red, the slice of pizza in her other hand quivering. Her eyes are wild. She looks the exact opposite of how she usually looks, and while I've always been a bit put off by her primness, I far prefer it to this nightmare.

I want to tell her that I'm not sure what that means, but then she'll keep talking, and based on her level of drunkenness, I don't think we're going to get anywhere tonight. I have enough experience babysitting the drunk to know that the thing to do right now is to get her to bed. "Susan, why don't we—"

"Because here's the thing, Patty. Thomas was her *boss*. How could he be such an idiot?"

I blink. It would seem that my innards have been vacuumed out of my body. *Patty*. Intellectually, I know that our names are close enough that a drunk person who knows—knew—both of us could make that mistake. Especially when that person is having a conversation with me that would be much better suited to someone my mother's age. Regardless, hurt spreads through me like a contagion.

Susan, who clearly didn't catch her slipup, goes on. "I mean, I'm sure you agree with me, Presley, this is the kind of thing your generation is talking about all the time with all this 'Me Too' stuff. *Power dynamics.* And you know what? There are a lot of things about your generation I don't quite get, but that? That, I get. But this is different than the 'honey, sweetie' thing."

I pinch the inside of my arm to bring myself back into the room, shake my head a little. "Uh, what do you mean?" I ask, in spite of the fact that I know I've got to get this woman to bed.

"I mean that *he* was her *boss.* Her boss, Presley! She's an ambitious woman and he was her boss! She claims to have wanted the affair to start, too, that it was mutual. Which, I mean, God bless her for admitting that to me. Now that I'm saying it to you, I can't quite believe this lunch actually happened. But, anyway, apparently she also wanted the affair to start, and then, you know, they slept together, like, three times, and then she wanted it to end, but ending it was much trickier for her than it would have been for him, because how was she supposed to know that spurning him wouldn't affect her career? I mean, don't get me wrong. I'm not on her side. Because my response to that question is: 'Well, honey, maybe you shouldn't have slept with your boss in the first place.' Maybe that makes me a bad feminist or something, but I don't care. Don't sleep with your boss. That's a great way to avoid a situation like this."

"Totally," I say, not that I necessarily think, as Susan herself is acknowledging, it's that simple. The one simple thing I do know is that this day needs to end for this woman right now. "You know, Susan, it seems like today was a lot. I know I had a big day. I had to clean up a greenroom after Skrillex, and let me tell you, that really took it out of me."

Susan blinks thoughtfully. "I think I saw a skrillex on the Food Network."

"I'm sure you did. Come on, now." I gently put my hands on each of Susan's bony shoulders, and she hops off the kitchen stool. I hold her up when she inevitably stumbles, which isn't difficult, considering she weighs around forty pounds. Once she straightens up, I follow her down the hall into her bedroom.

She turns to me and pulls me in for a hug, though it's not as bone crushing as usual. She's slack in my arms, but I don't have to hold her up entirely. She's just leaning into me, and she sighs. "Will you spend the night, Presley?"

"Well, I have work in the morning," I say.

"Okay, of course," she says, and she tearfully pulls herself out of my arms and walks into her closet, which is bigger than my bedroom. "It can just be so lonely here, is all."

I grimace, resentment bubbling and sloshing around in me like soup. Goddammit. I won't leave her, but I certainly won't be happy about it. "You know what, I'm actually super tired, so crashing here might be a good idea. I can just get up early to go home and change. People come in late on Fridays, anyway."

She pokes her head out from her closet door and grins through her tearstained face. She looks like a damn nightmare. "You can stay in Lawrence's room, end of the hall on the right. Michael's room is full of my off-season clothes."

I give a thumbs-up, feel my face cringe. She disappears back into her closet for a few minutes, and stumbles out in long-sleeved silk pajamas that I thought people wore only in movies. She blows me an air kiss and disappears into yet another room off her bedroom, which according to the buzz of an electric toothbrush is her bathroom. If the woman has her wits about her enough to remember to brush her teeth, then my work here is clearly done.

I slip back into the kitchen, where I wipe down the counter, shiny with the pizza grease Susan dripped all over it. I place the box in the fridge, which isn't difficult considering it's mostly empty. I refill my water glass, and it occurs to me to refill Susan's, an instinct left over from taking care of Patty, before I remember that Susan's hangover is not my responsibility. I guess Patty's weren't either, but the consequences were mine to deal with, whereas I'll be out of this place at the ass crack of dawn. Also, the thought of going back into that bedroom, of seeing Susan passed out in her bed, or of what she might say if she's awake, is enough to deter me.

I slowly push open the last door on the right in the hallway to a simple enough bedroom. Neutral-colored carpet, mahogany bed with a navy-blue duvet. Framed UVA paraphernalia above the bed, a signed Yankees poster on the wall perpendicular to it. Even though it's undeniably shittier, I long for my East Village closet-of-a-bedroom. I open a wooden dresser next to the bed in search of something to sleep in. I guess it'll be an oversize T-shirt and the granny panties I already have on, aka my exact sleep uniform every night, except usually the T-shirt belongs to me, not Lawrence Clark. Sure enough, in the only stroke of luck I've managed to have all night in this apartment, the drawer I open contains T-shirts. I pull out the first one I see, a Vanderbilt T-shirt that looks old and soft. I press it to my face, inhale that Tide smell. My shoulders relax. Then it occurs to me how fucking creepy this is, and I yank it away.

I know Clark is tall, but it still surprises me how low the shirt's hem dangles over my thighs, and my media-sickened brain can't help but feel somewhat adorable, as a girl sleeping over at some guy's place in just his T-shirt and her underwear, all long hair and bare legs and with no choice but to swim in some big man's clothes. Except that I haven't just hooked up with anyone; I'm alone in the bed of a guy with whom the most intimate interactions I've had involved *Pokémon* and discussing his sexually inappropriate father. Not to mention that I'm here taking care of his drunk, cuckolded mother.

I slide into bed to find it mercifully comfortable, the sheets clean and soft. I go to turn off the bedside lamp and notice that there's a lava lamp beside it. Retro. I pull up my texts with Clark and realize that he sent me a YouTube clip of John Early and Kate Berlant and had written, Do you know these two? with the crying-laughing emoji. I check the time stamp—last Thursday, right in the rush of a two-show day when Emma or Peanut or the interns were likely blowing up my phone and I must have totally missed it. I feel a tingle of guilt, but it's too late to address it now.

I snap a photo of the lava lamp, write, Pretty groovy, and send it to Clark. I start typing out a text to Izzy that I won't be home tonight but switch apps and check her location first: the dot hovers on Lorimer Street, in Williamsburg. Julia's place. So she won't be wondering where I am anyway. This disappoints me, and the disappointment is humiliating. I set my alarm for six thirty to give myself enough time to wake up, get the hell out of here before Susan is awake, rush home, change, and double back to midtown for work. I turn the light off, close my eyes. Dreamland does not take me.

I see Susan looking me dead in the face and calling me Patty. Pressure builds behind my eyes. I don't want to be here, in this apartment. I want to be tucked away in my room that would make a much better closet, Isabelle on the other side of the wall. I don't want to have this familiar feeling creeping in, the worry that down the hall things are not okay. That Susan is drunkenly weeping, that she'll choke on her vomit, that she is going to wake up with a hangover both physical and moral, making things awkward between us, when I asked for none of this.

The familiarity in it brings its own distinct brand of agony, too. Like pressing on a bruise. I dig the heels of my hands into my eyes to keep it all in as I'm consumed with the wash of knowing, even though it's nothing new, that Patty is gone. I won't take care of her ever again.

....

I must have fallen asleep at some point, because my alarm goes off and I have no idea where the fuck I am. As soon as I silence it, last night comes seeping back in like blood through a Band-Aid. This bed is so soft and warm it's like it's physically holding me in a hug, enveloping me like Clark himself did that time he hugged me before Susan and I saw *The Band's Visit*. The intimacy of that, of thinking of him hugging me while I'm lying in his bed, is bizarre and humiliating enough to propel me up. I need to get dressed and sneak out of here before Susan's up anyway.

I make the bed and fold Clark's T-shirt, leaving it on top of the duvet. I creep as quietly as I can down the hall. There's a series of ornately framed little drawings of flowers hanging on the wall, and I can't help but pause when I see the artist's signature. Mo-fuckin'-net.

I have to pass through the kitchen to get to the front door. Susan and I make eye contact right as I walk in. We both ignore the fact that my careful tread was a clear indication that I had been trying to sneak out. Susan smiles at me, but it's heavy and sad—I can see the effort her face is making. While she doesn't look as bad as she did last night (I'm not sure how that would be possible), I can't say she looks *good*. Her face is swollen, her eyes puffy. Her hair is pulled back in a banana clip and she's wearing a terry cloth headband in what I can only assume is an attempt to tamp down her frizzy flyaways. It isn't helping much. She's wrapped in a fluffy bathrobe that makes her look twice, maybe three times as big as usual. Still tiny, though.

"Good morning, Presley," she says.

"Hey, Susan."

"Do you want some coffee?"

"I think I better head out, actually. Thanks, though."

She nods. Takes a breath. "Listen, I know you have to skedaddle, but could you sit down for a minute?"

I swallow, wishing I knew how to say no to this woman. I take a seat at one of the stools on the kitchen island, while she stirs milk into her coffee. "If we're going to chat, I actually would like to revise my previous answer to the coffee question." She nods, her back to me, and reaches for a cabinet. She sets a steaming mug down in front of me, remembering from Christmas that I take it black. She leans on the other side of the kitchen island, and I'm glad she's not sitting in a stool next to me. I take a sip. It burns my mouth.

"I want to apologize for last night," Susan says. "Yesterday's lunch obviously . . . rattled me, but it was really inappropriate for me to ask you to come here and listen to me rant and rave and stay the night just because I didn't want to be alone."

Her humiliation is so plain on her face, my heart splinters. "It's all good, Susan. Not a big deal."

"I'm really embarrassed."

"Well, there's no need for that. We're friends, right? Friends call each other when they're in a bad spot."

She smiles a little at this, but it doesn't reach her eyes. "That's kind of you to say, Presley, but it would have been much more appropriate for me to have called a friend my own age, but all those women are mostly the wives of Thomas's friends and I just . . ."

"Totally get it."

"I'm still sorry you had to take care of me like that."

"Don't sweat it. It's not like I'm lacking experience in that arena." Susan looks stricken, her brows flying up her forehead as much as her Botox will allow, before her face crumples and she puts her head in her hands.

"Oh, Presley," she says through what I'm sorry to report are choked sobs. "I know Patty had her de-de-demons. I know she made things hard for you. I'm so, so sorry for that. But I re-really hate that she's gone."

I freeze. My throat is a pile of wet towels. The dual darknesses I felt last night, missing Patty and hating Patty, are piling up behind my eyes again. If I utter one word, if I blink even one time, it'll all come tumbling out.

Luckily, Susan carries the torch. "I really left her behind, you know? I could, just, ugh . . ." She pulls her head out of her hands and looks up to the ceiling, wiping her eyes. "I could feel her *hating* me for making Vanderbilt work for myself, after she left Nashville to go back to Eulalia. But I could have called her more, visited more. But I just avoided it. I told myself it was normal for childhood friends to grow apart. But why is that considered normal? What's normal about distancing yourself from the people who knew you at your core, your deepest and truest self? And the joke is on me, you know, because now I want to talk to her more than ever. I want to talk to her so badly. And I can't." She grabs a nearby dish towel to dab at her eyes.

"She didn't hate you," I say. Mortifyingly, several of my own tears spill over with the words. I wipe them away quickly with the heels of my hands, even though there's a surprising relief in them falling.

"Oh, honey," Susan says, hurrying around the island and closing the distance between us. She has to reach up to the elevated stool, and her tiny arms encircle my neck. Before I know it, my face is in the fluffy collar of her robe, and it smells clean and it's a relief to be buried somewhere, though I can feel it getting wet as I cry on it. I know it's time to pull away when I feel snot racing to join the mix as well.

She lets go and turns to grab a box of tissues sitting next to a neat stack of mail on the counter. We blow our noses and wipe at our eyes. "I don't mean to usurp your pain," she says to me.

Something like relief, a satisfaction in being recognized, announces itself in my chest. I nod. "It's good to share it," I say. "I feel like . . . I don't know. Because of how hard everything was with her, and I guess there was always a part of me that was, like, waiting for her to get better or something." I choke on the words. Take a breath. "It's like, we both have unfinished business with her, and I guess it makes me feel better to know I'm not the only one, maybe."

Susan nods. "I think this is a normal part of grief. To feel all the unfinished business."

"But you shouldn't feel bad, though, about not calling more, or whatever. She could be nasty to people she was jealous of." I exhale, and Susan hands me the dish towel.

"I don't know," Susan says, echoing my sigh. "A part of me knows you're right. It would have been strange for me to be checking in on someone who didn't seem to want much to do with me. But I never stopped loving her, so . . ." She wipes at her eyes, somehow still having tears left in her tiny body. "And I owed her, is the thing."

"What do you mean?" I ask, taking a sip of my coffee, trying to anchor myself to something.

"She saved my life once."

"Oh. Right." I've been curious about this since the first time she mentioned it, the first time I was here in this apartment, actually. But I haven't pressed, and it's migrated to the back of my mind.

Susan looks down at her hands on the counter. "It's a pretty harrowing story."

"You don't have to tell me," I say.

She sits down on the stool next to me and takes a breath. "We were seventeen." Here we go, I guess. "You know the swimming hole in Eulalia? We had gotten kinda sick of it, and there was a, kind of an estuary in Tutton, nearby, that apparently a lot of kids from Tutton High frequented. I had met a guy from Tutton High that past fall, and I had a little crush on him." She shakes her head, smiling a little. "We would talk on the phone sometimes, but I hadn't seen him in a long while, and he called to say a bunch of guys were going to the Tutton swimming hole that Saturday, and invited us to join. So we got in my little Datsun and drove out there. There were a few girls swimming, but we didn't really talk to them. They eventually left. Patty and I waited and waited, but the guys never showed up. Patty wanted to stay out later than I did. At the time, I thought it was because she was eager to meet my guy's friends, and I was frustrated, because I wanted to get home. But I think now she was probably just trying to be a good friend to me. She knew I really wanted to see that boy." She looks down at the counter and sighs.

"Anyway, night was starting to fall, so we decided to go home, and my car broke down on the way. We probably shouldn't have driven it out there in the first place, it had all these problems. But I loved that car. This was way before cell phones, mind you, so there me and Patty were, in the middle of a country road somewhere between Tutton and

Eulalia, with no way to get in contact with anyone. We didn't really have a choice but to wait and hope someone would help us. Eventually, this guy, middle-aged, kinda balding, gross, redneck type, pulls over to help us. We pop the hood for him, and he takes a look, and says we'll need to have this car towed probably, and luckily for us, he's happy to give us a ride back to Eulalia. I readily agreed to this, my naive self happy to have found a way out of this situation, much as I didn't want to leave my car by the side of the road."

A sick dread winds its way through me. Two teenage girls, alone, on a dark country road, picked up by a man. A stranger. Susan continues, "I could tell that Patty didn't want to get in the car, but we really didn't have much of a choice. So we got in, and after a while, he tells us we have to make a stop at his house, first, because he has to give his mother her medicine. I didn't think much of this, but Patty started hollerin'—screaming. God, I really remember it. There was a gas station in the distance, and Patty was yelling that if he didn't pull over and drop us off at the gas station she was going to, excuse my language"— and Susan starts laughing a little here—"piss all over his truck bench. She was making such a racket, he probably thought she was completely crazy. I know I did. But he pulled over, and we got out of the car in our wet clothes, went into the gas station, where Patty called home and your grandfather came and picked us up. To be honest, I thought she was being paranoid. But then about a month later Patty called me and told me to come over right away. She shoved a newspaper in my face. There was a mug shot of the man who had picked us up, he had been arrested for the rape and murder of a Tutton girl who had been missing."

I close my mouth, as my jaw had basically hit the floor. Susan sighs. "It's crazy to think I was ever that naive. But Eulalia was a safe, small town, and I was sheltered, and it just didn't occur to me that something like that could happen to us. But Patty was always so street-smart, always one step ahead."

"God," I say. "I don't know what to say. Holy shit. Men are *trash*." Of course, my first reaction should be gratitude that nothing happened to Susan and my mom. But also of course, the thing that flies out of my mouth is that.

Susan looks at me, surprised. Then a smile spreads over her face. She starts laughing, a low rumble that comes from her belly, and covers her mouth. I can't help but laugh, too. It is not funny that my mother and Susan were almost raped and killed by some redneck murderer, that Susan feels she can never repay my mom. It isn't funny that men do this shit, that they're violent and they cheat. But from the way Susan and I sit at her kitchen island laughing our asses off, you wouldn't know it.

CHAPTER 28

It isn't unusual that I'm headed to an open mic to hear Agatha on a Wednesday night, and it isn't unusual that Izzy is accompanying me. What *is* unusual is that Izzy is bringing a date. That's right, tonight I'm meeting the famous Julia. When she first walked into our apartment, fresh off the L train from Williamsburg (but thankfully not in one of those tiny beanies everyone who lives in Williamsburg seems to wear), my first thought was that Izzy's creepy pool photo was cute but did not do her justice. The girl is stunning. She's got this curly, shoulder-length brown hair, clear skin, exactly Izzy's model height, a nose that really makes itself known but works. She and Izzy do a chaste little peck when she enters, and it jolts me. I didn't know Izzy had become a pecking person.

"The famous Presley!" Julia said as she gave me a quick hug and a kiss on the cheek, a move I would never have been able to pull off gracefully. "It's awesome to finally meet you."

"Yeah, likewise," I said, my eyes sliding over to Izzy, whose eyes hadn't left Julia since she walked in.

Now we're sitting at Old Man Hustle, thankfully just a few blocks over from our apartment. This show, "Mystery Meat," hosted by up-

and-comers (or so they'd like to believe) Isaac Hoffman and Jonah Kurtz, has been getting good lineups, though I don't think half the people in this tiny bar knew they were going to be attending a comedy show tonight. Agatha is a regular here.

"Bell told me about Agatha, and about how you're hoping to get her on *Gary Madden*. I looked her up on Instagram and was cracking up at her Cate Blanchett impression," Julia told me as we power walked across First Avenue, the red hand blinking.

I didn't realize my face had screwed up in confusion until Izzy explained with something akin to bashfulness, "Julia calls me Bell sometimes." *Bell*. A bit cutesy, no? But the rare softness in Izzy's voice sparked an immediate effort to smooth over my face. I didn't want her to feel embarrassed.

Now a small girl in glasses I haven't seen before takes the stage. "Hi, I'm Christine. And I'm unemployed at the moment, anyone else? 'Fun-employed' I believe they're calling it these days." She gets one whoop from the back and nods at that person. "Nice, shout-out to us. Yeah, I used to have a job, but I got fired. I know. Boo. I worked in publishing, because like most people in that industry, I'm privileged but poverty curious." I let out an appreciative laugh. I am one of the only ones. "Anyway, so I love books. Or I used to, before I got fired for not reading them fast enough. Or maybe it was for being late. Or maybe it was because I didn't quite get that emails addressed to you from your boss are meant to be either responded to, acted upon, or both." Julia laughs. It's sharp, high-pitched at first—a yelp, followed by quiet chuckling. It's unattractive, which makes me trust her a little.

"Anyway, books. I've always really loved the *Sisterhood of the Traveling Pants* series. Where my Ann Brashares heads at?" Izzy whoops and claps, and there's a smattering of applause from a table to the left, full of girls who look to be about our age. "So, for those of you who don't know, *The Sisterhood of the Traveling Pants* is a series of books—nay, life-changing works of art—about a group of four best friends, high school girls. They're about to embark on their first summer apart, all going off to have their own separate adventures, and they're thrift store stopping. And they find a pair of pants that magically fits all four of them perfectly." Her eyes bug out and she makes a face of mock shock. "It's really crazy. I mean, other than the fact that one of them has a bit of an ass on her, they're all thin and approximately the same height, but we're meant to believe the only possible explanation has to be divine intervention christening their friendship as something greater than all of them. These books are—" She makes a chef's kiss motion.

"These books are not, like, overtly feminist, I guess especially not by, like, today's standards. But in my fledgling preteen years they felt kind of radical? Like, yes, there are guys in the books and some of them have some love story action, but really these books are just about these girls. Their relationships with each other, their personal growth as they navigate tough family stuff, figuring out where they want to go to college, who they want to be in the world, et cetera. Not told through the lens of a romance. The guys are secondary." Julia claps along appreciatively. "But something occurred to me the other day. Something disturbing. I want to remind those of you who are unfamiliar with the series, and even those of you who are, that the author's last name is Brashares. And these books are about a shared article of clothing. A *shared* article of clothing. And her last name is Bra. Shares. Say it with me: Bra. Shares. And she wrote about *legs* instead of *boobs*!" Izzy, Julia, and I laugh, but she's definitely lost a few tables here. Apparently, people didn't show up tonight for feminist wordplay.

I keep sneaking glances at Izzy and Julia. Despite the fact that Izzy warned me she was falling in love, I find myself aghast at their obvious mutual obsession. They're holding hands under the table and keep looking at each other every time they laugh at something, which is often. *Too* often, considering the quality of some of these jokes. Don't get me wrong: Julia seems great. Kind, beautiful, with this calm energy. She probably meditates. Or worse, probably doesn't even need to. I know she has some job that involves coding, so she's also a genius, I guess. And in addition to all these objectively good things, I know, I can *see*, that she makes Izzy incandescently happy. I should be thrilled, relieved even.

I am not.

I'm uncomfortable. I keep shifting in my seat, averting my eyes so it doesn't look like I'm staring at the practically visible chemistry streaming between them every time their eyes meet. I realize I'm *embarrassed*. I mean, here she sits with her googly eyes, just exclaiming to the world, to New York City, a famously mean place, that she has feelings for Julia. It's all so *naked*. And she barely even knows this girl!

"Want another?" I turn to Julia's smooth voice as she nods at my empty pint glass. The smooth voice that has apparently coaxed my supposedly anticommitment best friend to fall in love in a matter of minutes.

Then again, if she's buying . . . "Sure," I say. She gets up, ducking her head so as not to block the view of the makeshift stage as the hosts step up to announce the next comedian, and I turn my attention to Isabelle. She watches Julia approach the bar as though she's rescuing a baby from a burning building. My attention is ripped back to the comedy when the hosts call out Agatha's name and she rushes up to the stage, smoothing her short black hair down. She grabs the microphone and pants into it. She rushed here from another open mic and will have to hurry to a different show after this one, but I know that's not the reason she's short of breath. I start filming, just as Julia walks into the lens frame with our drinks. Involuntarily, I huff out a bit of air, which Julia hears. She murmurs an apology as she sets my drink down, then ducks her head, basically army crawls back into her seat.

I jerk my eyes back to my phone, watching Agatha through it. She has her hands on her knees as she continues trying to catch her breath. The audience isn't quite sure how to react. Just as her breathing starts to slow a little, she holds up one pointer finger, asking for a sec. A ripple of nervous laughter. More panting. Then she looks up, sort of smiles, sort of grimaces, as the audience tentatively starts to believe she might say something, before she starts panting again. She suddenly pulls the microphone to her mouth, and the crowd leans forward slightly in anticipation. But instead of saying anything, she takes in another gasp of air, like she hasn't actually caught her breath yet. Several people laugh softly, but most people are confused.

Slowly, she straightens up, stretches out her neck, and lets out a few long exhales, like she's cooling down after a sprint. "Sorry," she huffs into the mic, shaking her head and widening her eyes. "I was somehow already out of breath from the circles I'm about to run around our dumbass hosts here." And like a twig, the tension is snapped, and everyone laughs, warm and loud. "I'm joking, I'm joking, I'm a *comedian*, for fuck's sake. Please give it up again for Isaac and Jonah. They're mensches for organizing this. Am I allowed to say 'mensch'?" She gets a small laugh here, then rolls her eyes. "Sorry, I obviously am. I just love asking white-guy questions." Putting on a deep, silly voice, she continues: "*Am I allowed to say that? You can't say anything anymore!*" She makes a frowny face and crosses her arms. Dropping the face, she says, "I'm like, 'Chad, you even *saying* you can't say anything is actually just highlighting the fact that you can actually say whatever the fuck you want without fear of repercussion.' Know what I mean?"

Someone whoops from the back, which Agatha ignores. I sit up straighter in my seat, knowing that everything she's said so far was just her getting into this crowd. Her practiced set, the one she would do for *Late Night Show* if we cinch the Friday slot, is about to begin. "Anyway, as our lovely hosts said, I'm Agatha Reddy. Yeah . . . my name is Agatha . . . I know that it's a very . . ." She looks down at the ground demurely for a second, then looks back up at the audience coquettishly, batting her eyelashes, tilting her head just so. "Sexy name." The audience laughs.

She slowly walks back and forth on the tiny makeshift stage, swinging her hips and twirling the mic cable slowly. "I know what the name evokes," she says in a silky voice. "You're thinking . . . knitting. Yarn. Gnarled fingers. Cozy murder mysteries . . ." Her voice is climbing higher and higher with each item she lists, as though she's reaching climax. "Throat lozenges. The faint smell of . . ." And now she actually yelps: "*Kitty litter!*" The audience roars at this, and she looks out over the crowd for a moment, soaking it in, giving them a beat to let it all out, before she abruptly clears her throat. "All right, all right, don't make it weird. Chill out. I know it's an unsexy name, okay? Even I hear it in bed and have to immediately dissociate." Good laugh here. "That might make it sound like I get laid a lot, which . . ." Some anticipatory chuckles here as Agatha pushes her face into a cringe. "I do!" She smiles, and the audience laughs. "Not a big dater, though. Because I am straight, and men aren't exactly people I trust. I can't"—she squints her eyes here and starts to draw out her words—"figure out . . . exactly . . . why that might be, though." The girls' night out group next to us is hollering and eating this up, definitely connecting with this sentiment more than the idea of *The Sisterhood of the Traveling Bra*.

"No, but literally the other day," Agatha says as she drapes a wrist over the empty microphone stand, "I had *just* had a breakthrough in therapy. The mother lode: dad stuff. Yeah. So I'm thinking . . . trust issues with men . . . we are on the way to solving that shit. Fixing things for the future. But then, of course, just as I leave the therapist's office, I get yet another news notification, baby. Another one has bitten the dust. And let me tell you: this was a bad one. Because nothing kills a boner harder than finding out that someone you looked up to as a comedy god is obsessed with not something disgusting but previously normalized, like forcing young women to have sex with him, but randomly whipping out his dick and masturbating in front of them." Some guy lets out an "oof" here, which causes Agatha to roll her eyes. "Please," she says, much to the joy of the girls' group. "I was so shocked, though. And I mean, other than the fact that it was something he talked about all the time, onstage, in interviews, on his TV show . . . it was totally out of left field." She holds for a laugh.

"No, but yeah, I don't really trust men or anything they really . . . do or say. Hard to picture myself getting married with that kind of baggage, do you know what I mean? But like . . . am I wrong for that? Or is anyone who willingly chooses to trust and spend the rest of her life with a man wrong? For instance, despite my youthful glow, thick head of hair, and general air of immaturity, I am at an age where a lot of my friends are signing up for old haggery and choosing to get married. A friend of mine recently got sentenced—excuse me, engaged—so I called her up to say congrats, hear the story, squeal when appropriate, et cetera. And after she tells me the story she goes, 'You know, A'—she gets too turned on by my full name—'I feel bad for complaining because it was all nice, but I'm just sort of bummed, because I wasn't surprised at all. Like, I fully knew exactly when and how it would happen.' And to *that*, all I have to say is: if I ever somehow get over my issues and fall in love with someone, and decide to spend the rest of my life with him, and then he manages to completely pull one over on me with a whole-ass proposal, I will be back to square one with the trust issues immediately, my friends." The audience is tittering, loving her, which is only going to make my video more convincing. Adrenaline pumps through me: I really think this could be the set I show Emma. The one that will get everything started for me and Agatha.

"I mean, think about it: if this man is able to carve out a time to talk to my parents (by the way, if *they* don't give me a heads-up, that's a whole other thing), buy a ring, plan some elaborate scheme, without me picking up on *any* of it? No. My response will not be to put my hands up to my mouth and scream and say yes. My response will be to immediately hold a knife to his throat and growl, *'What else have you been hiding?'*"

Yelps of recognition, laughter, claps. God, I love this. It's a shitty bar in a rat-infested neighborhood with sticky tables and a lip smudge on my beer glass I'm fairly certain I didn't leave. There can't be more than thirty people in here, most of whom probably don't give a rat's ass about any of these comedians. It might be disappointing to think about the amount of work that's gone into these jokes and for this to be the payoff. But it's glorious, to be led into laughter like this, for all of us to witness Agatha turn her dark thoughts into something funny. It's just the beginning for her, and we get to see it.

I know the show will book her. The exposure she'll get from it will be blinding, and she could go on to be in a writers' room, then produce a show, then run her *own* show that could be about whatever the fuck she wants. She could get slotted into more festivals, go on tour, get a special on Netflix or HBO one day. She could pay her bills with this shit.

"Amazing! She's totally amazing," Julia says as she leans closer to me, eyes sparkling and cheeks red with laughter. I have no choice but to agree with her.

CHAPTER 29

Clark and I have been texting here and there since he responded to the photo of his lava lamp with: Having another psychedelic experience with my mother, are we? He didn't press when I informed him that I was not, in fact, there to trip with Susan. I do find it a little strange that he didn't question why I was having a slumber party with his mom, but I guess I shouldn't be surprised. All evidence leads to the conclusion that he is a go-with-the-flow kind of guy. Our texts have been about lighthearted, random stuff. Like the other day:

Clark: What's your favorite movie?
Me: Why?
Clark: Because I want to know?
Me: I hate this question.
Clark: How come?
Me: Because if I tell you, you're going to assume something about me.
Clark: And what's that?
Me: Well, I don't know. But I have a whole theory around this.
Clark: Which is?

Me: Too long to type.

Clark: Tell me in person this weekend? I could use your help picking something for my mom's birthday, considering you two are
besties these days.

And so, yet again, I find myself shopping. Apparently, Susan's birthday is coming up, and Michael's already called in an order for some
fancy basket at this absurdly priced soap store and it needs to be picked
up by a certain time. It smells like a headache in here, this place in
Gramercy. Not far, actually, from where I first ran into Susan all those
months ago.

"Maybe I should get her something from here, too," Clark says. Just
then the guy behind the counter plops down a gigantic basket, filled
with seemingly everything in the shop: bottles and bars and fancy little
balls. "Or not," he says.

I turn over one of the bars of soap displayed on the counter. Forty-
five dollars. "Seems out of our assistant price range anyway."

Clark nods. "Yeah, especially now."

"What do you mean?" I ask.

"Oh, um . . . ," Clark says. "Thanks," he mutters to the guy behind
the counter as he takes the basket, which requires both hands. At least
now his embarrassingly basic outfit of khaki pants and a Canada Goose
coat is somewhat concealed. We leave the store. "Nothing."

"No, what?" I'm curious.

"Well, just, you know . . ." A blush is making itself known on his
cheeks, and I don't think it has much to do with windchill. "I'm not one
of those kids whose parents pay their rent or whatever. Or my credit
card bill, or anything like that. But there are certain things, things like
Mom's birthday, where I would have, before, used my dad's credit card."

"Ah," I say. "Thomas."

"Thomas," he says. "I just haven't. I mean, it's not like I'm shutting
him out entirely, we talk on the phone some, and he's come into the
city for a few awkward dinners. Like I told you at Christmas. Taking

his money feels sort of strange, I guess, though. Especially when it's for Mom."

I nod. "Or you could stick it to him by buying something outrageously expensive for her."

Clark laughs a little, trying and failing to shift the weight of the basket to one hip as we walk down Park Avenue. "I doubt anything I'd pick out would be up to snuff for Susan. Besides, you know how she is. She would way rather macaroni art than Prada, if it was something I made."

"Yeah, your mom is pretty obsessed with you."

"My mom is obsessed with *you*," he says. "It's like you're both in seventh grade and you're the coolest girl in school. Which I guess is just your energy, you know, generally."

I snort. "I was not the coolest girl in seventh grade. Or eighth. Or ever."

"You might not have known, but I bet you were."

I rub my ice-block hands together and blow on them for something to do with myself. "So, what *are* you gonna get your mom for her birthday? Shit, what should *I* get your mom for her birthday?"

"That's the problem," Clark says. "I have no idea. Also! What's this theory about people's favorite movies?"

"Oh, um . . . ," I say, adjusting to the sudden change of subject. The boundless energy of this guy. "I just think it can be a useless thing to ask someone, because I think— *Wait!*" I stop walking and Clark turns to me, his brown eyes wide.

"Are you okay?" he asks.

"I have an idea."

The basket makes it challenging to get through the door of the tiny East Village vintage shop. Thank goodness people have no taste: the Dolly Parton poster is still here. "Voilà," I say to Clark, flourishing my hand beneath the print like it's a new car he's just won in a game show.

"I don't get it," he says.

"What is there to get? A black-and-white portrait of Dolly Parton. Forty bucks. For Susan."

"Does my mom even like Dolly Parton?" he asks me.

"Yeah, it's a certified fact," I tell him. "We came here a few months ago and both kind of obsessed over the poster. She's a fan."

Clark puts the unwieldy basket down at his feet and looks at the print thoughtfully. "Are you sure?" he asks.

"Yes."

He looks at me, a question on that expressive, almost cartoonish face. "Should I be freaked out that you know something about my mom that I don't?"

I shrug. "It's perfectly normal for two women of southern origin to discuss the undeniable cultural contributions of Dolly. A bit weirder for a woman to do it with her son, I guess."

He shifts his weight from New Balance to New Balance, looking a bit agitated. Rather jarring, as I've never seen him look anything other than pretty damn affable. The whole golden retriever thing. "Well, maybe you should just get it for her, if it's, like, a thing between you two."

I'm not sure what to say to a twenty-six-year-old man who might be jealous of the time I'm spending with his mother. "No, it's all you" is what I go with. He picks up the basket and turns away from me.

"I'll think about it," he says as he abruptly exits the store, the drama of which is ruined by the doorframe clotheslining the ridiculous basket. I wait a beat, unsure what to do, then follow him out. He's standing on the sidewalk, shoulders hunched in the cold, still holding all that soap.

"Do you want me to take that?" I ask him.

"No," he snaps. I jump back a little, not that he said it loudly. But I don't know what to do with moody Clark. He slumps his shoulders, seeing my reaction. Looks down at his shoes. "I'm sorry, I didn't mean to sound harsh."

"It's fine." We stand in silence for a moment.

"Want to go get a beer?" he asks.

"Not if you're gonna be a jerk."

That blush is back in his cheeks again. "I won't be a jerk, I promise."

I'm not exactly in a rush to get home. Izzy is painting her dresser, had mentioned Julia was going to help. I'm not sure I'm ready to be zapped by the electricity flowing between them again.

We go to one of my favorite spots, the Gray Mare on Second Avenue. Izzy and I had been awaiting its opening with much anticipation, and we were right to: it's perfectly pubby and cozy. Pleasant without being cutesy. No frills. Darker the farther you get back into the bar but bathed in warm light by the windows in front. Which is where we sit, at a little table. I would have preferred to sit side by side at the bar like we did at Analogue, but this table provides a little spot for our third entity, the damn basket. Plus, it's nice to have an extra stool for our coats and scarves and hats. That's the thing I hate most about winter in New York: I'm always so weighed down by all my shit.

The stools are on the smaller side, and I laugh a little at the way Clark has to fold himself over to sit and rest his elbows on the table, crumpling his plain navy-blue pullover. I take my beanie off and immediately wonder how fucked up my hair looks. Then I'm annoyed with myself for wondering. Why should I care?

"I'm sorry for getting weird for a minute there," he says.

"It's okay," I say, shrugging, like it didn't put me on high alert.

"No, seriously. I was weird, and then rude, and I'm most sorry for being rude."

"It's seriously fine, we really don't have to have a whole conversa—"

"I think, if I'm being honest, I'm pretty shaken up by the whole—by everything going on with my family. I don't, like, talk about it much." Doesn't seem that way to me. "I don't want to make other people feel weird by talking to them about it, because the whole thing is so uncomfortable. I'm so glad I have Mike, who's way smarter than me. Mike wasn't super surprised by the whole thing, but I was. I really was. And I think that's the thing that's really getting me, like I thought I really knew my dad. And I clearly just didn't. And then back there . . . it's obviously so stupid, I mean, it's not actually a big deal that I didn't know my mom likes Dolly Parton. But it just . . . I don't know. It 'triggered' me, I guess," he says, throwing air quotes up around the word "triggered."

"That makes sense," I say. Maybe it's that I know his family. Maybe it's that he's met my family. Maybe it's that something about the way he tends to look at me when we talk, so simply open, like he is interested in what I have to say without any trace of anticipating how he will respond to it, makes me want to contribute. Whatever it may be, I say, "I get it. It's one thing to know, like, intellectually that your parents are full, independent people, and that you only know a specific chunk of them. It's another thing to really be confronted with that." Clark nods enthusiastically, silently urging me to go on. "Your mom just told me a story the other day about my mom that just, I don't know. It showed me a side of her I didn't know was there." A side where she took care of someone, instead of demanding care from someone else. Both because I do not want to answer follow-up questions about this and because I would like to know, I ask, "How are you, like, doing with all of it?"

"Um . . . ," he says, slouching in his seat. "Honestly, I go back and forth. Sometimes, I just want them to figure it out, one way or another. Like, the limbo is tough. But then I think about how it'll actually be if they decide to split, and . . . yeah, I can't say I like that. Makes the waiting not seem so bad."

Divorce: both a word that defined so much of my generation's childhood and a concept with which I am not even in the same hemisphere. The only firsthand experience I have with a marriage is my grandparents'. My grandmother would occasionally snap at my grandfather for, like, not being able to find the cheese in the refrigerator even though it was *right* there. "If it were a snake, it'd have bitten you by now" was as testy as they ever got with each other, to my knowledge. Mostly, each was always patting the other's hand while it rested on the kitchen table, grocery store flowers brought home for my grandma just because. I know there had to have been intense arguments about Patty, but they happened behind closed doors. I think my grandparents felt like I had been through enough, and they didn't want to add exposure to their fights to the list of my childhood traumas. Whatever their disagreements were with regard to how to handle Patty (kick her out, cut her off, give ultimatums, give her another chance, raid her room, follow her after work, etc.), I suspect they always put each other first in all of it: my grandpa worried about how Patty's condition or latest fuckup would affect my grandmother's emotional state; my grandmother was concerned about how the Patterns of Patty would affect my grandpa's day-to-day.

They're a team, a unit. And the value of that is understandable to me: I'm sure it's nice to be taken care of, to know you're someone else's top priority. Whole families and so much love can sprout from that kind of partnership, and fracturing it is a tragedy. But also life is possible to get through solo, and sometimes another person is just yet another thing to tend to.

And for Clark, I mean, the kid has had a pretty charmed life. I'm guessing Susan and Thomas didn't fight in front of him and Michael, what with Susan's pinched smiles and refusal to be visibly ruffled. They were probably a shiny emblem of love in Clark's head, probably what he aspired to with that lawyer ex-girlfriend of his. Focused, successful, social, in love. Sympathy and resentment braid themselves together as I look at him, using the back of his large hand to wipe his mouth after a particularly foamy sip of his beer.

He says, "Michael's been helping me see that, like, as mad or hopeful or whatever as I am, this isn't about me. The person who's the most hurt in all this has got to be Mom. And so that's what I tell myself: I don't know what's going to happen, so the top thing I should be doing right now is trying to be there for her. And I'll support her whichever way she ends up deciding to go. And trying to support my dad, too. Don't get me wrong," he says, looking earnestly into my face, "I think he's an idiot. I obviously don't think it's okay to be weird to women at work. Or cheat on your wife. But he's also my dad. And he was being selfish, for sure, but I don't think his intention was to hurt anyone, or make anyone feel bad. And he should have known better, but I don't know that he did. He was being a dumbass."

"Yeah," I say. I balk at the idea that men like Thomas can be misogynists to their subordinates at work and then have their sons explain it away as them being "dumb." Then I think, Emma and I do that all the time, with "Dumbass or Devil?" And *then* I think about Patty and the time she drunkenly backed her beat-up Mazda into my neighbor's new Lexus. The neighbor had a kid in my grade. I was angry and embarrassed, sure that what she did was wrong. But I also know she didn't intentionally destroy anyone's property, and maybe that matters, somehow.

"Anyway," Clark says, shaking his head and leaning over his beer, peering into it. "What's this story about our moms?"

"Oh. Nothing," I say, unsure how to be socially graceful while explaining that our mothers narrowly avoided rape and murder in the seventies.

Clark shrugs and looks up at me, and the way the weak afternoon light streams through the windows makes his brown eyes look almost golden. "I was hoping for something scandalous," he says. He's smiling, his earlier annoyance at my knowing things about his mother that he didn't clearly gone.

"Sure," I say, "because that's what your family needs. Another scandal."

Clark laughs, the laugh I noticed at the Cellar, where he throws his head back, the one that comes from deep within his gut. He doesn't think twice about it, doesn't try to tamp it down or make it palatable or cute. As far as laughs go, it's a very good one. "I meant, like, cow tipping or drinking moonshine or something," he says.

"There aren't that many cows in Eulalia, city slicker."

"Moonshine, though?"

"Delicious beverage."

"I'm sure. That's all I'm saying: I'd love to know if Susan's tried it. When Susan decides she's gonna be a good time, there's no stopping her. You should have seen her on my twenty-first birthday."

"What did y'all do?"

"Karaoke."

"No way. Susan?"

"Yeah, she took one tequila shot and was, like, bombed."

"She's the smallest woman in the world, so . . ."

He laughs again. "Exactly."

"What did she sing?"

"Céline Dion. 'That's the Way It Is.'"

Thankfully, Clark tips his head back to drink his beer, and I follow suit, so I have a cover for the knot that's formed in my throat, the squeeze in my chest. Patty spinning around in our living room, drunk off her ass, crooning that song. Sounding pretty good, actually. I swallow.

I say, "I'm trying to decide whether I want to make fun of you for spending your twenty-first birthday with your mom, or if I think it's kind of cool."

"You can't make fun of me, because as I recently pitched a fit over, you two are friends yourselves."

"Touché. And it was hardly a fit."

Clark shrugs, taps his pointer finger in a quick staccato on his beer glass. "So. The movie thing."

"Ah, yes," I say, repositioning myself on my stool, preparing to pontificate. "I just think the whole conversation that follows that question is usually bullshit. Because most people use it as an opportunity to, like, brand themselves, or seem impressive, or something, by saying what they think the *best* movie they've ever seen is. But appreciating a great movie is not the same thing as it being *your favorite* movie. And I think most people's favorite movie is probably something they're comforted by, which is pretty personal, and probably not something that's, like, critically acclaimed."

Clark blinks. "Maybe most of the people you hang out with take it that way. I have no qualms about readily telling anyone who asks that my favorite movie is *The Emperor's New Groove*."

I blink. "The one with the talking llama?"

"Emperor Kuzco, yes. And don't forget Yzma. *Is that . . . MY voice!*" he says in a high-pitched yelp, I guess quoting the movie. People from the next table turn their heads in confusion, and I put my left hand up, shielding my face in embarrassment but also laughing.

"Okay, but maybe you're just being ironic. Maybe you just want me to know that you're too confident to care about appearing impressive in the face of film snobs. To seem above it all," I say.

He furrows his brow and looks at me as though I've just brayed like a donkey instead of making a valid point. He shakes his head. "No, freak. It's just my favorite movie. I saw it in theaters when I was a kid and was obsessed with it, apparently demanded to be taken back to see it *three times*. I was Kronk for Halloween. Watching it feels like, I don't know, putting on a warm blanket. I watch it sometimes when I'm hungover. And it holds up. It's so funny. And sweet. I love it more than any other movie. Which is what a favorite movie is. Despite your theory."

"Okay, fine. I agree that that's what people's answer *should* be, I'm just saying a lot of people probably aren't real about it."

"Well, fuck those people," Clark says. Adam tells people his favorite movie is a Jean-Luc Godard film, French New Wave cinema. I'm relieved, perturbed, and a little sad that I can't remember the title.

"Yeah, fuck those people," I agree.

"So. Presley, I will ask you again. What is your favorite movie?"

I take a long sip of my beer. I'd really rather not do this. I usually avoid this question by turning the conversation into the meaning of the question itself. Adam was persistent in asking, but it was easy enough to distract him by discussing films generally, how there are too many factors at play in a single film to narrow it down to one. But I know my answer.

"Oh, come on," Clark says. "Do you think I'm gonna judge you? My favorite movie is about a talking llama, as you so disrespectfully pointed out."

"I don't want to say."

"Okay, I'll guess. Is it *Bridesmaids*?"

"Because I'm a woman and love comedy? No, but I do love that movie."

"Me too. Is it *Pulp Fiction*?"

I shake my head.

He thinks for a minute, staring at me with narrowed eyes. "*Forrest Gump?*"

"No, but you're getting warmer."

"Interesting," he says, putting his big face into one of his big hands. He sits up straight suddenly, snapping his finger. "I know! What's that one with Dolly Parton, where she's the hairdresser, and the girl dies?"

"It's not *Steel Magnolias*. Which, how are you familiar with that movie, by the way?"

"Susan. I guess somewhere in my mind, I did know she was a fan, after all."

"Ah."

"I was thinking southern. . . ."

"The movie's not southern. I said warmer because of one of the actors."

He narrows his eyes at me, studying me, a smile tugging at the corners of his mouth. "*Saving Private Ryan?*"

I shake my head. "Nope."

He throws his hands up and looks to the ceiling in mock exasperation. "Presley, for the love of God, please just tell me!"

I swallow. "It's *Sleepless in Seattle*."

"Well, Christ!" he says, slapping a hand down on the table, again inviting looks from the people next to us. "Why wouldn't you just say that?"

I sigh. "Because. Okay. I love Nora Ephron, of course. Duh."

"My mom has a great story about how she was rude to her at a dinner party once."

"Susan was rude to Nora Ephron?" I ask incredulously.

"No, other way around."

I nod. "That tracks."

"So, anyway . . . ," Clark says, making a rotating motion with his hand, encouraging me to keep going.

"It's just so blatantly her most . . . *romantic* movie. I mean, it's ridiculous. Two people agreeing to meet on the top of the Empire State

Building, based off just vibes basically. In *You've Got Mail* and *When Harry Met Sally*, those characters spend tons of time talking. They talk and talk and talk and roam around the city and talk some more. Even when they don't know they're talking, they're talking. They don't fucking talk in *Sleepless*. It's basically a fairy tale for adults," I explain.

"And what's wrong with that?" Clark says.

I blanch, and Clark laughs. "It just doesn't really feel like me, I guess." It does feel like Patty, though.

"I don't know that I've ever seen it," Clark says. "How about we watch it sometime and I can let you know if I think it's as far from you as you think it is."

I'm reaching for my beer when he says this, and I accidentally flinch at the suggestion and knock over my pint glass. Luckily, it's not totally full and I catch it quickly, but some of it sloshes onto the table. "Oh shit, my bad," I say, getting up and heading to the bar. I tell my heart rate to slow down and take a deep breath as I pinch a pile of napkins. There's no reason to panic. Surely he meant that we could watch the movie together as friends. Family friends.

I return to the table and mop up the small beer puddle. "You good?" Clark asks.

"Yeah, yeah," I say, setting aside the soggy pile of napkins. "Anyway, I comfort myself with an article I read recently, talking about how Nora said *Sleepless* isn't meant to be a straightforward romantic movie, it's meant to be a movie about romantic movies. When I think about it as cultural commentary, and not just a sappy love story, I feel better about myself."

"Ah, yes, as long as someone who works at a fancy magazine has given you permission to like it," Clark says, a playful, annoying grin tugging at his mouth. I give him the finger and he laughs.

"You'd think the actual New Yorker would have some respect for *The New Yorker*," I say.

"Hey, you're just as much a New Yorker as I am. You live here, don't you?"

There's a small bloom of pride in my chest. I know my address.

And not that I need approval or to be, I don't know, *ordained* by this frat boy, but something about someone from the city stamping off on my New Yorker status is satisfying.

We finish our beers, chatting about movies, about Clark's visits to Eulalia, how jarring it was coming from the city. Work (bosses), and how Clark's promotion being made official has been delayed. I don't ask Clark how his journey with the apps is going, don't make sure that ex-girlfriend of his is letting him be. That's none of my business.

CHAPTER 30

Surely, it's no surprise to learn I'm not a Valentine's Day person. I don't care enough to be overtly anti; I don't feel shamed or indignant for being single. Patty, on the other hand, annually took the day pretty hard, except that she got to use it as an excuse to drink her daily vodka cranberries, because on that day the drink was festive instead of a red (pink) flag. Isabelle, who loves a theme, usually gets me a little card and some chocolates or something, which is nice. Except there was nothing left out on our coffee table this year when I stumbled out of my bedroom, Izzy having gone straight to work from Julia's, where she spent the night. I'm seeing her later, as Susan is taking the two of us out for a postwork drink.

Fret not, the day does not turn out to be giftless for me—like all the women in my office, I receive a rose with a little generic printed card from Gary (really from Cora, his assistant). It's pandering and strange, but the intentions are pure. Peanut almost immediately steals mine and keeps holding it between his teeth and doing a likely culturally inappropriate imitation of a matador dance.

Adam and I have a run-in at the coffee machine, more awkward than usual, I think, considering the day. A day when the feelings he knows I had for him are meant to be celebrated and reciprocated (according to Hallmark, anyway). The ache in my chest that's replaced our nightly phone calls is getting duller by the day, but now there's a pang in noticing that he's wearing a sweater I haven't seen before, a sweater whose acquisition I would have been consulted on two months ago. We approach the machine at the same time, and even though I've asked him not to speak to me, there are people milling about, and besides, it would just be plain noncollegial for one of us to actually leave. Plus, I don't want him to think it would, like, *kill* me to converse with him.

"Uh, after you," he says, making a weird bow gesture I would have teased him for were we still friends. Or whatever it was we were.

I shake my head. "Emma's not even here yet, so you go ahead." He nods a little, blushing, and pulls a mug from the cabinet. He opens his mouth to speak but says nothing, and I can see his mind spinning, wondering how literally he's supposed to take the mandate to not speak to me. "So, how are things?" I ask pointedly, to prove that I am capable of a kitchen chat. May even be indifferent to it.

He nods in quick succession while he punches his desired coffee (almond milk latte) into the fancy machine. "Good, good. Things are good. Can't complain. I mean, everything isn't, you know, like, hunky-dory. Like I . . . but I know I can't. Yeah," he says, blushing furiously and staring at his mug as it fills with his pansy drink.

"Sounds cool," I say, just to fill the air.

"How are things with you?" he asks.

"Good." He nods and grabs his coffee the second the machine has emitted its final spit. He opens his mouth, then closes it, then repeats the process. It's painful to watch.

"Catch ya later," I say, dismissing him. "And happy Valentine's Day," I add to his back as he exits the kitchen. I see those narrow shoulders tense, and I feel scooped out, hollow.

The midtown St. Regis for Valentine's Day drinks was Susan's idea. Apparently, they make an excellent dirty martini, but I am not in the world of Don Draper, so this does not appeal to me. Susan's been dying to get to know Izzy, and vice versa. Isabelle is going to go meet up with

Julia after our girls' heart day happy hour. Usually, Izzy and I would have gotten a drink or caught a movie or something for the occasion. Last year, we saw *Casablanca* at Village East by the Angelika, just up the street from our apartment. They were playing it in eight millimeters, and it was a cheesy thing to do, but special.

Susan and Isabelle hit it off immediately, of course. I'm trying not to throw up at the hearts and red candles everywhere, sipping my old-fashioned, while Izzy fills Susan in on her job, and then Susan compliments Izzy's shirt, and now she's telling Susan about some sample sale she hit two weekends ago, and they're off to the races.

"The thing is, Susan, I had to know you were some kind of retail hero if you managed to get this one to spend a Saturday afternoon shopping," Izzy says, reaching across the little corner table we're smushed in to squeeze my shoulder.

"Well, clearly the hero is you, considering that fabulous vintage shop she took me to. Did she tell you about what we found?" And now they're talking about the Chanel doll-from-a-horror-movie monstrosity of a dress.

"I'm the lucky one, though," Susan says, snapping me back to the conversation. "Presley really has been such a wonderful friend to me, and it means the world. I know she has better things to do than spend time with an old bat."

"You're not old, Susan," I say, shifting in my seat.

"She's the best of the best," Izzy says.

"Agreed," Susan says. Her cheeks are flushed, and I wonder if she's tipsy. "Oh gosh, I called this one in a real pinch the other night, and she was right there. I had been a tad overserved after a rough day, and Presley came and took care of me. It was horribly embarrassing, but Presley was a dream."

It's subtle, but I see Izzy cock her head a little and give me a sidelong glance. I haven't told Izzy about that night, because I don't want to get into the details, meaning the shared breakdown we had over Patty. And the story of Patty's heroism. Plus, it's not like Izzy's been home much anyway. She's at Julia's most nights. Julia has a *studio*. "It really wasn't a big deal," I say to her as much as to Susan.

"Well, I really appreciated it," Susan says. I can't believe buttoned-up, prim, and proper Susan is even bringing up her sloppy night in front of someone she just met. Then again, I guess when you're starved for female friendship, and you feel that warm, fuzzy line pulling at you, the stories just start coming up involuntarily. "And I'm so happy to be officially meeting *you*, Isabelle, on Valentine's Day of all days! I'm sure you young single gals have far better things to be doing."

"Please, Susan, the pleasure is all ours," Izzy says, holding her glass up to clink ours. She continues, "Though, for my girlfriend's sake, I should probably fact-check and mention that I'm not single."

I might have to physically pick my jaw up off the table. My insides are suddenly freezing, like ice has replaced my blood. After seeing them at the open mic, I knew they were the personification of the cheesy decor that currently surrounds us. But I had no idea we were throwing *labels* around here, that things had been solidified like that. Shouldn't gaining your first girlfriend warrant an entire conversation with your best friend? Surely Isabelle would've had some fears around commitment she would have wanted to talk through with me; I always sort of assumed that she and I would have to convince each other it would be okay to make things official with someone we really liked. She's barely told me *anything* about this girl and how things have been going between them.

"Oh, P, don't look so surprised," Izzy says in a playful tone, though she's looking into her cosmopolitan and not at me.

"Well, I just . . . ," I start to say. Susan's eyes dart back and forth between us like she's at the US Open. I shake my head a little, try to drop back in. "Izzy, that's great!" I say, though I can hear the strain in my own voice, and I know Izzy can, too. "I just didn't realize things were official."

"We just had the conversation last night," she says, apologetically, I think, finally looking at me. "I wanted to tell you in person."

I nod, some of the sting relieved. Susan claps her hands together. "Well, that is just fantastic. Love wins!" Christ. "Tell me about her!"

I take a hearty sip of my cocktail while Izzy launches into Julia's bio. Susan nods, eyes wide. It might just be me, but I think I see some tears gathering in those brown peepers. Either she really is moved by a same-sex love story or she's feeling the canyon between the blossoming new romance of two twentysomethings and the broken, withered thing between her and her sort-of-husband-sort-of-ex-husband. Swallowing, she says, "She sounds just wonderful. And in this case, I doubly appreciate you coming to meet me on Valentine's Day, then."

"It was truly my pleasure, Susan," Izzy says. Then she winks at me, turns to Susan, and says playfully, "Tell me. What's that son of yours getting into tonight?"

"Oh, have you met Lawrence?" Susan asks, perking up, glowing the way she always does whenever one of her sons comes up in conversation.

"No," Izzy says, eyes sliding over to me. I don't know where she's going with this, but I don't think I like it. "But I'm sure our paths will cross soon, what with him and Presley hanging out."

Susan whips her head around to me, almost manic. "Oh, really? You two have been spending time together? That's great." She looks far too pleased for my liking.

"I mean, not really," I say, my eyes throwing knives in Izzy's direction. "We just hung out recently, hunting for a birthday gift for you, actually."

"Oh," Susan says, her joy dampening a bit but continuing to nod. "Well, you two certainly didn't need to get me anything."

"You know men," Izzy says. "I'm sure he was glad for the help." Susan giggles and Izzy sets down her empty glass and swipes some lip gloss over her mouth. "This has been a blast. Nothing better than a Galentine's celebration. But I gotta jet. The ball and chain awaits," she says with an eye roll.

It's childish, but I don't want Isabelle to go. Even though Izzy had already told me she'd have to leave after one drink, even though it was nice of her to show up at all, considering she has a *girlfriend*, I'm indignant that she's just rushing out like this. She tries to take out her wallet, and Susan stops her, of course. She kisses the air near Susan's cheek and gives my shoulder a squeeze before rising from her stool. She doesn't make eye contact, though. "Thanks for the drink, Susan. On me next time. Or maybe you could come over!" Susan claps her hands together like a toddler at the suggestion, watches Isabelle go like she's a pop star leaving the arena.

"Well, she is just fantastic," Susan says. "You're lucky to have a friend like her."

I thought so, too.

CHAPTER 31

I'm squeezing a leftover packet of delivery soy sauce over Trader Joe's fried rice when a snow-dusted Isabelle walks in the door, big tote bag slung over her shoulder, I guess to hold all that she's been wearing the last several days she's been sleeping at Julia's. "Hey, P," she says a bit tentatively. Or maybe that's just in my head.

"Hey." There's an urge to go eat dinner in my room, though I never do that. But I don't want to fake excitement for Isabelle's new relationship, act like finding out about it at the same time as Susan made me feel anything other than alienated.

But, ever an air clearer, Izzy brings it up as she flops down on the couch. "Look, I didn't mean to blindside you last night with the whole girlfriend thing," she says. "I really did just want to tell you in person, and that was the first time I was seeing you."

I shrug, sinking into the couch, using my fork to break the fried egg on top of my rice. "It's fine," I say. I cast my mind for something to say that will stanch the tension buzzing between us, but I get nothing.

Izzy sighs, clearly frustrated, as though I'm the one who's in the wrong here. A sour fear grips my chest, because I don't know what's going on between us, and what's between us is usually the only thing I'm sure of. "It doesn't really seem fine," she says.

The need to make things okay pushes itself to the forefront of any other thought. "Seriously, don't worry about it. You don't need to feel bad."

Izzy throws her hands up in what I can tell is frustration, and anxiety licks me like a flame. "I know that! But I do! Which is so unfair! God, P," she says, and she looks up at the ceiling and massages her temples. She takes a breath and turns to me. "Look, I really am sorry not to have told you one-on-one, that was clearly my miscalculation. And I know this is happening really fast, but I'm excited, and it's like you're not even happy for me at all, and it sucks."

It's like I'm suspended in amber, numb, floating in time. Fighting words are foreign to us, and I'm drowning between the islands of how I feel about this. On the one hand, how *can* she expect me to be happy for her? I thought we were in agreement: we had everything we needed. Including each other. Fear gurgles in my stomach. Everything could change, with this. Our entire relationship. I thought it was bad when I was demoted from being *Adam's* first call, but getting kicked off the top of Izzy's pyramid? Unimaginable. Well, until now.

But also? Anchors of guilt drop in me that, of course, she's technically in the right here. Love came thundering into my best friend's life, and I'm unequivocally, undeniably, without question a piece of shit for doing anything other than jumping up and down and squealing and demanding all the details of the conversation that led to their mutual christening of "girlfriend."

To my horror, I feel tears rushing into my eyes. I know I need to say something, but I'm having trouble accessing language. I shake my head. Izzy squeezes my shoulder, and it helps bring me back into myself. She's looking at me with such pity; I never knew I could be grateful for something and hate it so much at the same time. I want to tell her I'm happy for her, but my voice could break and allow the guilt and fear to obliterate me into a crying mess.

"I'm really sorry," I manage to choke out.

"Thank you," she says, nodding. "And there's something else."

I swallow. "Oh God, more?"

She nods solemnly, takes a breath. "I want you to be more open with me."

I turn to her, confused. "I tell you everything."

"No, you don't, babe. We both know there are things you don't talk to me about. Like, Susan telling me last night that you took care of her recently was a surprise. And I'm guessing that that's connected to . . . well"—she swallows, as though pulling in courage—"the main thing you don't talk to me about. Patty."

At this, my earlier indignance regains its footing, and it's a relief. I tear my eyes from her face, scoot farther from her on the couch. "What the hell?" I say. "You know I don't talk about that with *anyone*. You know what you're doing right now? You're doing that thing that I hate. That thing I have *told you* I hate. The thing where you're making my mother's death, my grief, about yourself."

Izzy sighs, and I see her plant her feet firmly on the floor. "That isn't what I'm doing. I'm bringing this up because you're going through something scary and unfathomable, and I want to help you with it. I'm bringing this up because I *see* you, Presley, and I care about you."

"Oh my God," I say, shaking my head. "This is so classic. Gets into a relationship and suddenly thinks everything has to be shared, all the time, all the touchy-feely stuff. We don't have to do all that to be close!"

"I know that!" Izzy says, clearly exasperated. "This isn't about our friendship. It's not! It's about you. And I love you, and I want you to be okay. And I think all this not talking about her isn't making you okay. I had to say it sometime, and being on the subject of not sharing things with each other feels as good a time as any."

I can physically feel them, my barriers extending out of the ground, rising to meet the sky, to create a wall that will not allow this to happen. Keeping me safe from having to do the thing I don't want to do, to talk about her, and remember her, and feel it all. The horror, the guilt, the shame. All the bad shit. Patty. The shared moments on my grandparents' couch, the few inside jokes, the way her eyes would widen when she looked at me sometimes, the love dilating her pupils. The good shit—that's harder.

But here, on *this* couch with me now, is someone else whose eyes also widen with love for me, who takes care of me, who carries me with her everywhere she goes. It's like her willingness to bring this up with me now, in this moment when I'm most fearing things will change, gives me a rock-solid certainty that I can trust her with it. This moment should be all about her, and she just wants to make it about me. To help me.

I sink into the couch. If I open my mouth, I'll cry. I do it anyway, and sure enough, my cheeks are quickly coated. "I don't know why, but it's really fucking scary."

"I know," she tells me. She gets up and brings me a roll of toilet paper from the bathroom. "You can start wherever you want, though. There's nothing you can say that's wrong."

We talk until two in the morning. First about Patty. I say that sometimes I miss her, sometimes I don't. I tell her about how we used to sing along to the Dixie Chicks in the car, about Atticus the cat. About a trip we took with my grandparents to Florida when I was eight, when she was really on her AA shit, and we built sandcastles and bodysurfed and I remembered thinking maybe everything could be normal. And Izzy listens.

And then I make her tell me everything about Julia. I ask all the questions I should have asked weeks ago, and she gives me the details. She tells me about how they've started playing pool in Julia's neighborhood at this dive bar and whoever wins gets to be little spoon that night (I pull a neck muscle from fighting the urge to cringe at that one). About Julia's shellfish allergy, which is a real bummer because sushi is Izzy's favorite food (I am secretly relieved that this means there will be at least one activity reserved for just me). About how close Julia is with her twin brother (not single, Izzy tells me sadly, though we both agree quickly that would be a bit much, even for us).

I'll be tired tomorrow. My voice will be scratchy from all the talking, my eyes will be puffy from the crying. But I won't curse myself for staying up late, I won't be embarrassed by my swollen face. I'll be grateful, actually, for the proof of how Isabelle refuses, full stop, to allow me to push her away. I could easily spit out a laundry list of reasons why I'm not like Patty. But I think Isabelle's love might be the most important one.

CHAPTER 32

It's surprisingly difficult to find a decent place to get a drink in midtown. There's no shortage of bars, but to find a spot with even an ounce of charm is damn near impossible. This is a conundrum Adam and I used to face when we felt like a postwork drink, and one that Emma and I face now, as we want to have a proper drink after work tonight instead of just guzzling wine in her office. We have something to celebrate.

Earlier this afternoon, Emma called out to me from her desk, which inevitably gave me that classic principal's-office feeling. But when I sat on her plush couch, she grinned at me and said, "You're going to get to give Agatha Reddy a very fun phone call. Congratulations."

I am not a squealer, so it took me a second to realize the high-pitched sound of delight destroying my eardrums was coming from me. Emma was laughing. "No way!" I think I said.

"Way. I showed the video you sent me to Gary in today's talent meeting and he's in. We'd like to have her on to tape two weeks from today, to air that Friday, if that works for her."

"Oh, it'll work for her," I say, heart racing, feeling coming back into my limbs, certain that Agatha would cancel her own wedding if it meant making this opportunity. The giddiness that had been coursing through my veins was replaced by relief, and I leaned back on Emma's couch and exhaled. I did it. *We* did it.

"So, here's what happens now," Emma said, putting on her business voice, but it barely cloaked the pride that was thickening her vocal cords, and a rush of warmth invaded my chest. "I'm going to walk out of here so that you can use my office to call Agatha and tell her the news, then you'll email her and make the booking official, and then you and I are going to celebrate."

She paused by her door. "I'm proud of you, Presley. And excited for you."

I couldn't stop smiling even after she left, even after I pulled up Agatha's contact in my phone and wondered if she'd be able to hear it when she picked up.

"Am I in?" she said instead of hello.

"You're in," I said in a voice that hopefully conveyed both joy and professionalism. She screamed, and I laughed, and then she said she had to tell her sister and hung up, and then she texted me a million exclamation points and nonsensical emojis. I stood in Emma's office for a moment before going back to my desk to email her all the details and make it official. It was like there were golden bubbles boiling in my chest. Triumph. Victory, of the sweetest kind, because it's dual: I'm on my way to getting promoted, just in time for my two-year anniversary as Emma's assistant, and Agatha is on her way to becoming the star I know she's meant to be. I called Izzy, and she screamed so loud her colleague in the office next door rushed in to check on her.

And now Emma and I are going out to celebrate. Emma settles on an uncharacteristically big-for-Manhattan bar with a French name that's packed to the brim with finance bros, as we knew any bar in this area would be. We squeeze onto two stools at the bar, and Emma shouts over the din that we'd like a dirty martini (for her) and an old-fashioned (for me), please.

"So, now that Agatha's booked, there's this other comedian I've been keeping tabs on. Her name is Naima," I say after we clink glasses.

Emma mock slumps over the bar and sighs. "Hustle, hustle, hustle," she says. I grimace, feeling like a brownnoser. "Enough about work." Straightening up, she slides her martini's olive off its toothpick and into her mouth. She chews. "Entertain me, I'm old and boring. Are you see-ing anyone?"

I snort, and Emma looks surprised. "Sorry," I say quickly. "It's just that I don't really date."

"Well, you shouldn't feel any pressure at your age," Emma says. "You should be young and single and meet lots of people and do a lot of stupid shit."

"That I can say I'm doing successfully," I say. I sigh, appreciating how the whiskey immediately loosens my limbs. "My best friend just started dating someone, though."

"Do you like him? Or her?" Emma asks.

"She seems great," I say truthfully.

"But you're worried things will change," Emma says correctly. Even though I am officially on Team Julia, this is still uncharted territory for me and Izzy. "I get that. They probably will, to be honest." She takes a big gulp of her martini. "One day, you're dancing on a table, looking out over a bar, wondering which guy you're gonna go home with. Then you blink and you're suddenly married and putting a down payment on a house upstate and you spend your Saturday nights researching kindergartens and googling 'age when full sentences are a thing.'"

I wince dramatically. "Yeah, a second home, a family, that sounds so tragic."

She swipes at my shoulder and I laugh. She sighs. "I know I shouldn't complain."

"Nah, dude, you can totally complain," I say. Then I feel a hand on my shoulder. I turn and look up into the face of Lawrence Clark.

"Hey there," he says.

"Whoa, hey," I say, taking him in, in all his loosened-tie glory. He wraps an arm around my shoulders, pulling me in for a little side hug.

"Hi," he says, extending a hand to Emma. "I'm Lawrence Clark, a friend of Presley's."

"Hello," Emma says. I can practically see the delight dancing in her eyes at the idea that I would know this man. Even though this bar is forgettable, and the clientele are not people I would be proud to associate with, I'll admit there's something a bit delicious about running into someone in front of Emma, like I'm proving that I'm the young-woman-about-town she was just encouraging me to be. And it doesn't hurt that Clark is friendly and handsome and . . . Clark. "I'm Emma. Presley's colleague."

"She's my boss," I tell Clark, rolling my eyes at Emma. I appreciate that she tries to soften the hierarchical weight between us with her word choice, but I picked up the woman's dry cleaning today. She is my boss.

"That's awesome that you two are hanging out," Clark says. He leans forward as he says this with great emphasis, and it would seem he's already a few drinks in. "My old boss never would have gotten a drink with just me after work."

"Old boss?" I ask.

Clark nods, a slow smile spreading on his face, that gleam in his eye. "Yeah. I finally got promoted today. After months and months."

I thump him on the shoulder, and he fake winces. "Clark! That's amazing. Congrats."

"Congratulations," Emma echoes. "Where do you work?"

"CAM," he says. "Sports! So you don't have to get mad at me. I've never been annoying to you like my colleagues in talent probably have."

Emma nods approvingly. "Good."

"Well, anyway, some of us are out celebrating," Clark says, jerking his head over to a group of guys who all look laughably similar, same gelled hair, same loosened tie, same beer stein in front of them. "You ladies should come join us."

"Oh, we're actually just—" I start to say when Emma cuts me off.

"That sounds *great*," she says, and drains the last of her martini. "I'll just be needing another one of these, is all."

"I got you," Clark says, pulling out his wallet. He sees the look on my face, the one that probably looks pained, and he leans in. "On CAM. Your boy can expense now."

"In that case, I'll take an old-fashioned," I say.

"Like I don't know your drink," Clark says.

I can feel Emma's eyes on me, can practically feel her glee in seeing me out in the wild, witnessing an activity she probably thinks is flirting. Her thinking she's living vicariously through me.

For the sake of, I guess, Mom's Night Out, Emma and I cram ourselves into a booth with Clark's coworkers, whose names are, God help us, Chad, Brad, Justin, and Jake. Clark sits between me and them, and our thighs are pressed against each other in the booth. I get a good nostril full of Clean Boy smell, a feat considering the aftershave and cologne wafting off these men, commingling over our small table.

Emma, of course, starts immediately giving them all shit, especially when she finds out that one of them represents someone having something to do with the Baltimore Ravens. I can feel Clark's slight turn as he keeps looking at me, I guess to check my expression while Emma verbally assaults his colleagues. "So, Presley," Chad, I think, or maybe Brad, says with alarmingly unwavering eye contact. "How do you know our coordinator, Clark, here?"

"We're family friends," I say.

"Oh, are you also from the city?" another one asks me.

"No."

"Presley is from the same town in Georgia my mom is from," Clark says.

Apparently bored by this answer, Justin or Jake nods and turns back to the other one, saying something about a Georgia football player I've never heard of. More drinks are consumed at CAM's expense, and Emma and I settle into a discussion about when she started drinking martinis (when she was single, to seem impressive), until she eventually concedes that she should probably return home to her family. The Chads are all off to watch some game at a sports bar downtown, so I turn to Clark to say goodbye.

"Wanna get one more drink, just you and me?" he asks.

I nod in the direction of the Neanderthals with good eye contact. "Don't you want to go with them? Keep celebrating your promotion?"

He shakes his head. "Not really."

"Okay, sure." After goodbyes with his colleagues that quickly turn into leers that make me uncomfortable and Clark downright humiliated, we head down the street to some gross bar Clark suggested called Cassidy's. We order beer-and-shot combos and steak fries that clearly came from a freezer. It's kind of glorious.

"Your boss seems cool," Clark says. "My boss wouldn't come out for even one drink tonight to celebrate."

"That's so shitty," I say, the words pouring out in a slightly sloppy way, and I realize I'm drunk. "But at least he's not your boss anymore!"

"That's the thing about being coordinator," Clark says, tipping his Bud Light back into his mouth. "No one is my boss, and everyone is my boss."

"I wouldn't know. Still haven't been promoted," I say, some of the earlier sparkle from today's victory wearing off. Booking Agatha had been my goal to become *closer* to getting promoted. Now that it's happened, I'm wondering what that timeline will actually look like.

"What? But you're so smart," he says. I laugh. How would this kid know whether I'm smart? Plus, we both know intelligence is not often related to who moves up the ladder and who doesn't at workplaces like ours.

"Come on, you know how hard it is," I say. Especially when you're not a good-looking white guy with a fancy family, I refrain from adding.

"Yeah," he says, nodding.

"Especially when you're not a good-looking white guy with a fancy family," I do actually add now, my drunkenness eviscerating my filter.

He blows air through his lips. "Yeah, I'm sure as a pretty white girl you're a total stranger to privilege." It wasn't unkind, and I can't deny my privilege, so I laugh. I try not to notice that he called me pretty.

"They sure did make me wait for it. It's been almost three years," he says with an exhale. "Though some of that is on me."

"Doubt it, you know how long these things take," I say. I feel for him, though; I've been stressed about nearing my two-year mark. My stress level would be sky-high if I were approaching three.

He shakes his head. "It took me a while to get the hang of things. I'm not, you know . . . always the sharpest tool in the toolbox."

"Shed."

"My point exactly."

"That's not true, Clark," I say. It's not like I've been blown away by his intelligence, but it's clear he's no dummy. Either way, perhaps the self-awareness or self-deprecation he's showing right now impresses me more than cleverness would anyway.

He shakes off my assurance and we move on to talking about our weird coworkers, then he's telling me a story about slipping in the office kitchen and face-planting on his second day at work, then he says he wants to do karaoke, and suddenly he's on the phone with Susan.

"Mom, Mom," he's saying into the phone. "Presley and I are gonna do karaoke—"

"I'm not doing karaoke!" I insist, trying to speak loudly into the phone, which Clark jerks away from me and presses to his other ear.

"We are. We're gonna go to that spot we went to on my twenty-first. Come meet us. It'll be fun! We're celebrating!"

I've reached the level of drunkenness where I'm sort of floating above myself, and it's a unique pleasure to be unbothered by the events unfolding here. Am I a karaoke girl? No. Am I in a state fit for interacting with Susan? I am not. Should I have been home an hour ago, considering I have work in the morning? Absolutely. But all this seems insignificant, these needling things that I let weigh me down in the sober light of day.

Next thing I know, we're in a cab. We go somewhere on the Upper East Side, on Second Avenue, in a bar with a disco ball and a stage and very few people. In prances tiny Susan, wearing leggings and a gigantic fuzzy coat, and she squeezes each of us and reaches up in an attempt to plant kisses on Clark's cheeks. He has to bend down to receive them. "I am so proud of you!" she says. She takes each of our hands in her own.

"I cannot believe you two dragged me out late on a Thursday night, but I'm so flattered, and I just had to celebrate my Lawrence for his big promotion!"

"Cheers!" I say, even though I don't have a drink in hand. Which should be rectified.

At Clark's insistence, I guess in some weird desire to relive his twenty-first birthday, we each take a tequila shot, which given Susan's size should have her blacking out within the next twenty minutes. Clark and I have a race to see who can gulp down a glass of water the fastest. I believe this was his idea, and it is a good one.

"Wooo!" Clark turns and cheers for the scrawny, bespectacled dude on the mic earnestly singing a song from *High School Musical*.

Susan, taking a sip of sauvignon blanc that must be so far below her standards I'm shocked she can keep it down, turns to me, eyes wide, already swaying a bit. "We should do a duet," she says.

"Genius," I say.

"Do you know the Dixie Chicks?"

Do I know the Dixie Chicks.

In what could have been several hours or no time at all, I am onstage with Susan, microphones gripped in each of our hands. There are about ten people in the bar, none of whom are paying attention to us. Except for Clark, who stands on the floor, arms up, cheering as though we're Rihanna. Susan selected the song, but as soon as I hear that opening guitar strum, I know we are both fucking in for it. There's a TV to our left, facing us with the lyrics, but neither of us needs them.

For those unfamiliar with the masterpiece that is "Not Ready to Make Nice," it starts off slow, reserved. According to YouTube videos Isabelle and I used to watch late at night in our dorm, when Natalie Maines begins to croon, she's usually pretty still in the beginning, eyes smoldering, looking out over the crowd or into the camera. This is not Susan's approach. The thrill of doing this is all over Susan's face: her raised eyebrows, the way she keeps turning to me and smiling her huge, somewhat gooney (considering all the Botox and this lighting) smile and nodding like, *Can you believe we're really doing this?* Susan has a pretty, choral kind of voice, which is easy to hear over my murmuring the first verse.

We get more into it when the chorus comes around, singing about how we're not ready to make nice, not ready to back down. I sneak a peek at Susan, who is a little crouched, bouncing her weight from foot to foot, like a boxer fresh in the ring. I find myself doing it, too, and laughing a little when I make eye contact with Clark, who is pumping his fists at us and jumping up and down like a child.

As we head into the second verse, our energy builds. And now: the bridge. Maybe it's all the drinks (it is), maybe it's all the latent anger that lies dormant in me (that, too), maybe it's the fact that this part of this song opens up a black hole that gives no choice but for the listener to be sucked in, taken over by it, and thrashing around in it, but for this next part, the neon-colored disco light dots fall away, the ten mellow patrons fall away, Clark and Susan fall away. I'm thirteen again, my purple headphones over my ears, Walkman clutched between my hands, head bobbing and whispering the lyrics in my childhood bedroom, drowning out the sound of Patty drunkenly arguing with her parents. Or I'm in Isabelle's freshman-year dorm room, the two of us having just taken warm whiskey shots and screaming the words, inviting a noise complaint from her hall mates just before we're about to go use our fake IDs. Or maybe I'm Natalie Maines, playing to a stadium that's marveling to themselves that after all the times they've listened to this song in their most private moments, they're now getting to hear it from the person who made it possible. We're screaming halfway through the bridge; then we're practically howling those last few lines. It's like we have no choice, what with the necessary heart that must be put into the second half of that last verse. I also cannot overemphasize the affirmation of the swelling violins after every last particle of breath has been spent on that last word, that "over" word. The drama of the music validates the drama of my feelings, and based on the out-of-tune screeching from Susan that managed to cut through some of my isolation in that last moment, I know she's feeling it, too. I turn to look at her as we loop back to the chorus for the final time.

The sight of tears shining on her face snaps me back into myself. She swipes at her eyes and sniffles, belting out the final words before turning to me and smiling, the tears lingering in her eyes. She grabs my hand, nods to the crowd (which consists basically of just Clark at this point), and bows. I'm pulled into following suit. Clark whoops and hollers, and I realize how emotionally spent I am and wait for the embarrassment to creep in. I just displayed a vulnerability shown previously only to my childhood bedroom and my best friend to a room full of strangers, my mother's Waspy friend, and a city bro. A city bro who's looking up at me, offering a hand to help me off the stage after helping his mother, a city bro who smells like Tide and works hard and knows what it is to be let down by the person who's supposed to take care of you and who has a smile so big it takes up my entire vision.

He hands me a Bud Light and I sip it gratefully—"Not Ready to Make Nice" really dried out my pipes. "That was revelatory!" Clark tells us, so charmingly that the fact that he butchered the pronunciation doesn't bother me. We move off to the side of the bar, nodding along politely, Susan full-on clapping to the beat of a hopelessly tone-deaf thirtysomething woman singing Ariana Grande.

After she's done, Susan says her goodbyes, hugging us close and thanking us again for including her. Clark plants a kiss on top of her head, and it's like he plugged her in, the way she immediately lights up, her previous tears gone. We realize we should go, too, it's late, and we stumble out of the bar. Susan spots a cab with its numbers lit up and hails it, Clark closing the door softly after her. I wave as Susan rolls down her window and blows a kiss at us, headed west.

Clark steps back onto the sidewalk, hands in his pockets, and smiles at me. "Hey," he mumbles, and immediately starts laughing. I laugh, too, more like a *giggle*, actually, humiliatingly, but we're both drunk, and there's a sugary, tingly feeling zapping in the air back and forth between us. Maybe it's the alcohol, maybe it's the fact that we've technically known each other for a long time, maybe we're just horny. For whatever reason, or combination of those reasons, he steps close to me, and when I look up into his face, I know we're going to kiss.

And we do. He leans down and I stand on my tiptoes and he presses his mouth into mine, and even though the idea of kissing is something I find stressful if I think about it, right now I'm not thinking about anything. Something I didn't even know was coiled deep in my gut releases and unspools, and we lean into each other, relaxed. It feels like the most natural thing in the world, like this is the millionth time we've kissed. His hands are on my face pulling me up, and my hands are around his neck pulling him down, and I'm just fully making out with him in the street moments after having a cathartic emotional experience with his mother.

This strikes me as funny enough to point out, so I pull back to tell him. But now I'm looking at him and he's looking at me and my liquor-muddled brain can't fish out what it was I was going to say. "Will you come home with me?" he asks. I nod. He hails a cab, and we fall in. He immediately puts his arm around me, drawing me to him, and we resume making out. We each have one hand on the side of the other's face, and our tongues are in each other's mouths and he pulls me closer to him and somehow I'm in his lap now, and I feel him hard beneath me, and as strongly and suddenly as an avalanche I realize how badly I want him.

CHAPTER 33

My hangover is bad enough that when I wake up and the slow realization creeps in that I'm not in my bed and do not, in fact, know where I am, I don't even panic. I don't care. Hopefully I'm in a dangerous enough situation that I may be murdered, which feels like the only way to end the jackhammer going off in my skull and the nausea falling over me like rain. My back is warm, and I become aware of an arm draped over me, pulling me in. The hand of said arm is somehow intertwined with mine. I'm comfortable and warm and this arm around me and this pressure of another body behind me is the lifeline keeping this hangover from pulling me into a whirlpool of death. I snuggle in closer in gratitude.

Then I remember that I'm in bed with Lawrence Clark.

The old-fashioneds. The tequila shot. Oh God, the Dixie Chicks.

We kissed in the street, that I do know. We kissed in the cab, too—oh no, we were *sloppy*. I remember us laughing, and trying to keep quiet as he poured us cups of water in his dark kitchen so we wouldn't wake his roommates up, creeping back to his room, and then . . . not much else.

I need to get out of here. I slowly, gingerly, start to move his arm off me, and Clark sleepily grunts and pulls me in tighter to him. His body felt like home mere seconds ago, and now it's a trap. I try again to push his arm off, and this time I succeed. I lift the sheet up, curious to learn what I'm wearing. A US Open T-shirt and a pair of Gap granny panties I've had for at least seven years.

"C'mere," Clark says lazily, and turns me over, pulls me into him, tucking me into his side and sliding his shoulder under my head so I'm now resting on his chest. I give in, too groggy to protest. He starts scratching my back, and shit, does that feel good. It's like he's hypnotizing the hangover right out of me. My very own dopamine IV.

I'm tired, so tired, and the scratching and the gentle hiss of his radiator and the warmth of him is pulling me to rest. Then I remember it's Friday. A workday. "Shit!" I sit up immediately, and the jackhammers start going off in my skull at twice the intensity. "Where's my . . ." My eyes are ravaging the room, looking for my phone.

Clark sits up, too, shirtless. He leans over to his bedside table, where my phone is plugged into his charger. He hands it to me, and I see that it's not yet seven a.m., and I breathe a sigh of relief. I don't need to get to work until ten on Fridays, so this is a salvageable situation. "Time?" Clark asks.

"Six forty," I say.

"Ah, so you woke up twenty minutes before your alarm."

"I set an alarm?"

He nods, slipping back under his sheets, tugging at the back of my (well, I guess, his) T-shirt, indicating that I should lie back down, too. For some reason, I do, returning my head to his chest, my right arm draped over him. "You set an alarm for seven, you said that would give you enough time to go home and get ready for work."

"Good for me," I say.

"You were adamant that you had to get up on time. You almost went home."

This is coming back to me now. My debating calling an Uber, him rolling onto his back, pulling me onto his bed, me straddling him and kissing him, clearly staying. The memory fades around there. "We didn't . . . ?" I ask.

I feel him shake his head. "No, we were too drunk," he says. "But you insisted I take your clothes off and put this T-shirt on you so that I could at least see your boobs. Which was sweet."

I cringe at how transparent that attempt to be cute is, how needy it seems. *Help me, I can't even undress myself, pouty face.* "Yeah, I'm a real peach."

"A *Georgia* peach," he says, pulling me closer and letting out a fake laugh at his bad joke.

"Ugh," I say, unable to muster the energy to give him proper shit for such a dumb line. He chuckles and kisses my forehead, which some- how has a kind of Dementor effect in that it sucks out some of my hangover. He's scratching my back again.

"Twenty minutes, twenty minutes," he murmurs. "What can we do in twenty minutes. . . ."

"Sleep," I say, even though that's suddenly not what I want to do.

He rolls over on his side and pushes me gently onto my back, so now he's hovering above me, looking down into my face. He kisses me. Our morning breath is criminal, but I don't care. Kissing him, I'm not in this hungover, bloated, smelly carcass of a body. I'm floating, practically celestial.

He's kissing my neck, pulling the T-shirt up and kissing my chest, each nipple, my stomach, and suddenly I am *very* in my body, but he's healing it, transforming it from a hungover corpse into something else entirely. "Can I?" he asks, and I feel his breath on my underwear and I want him so badly I'm surprised that when I say "Yes" it's not a scream. I lift my hips and he slides my underwear off. He tosses them over his shoulder, and as I go to put my legs back down on the bed, he catches my left ankle in his hand. He's kneeling between my legs, and we make eye contact, my head propped up on a pillow soft as a cloud. He's look- ing right at me, and I'm looking right at him, and he does the most insane thing in the world and kisses my ankle, right on a really knobby bone. It's the most intimate thing a man has ever done to me, and I'd have thought that kind of intimacy would make my heart pound in panic, but I can feel it sitting in my chest, very, very still.

I'm about to open my mouth to say forget it, never mind. Because it was boyfriend-y, that move, weighted with the closeness it suggested. Like he wants every piece of me, every inch, and the truth is my ankles are knobby and weird and I'd like to keep them to myself.

But I'm too paralyzed by my own wanting to ask him to stop. He sets my ankle down and his head is between my legs and his mouth is on me and his tongue is in me and my hands are in his hair and I'm having to remind myself that he has roommates, that it would not be good form to cry out, so I slap my hand over my mouth because there's no way I can be silent right now.

Tiny sparklers are crackling all over my body even after I come, and he collapses next to me, pulling me onto his chest again. He plants another kiss on my forehead and I exhale. Damn, that lawyer ex-girlfriend taught him well.

His fingers trail up and down my arms, and I snuggle closer under the comforter so that he can't see the goose bumps he's given me. He tugs gently on my hair, tipping my face up toward his. He presses his lips to mine, rolls himself on top of me again, and I feel how hard he is, the fabric of his boxers pressing into my leg. "Do you want to have sex?" he breathes, and I'm momentarily tempted to laugh, to make a joke about the naked desperation in his voice.

But I don't. Or rather: I can't, because my mind is buzzing with too much ache to make a joke, and you can't make fun of someone for something you're feeling, too. "Yeah." I'm surprised by the sound of my own whisper.

I shiver as a draft covers my chest when he starts digging through his bedside drawer, navy-blue comforter going with him. "Sorry," he whispers, tucking the fabric under my shoulders before rolling a condom on. The cold air was a shock to the system: Do I really want this to happen? I search through my pounding head for an answer, and then his face is right above my face, and our eyes are meeting, and he's smoothing my hair away, and that automatically somehow quiets the pounding, and the pool of his brown eyes is enveloping mine, and I know unequivocally that I want this to happen.

I nod, and then we're kissing, and then he pushes himself inside me and my hands grip around the back of his neck and he moans and I moan and we change positions, and if you had told me three minutes ago that I would be moments away from having another orgasm, I would have laughed, but here we are, and here I am, and he's saying my name and I'm thinking that it's never sounded quite like that before, so pristine and so utterly filthy at the same time, and then he's shuddering into me and I'm shaking, overwhelmed, exhausted, not myself and *so* myself, and then he's taking the condom off and I'm lying there, an oversexed shell of a person, all raw and vulnerable like I'm wearing my innards outside of my skin.

My alarm sounds and I scramble to turn it off, Clark exhaling a laugh. "Quite the timing, there," he says, like this was all my own calculated play. I sit up, paw at my phone, and he tugs on my arm, pulling me back down. I don't have time for that, so I give his flat, hard stomach a quick pat and stand to find my clothes. "Aw, no cuddles?" he asks. Cue the rapid return of my nausea. It must show on my face because Clark laughs, then puts a pillow over his face and groans. He takes it off. "Fine, fine," he says. "They're over there." And he nods over to his dresser, where my jeans and black T-shirt are folded, neatly stacked, with my jacket laid out next to it.

"Well, isn't that fancy," I say.

"Only the five-star treatment at Hotel Clark," he says. I fake retch and he rolls his eyes, smiling. I dress quickly, suddenly not wanting to be naked in front of him, the sparkling intimacy from just moments ago fading like an apparition. I hear him scooting off his bed, the rustle of sheets and blankets as I lace up my Doc Martens. By the time I stand, he's standing right in front of me. At least one of us isn't self-conscious about being buck naked in front of the other.

"Um, hi," I say.

"Presley, hello," he says, reaching around me to open up a drawer. He pulls on a clean pair of boxers that has little dogs on them and I snort. So cutesy. He ignores this. "I'll walk you out."

"Is your apartment so cavernous I'm gonna get lost?" I ask.

"No, chivalry just isn't dead. Live with it. But hey—" He's standing in front of me again and he puts a hand on each of my shoulders. He bends down so he meets my eye level, searches my face. "Do you think . . . I don't know. Well. We should talk about this, right?"

I instantly step back, my body acting of its own accord. I drop my eyes, looking at the floor. "Uh, I don't think there's a ton to say here." Sirens are going off inside me, and I want to get out of this apartment, right now. Out of the corner of my eye, I see Clark straighten up, stiffen.

"Okay, then," he says, putting his hands up by his shoulders, as if I were trying to arrest him instead of avoid a conversation. He turns and opens his door, which I walk through. His living room is dark, but I can make out a couch, a TV, an array of hot sauces sitting on the coffee table. I open the front door and force myself to turn around. I give a little nod in his direction, which he does not accept. He pulls me in for a hug, and my head still fits on his chest under his chin like it did in bed. He holds me for a moment longer than is normal for family friends, which I'm not sure is something we can still call ourselves. He lets me go, I mutter, "Bye," and take off down the hall.

A quick ride on the F train later and I burst into our apartment, half excited to dish with Izzy and half resentful that she was right to tease me about Clark after all. But her bedroom door is open to a dark, lifeless room. I pull up my location app to confirm what I already know: she's at Julia's. I toss my phone on the couch and turn the shower on. Nausea overtakes me and I lean over the toilet just in time. When I'm done puking, I sit on the floor as steam fills the bathroom, wishing this loneliness would evaporate with it.

CHAPTER 34

I had been hard-pressed to find a single problem with hooking up with people I would never have to see again, but now I see a glaring one: being completely unprepared for this situation. You know, that classic situation in which you hook up with the son of your late mother's friend, a woman who has also become your friend, and then one week later she expects both you and that son to spend an evening in her apartment for her fifty-eighth birthday.

Clark is cooking spaghetti and meatballs. Or, excuse me, as Susan said in her texts (all of which are still signed xx Susan, by the way), he's cooking his "famous" spaghetti and meatballs. Sour anxiety courses through my veins, and I notice as I ride up the elevator, accompanied by Roger (Jennifer Aniston this time, which is truly insane), that my hands are slightly shaking. I need to buck up. I'm acting like I'm in middle school. Clark and I are adults who bumped uglies because we were drunk (well, technically, it was the morning after we were drunk, but the effects of the alcohol still lingered). This is no big deal. At least, that's what Izzy told me this morning when I was pacing around our apartment with my coffee. She screamed into a pillow last Friday after work when I told her what had happened. Not in an angry way, in an I'm-so-excited-but-I-know-my-excitement-will-deter-you kind of way. Which I appreciated. We tried to unpack how I feel about the whole thing, but the truth is I have no idea. Though I accidentally fucked my own case for ambivalence two days later when she caught me smiling at my phone when Clark texted me a photo of the Dolly print, confirming he bought it for Susan's birthday (he predicted she'd hang it in her closet, out of sight).

Susan opens the door and throws her arms around me, nearly crushing the bouquet of flowers I'm holding. I'm not bragging when I say the bouquet is gorgeous, because I stole it from a greenroom the second Daniel Radcliffe left today. "Happy birthday," I tell her when she pulls away and I'm able to catch my breath.

"Thanks, wow, these are stunning!" she says, taking the bouquet out of my hands, shutting the door behind me, and marching me back into the apartment. "Let me go put these in water. And what can I get you to drink?"

"Glass of red would be good." We're having spaghetti, after all.

"A bottle is breathing in the kitchen, great!"

I can't help but burst out laughing when we enter the kitchen and I see Clark in an *apron*. He's standing at the stove, plopping lumpy meatballs in a pan of red sauce. He spins around upon hearing the laughter, gives some jazz hands, looks down at his apron and back up at me, grinning. He holds an arm out to me and I slap him with a high five. He looks at me quizzically, and I realize the arm was meant to open himself up for a hug. I can feel a blush rising in my cheeks and he gives the smallest headshake, but also a little chuckle, then returns to his sauce. "Hope you like meatballs," he says.

I peer over the saucepan, and the smell of garlic and tomato and basil wafts into my nose. My mouth waters; I haven't eaten in hours.

As if she can see the saliva gathering in my mouth, Susan says, "Lawrence's spaghetti and meatballs is just *wonderful*."

"It's the one thing I can make," Clark says modestly, shrugging, though a grin tugs at the corner of his mouth. He turns to face me. "Ina forever."

Ina Garten came on the show to promote her last cookbook and did a demo with Gary. She was a goddamn delight. Susan hands me my wine and I follow her to a counter stool. We sit, watching Clark salt the pasta water.

"Do anything special today, Susan?" I ask.

"Actually, yes," she says. "I went to a spa! In Brooklyn, of all places, and it was excellent. It was Michael's gift to me." A spa day *and* that bulky bath basket? Damn, Michael.

"Always showing me up," Clark says.

"Oh hush, you're actually here," Susan says. "And he brought me that!" She nods to a shoddily wrapped rectangle on the counter. The Dolly print.

"A spa sounds like the perfect birthday activity," I say. I've never been to a spa, obviously. But the idea of the solitude appeals to me. I like the idea of purposeful touch, of a space where the way to succeed is to relax. A ringing pings suddenly through the kitchen, and Clark leans over to look at a lit-up phone, plugged in next to the stove.

"Oh, who's calling me?" Susan asks.

"Uh . . . Dad," Clark says. I feel Susan stiffen next to me, and I immediately study the inside of my wineglass as though it offers an escape route. "Do you want me to pick up?" Clark asks when it becomes clear Susan isn't going to say anything.

"No," Susan says.

"Mom—"

"I'll call him back," she says in what I can tell is supposed to be a light tone but sounds weighted down by a net full of elephants. The air is thick with the words Susan and Clark aren't saying to each other— and to think I felt like an intruder at Christmas. Not to mention the suffocating crisscrossing of the entanglements between us: I doubt Clark knows about Susan's lunch with Thomas's former lover. I have no idea what she's told him about where she stands on the Thomas situation; *I* don't know where she stands on the Thomas situation. I know that Clark wasn't taking Thomas's money but don't know how much he and Thomas have discussed directly. I might be Susan's only friend. I slept with Clark.

Speaking of, Clark is considerably more skilled in bed than he is in the kitchen. The meatballs are a little burned, the pasta a bit undercooked, the sauce fairly runny. It's edible, but not great. Looking at Susan's reaction, though, you'd think she was in Rome or one of those fancy Italian restaurants in the West Village Izzy is always showing me on Instagram. "I appreciate you, Mom, but you really don't have to do this," Clark says after her third exclamation about how delicious it all is. "This is certainly not my best. Maybe one of my worst, actually."

"I think it's good," I say, taking a sip of my wine to avoid eye contact.

"You're a terrible liar," Clark says. I snort into my wine. "All right, Mom. What was your favorite birthday ever?"

Susan tilts her head in thought as she saws into one of her meatballs (with not an inconsiderable amount of effort). When she slices her knife through, she just separates the pieces, then starts cutting another. "Hm," she says. "Well, actually, Presley, my seventeenth birthday is a particularly memorable one, mostly because of Patty."

I open my mouth, a quip about whether they almost got abducted that night as well on the tip of my tongue. But I swallow it. "Oh?"

She nods, leans forward, chin in her hands, eyes starry and far-off. "It was a Friday. Patty and I watched the football team do spring practice in the afternoon, through the slats in the bleachers. We hid under them, sneaking cigarettes and beers."

"Whoa, Mom!" Clark says, nodding his approval. "Bad Susan. Nice."

Susan rolls her eyes, but she's blushing. "And then there was a party that night in this field everyone in Eulalia would go drink in. We'd line up our cars and turn the headlights on to illuminate it. Do the kids still do that?" she asks me.

I nod. "Yep." I suppose now would be a charming time to tell her about how I had my first beer there or whatever, but the truth is I just went as a designated driver. I didn't drink in high school. It took me a while to warm up to the idea of alcohol.

"We'd blare the radio from someone's truck speakers. And then, at one point, Patty had everyone sing 'Happy Birthday' to me. She stood on a cooler, told everyone to stay hushed, she was going to serenade me. And she sang— Oh, do you know 'Somebody Somewhere,' by Loretta Lynn? From *Coal Miner's Daughter*?" Clark and I look at each other, shaking our heads. He's leaning on his elbows, square on the table, his big frame hunched over. I swallow. "No, you're too young, of course. Well, Presley, you know what a beautiful singer your mother was."

I swallow for a different reason now, a knot popping up in my throat that must be pushed down immediately. Clark's eyes may as well be his hands for how I feel them on me. "Well, in her mind, anyway." My voice comes out high-pitched, my attempted lightness less believable than Susan's exclamations over Clark's cooking.

"It's a pretty song," Susan says. "Lawrence, will you play it on your phone?"

"Sure thing, birthday girl." A few seconds later warbly, tinny music starts dribbling out of his phone. I've definitely never heard the song before. Susan closes her eyes and starts swaying back and forth slightly. She opens her eyes right into mine with a small gasp, just as I'm wondering whether I was correct in thinking I heard Loretta Lynn sing the words "late show."

Susan closes her eyes again and I catch Clark watching me, smiling at me, as Loretta Lynn sings about being lonely and sad. Loretta says she kept getting bluer with each little drink she had, and I'm tight, agitated, my strings plucked. Lord, Loretta says, she needs someone, someone who's with someone else who doesn't know what he's missing. I'm pretty sure I've never heard Patty sing this song, but my God, listening closely to the lyrics, she could have written the damn thing.

An Ocean Spray stain on a tangerine tank top. Weeping over the Winn-Dixie butcher. Pops sitting on the edge of my bed, patting my foot and saying, "It could be different this time, you never know, kid."

I'm surprised by a screech, and it takes me a second to realize I'm the one who caused the noise, pushing my chair back and standing abruptly. Clark and Susan are both looking at me, their almost identical big golden-brown eyes wide. "Bathroom," I manage to squeeze through my vocal cords. I drop the cloth napkin I don't remember picking up on the table and bolt.

Sitting on the toilet, I plant my feet firmly on the ground, like Izzy taught me. I take deep breaths. There's this loud noise in my head, this ringing in my ears, a deafening white noise. My chest is squeezing and my hands are tingling, but I focus on my breath, I picture my lungs taking in the air, pushing it out. There's no one in here to say anything to, but if I had to speak, I know there's only one word I'm capable of forming and it's her name and I'm choked by my anger and my chest is splitting open from the jagged, unattached pieces of my heart floating around in it. I picture my lungs again. Filling, emptying. Feet on the floor. *Get ahold of yourself, Presley.*

After what I hope hasn't been a lot of time, I return to myself enough to stand and wash my hands, face myself in the mirror, surprised to find I look normal considering my insides have become stew. Another breath.

The song is mercifully off when I return to the table. "Sorry about that," I say as I sit down.

"No, Presley, I'm sorry," Susan says. "I—"

"No," I say simply, shaking my head, and tears rush into my eyes because she's looking at me with so much tenderness. I don't dare look at Clark. I take a sip of my water. I clear my throat. "It sounds like a fun birthday, though. Let me know if you want to re-create it. We can go to Sheep Meadow, and Clark and I can shine our phone lights on you."

It does the trick. Susan laughs and I hear Clark let out air somewhere to my left. He says, "Do you remember that birthday, Mom, I think I was, like, nine, when Michael choked on a piece of steak?"

"Oh my God, don't remind me of that," she says. Looking at me: "Thomas had to give him the Heimlich. It was awful."

"I bet we can trace Mike's vegetarianism to that exact moment, now that I'm thinking about it," Clark says, and Susan lashes him playfully with her napkin. The conversation carries on, thankfully, and my shoulders start to drift away from my ears, the knot in my chest loosens.

When we're done, I take everyone's dishes and start cleaning the kitchen. Clark cooked and it's Susan's birthday, after all, but it isn't long before Clark is standing next to me at the sink, taking rinsed plates from me and loading the dishwasher. Susan, who had been sitting at the kitchen island looking at her phone, goes to the bathroom. Clark dries his hands off with a dish towel and yanks lightly on my ponytail.

"Hey, you," he says.

Hey, you. "Hey, you" is the kind of thing a wife says in bed to her husband in a movie, in a flashback to a time before her untimely death. "Hey, you" is the kind of thing a male model says in a weirdly sensual perfume or razor ad. "Hey, you" is the kind of thing a tweenage girl would be charmed by the idea of a guy saying to her.

"Hey, you" is not the kind of thing two adults who drunkenly (basically) fucked say to each other.

"What?" he asks, in response to what I'm guessing is a look of disgust on my face.

I don't even know where to begin. "'Hey, you'?" is what I choose. "Isn't that a bit . . . flirty?"

"Yeah," Clark says, like I'm an idiot for asking. "You okay?"

"Yes," I say quickly, unsure if he's referring to my clear disdain at his attempted flirting or my near mental breakdown moments before.

We're standing in front of the running sink, looking at each other. The only flirting I've ever done in my life—namely all the verbal sparring I did with Adam—wasn't something I would even admit was flirting until it was all over. I have no idea what to do with this: this guy standing in front of me, declaring flirtation. I'm scanning my brain, but no appropriate responses are coming up. Do I flirt back? Do I draw a line, saying we probably shouldn't flirt, considering we're family friends who slept together and there's no need to inflate this into anything more?

There's no room for words to come out of my mouth, however, because Clark kisses me. I'm so surprised I almost jerk away, but his hand is on the back of my head, trapping me. Somewhere in the depths of my mind there's an awareness that this could be deemed problematic, but the truth is I'm glad for my inability to ruin this. The kiss is hard and deep and fast, as he pulls away quickly and turns back to rearranging the dishwasher just as I hear light footsteps walking down the hall.

"What'd I miss?" Susan asks as she walks in, and I immediately drop the wineglass I had been rinsing. It clatters loudly in the sink but thankfully doesn't break.

We're all leaning over the kitchen island when Susan opens the Dolly print, which she predictably gasps at as though it were round-trip tickets to Bali or something. "Do I have you to thank for this?" she asks, booping my nose with her pointer finger like I'm a puppy.

"Yep," Clark says.

"Well, I just love it," Susan says, holding it up and admiring it, the kitchen chandelier reflected in its plastic covering. "I'll have it framed, and it'll look gorgeous in my closet."

I try to stifle a snort, and Clark grins at me, eyebrows raised: *I told you.*

We eat the cupcakes I brought (another greenroom leftover) after lighting one and singing to Susan, Clark in a baritone, with Michael FaceTiming in. By "we," I mean Clark and I eat, while Susan politely nibbles. I say I have to go, it's a work night, as if on this exact work night last week I wasn't belting the Dixie Chicks with one of them and being undressed by the other.

"Lawrence, you go, too, and make sure Presley gets home safe," Susan says.

An icy hand grips my chest, nervousness settling in me like fresh snow. I don't know if Clark's earlier kiss is going to extend into something else this evening, and I don't know if I want it to. And by that I mean, I do know that I want it to, but ideally it would happen in a vacuum where it would mean absolutely nothing and there would be no consequences.

And by "it," I do unfortunately mean everything, including the cuddling and the giggling and all that shit I've built a brand around hating. Susan kisses us on our cheeks, crushes our ribs in her hugs, and sends us on our way.

"So," Clark says as we exit the building and start walking toward Lex. "Do you want to get a drink or something?"

I pull my coat closer around me and shove my hands as deep in my pockets as I can get them. It's freezing. "I should just get home and get to bed," I say, thinking longingly of warmth. And of solitude, after hearing that damn song.

"Hm," Clark says. "Would you like company for that?"

My voice is stuck in my throat, not that I know what I want to say anyway. I recognize that he has been inside my body, but somehow the idea of him inside my apartment seems more intimate. "I think I'm good," I say. We stop at a crosswalk. He turns to me, and I look at him.

"Well, okay, then," he says, clearly stung.

"It's not that I don't want to hang out," I say carefully. "Tonight's just not . . . I just can't tonight." My heart is drumming away in my chest and I feel hollow. The light changes and we cross the street.

He shakes his head. "All good," he says, but I can't read his tone. "Listen, I'm sorry about playing that song."

"Nothing for you to be sorry for," I say, eyes trained on the ground in front of our walking feet.

"Okay, but I'm sorry for what you're going through," he says quietly. He squeezes my shoulder. It's quick and comforting, like when Isabelle does it.

"Thanks."

"You know, you can talk to me about it anytime you want. I'm here for you, Presley."

"I'm good." I'm not sure how I meant that: like I'm fine or like I'm passing on the opportunity. I suppose I want him to think both, though one is clearly a lie.

He sighs. "I just—"

"Let's just not." I quicken my pace, and he matches me with ease. Those damned long legs. A crosswalk stops us in our tracks, and I check for cars and, seeing none, continue walking.

"All right, subject change needed, noted. Got a question for you," he says.

My heart rate speeds up. "Yeah."

"I may or may not have encouraged my dad to call my mom today. Bad idea?"

My exhale of relief is visible in the cold air. Much easier to talk about his parents' complicated marriage than to reference a sexual future with him or discuss my grief. I have time to think about my response, too, as we start digging through our pockets for our MetroCards as the Seventy-Seventh Street station comes into view. "I'll ride with you to Union Square," he says.

We rush through the turnstile, a 6 train already at the platform. Clark beats me to it, then turns, holding a hand on the door to keep it open as I hop on. We plop down onto a bench just as the train starts moving. I immediately begin to thaw, from the change in both temperature and subject. The car is nearly empty except for a large man openly staring at us from the corner, and I'm grateful for Clark's presence. And frustrated by the idea of needing protection.

"I don't think it was a bad idea," I say. I think about Susan's anger the last time I was in her apartment, how disappointed and disgusted she seemed in Thomas. But she hasn't left him yet either. "I mean, they're married. Doesn't seem like she's made up her mind about what she wants to do, right? So if he wants to be with her, I'd think calling her on her birthday would be square one, you know?"

"Yeah," he says. I knew Susan and Thomas weren't talking, but it occurs to me now that I didn't know the effort he had or had not been putting in. "I wonder if she's actually going to call him back or not."

"Me too," I say. "Though, you know . . . different stakes for me."

Clark pushes out a quick little "ha" as he shrugs out of his coat, the train considerably warmer than outside. I see our reflection in the train window, like I did that first time we got a drink after the Comedy Cellar. He looks tired now, asking about the phone call, and I realize I've never experienced anything other than his seemingly boundless energy, even when we first woke up almost a week ago. An urge overtakes me, and without thinking about it, I squeeze Clark's hand. When I go to pull it away, he holds on to it, and we ride the rest of the way to Union Square like that.

CHAPTER 35

"Big day today," I hear behind me. It's been a while since I've heard his voice, and I'd be lying if I said I hadn't missed it. I turn, and Adam is standing there, clearly unsure of what to do with himself. In the old days, he'd sit on my desk, and Peanut would eventually make his way over from outside Mark's office. Now he bounces from foot to foot, his skinny frame vibrating with nervous energy.

He's right, though. It is a big day. The whole office is buzzing with the energy of it—at least in my head they are. I'm wearing my best dress, one that Susan got me for Christmas. I'm even wearing mascara.

Tom Hanks is here today.

"That it is," I say.

He smiles, and there's that beam, that old Morse code feeling. But I feel differently about it now. I used to think *I* didn't know what it was he was trying to say, but now I suspect he has no idea either.

"Remember last time he was here?" he asks. I do, of course. It was the day we met. I nod. I wait for my heart rate to become irregular, for my breath to catch. Adam. Talking to me about the day we met. The full beam of his attention pointed at me.

Maybe it's because I asked him not to speak to me and he's blatantly breaking that. Maybe it's because there's no fog to peer through anymore, trying to make out the shape of what we are: he has a girlfriend, who isn't me. Maybe it's because I held hands on the train with Clark, and when I felt something as solid and real as that, the aura around the make-believe of me and Adam dissipated. Whatever it is, my body is behaving as indifferently as if he were the guy behind the counter at Ray's or some dude on the B train. Nobody special.

"Look," he says, exhaling and raking a hand through his hair. I used to find that so endearing, and I notice now that it seems like something of a studied move. "I know you asked me not to talk to you, and I want to respect that." I open my mouth to ask him, if that's true, why the hell is he doing it? But I close it. Arguments are for subjects, and people, you care about. He goes on: "But I just want to say that I've thought about everything, and I'm really sorry."

I feel my eyes squinting, confused. I try to remove the acid from my voice and say, "Yeah, you said that when we talked. I know you're sorry." He looks at me, and it dawns on me suddenly what he wants. He wants me to tell him that I forgive him, he wants to be exonerated from the guilt he feels. This is classic Adam: needing to be verbally affirmed, unable to function thinking someone he cares about is angry with him. I used to see this as valiant, an act of caring, and I appreciated his dedication to his relationships. But he's not my pal sitting on my desk anymore, he's a former whatever-he-was standing in front of me, and from this new angle I see it differently. The selfishness of it. The space I asked for doesn't matter to him, because *he* doesn't want it.

I'm aware that I don't actually know Tom Hanks, but I wholeheartedly believe that if a woman asked him for space, he would give it to her. For some reason, this makes me feel better.

Solely to placate him, not for his sake but for mine, so this can be over, I say: "Yeah, we're good, Adam."

He sighs, visibly relieved, and I try not to laugh out loud. Pathetic. He raises an eyebrow. "Friends again?" he asks.

I can't help but scoff. He seems to take this in jest and laughs, too. Jesus Christ. "Off you go," I say, and he skips away, like I was making a little joke. I sigh. Relief that there isn't this phantom of tension floating between us. Frustration that it took me as long as it did to recognize his selfishness. I turn back to my computer, tracking a flower delivery. I'll be damned if there aren't fresh orchids in Tom Hanks's dressing room.

·················

Finally, *the* Thursday comes around. I can tell Agatha is nervous when I walk into the greenroom and see her standing in front of the mirror, fidgeting with her high-waisted, brightly patterned suit.

"Hey!" she says to me when she sees me in the reflection. She rushes over and gives me a hug.

"You excited?" I ask.

"I feel like I'm gonna ralph," she says. She does look a bit green, despite the great work the hair and makeup team has done. "Plus, I feel like a fraud in this getup."

"You look fabulous," Agatha's sister, Priya, says from the couch. She stands and walks over to me, hand extended for a shake. "The famous Presley. I'm Priya."

"Great to meet you," I say. She nods and walks over to her sister, dusts something invisible off one of her shoulder blades.

"Are you sure you can't see the tags?" Agatha asks, staring as she pokes her ass out in the mirror, searching for a rectangular imprint.

"No tags in sight," I say. I take her by the shoulders and look into her brown eyes, ringed with sparkly liner. "Listen. You are going to be amazing. You've practiced this set so many times, and it's perfect. Gary loves it, and soon the whole world is going to love it." She takes a deep breath and nods. "Obviously, help yourself to anything in the fridge."

"Thanks for the sick swag bag," she says, grinning, holding up the *Late Night* tote bag filled with merch that all our guests get.

"Sure thing. I gotta go run around, but just text if you need anything at all, okay? Otherwise, I'll be back in an hour to get you."

I'm rounding the hall to go make sure the interns aren't somehow fucking up door duty when Peanut stops me, and I know immediately something is wrong. He looks terrified, his usually sparkly eyes wide with fear. "Bit of an issue," he says.

"Okay?"

"Oh God," he says, taking a shaky breath and looking at his feet. "You're gonna fucking kill me. I'm scared."

"What is it!"

"Mark," he begins. "So, you know how Mark has a nephew who lives in LA and is on the stand-up scene there?"

"No?"

"Well, he does. And I guess . . . I'm so sorry, Fry, I didn't know. But Mark's been telling Gary about this guy, and he happens to be in town this weekend and so . . . so, um . . ." Peanut takes a visible gulp. "So, he's actually gonna do the stand-up slot tonight."

Everything freezes. My body, my brain, my heart.

"I swear I had no idea he was talking to Gary about this, and it was so last minute, and it's fucked up, I know it's fucked up, but I'm sure Agatha can come back another time. I mean, she's local, I'm sure she could come back as soon as, like, next week."

Waves of nausea crash over me, and I can't feel my face. I'm enveloped in a swirl of shit: stomach-dropping disappointment for Agatha, acidic guilt that I'm going to let her down, and, most prominently, anger. Oh God, the anger. I could flip a motherfucking car with my bare hands right now. *Mark.* That prick. Emma. I need Emma. No. I can handle this myself.

I take a deep breath, and Peanut puts a hand on my shoulder. I nod and he removes it. "Okay," I somehow say through clenched teeth. "Well. I'm going to go confirm with Mark and handle it from there. Thanks for the heads-up, Peanut."

Fire courses through my veins as I exit the theater and make my way upstairs. Mark is sitting in his office, looking at his computer, probably just pretending to work. I clear my throat when I enter as a greeting, and he looks up. "Hey, Presley," he says. "Glad you stopped by. I was about to come and find—"

I cut him off. "Peanut told me. I'm just here to confirm that your *nephew*"—I can't keep the venom out of my voice as I spit that word—"is here to do the Friday stand-up slot?"

He shifts in his seat a little, and I swear I see a bit of a blush tinting his cheeks. Good. He should be ashamed of himself. "Yeah, I know it's pretty last-minute, but I showed Gary some of his stuff, and he happened to be in town, so it just kind of worked out this way."

A myriad of responses boils in my closed mouth. Such as: *And you didn't think to tell me yourself? And you've never mentioned him before? And won't he be back in New York at some point, preferably when we can book him in advance like professionals? And you knew we already had someone, someone who's been working her ass off, someone who actually deserves to be here?* But I swallow them all. We have a show to put on; there's no time for anything other than efficiency.

I don't even need to respond, because, of course, he just keeps talking. "I know you were excited about your comedian going on today. But she's local, so it won't be hard to have her back soon. You know how these things go. Show business, baby!" he says, pointing little finger guns at me as if this is nothing, instead of nepotism at its most disgusting.

I nod curtly, grit my teeth, biting back the urge to spew my anger. It won't be helpful.

He nods back. "Do you want advice on how to deliver the news?"

"Not from you," I say just before I turn on my heel and stalk out. Politically, that was a bad move. But I'm too riled up to give a fuck. If I'm going to become a producer on this show, it won't be because he helped me.

"Oh God, what is it?" Agatha asks as soon as I enter her greenroom, and I inwardly curse myself. I had hoped my face gave nothing away.

"We're going to have to reschedule." I figure it's best to just get the hard part out first, for both her sake and mine. "I'm so sorry. There was a last-minute change, which can happen with shows like these. Everyone here is excited about you, truly. We want you to do your spot here. It just can't be today."

"Why?" she asks, her previously wan face rising in color, frustration buzzing around where nerves had been just moments before.

I blink. On my way from the offices to the greenroom, I had tried to figure out how to phrase this. I want to be professional. I don't want to make the show look bad; I don't want to slander my higher-ups. Well, actually, I really would very much like to do that, but losing my cool isn't the right call right now. But it's also important that she trust me, and that I build a good reputation among the comedians I respect, and that has to involve honesty. She should know that I know that this is unfair.

"There's a comedian a producer has had interest in who's West Coast based. He's in town this week, so it makes sense from a budget standpoint to go ahead and put him on today, with the plan to bring you in a different week. As early as next week, honestly. It was a total breakdown in communication that all this got sorted out so last-minute, and I'm really embarrassed that it's going down like this. This isn't how we like to do things here."

"'He,' yeah," Agatha scoffs. "Straight, white, check, check, check. Do we know him?"

I shake my head. "I hadn't heard of him. I don't cover West Coast."

Agatha swallows and looks at her sister, who has remained calm, eyes flickering between me and Agatha like she's at Wimbledon throughout this whole exchange. She sighs. "Well, okay, then. This blows, but it is what it is."

"I'm sorry, again," I say. Pathetic. Like me mumbling that I'm sorry is going to fix anything.

Agatha starts methodically wrapping each doughnut in a paper towel and placing them in her tote bag. "May as well make the most of this," she mutters.

CHAPTER 36

I won't lie: I may have pitched a fit about it at first, but I'm starting to appreciate the alone time I get in our apartment now that Isabelle so often sleeps at Julia's. Though tonight, eating a chicken salad sandwich (Trader Joe's Wine Country Chicken Salad is the only tolerable chicken salad in this city) with as much rage as if *it* had been the one to cancel Agatha's performance today, I would love to vent about it to her. I texted her that I had an awful story for her next time she was home, and she offered to come home tonight instead of going to Julia's, but I told her not to worry. My rage isn't going anywhere. It also helps that Emma got approval for me to take Agatha out for a nice apology dinner on the show's dime. I'm texting with her now about where we want to make a reservation (and about how Mark's nephew bombed, much to my satisfaction), so that we can spend oodles of someone else's money two Thursdays from now, after she actually gets to do her set.

Our texting is interrupted by an incoming call. "Shit," I say out loud, to no one, when I see Clark's name on my screen. I'm out of my depth here. I don't have a handbook outlining the appropriate next move in the sleeping together, then rejecting someone's sexy invitation, then holding hands on the train pipeline. The temptation to not answer, then text him that I'm heading into a show is overwhelming, but a cop-out doesn't sit well. Plus, hearing his voice doesn't sound exactly bad.

I answer. "Hi."

"Hey," he says, and I can hear the din of the city around him, can practically see his breath in the cold air. "I'm calling because I'm in your neighborhood. Wanna meet up?"

I swallow and look down at my sweatpants. I'm fresh from the shower—wet hair and braless. I think I'd rather be bludgeoned than put on real clothes. The idea of donning my puffy coat and heading back out into the freezing night is far from ideal. There's also something bulky and awkward sitting in my throat, blocking me from making up an excuse and saying no. I realize I do want to see him. "Um," I say, "I'm sort of, like, already in my comfy clothes." Comfy clothes?

"Okay," he says, and I hear him sigh. "Look, Presley, I want to see you, and I don't care if that means sitting on your couch and just chilling. If you don't want to see me, tonight or ever or whatever, then just tell me. I'm not gonna play some game with you here. So, let me try this again. I want to see you. Do you want to see me?"

My body goes very cold, then very hot, and I fear I might be blushing like a schoolgirl, and thank Christ no one is here to see it. I look around the apartment. Clean, per my usual work. I should have time to wolf down my sandwich and brush my teeth and hair. My mouth seems to decide to go with my gut before my brain does. "Do you want to just come over here, then?"

I swear I can hear him grinning his big, stupid grin through the phone, like his large features project it through the line. "See you in a bit. I know your cross streets but text me your address. Be there in five."

After texting him my address, shoving my plate in the sink, and yanking the appropriate brushes through my teeth and hair, I light a candle. Then I blow it out. Who do I think I am, a *seducer*? I'm still working toward open flirting; open seduction is a bridge too far. My buzzer sounds, and suddenly a winded Clark (those stairs) is standing in my doorway, the rush of cold air he brought up with him rolling over me. He immediately engulfs me in a hug and I shiver, awkwardly failing to properly fit my arms around his big coat and backpack.

He steps in and looks around. "This is nice!" he says, shrugging out of his backpack and coat.

"Do you want a drink or anything?" I ask. If he does, I hope it's whiskey. That's all we have at the moment.

"Nah, I'm good," he says, shaking his head and plopping down on the couch. His knees come up so high with the way he sinks into it, I can't help but smirk. I don't think we've ever had someone his size in our apartment before.

I sit on the hand-me-down yellow armchair, and he frowns and shakes his head. "What?" I say. I think I meant the word to come out flirty, maybe even suggestive, but it certainly did not. It sounds like I'm trying to start a fight.

He pats the spot on the couch next to him, and I roll my eyes and sit there. He grabs my knees and swings my legs so they're over his lap. Rotated, I lean back against the pillow on the armrest. "So. How are you?" he asks.

For some reason, this feels like a shocking thing to ask. Like he came here to talk. I'm not used to being alone in apartments with men who want to talk. "Uh," I say. "Good. How are you?"

"Eh, I'm okay." He looks down at my knees, resting on his lap, and gives each kneecap a squeeze. It's not something I ever would have expected to feel good, but it does. To be touched in a place I don't think about. "My dad is in the city," he says. "At home."

"Whoa," I say, expelling air I didn't realize I had been holding. Thomas is back. Susan is just taking him back? "How do you know?"

"I have his location, which I don't think he realizes," he says. "I was helping my roommate look for his phone on Find My Friends, and there Thomas was, on Eightieth."

"When?"

"Yesterday. And he's still there now." He's drumming on my knee-caps and must hit my reflex, because I involuntarily kick my left leg a little. Clark chuckles softly to himself, and it's a laugh I haven't heard before. High-pitched and goofy, like he's utterly delighted. My heart rate picks up at how completely ridiculous, but also wonderful, the sound is. I swallow, root myself back to the moment. Susan. Is Susan resolving things with him right now? Or ending things? Has he been coming back regularly and I just didn't know? Did she invite him back, or did he show up unannounced? Is he just getting clothes, or are they, like, having sex right now? I shudder.

Then I remember that I'm sitting here with the product of such a union. "Did you, like, reach out?" Clark shakes his head, continues his drumming. "Are you okay?"

He nods. "I called Michael, who was just like, 'Well, I guess we'll see. I mean, it's his apartment, too. He had to come back sometime. Could be for any number of reasons.' And he's right. So now, I'm just, like, waiting for one of them to say anything, like if this was a we-made-a-decision-and-the-decision-needed-to-be-made-in-person kind of thing. Or if it's . . . something else."

"Yeah, wow," I say. I'm disturbed to report that in light of this news that will deeply affect the futures of Susan and Clark, my friend and my who-knows-what, my primary concern is whether *this* is the reason Clark came over tonight. Assuming he doesn't want to ask Susan about it before she brings it up herself, I'm the only person in the city he can really talk to about this. Instant humiliation engulfs me that I thought for even a second that he was here for anything other than his family troubles. I'm his *family friend*. I reorient myself around this and hope none of that is visible. "Well, what do you think about all this?" I ask.

He shrugs and looks at me, eyes wide, like *who the fuck knows*. "I don't know," he confirms. "Part of me wants to know, and part of me doesn't, and I guess I'm just closer to knowing now. But I'll probably start asking questions of ol' Suze if no one tells me anything soon."

I nod. "That makes sense. For what it's worth, Susan hasn't said anything to me about it." Not that I would necessarily tell him if she had.

He smirks. "That actually is good to know." Further evidence that he's here to vent and/or retrieve information. "Whatever, we'll see. Anyway. How was your comedian?"

I groan, tilting my head back. I had forgotten I mentioned Agatha coming to the show at Susan's birthday dinner. I tell him about what happened, and he is appropriately horrified on behalf of both Agatha and me. "I'm sorry, Presley," he says, squeezing each kneecap at the same time this time, and I will myself not to blush, but I feel my legs relaxing into him when he lets go. "That's crap. But it's just a speed bump, not a dead end."

"Yeah," I say, oddly encouraged by the analogy. "Tell me about your new coordinator life." And he does. And we talk and talk, and then he wraps his arms around my waist and scoots me closer to him, wrapping an arm around me, placing my head under his chin.

"I wanted to talk to you about something," he says. I tilt my head back and look at him.

"Okay."

He smiles. "You don't have to look so scared."

"I'm not scared." The quickness with which I reply does little to help my case.

"Right, totally," he says, clearly teasing, and suddenly I want distance, so I scoot back to where I was resting against the edge of the couch, and he puts his hands back on my knees. His eyes search my face, like Waldo might be hiding on my lash line.

"So, shoot," I say, waiting for him to tell me he doesn't want me to read too much into what happened after karaoke or he has gonorrhea or whatever.

"I've been thinking a lot about what happened the other night, at my parents' place. When my mom told that story about your mom, and we listened to that song and you . . . you got upset."

I might prefer gonorrhea.

And I don't think I was visibly upset. I mean, I'm sure I didn't look happy, and I know I left the table, but I came back, and the night went on. My instinct is to defend myself, to correct him. My conversation with Isabelle springs into my mind, and I stop. I don't think he's here for us to argue about whether I *looked* upset. I brush something invisible off my lap. "So?" I say, congratulating myself on my bravery for not covering up the fact that it was a tough moment.

"So, are you okay?" Clark asks me.

"Am I okay that I had to listen to a song my dead mother sang about being sad and drunk, before she was even sad and—well, I guess she was drunk." I look up at Clark quickly and shake my head. "Fuck, I'm sorry," I say, instantly covering the tracks I had just made in my own mind, the ones about sharing my grief.

Clark shakes his head, just once. "Why are you sorry? I asked."

"Why?"

"Why what?"

"Why did you ask?" It accidentally comes out accusatory.

He tilts his head, looks so confused. "What?" he asks.

"I just mean, like, why are you asking me about this?" He still looks confused, but the corners of his mouth turn up, and the look is sympathetic, almost condescending, and it bothers me so deeply it's like a claw has scraped through my kidney. "Whatever," I mutter, and I lift my legs off him, attempt to pull them into me, but he grabs my ankles, and it knocks the wind out of me, thinking about the last time he did that, and now I'm not only defensive and bruised but also horny? It's all very confusing.

He sets my legs back down across his lap. My hands are folded over my middle, and he places one of his big hands on top of them. His fingers are spindly and delicate, which is very at odds with the rest of his oafish presence. "Don't do that," he says, and for perhaps the first time in my life, I find myself not incensed to have been given an instruction by a man. He exhales, frustrated, I think. "Let me start over. I am checking on you because I care. You've been through something really hard, and I want you to know you can talk to me about it. I *want* you to talk to me about it. You can trust me. I mean, I trust you."

I blink, just for something to do. I let some air out. Maybe it's because we're in my apartment, on my home turf. Maybe it's because it's easy to conjure Isabelle here, to hear her telling me to open up. Maybe it's that I already got upset in front of him, so what is there to lose? And maybe I want to talk about her. Not talking about her hasn't helped the way I thought it would. I need to suck out my own poison, maybe.

"I sometimes . . ." I grab the cup of water sitting on a Pamela Anderson coaster and take a sip, not looking at Clark. I study the inside of the cup. "It's hard to think about her like that."

"Like what?" Clark asks me quietly.

"Young." I sneak a glance at him, and he's looking at me so fastidiously I have to look back down. I won't be able to say anything while confronting that gaze. "My mom and I didn't always have the best relationship. I'm not sure what your mom has told you, but she didn't have the easiest time of things, my mom." Clark doesn't confirm or deny, but he does squeeze my kneecaps again. I take another sip of water, but it doesn't loosen the knot sitting in my throat. "And I guess it's pretty selfish, but kids are selfish, and when I was a kid I didn't think a lot about what she was like when she was my age. I was always just, like, so pissed at her, and, uh, embarrassed by her, I think." Fuck. I'm crying, the tears have spilled over, and I wipe at them furiously, not even giving my tears a chance to hit my cheek. I don't apologize, though. "But lately I've just been thinking more about when she was young, before life got so hard for her. And it just . . . It's just so devastating: all the things she wanted and never got." I sniff, trying to force all the snot back into my face. I feel Clark return my legs to me and he stands, walks the three steps to our kitchen counter, hands me a paper towel on the way back. I blow my nose, and it's a real honk.

"Nice one," Clark says.

"Thanks."

"Come here," he says, and I didn't know words could be so soft. He pulls me into him, and my head is on his expansive chest again, and my tears must want to feel privy to it, too, with the way they rush out of me and onto his button-down. Somewhere in the depths of my mind my familiar embarrassment lurks, but I'm pleased to report it's not mortification. It feels good, actually, to sit here and cry on him. A release. Well, as good as crying about my mother's wasted life can feel.

Clark kisses the top of my head. "I remember her, you know. She snuck me an extra piece of cake at my grandmother's funeral."

I laugh, and it's snotty. Of course she did, probably to piss Susan off. I press the back of the paper towel to my eyes, blow my nose again. I deposit it on our coffee table and he pulls me back into his arms. We're quiet for a moment, and then he says, "I'm sorry, Presley." I feel him swallow against the side of my head. "I'm so, so sorry." And his voice is low and quiet and I believe him.

I take a rattly breath. "Thanks," I say.

Eventually, I pull my head back and look up at him. "You know we played *Pokémon* together after that funeral?"

"Was it *Pokémon*?" he asks. "I thought it was *Super Mario*."

"Shit, you might be right," I say.

"I'll bet you were obsessed with Princess Peach," he says, and my jaw drops in offense and he tilts his head back and laughs and we talk about video games and other stupid shit we did as kids, and my face dries and I laugh at how excited he was to go visit his grandparents in Eulalia because it meant Chuck E. Cheese, which of course they didn't have in Manhattan, and we just sit like that, telling each other stories, until he pulls me up and onto him, so I'm basically on his lap, just like we were in the cab coming home from karaoke. And he puts his hand, the one that's not supporting me teetering on him, on my face, and in my hair, and he's looking at me and I'm looking at him and my breath is stolen and he kisses me and something inside of me unwraps and I'm melting directly into him, not a drop of me spilling anywhere else. My hair is still damp from my shower, and my sweatpants and Boar's Head T-shirt and this drafty living room feel so comfortable, and so does Clark.

Clark stands, cradling me to him, and I wrap one of my legs around his waist, and just as I'm silently celebrating how suave and sexy the move was, he rears his head back. "Presley?" he asks.

I swallow, nervous. "Yes?"

"I want to be all smooth and cool, but I don't know which room is yours."

I tilt my head back and laugh, and he's laughing his Clark laugh, too, and then I point and he carries me to my closet of a room, swinging my door open with his foot. He lays me down on my bed, so gently I'm worried about the effort it must take. He climbs on top of me and kisses me deeply, gravity pouring him into me. My hands are in his hair, on his chest, around the back of his neck, and then he rolls over and I go with him and now I'm the one being poured into him.

My fingers find the button of his pants and pop it open, the zipper easy to pull down. Before I can get any further, he rolls over me again, and his kisses drift from my lips to the corner of my mouth to my jaw to my neck and back up again as his hand slides beneath the elastic band of my ancient Champion sweatpants. The second his finger meets me he lets out a breath so euphoric and relieved I think he surely must be exaggerating, but as his finger starts moving it becomes impossible to think about what he's thinking: I'm suddenly only every buzzing, electric, vibrating nerve ending in my body. And I'm struck by how I had forgotten, with my get-in-get-out way of doing things, as his fingers move assuredly and fluidly in me, what it's like to take time, to have this teased out of me. I'm drowning in myself, in my body's ability to feel this way, and I'm suddenly so in love with myself I could scream. And then it happens: I'm blinded and shaking and Clark is breathing into my neck so hard I'm a little worried he came, too.

You'd think it would be enough. And it is, but also, as I'm lying here, trying to catch my breath and feeling him collapse next to me, and I'm looking at his flushed face and those big eyes looking into mine, so bright I'm almost scared my room will catch flame, what a waste it would be not to keep things going. So I swing my leg over him and yank his pants down and touch him so gently I'm surprised by his moan, and then I see the way he's gripping my duvet cover and all my thoughts stop making sense.

I kiss him, then pull away. "Do you want to have sex?" I ask him, knowing the answer. I feel him nod beneath me, grab a condom from my bedside table, and hand it to him, yank his pants and boxers all the way down while he rolls it on. I step out of my sweats, too, straddle him again. I look down at him and a smile plays at his big, cartoon mouth. He shakes his head slightly and tugs at the hem of my T-shirt.

"Off," he says.

I roll my eyes. "I let you see my boobs one time, and now . . ." But I pull it over my head, shiver as the air hits my chest.

He looks at me, swallows hard, his Adam's apple bobbing down his neck as his eyes scan my naked body. Suddenly self-conscious, I tug at the hem of his shirt, and I lean back as he sits up and takes it off. He lies back down, expression the same. Looking at me so seriously, none of his affable Clarkness on him at all. His eyes big like UFOs, and I'm pretty sure I could disappear in them. Pretty sure I want to.

"Presley," he says. My throat is so thick I don't think I can say anything, so I just keep looking at him. His eyes keep searching my face, and I know he can't figure out what to say, so I lean over him, smoothing his wavy hair away from his face, resting my forehead on his, like I know what romance is. And then I lower myself onto him and his hands crisscross against my back, pulling me in close, until I sit up and pin his hands down with mine and our breathing syncs. I'm lost, I'm so lost, but I'm also completely aware that I am in the exact right place. I hadn't realized sex could be like this, so full of contradictions. Like how I feel both so powerful and so vulnerable, am both starved and satiated. Clark moans into my neck and I curl around him, then collapse next to him, trying to catch my breath.

By the time I do, Clark is standing over me, condom deposited in the trash, butt-ass naked (but for his socks), tugging at my covers. I shimmy under them and he does the same, pulls me close. My head is on his chest and he kisses my forehead. I take a deep breath, unsure if I've ever felt this relaxed in my life.

"Presley?" he whispers.

"Mm-hmm?" I say, and am surprised by how raspy I sound, like my vocal cords have thickened.

"I need to say something." I lift my head off his chest, prop myself up on my elbow. I'm taken aback by how serious he looks, and I lie back down on my pillow, busy myself with the top of my ratty IKEA duvet, smoothing the lumps out. He puts his fingers under my chin and pulls it up, forcing eye contact. "I like you," he says, and suddenly there's pressure from his fingers because I'm jerking my chin back down to my chest, unable to look at him, or anything, other than my own body beneath my covers. "Hey," he says, and my eyes jump back to his face, considering my own is held in place. "Don't do that. Please just listen to me. I like you, Presley. I really like you."

A ribbon of something warm inflates in my chest, spreads into my limbs. His directness, his vulnerability, hits me like a gust of wind. I automatically look away from him, then force my eyes back to his face. I commit to avoid the disservice of looking away now. "You're obviously beautiful, but what I like about you is, like, the fact that you're hot is almost the most boring part about you. I just mean, you're so smart and so funny and so sweet. No. Listen!" he says, playfully putting a hand over my mouth as I gag at being referred to as "sweet." He goes on, "I know you try and, like, fight people from seeing it. But you're just so full of goodness. You, like, shine with it. I think it's because you care about all the right shit. And I just . . ." His eyes had drifted up to the ceiling, but now he turns, looks dead-on at me, and grins. "I wish I could say something smarter about it all, but I'm just fucking smitten, okay?"

A sound comes from my throat, and I know it sounds an awful lot like another gag. But I don't mean for it to, and I instantly regret it. Because something like shame flickers across his eyes. But also: What am I supposed to do with this? Coming from him, Clark, this man who took one look at a girl one time and then dedicated, like, eight years of his life to her? I swallow, feel like I'm caving in on myself.

"I'm sure you say that to all the girls," I say as I study my duvet, trying my damnedest for my voice to sound light, floaty.

I hear the scratching of his head on my pillow as he shakes it. He cups my face with his hand again, pulling me back into his gaze. "There's no girl like you, Presley. Don't act like you don't know it."

Even though it makes me lose my breath, it rings some bell in me, that sentiment. My heartbeat rings deafeningly in my ears. I know that this isn't some weird fever dream because of how in my body I am, but I can barely see him, I'm so blinded by my own disbelief. I had no idea that a man could be this blunt, that it could sound easy to be this sure when speaking about these things. Feelings. *Liking* someone, and *why*. I know I need to say something; I *want* to say something, because I see, in those big, golden retriever brown eyes, a flicker of something that I think might be fear. The ever-confident Lawrence Clark: nervous. And I want to snuff that out for him. I clear my throat, but something rattles, and then I'm coughing. I sit up and reach over him for a cup of water that's been sitting on my bedside table for at least two days and gulp it down. "Sorry," I say.

He reaches around me and theatrically thumps me on my back, then pulls me down so I'm supine again. "You good?" he asks.

"I don't know, man," I say.

He nods. We're both propped up on my pillows, facing each other, sleepover style. He looks sad. "Well. I just wanted to be up front, be-cause if you're not interested, that's fine, but it's information that would be good to know."

Now it's my turn to nod. This, the needing to know, I understand. "I totally get that." I take a breath. He looks at me expectantly, but the right thing to say eludes me.

"Okay," he says, and his eyes rip away from mine and he sighs.

"I don't know what to say," I say, frustrated by my inability to artic-ulate. I think of the anger, the postmortem longing I had for Adam to have been this direct with me. The pain I could have been saved. And now here someone sits, and I'm drawing things out and being silent, and I'm sure he's assuming that I'm trying to figure out how to let him down easy. And I do like him, but . . .

Oh, the *buts*. *But* how can he be sure he likes me? It's not like he knows me *that* well. *But* how can I be sure I like him, when, like, five minutes ago I was in love with an asshat? *But* it's a complicated situa-tion, what with my friendship with his *mother*. *But* how can I be sure

he's over that ex-girlfriend of his? *But* what if we're just in a complicated soup of feelings, given the little breakdown I just had, what he's
dealing with in his family? *But* what if we're being rash, and then we
make a really big mess that could have been avoided had we not given
in to a silly impulse?

But what about the way he's looking at me now? But look at how
open and vulnerable and *sure* he just was, telling me these things. But
maybe he *does* know me, really does see me. And this: the thumping
of my heart and the warm, fuzzy feeling bouncing off him at all times
that envelops me like a blanket and that laugh and those hands and
how nice he is to his mom . . .

"Um . . . ," I say, trying to quiet the din in my own head enough to
get some words out, to save him from my silence. "I'm not, like, good
at this." He laughs. Hooting, head thrown back, obliterating some of
the tension. My shoulders drop a little, but I still dig for words while I
wait for him to quiet down. The craving to be in my room, alone, hits
swiftly. This is a lot to think about and I can't do it in front of him. I
can't feel my feet on the floor, so I anchor them to my mattress. "Is it
okay if I take some time to think about it?"

For a moment, there is only silence, as neither of us breathes. And
I have the crazy thought, What if I suffocate? What if it kills me, this
inability to say anything? Then a slow sigh leaks out of him, and he
nods. Like two psychos, we're fully staring at each other, and I swear I
can see his brain buzzing as he tries to figure out what to say now. He
doesn't say anything; he just keeps looking at me and strokes my hair.
I almost open my mouth to tell him I'm not a dog, but it feels pretty
damn good, so I refrain. I close my eyes and he plants a wet smooch
on my forehead. I open my eyes when I feel him leave the bed, sit up
and watch as he gathers his clothes off the floor and starts putting
them on. My heart floats up to my throat, because suddenly, I don't
want him to leave. But I'm sure as hell not about to beg anyone to stay.
Especially when I have no right, considering how I just responded to
his proclamation of like.

I join him in dressing, though I catch him staring at me as I pull my shirt over my head. "Perv," I say.

"Definitely," he says. I walk him to my front door, and he pulls me into him, my arms again struggling to fit around his big puffer jacket. He pulls back, takes my face in his hands, and looks at me. "*You* have to call *me*, okay? If you want this."

"Okay," I say quietly.

Then he kisses me. And leaves.

CHAPTER 37

Two mornings later, I'm staring at my phone in bed, somewhere between asleep and awake, scrolling Instagram: Julia holding up a beer, toasting some cocktail Izzy is holding in front of her camera; a *New York Times* article about the Bill Cosby trial; the toddler of a kid from my high school I really have no business following these days. I minimize the app and in doing so catch today's date. My stomach drops.

It's officially been two years since my grandma called me when I was walking home from that show, two years since I saw that Elvis graffiti. Two years since I drove from the Atlanta airport to Eulalia in a daze, focusing on the mission to get there so that no other thoughts or feelings could permeate. Two years since it was already too late by the time I showed up.

Two years since Patty died.

"Hey, darlin'," Grammy says after picking up on the second ring. She must have already been sitting in her La-Z-Boy to have been able to pick up the home phone from its cradle right next to her chair so fast.

"Hi, Gram."

"How are you doing?" she asks me.

"I'm okay," I say, rolling onto my back and staring up at the water-stained ceiling. "How are you doing?"

"I'm okay, too," she says. She sounds tired, weary.

I swallow a lump in my throat. "What do you think Mom would have wanted to do today, if she were . . . ?" I don't finish the sentence, because I can't.

"Hm," Gram says. I want her to say something about going to the park, about catching a movie, about eating a good dinner. Maybe visiting the Humane Society—that was something Patty liked to do. But we know that Patty probably would have gotten drunk today, slowly, during her shift at the Winn-Dixie or the hardware store or on the couch alone. She would have picked a fight with one of us, or yelled at the TV, or cried on the phone. "Well, it's raining here," Gram says. "Good thing, too, plants need it. So, maybe she wouldn't have had work, and maybe we would have had a lazy day and watched TV. Maybe a marathon of something. One time when it was raining, I swear we watched seven episodes of that Olivia Benson in a row."

I sit up in bed, pulling my covers over my chest. It's cold in my room. "She's good at her job, that Detective Benson."

Gram chuckles a little into the phone, and neither of us knows what to say. You might think after two years we would have the words. I'd say anything I think she would want to hear, but I don't know what that could possibly be. Besides, there's no way I can get away with anything besides honesty with Grammy, but nothing honest sounds nice or original.

So I say something true. "Well, I love you, Grammy."

"I love you, too, Presley. Very much. So much." Her voice cracks.

The sound of a phone being picked up off a cradle, a throat clear, then, "Well, hey there, Miss New York City." Pops must have picked up in the kitchen.

"Hi," I say, my voice thickening, my room suddenly looking blurry. "How are you?"

He sighs. "'Bout as good as I reckon I can expect. You?"

"'Bout the same."

We all just sit on the line, breathing. We'd always felt something like a team of three. This group feels wrong without Patty, though. I guess it's hard to consider yourself a team when the thing that brought you together, the issue you've been tackling, no longer exists. But that doesn't mean there isn't a lot of love here, crackling through their corded phones and throughout the house in Eulalia, traveling across the airwaves into my ear in the East Village.

"I know she wasn't always the best at showin' it," my grandfather says, "but I hope you know that your mother loved you. She loved you so much. She loved you with her whole heart. And while she was gone too soon, I don't think she would have lasted as long as she did without you."

The tears that had been gathering in my eyes moments earlier now fully coat my cheeks, plopping onto my chest. I wipe them with the back of my hand and take a breath, which makes a shaky noise. "I know," I manage to get out before I'm keeled over, shoulders shaking, because I *do* know. And somehow that's the most painful part of all. She didn't drink herself to death because she didn't love me or because I didn't love her. She drank herself to death because, well, I don't know why. There are zero reasons and a million reasons. The tragedy is that she loved me, and it wasn't enough. It wasn't enough to stop her dying, it wasn't enough for her to be a good mother, it wasn't enough to overshadow the dim sum menu of emotional issues I carry around day after day. It was a broken love, but it was something, and now it's gone.

My buzzer sounds, snapping my spine upright. I wipe my eyes again and try another breath. It's still shaky. "She loved you both, too," I say through sobs. Nothing I can do to hide it anymore. "And even if she didn't show you how grateful she was to you for everything you did for us, I hope you know how much I love and appreciate it. You're my family, and I'm so glad I have you. I'm so, so lucky."

"Oh, honey," my grandma says in a wet voice. "We're the lucky ones."

"And we love you so much," Pops says. I nod, even though he can't see me, and try to inhale again, but my nostrils are blocked with snot. The buzzer sounds again.

"Um, I gotta go, someone's at my door," I say.

"Someone you know?" my grandma says, perpetually on edge that city life has me under constant threat of murder or robbery.

"Yeah, yeah, Isabelle's just coming in," I lie. I don't have it in me to explain delivery and our broken buzzer. We say more I love yous, hang up, and I buzz what I can only assume is a delivery meant for a different apartment. There's a knock at my door not a minute later, and I open it to a bouquet of flowers so large and colorful I'm embarrassed just looking at it. A deliveryman tries to stick his head around it.

"Presley Fry?" he asks me, not waiting for me to answer and shoving the flowers into my hands.

"Thanks," I call down the hall as he takes off in a flash, eager to get away from the girl who probably looks like she just got hit by a train.

The card on the flowers reads, unsurprisingly: "Thinking of you today, a bit more than most. I know your mother is looking down on you and smiling. Love to you and your family xx Susan." It's so painfully Susan, but I'm basically just a walking open wound right now, so the tears I thought I was done with rush back to refill my eyes.

When I go to set my phone down on the coffee table, I notice a Daily Provisions bag and a card. The card, of course, is from Izzy: "Wanted to respect your space today, but you know I'm just a phone call or text away. Please enjoy these donuts, which will surely heal all the pain you're feeling. On the real, I love you so much, P, and I know Patty did, too. I wish she were here to see how fucking fantastic you're doing." I peer into the bag. Maple crullers. I stuff as much of one as I can in my mouth immediately, and while Isabelle was kidding about it healing all my pain, it's so good that for a split second I think it might have.

I sit in the armchair and finish the doughnut. I open my messages to thank Izzy and Susan, when I see I missed a text that came in while I was on the phone with my grandparents. From Clark, whose mother undoubtedly told him the significance of today. It's a hunk of blue on the screen, the novel type of text that was probably crafted in the Notes app, then copied and pasted into iMessage. It plucks a string of tenderness in me, that thoughtfulness in caring about getting it right. It reads:

> Hey Presley, I wanted to tell you that I'm thinking about you today. Well, I think about you a lot, but it's extra today. I wish I knew what to say, I wish I could say something that would make you feel better, that would show that I get what today probably is for you. But I have no idea. So just know that I'm thinking of you, and Susan is, too, and I know a lot of other people probably are, because you're the kind of person people want good things for. And I'm here, if you want to talk.

I have to blink several times to get through the last bit, because these fucking tears are back again. The text is nothing eloquent. It's repetitive. It's honest. It's so *Clark*.

It's perfect.

I put my head down on the secondhand coffee table, and a puddle of tears forms immediately. I'm overwhelmed by the kindness and the love from these people. It feels so big, and so bright, that even though the pain from two full years without Patty is undeniably *there*, sitting in me like a trash island, it feels smaller, looser, weaker, like it could possibly be pushed out by something new.

CHAPTER 38

It's the first day of spring. I mean, not officially, I'm hardly a ground-hog. And I'm sure it's just temporary, a fake-out, and we'll all be reaching for our coats again in no time. But the sun is out, and it feels warm, and all us New Yorkers have our faces tipped up to the sun, soaking it in. I'm walking through Central Park with Susan, and we're laughing at the people who are acting like they just arrived at the beach: shirts discarded by people lying prostrate in Sheep Meadow, runners with legs exposed and skimpy tank tops. The visible hope of it all, that winter is gone.

On a less sexy note, I can't stop blowing my nose into the disgusting wad of bodega napkins I have wadded up in my jean jacket pocket (spring allergies are a bitch), which I have to reach farther for than usual considering my jacket is tied around my waist. I realize how little walking around I've done with Susan: our height difference feels ridiculous. I thanked Susan again for the flowers as soon as we started walking, to which she replied, "You're welcome," in a voice I could tell was choked with tears, which, considering my display in my apartment yesterday, I understand. I also told her that Clark had sent me a lovely text, so he would get credit for following through on her reminder. She replied in surprise, saying he had asked about the anniversary months ago, but she hadn't mentioned it to him again.

We're approaching the Great Lawn, more people sprawled out with minimal clothing, although in a more wholesome, family-fun kind of way. "There's something I wanted to tell you," she says in a pinched voice. I look down and over at her, and her Dior sunglasses conceal her eyes, and her head is tilted toward the fancy tennis shoes I believe she was wearing the day we ran into each other all those months ago at Daily Provisions.

"Shoot," I say, and I'm suddenly filled with the completely irrational fear that she's going to say something to me about sleeping with Clark.

"Thomas is coming back."

Selfishly, for just a quick moment, my chest loosens that this isn't about me and anything sexual or secret I've done with her son. Then it quickly retightens: concern, and what this could mean for her. And beneath that, what it means more widely, considering the moment we're in. She's something of a cultural guinea pig. What are women to do when their shitty media-men husbands come crawling back, begging for their forgiveness? *Well, Susan Clark let Thomas Clark, disgraced former head of American Network, back into their three-bedroom apartment on the Upper East Side.* Unless she just means he's coming back to the city, but solo?

"Into . . . our home," she says. So, not.

"Oh," I say, unsure of how I'm supposed to respond. I blow my nose again.

"I don't . . ." She sighs deeply, a sound gravelly with frustration, nearly a groan. "I don't want to bore you with the details, but I will say, he is my husband. He is my family. And yes, he made a big mistake. And, well, some others. But when I married him, I said vows, and I meant them. And I choose him. I choose my sons. I choose them over think pieces in *The New York Times*, I choose him over what Gary Madden and whoever else has to say on television, and I choose him over what anyone at goddamn Michael's thinks about it, that's for sure." We both laugh. "I just wanted you to know, is all."

I nod as we continue walking. A dog walker with about thirteen different types of poodle mixes splits us up and buys me time. Clearly, I'm not meant to comment here. All that's left to say is something perfunctory. I suppose something happy, even, some vocal relief that her husband, her other half, the love of her life, is returning to her? Surely she's comforted by the fact that this in-between time is over, that she can move forward with the confidence only clarity can bring?

But there's this: this nagging disappointment, this tug of anger that he'll escape this nightmare relatively unscathed. Yes, he's been humiliated; yes, he's lost his job; yes, he's had to have horribly uncomfortable conversations. The cost of his mistakes has not been cheap. And yet he's emerging from it all with a family who will spend every holiday with him, who will have dinners with him, tell him that they love him. He has a wife who will take care of him, who will gently place a thermometer in his mouth when he feels ill, and who will remind him of upcoming birthdays and the dish he loved at that restaurant that time. His T-shirts will be folded, his apartment sparkling, his ego saturated, and yes, these are all things he could pay for at this point, but he won't have to, and that's the whole thick of it, isn't it? He'll get it for free, day after day, from this woman. This woman who loves him.

This woman who has taken me in, who has brought pieces of my mother back to me, who has given me a home in a city in which I thought I would have to claw and scrape for anything I would ever have. This woman who is my friend.

Our hips are inches from each other again, after each poodle has sashayed its way past us. "Are you happy about it?" I ask carefully.

I see her shadow nodding on the pavement ahead of us. "It's a long road ahead, between here and normal. But yes."

I nod back. "Good, then. I think that's great."

"Really?" she asks, and her tone betrays her declaration from moments earlier that she doesn't care about what anyone else thinks.

"Yeah. I just want you to be happy, Susan. If this will make that happen, then I'm all for it." She rubs my arm a little, then drops it back by her side, and I'm thankful she'll let me get away with that instead of having to hug it out. "Although, I hope you'll still make time for me," I say, and she practically bursts into a ray of light upon hearing me say that and throws her little arms around my middle, squeezing the breath out of my lungs.

"Oh, Presley, of course!" she says. When she lets me go and I gasp dramatically, gulping down air, she laughs. But I see her wipe a tear away, and she asks for one of my pocket tissues.

We continue meandering up the park, walk the east side of the reservoir. I tell her about Agatha and Mark, and she is horrified by how very *rude* it all is. She asks if she can take me shopping for spring clothes, and I groan but then tell her sure. She asks if I've seen Clark lately, and I tell her I have, and we both leave it at that.

When we're walking toward the park's exit, I put out an arm to stop Susan before we're taken down by a runner, a woman with a long, frizzy, bottle-blond ponytail, perfectly toned legs, in a ratty old pink T-shirt. I blink several times in a row—it can't be. And of course, it isn't. Upon closer inspection, she's more muscular than Patty was. Her ratty T-shirt is, in fact, a lululemon running top. Less than the clothes or the ponytail, though, it's the way she's running: like she's got competitors to outrun, a place to be, a record to beat, and if you're in her way, that's not her problem, it's yours. There's a confidence to her; the world can't touch her. She's fast and she's brash and she doesn't give a fuck.

"What are you smiling about?" Susan asks me.

I shake my head. "Nothing."

"Oh, by the way," she says as we emerge onto Fifth Avenue, "Roger wanted me to pass along a message for you. I have no idea what it means, but he wanted me to tell you he finally figured it out, and it's Meg Ryan."

I throw my head back and laugh.

CHAPTER 39

I could tell that Clark was already out when I called him. He answered on the second ring, and background noise immediately assaulted my ears. "Hey, hey, one sec!" he yelled, then I heard him muttering, "'Scuse me . . . 'scuse me . . ." Sudden quiet. "Hey," he says. "What's up?"

"Hi." It's been a little over a week since he insisted I call him if I decided I wanted "this." A week spent mentally pacing back and forth, talking it out with Izzy, and hiding my phone from her so she wouldn't dial him up herself. "What are you up to?"

"I'm at Village Tavern watching basketball. You?"

"Whole lotta nothing," I say. "Was wondering if you wanted to get a drink or something, but if you're busy—"

"Not busy," he says.

"Anywhere in particular you want to go?"

In less than half an hour, we're knocking tallboys in brown paper bags together, sitting on a bench along the West Side Highway, looking out over the Hudson. As predicted, the warm weather wasn't here for good, but sitting in the sun, nestled in jackets, the brown bag and our sleeves protecting us from the chill of our beer cans, it's not too cold. He's gotten a haircut since I last saw him, and with his wavy hair cropped shorter, there's more of his face to look at. Which I do, until he catches me, and I jerk my eyes out over the water, take a sip of my beer.

"So, you called," he says.

"I called."

"Did you call because you've realized you have a big, fat crush on me and wish to go on lots of dates with me and cuddle and stuff?" he asks. He scooches closer, lightly elbows me in the ribs, and rocks back and forth on his hips, which makes me spill my beer a little. I press the brown bag into my coat, hoping it'll soak the droplets up and buy me some time. The beer remains, and Clark is quiet. I take a deep breath and look at him. His eyes flicker down to the wet spot on my coat, and he digs around in the bodega bag, pulls out a napkin, and dabs my coat with it. "Shit, sorry," he says, his eyebrows furrowed in concentration as he turns the napkin over.

"Yes," I say, and his eyebrows unfurrow with almost comical speed and a shit-eating grin spreads across his cartoon face.

"Yes?"

"Yeah. I like you. But there's no need to, like, make some big deal out of it." I look out over the water, and he lets out a hoot and pulls me in. I'm sort of bent and crushed uncomfortably in his arms, but I don't mind. He loudly smooches my head and releases me.

"Coolest girl in school likes me, and it is, in fact, a big deal," he says, taking another sip of his beer, also looking out over the water.

I take a breath. "We're gonna have to go slow."

"I can do slow," Clark says with a nod.

"I'm talking, like, glacial."

"Well," Clark says, "you *have* already met the parents, so I don't know how glacial we can really go here."

I laugh a little, in spite of myself. Oh God, Susan is going to lose her shit when she finds out about this. There's a heat in my cheeks despite the windchill. "Seriously, though," I say. "This isn't something I really . . . do."

He turns, angles himself toward me, and our eyes meet. He kisses me, and when he pulls back, he says, "There isn't much to it. I'm gonna be me and you're gonna be you and we're gonna do that together. Nothing to be afraid of."

I narrow my eyes. Surely it isn't that easy. Then again, everything with Clark feels easy. Either way, I'm surprised to realize I want to find out.

"So, how was your week, babe?" he asks, and now he's the one with spilled beer because of how quickly I slug him on the shoulder. He's laughing, that laugh from his gut, that uproarious, head tilted back, so pleased with himself and the world laugh. "Fine, fine. But how was it, actually?"

I open my mouth to ask him how *his* week was, considering we have yet to discuss the return of Thomas, when I feel a buzz in my pocket. A long buzz, a phone call. "Sorry, one sec," I say, pulling my phone out, a photo of drunk, smiling Izzy eating a chicken wing lighting up the screen.

"Hey," I say, pressing the phone to my ear and wincing at the cold screen on my face. I'm met with silence. "Hello? Izzy?"

"Uh, hey," she says quietly. "I saw that you're on the West Side Highway, are you on a run or something?"

"God, no," I say, holding up my beer even though she can't see it. She squeezes out something like an attempt at a laugh, and my internal flags shoot up. Something's wrong. I move the mouthpiece behind my neck. "I'll be right back," I whisper to Clark, who gives me a thumbs-up, though his eyebrows are raised. I move away from our bench. "Izzy, what's wrong?" I ask.

"Nothing. I was just seeing what you were up to."

"Bullshit. I can hear it in your voice. One sec." I open my app that shows her location. She's at home.

When I raise my phone back to my ear, she's speaking, saying, "Seriously, not a big deal. I'm fine. Go back to doing whatever you're doing over there. Which is what, by the way?"

"Nothing, I'm just . . . Well, I'm hanging out with Clark."

"Ooh la la!" Izzy says, but she doesn't succeed in enlivening her voice as I can tell she meant to. "Juicy. Have you told him yet?"

"Izzy—"

"Oh, duh, you're with him right now. You can tell me later! Ta-ta." And she hangs up.

"Everything okay?" Clark asks as I approach our bench.

I nod. "I think so," I say. My wallet and headphones are in my coat pocket, which I'm wearing, so there's no purse to pick up, nothing physical I can do to indicate that I'm leaving now. The words feel harder to say just standing here, with nothing to do as a distraction. "I'm really sorry, but I think I have to go."

"Oh," he says, clearly disappointed.

"I feel shitty about it. I know I called and asked you to hang out, and took you away from your friends, and now I'm bailing. I wouldn't do it if it wasn't for a good reason. And . . . and I'll make it up to you, okay?" Before I can lose my nerve, I bend down quickly and rush my face to his, kissing him on the mouth. He grabs fistfuls of my coat, lightly pulls me in closer, almost not letting me go when I pull away.

"I'll call you later," I say quietly, because our faces are still close, eyes wide-open, inches from each other.

"Isn't something you do, my ass," he says, smiling. "Presley Fry, you're a natural."

CHAPTER 40

Isabelle jerks her head up in surprise when I rush into our apartment. The first thing I clock is her smudged mascara, the second the pile of crumpled tissues on the coffee table. I don't bother with shrugging my coat off before I throw my arms around her, and she makes a choked sound: I think it was meant to be a laugh but almost immediately becomes a sob.

I sink onto the couch. "Who do I need to kill?" I ask.

Izzy blows her nose and shakes her head. "No. I'm being stupid," she says. "It's not a big deal, it shouldn't be a big deal." She presses the heels of her hands into her eyes to keep more tears from falling. The effort is fruitless. She exhales. "Julia and I had a fight."

"What happened?" I ask.

Izzy sighs. "Want to go for a walk? I need to get out of here."

She grabs her coat, and we start walking up Second Avenue. We're out of tissues, so I bring a roll of toilet paper, which I have to continue handing her bits of as she fills me in. Over brunch, Julia mentioned something about her brother's wedding, which is six months from now, something about how one particular cousin would be a great person to keep Izzy company while Julia had to take family photos and fulfill maid of honor duties.

"And I don't know what came over me," she tells me as we continue walking up Second Avenue without direction. "I just sort of panicked. Six months from now feels like a long way away. I've never been in a situation where I was making plans *six months* in advance with someone who, like, isn't you." I nod. "And I get it, she's my girlfriend, we're in a relationship, that's totally normal. But it just sort of hit me all at once: like, oh, regardless of what's going on in the city that weekend, and even though it's half a year away, I'll be in fucking Vail for this fucking wedding surrounded by people I've never met before, all because Julia is my girlfriend. It just seemed like a lot, for some reason."

"I mean, you haven't even met her family," I say while Izzy blows her nose. "And it's a big adjustment, all this shit. I totally get being freaked for a second. It doesn't mean you don't actually want to go."

"Right!" she says, turning to me. "And I think if she had, like, texted me about this or something, I might have had a little freak-out, then calmed myself down, because she's just being a normal person in a relationship, and I'm the one who's having a weird reaction. But we were sitting there, at brunch, and the thing is, she knows me so well. She knows my whole . . . face." Izzy flicks her wrist in a circular motion around her face as she says this. "She could tell that I was spooked. And then she called me out on that, and then I tried to play it off like my face hadn't done anything, like she was being nuts, which was fucked up of me. And then I finally admitted that the wedding thing freaked me out a little, and she got defensive, and we were supposed to go to MoMA this afternoon because Julia's never seen *Drowning Girl*, but she said, she said . . ." I pass Izzy some squares of toilet paper as we turn left onto Thirty-Third for no reason other than the crosswalk is lit, and she tries to stop hyperventilating. "She said maybe we should take some space this afternoon instead."

I squeeze Izzy's shoulder. "Well, that doesn't sound like it's over or anything, Izzy," I say. "It sounds like y'all just had a rough moment, which all relationships do, right? And now you're just gonna take a beat and cool off before you talk about it again. I think it's really mature."

"I know!" Izzy wails into her soggy makeshift tissue. I pass her another. "It's reasonable, because she's amazing! And I ruined our day! And I know it'll be okay and I'll be able to explain myself, that I just had a weird flash of commitment phobia because I forgot for a split second how much I *do* want this relationship, but it sucks that I got in my own way and did this, because even though it might not be some huge deal, I know I hurt her. I could see it on her face that I did. And I never want to hurt her. I'm her girlfriend—I'm supposed to be the one who helps her when *other people* hurt her."

I bite back my knee-jerk urge to tell her that it seems to me that the people who hurt each other the most are romantic partners. Doesn't seem helpful right now. And I'm not so sure I believe that anymore. Or maybe I do, but I just see more clearly now that it's not *just* hurt and disappointment that get traded back and forth. Other stuff comes with it that makes it worth it. Maybe.

The group walking in front of us suddenly stops, blocking our way forward. They all take out their phones and tilt the cameras up to the sky. I suddenly realize where we are. Izzy and I both look up, then look at each other at the same time. "Should we?" she asks, a little glint of mischief shining through her tears. I nod.

Forty bucks and a crowded elevator ride later and we're atop the Empire State Building. It's a clear day, and we're high enough up that it feels like we're actually in the unobscured blue sky. We press our faces against the net, cold wind nipping at our cheeks.

"So, did you tell Clark you like him? Or was it just more holding hands in silence again?" Izzy asks.

I shake my head, take the toilet paper back from her. The wind is making my eyes water. "I told him."

She whips her head in my direction. "And?"

"Yeah. We're gonna try things or whatever, I guess." Izzy squeals and throws her arms around me, and I shimmy out of them, laughing, which is difficult to do considering she's also jumping up and down.

We meander to the southern part of the deck, angling for a different view. We start plotting romantic gestures Izzy can do to show Julia she's sorry, to show how all in she is.

Manhattan dances below us. Cars inch up and down the avenues; tiny ant-people wander around. The Freedom Tower gleams, the sun blessing it. Somewhere in the left field of our vision is our apartment. Somewhere across the river Agatha Reddy is probably writing, sending voice note jokes to Priya. Somewhere behind us Susan is probably bustling around, running errands, perhaps sitting down with Thomas, figuring out a way forward. All these people trying. The city pulses with the energy of their efforts.

I grab Izzy's hand and squeeze it.

ACKNOWLEDGMENTS

The first thanks now and forever goes to Andrianna deLone. I am so lucky that because of her partnership, I never feel I have to experience that writerly loneliness everyone is always whining about.

Randi Kramer will be incredible at whatever she chooses to do, but I'm so grateful that for the last few years she's chosen to edit my books. It was a joy to write this book with her insight and guidance. And I am also so grateful for Ryan Doherty stepping in and seeing this thing through. Thanks also to Faith Tomlin!

The Celadon team is the best in the game, and I cannot believe I have gotten to publish two books with them. Thanks to Rachel Chou, Jennifer Jackson, Anna Belle Hindenlang, Jaime Noven, Liza Buell, Sandra Moore, and Emily Radell.

Big thanks to Peter Richardson, Vincent Stanley, Morgan Mitchell, and Michelle McMillian for making this a real book. And thanks to Sona Vogel for her copyediting, a Herculean effort with this one. And thanks to Kathleen Cook for going through this with a fine-toothed comb.

I feel so lucky to have author friends. I'm so grateful to Becky Chalsen for her friendship and support as we navigate our double lives as authors and development execs. Big thanks to Avery Carpenter Forrey for the voice memo check-ins.

Thanks to Heather Karpas, the world's best reader and pal.

Thanks to Kristyn Keene Benton and Kari Stuart, who are impossible not to idolize. And thanks to Zoe Sandler for all her support.

Thanks to Sloan Harris, Esther Newberg, and Jennifer Joel, who ran a department I was lucky to be a part of and, unfortunately for them, still consider myself to be a part of.

Thanks to John de Laney for handling my contracts and entertaining me.

I adore Josie Freedman, and am so lucky she's my agent. And thanks to Nissa Kreitenberg for all her help as well!

I like to think of this book as an ode to female friendship, which is the most enriching part of my life because of these ladies: Caroline Ellis, Alex Oliver, Kaitlyn Nugent, Ali Pattillo, Adrienne Crow, Sydney Jeffay, Sarah Raymer, Katherine Green, Katie McKenzie, Erika Weaver, Lauren Buss, Gracy Juba, Kirby Mathews, Mary Luttrell, Laney Mallet, Mathilde Tribou, Abby Kovan, Katie Baumberger, Alexa Brahme, and Olivia Trovillion.

Boys can be good friends, too. Thanks to Ethan Carlson, Patrick Kelley, Scott Nugent, Nic Guerreiro, and Bruce Lampros for proving this. Special thanks to David Raymer, who allowed me to use the Frosty story. And thanks to Murphy!

Thank you to my cousins. I love you, Charlie Miller.

Thanks to Tim Dalton for his support. Which is unwavering, for whatever reason.

Thanks to my family: Nina, my mom, my dad, Roo, and Georgie. And my sister, the greatest person in the world.

ABOUT THE AUTHOR

Cat Shook graduated from the University of Georgia in 2016 with degrees in creative writing and mass media arts. Born and raised in Georgia, she now lives in Brooklyn. She is the author of *If We're Being Honest*, a *Good Morning America* Buzz Pick, and *Humor Me*.